IT WAS KILL-OR-DIE

The door closed behind Macurdy. Standing before him was by far the tallest man he'd ever seen. He wore a black coverall and a tall, black, bag-like cap that covered his forehead. His green eyes glittered coldly. Macurdy felt like a bug on a pin.

"So, Herr Montag," the giant said. "I am Kronprinz Kurqosz. Baron Greszak says you are a psychic. Show me what you can do."

Since he was wearing his retarded Kurt Montag persona, Macurdy stared speechless, slack-jawed.

Red eyebrows rose. "Nothing?" The crown prince grinned, then pulled off his strange cap and tossed it on the table. He had ears like a goat's, perhaps six inches long, clothed with the same copper-red hair that covered his skull, forming a crest on its meridian. "If you do not satisfy me," he said, "I will give you ears like mine. Now, show me how large a fireball you can make."

Macurdy made one an inch in diameter, floating a couple of inches from his fingertip, and reaching, Kurqosz tested it for heat. At ten inches it was uncomfortable, yet Macurdy showed no sign of pain. "Interesting! Interesting! Make it be fifty centimeters away."

"I cannot, Herr Kronprinz. I don't know how."

Kurqosz turned, gestured, and above a table, a hawk-like creature materialized, hovering on loudly thrumming wings that scattered papers from a table. Its head was like a great bat's. "It can be killed by casting your fire-ball at it," Kurqosz said. "If you do not kill it, I will have it attack you!"

Glowing red, the thing's eyes looked at Macurdy, its gaping mouth showing needle teeth. Then it darted toward his throat.

BAEN BOOKS BY JOHN DALMAS

Lion of Farside
The Regiment
The White Regiment
The Regiment's War
The Yngling and the Circle of Power
The Yngling in Yamato
The Lizard War

JOHN DALMAS

THE BAVARIAN GATE

BAEN

THE BAVARIAN GATE

This is a work of fiction. All the characters and events portrayed in this book are fictional, and any resemblance to real people or incidents is purely coincidental.

A Baen Books Original

Baen Publishing Enterprises
P.O. Box 1403
Riverdale, NY 10471

ISBN: 0-671-87764-X

Cover art by Paul Alexander

First printing, January 1997

Distributed by Simon & Schuster
1230 Avenue of the Americas
New York, NY 10020

Printed in the United States of America

This novel is dedicated to William Sullivan, Doyle Roberts, Charles Doyle, and the other World War Two veterans of the 509th Parachute Infantry.

THANKS

My thanks to fellow writers Jim Glass and Jim Burk, who read an earlier draft, asked numerous questions and made helpful suggestions. Also Bill Sullivan and Doyle Roberts, veterans of the 509th, who loaned me books, answered numerous questions, and read and commented on Part 2, "Airborne!" And to Heiko Wiggers, a graduate student from Germany, attending Eastern Washington University. Heiko not only corrected my atrocious German, but checked my handling of German geography, culture, and ethnicities.

I also want to thank Fred Larson of Anchorage for his advice on aircraft, and for reviewing parts of the manuscript.

These people are not responsible for my errors. On the contrary, they helped me avoid some.

CONTENTS

PART ONE — GROWING TO FIT

PART TWO — AIRBORNE!

PART THREE — ACTOR WITHOUT A SCRIPT

PART ONE
Growing to Fit

1

Washington County, Indiana

Curtis Macurdy gazed out the window of the truck at a field plowed and disked. Near the far end, someone, presumably his father, was walking behind the horse-drawn spike-tooth, readying the ground for drilling. Beyond stood the house Curtis had grown up in, the barn nearby, sheds, corncrib, and the ancient white oak that spread across the front yard.

"That's the place," he told the driver. "Just drop me off at the corner." He felt uncomfortable about his homecoming; had since he'd gotten off the train at Volinia.

The driver slowed, turning west on the township road. "Might as lief take you to your door," he said. "Ain't no trouble."

Along the roads, the maples, tuliptrees, elms had all been tinged with the fresh pale green of opening buds, but the yard oak, bare as February, showed no sign yet of wakening. The driver pulled into the driveway and stopped. "My thanks," Macurdy said, and taking the coin purse from his pocket, removed a fifty-cent piece.

The man waved it off. "That's half a day's pay, and this ain't been more'n a couple miles out of my way."

Macurdy nodded, put the coin back, and shook the man's hand. "Thanks," he said. "I'm obliged to you." Taking his suitcase from the seat, he got out, slammed the door, and waved as the driver left. Then he walked to the house. *Place needs paint,* he told himself. *Hard times.*

He opened the back door without knocking, took off his jacket and hung it on one of the back hall hooks. "Charley?" his mother's voice called.

"Nope." He stepped into the kitchen. The rawboned woman had turned from the big black kitchen stove. Seeing him, her eyes widened, her mouth half opening. For a moment he thought she might fall down, or worse, weep, but she recovered herself.

"Curtis!" she cried. "Blessed Jesus! It's you!" They embraced, then talked, she asking how he was, how long he planned to stay, her questioning marked more by what she didn't ask than what she did, as if fearing what he might tell her. His answers were brief: He had no plans yet, he said. If needed, he might stay the summer, and maybe through harvest.

His own questions were simply to catch up on the state of the family. Nothing had greatly changed, she told him, except that the price of everything had fallen, both for what they sold and what they bought. Max and Julie were still farming, and Frank had got promoted to shop foreman at Dellmon's Chevrolet, though they paid him less than when he'd started there as a mechanic, four years earlier.

And Charley had hired a man to help with the farming. "Your dad's not as young as he was," she added.

After a few minutes, Curtis put his jacket back on and went out to the field. Charley Macurdy saw him, and stopping the team, walked over, both his aura and his face showing a difficult mix of emotions—mainly joy and uncertainty, Curtis thought. And worry. Curtis was just now realizing what it was like for his parents, this return of a youngest son, who'd left with his bride, bought a farm in Illinois, then abruptly dropped out of sight, never writing for three years.

"Curtis!" Charley said, and reached out a hard-callused hand. "Good God! It's so good to see you again, son!" Then, startling Curtis, his father hugged him, hard arms clasping him against a hard chest. Perhaps, Curtis thought, he didn't want him to see the moisture in his eyes.

For a while they stood talking in the chill late-April breeze, his father as careful in his questioning as his mother had been. Like Edna, Charley feared the answers; most questions could wait till they'd got used to each other again. Curtis was welcome to stay as long as he'd like, Charley told him, but there wouldn't be much money in it. "Especially not while I'm paying a hand," he said, adding ruefully: "Not that I pay Ferris much; not what he's worth. He's been with us three years now, and it wouldn't be right to just cut him loose all of a sudden."

He looked questioningly at his son. "You are going to stay, aren't you? This place can be yours when I can't keep up with it anymore. Maybe sooner, if you want."

Initially Curtis had planned to stay, farm with his father, but the closer he'd gotten to home, the less real it had seemed. After where he'd been, and the life he'd lived there, it likely wouldn't work out. If nothing else, there'd be too many questions without answers—and sooner or later the question of age. Best to start new, someplace where he wasn't known.

"I'll stay till the spring work is done," he replied. "Harvest at the latest. Then I'll need to move on."

Charley nodded, looking at the ground, then brightened a little. "A few weeks ago, some folks stopped by and asked after you," he said. "A woman and two men. Moneyed folks; drove up in a big Packard. The woman did the talking. Seemed real disappointed you weren't here; thought you might have come back. Said they had a job for you. Didn't say what."

He paused, noting his son's frown. "She called herself Louise," he went on. "Kin to Varia, all three of them; I'd bet on it. Same eyes, same build. Hair not so red though. You know them?"

Louise? Not hardly, Curtis thought. *No Christian name like that. Idri maybe, with her long, unforgiving memory.* "I'm not sure," he answered. "Varia's got lots of kin, but I never knew a Louise. Most that I did know, I didn't greatly care for."

Both of his parents needed to hear something that made sense to them, which meant lying. He'd foreseen the problem and knew what he had to say, but didn't like it.

He'd been out of the country, he told them at supper. Varia's family was foreigners; he didn't say where from. She'd gone back to the old country with them; they'd insisted. He'd followed, had farmed there and even done some soldiering. Then Varia had drowned, he went on, had fallen through the ice on horseback, and the current had carried her beneath it. He'd recovered her body at a rapids downstream.

He lied, of course—wrong wife—but Charley and Edna believed him. They felt bad about it, but at least he hadn't abandoned her.

As the weeks passed, Curtis became more comfortable with the idea of leaving. Ferris Gibbs, the hired man, was a good hand—a self-starter who noticed things and knew what to do about them. He'd had a farm of his own, but lost it to the bank in '31, when he couldn't make the mortgage payments. "A casualty of the Hard Times," Ferris called himself, without apparent rancor. On Saturdays he left right after supper, and came back late Sunday. As Charley saw it, Ferris would leave when times got better—he'd want a place of his own again—but Frank's boy already liked to work with his Grampa Macurdy on the farm, when school let out in Salem. Said he wanted to be a farmer.

The first Sunday, Curtis went to church with his parents. He'd have preferred not to, but he knew it would please his mother. Folks looked askingly at him, but after the service they simply shook his hand, commenting on how good he looked. Pastor Fleming asked how old he was now, and told him he looked as young and strong as he ever had. The young part was ridiculous, Curtis told himself, considering the reverend had known him since he was fourteen.

As young as ever. A foretaste of problems to come.

Max and Julie and their kids came for dinner after church that day, and Julie, being Julie, asked questions his parents never would have, like "what country was it?", meaning where Varia came from. He thought of answering "Hungary"—that would do it—but he was tired of lying. "Yuulith," he told her instead, adding "that's their name for it." She'd look it up when she got home, he knew, and not finding it, would probably let be. Macurdies, even Julie, were pretty good at letting be.

✧ ✧ ✧

He got more and more settled in, and stayed longer than he'd thought he might—until one day Bob Hammond, who farmed Will's old place on shares, decided to sell his sheep. Said he "couldn't face another week of Baaaah! Baaaah! twenty-four hours a day." He hired Curtis to help him haul them to the railroad in Salem, unfinished lambs and all, and load them onto a car. It took all day—three trips—and when they'd finished, Hammond took his wallet out of his overalls to pay him. Curtis knew the man couldn't afford the two dollars he'd promised, so he said he'd just take one, and eat supper with them that evening: likely boiled potatoes and stuff from the cellar—home-canned beef, green beans, maybe fruit pie—a good twenty-five-cent meal.

On the way, they drove past Charley and Edna's, and there was a big expensive Packard in the side yard. Curtis stared as they passed it. "Whose car is that?" he asked.

"Darned if I know. Never saw it before." The tenant pursed his lips worriedly. It looked like a banker's car, and more often than not, bankers meant trouble these days. Though he didn't think Charley had any mortgage to worry about: The Macurdy land had been in the family for generations.

It seemed to Curtis it would be one of Varia's Sisterhood: maybe Idri. He wasn't afraid of Idri by herself, but she wouldn't be alone, and he wasn't altogether sure he could handle the men she'd have with her. Besides, this wasn't Yuulith; they might carry guns. And if they killed him, they'd kill his parents as witnesses.

He wasn't very good company for the Hammonds at supper. Half his attention stayed on whoever might have driven up in the Packard. He'd come close on the food: It was canned pig hocks and boiled potatoes, with pork gravy, canned green beans, and peach pie for dessert. Seemed like Miz Hammond kept her family pretty well fed. The coffee was weak of course, but coffee had to be bought.

When he'd finished, he paid his respects and left, walking east toward home. But before he'd gone more than a few chains, he left the road along the old line fence, screened by the growth of serviceberry and young sassafras in the fence row, until the barn cut him off from view of the house. Then he hiked through the potato field to the barn, skirting the manure pile. Trapjaw, Charley's old redbone hound, peered from the barn door, then sauntered out, tail waving, to greet Curtis. From inside, Curtis could hear the sound of milk on pail bottom as his dad began on another cow.

He looked in. Charley was hunkered on the one-legged milking stool, head against a fawn-colored flank, squeezing and pulling, the sound changing from metallic singing to the rushing "shoosh-shoosh-shoosh" as milk jetted into milk, broken just a beat as Charley squirted a stream into an expectant cat's face. With quick tidy movements the animal wiped it off, licking the paw between wipes, then waited primly, hopefully, for her next serving.

"Howdy," Curtis said.

Charley answered without pausing, merely glancing back over his shoulder. "You're back, eh? Your ma put your supper on the back of the stove. You've got company." Ordinarily Curtis saw auras simply as an inconspicuous, layered cloud of colors. Now, however, he focused on Charley's. It reflected distrust, a sense of betrayal. When Curtis failed to respond, Charley added, "It's Varia. The wife you said drowned."

The words struck Curtis like a fist in the gut, but he recovered quickly. "How sure are you it's her? She's got a twin." He'd almost said clone, then caught himself. "Named Liiset."

The barrier softened as Charley considered, and Curtis spoke again. "Did she say anything, or ask anything, that didn't sound like Varia? Maybe something Varia would have known but this one didn't?"

Charley grunted. "Now that you mention it . . . A twin, you say."

"And Varia wouldn't have brought men with her."

"You saw them then?" Charley asked.

He hadn't needed to. He'd turned Sarkia down on the other side, but obviously she wasn't taking no for an answer. With his reputation, she'd have sent men, very likely tigers, as the clone's enforcers. And if it came to a fight, and he succeeded in killing them, how would he explain to a judge, or even to his parents?

"No," he answered, "I just came from supper with Bob and

Hattie. So he wouldn't feel he had to pay me any two dollars. But I saw the Packard in the front yard when we drove by. And there's stuff I didn't tell you. About Varia's family. Stuff just about impossible to explain; stuff you wouldn't believe. Too foreign. I—kind of rounded off the truth."

The strong farmer hands continued squeezing and pulling. As the milk had deepened, the sound had changed to "choof-choof-choof." Charley said nothing, but he was thinking, putting together snippets of observation accrued over more than twenty-five years. The cat, ignored now, stalked off to wait with others by their milk dish.

"Did the men have an accent?" Curtis asked.

"Neither one of them said anything in English. Varia, or whoever she is, did the talking. I think you're right though; she's not Varia. Not by what she said, but what she didn't say. She didn't ask about Julie, or Max, or Frank . . . none of them. And didn't tell us anything about you, except they had a good job for you. She excused the fellas with her, said they'd just come from the old country and hadn't learned English yet. Said she's taking them around with her to learn about America. When they talked, I kind of thought they might be Eye-talian."

"Big hard-looking men?" Curtis asked. "Hair somewhere between carrot and bay?"

"I guess you know them."

"Probably not them specifically. But they're not Eye-talian." He spoke a line of Yuultal then, ending with, "It sounded like that, right? Their part of the world is full of old rivalries, with people trained to kill. Finally I had enough of it. More than enough."

Charley nodded, not knowing what to say, his hands still pumping milk into the four-gallon pail.

Curtis continued. "And Varia's not dead. Her family traced us from Evansville to Illinois, and stole her back. She never imagined I could find her, so she ran away from them, and ended up married to someone else, a man who saved her when her kinfolks caught her again. So I joined another group, separate from either of those, and married a woman whose name translates out to Melody. It was Melody fell through the ice, a good good woman, that I came to love maybe as much as I had Varia."

Charley's aura had shrunk from doubt and concern, shrunk halfway to his skin. He'd even slowed his milking, looking over his shoulder at his youngest son.

"But Varia wouldn't have come here with two men," Curtis went on. "If she'd come after me, it would have been alone and it would have been enough."

Soon the jets of milk thinned. After another half minute, Charley rose from the stool, picking it up with one hand and the pail with the other. Together the two men walked to one of the ten-gallon cans, and Charley emptied the pail into it. "What are you going to do now?" he asked.

"Leave. Go somewhere they won't have a notion of. Or you either; that's the way it's got to be." He paused, his eyes intent on his father's. "Did it ever seem to you that Varia was—a little bit witchy?"

Charley nodded. "In a manner of speaking. A time or two. Ask your ma."

"Liiset's got her own witchy powers, so I need to be gone before you go back in. I'll saddle Blaze and ride to Max and Julie's. Leave Blaze with them, tell them I'm in trouble, and borrow some money; maybe twenty dollars. That you promised to pay it back for me. My money belt's in my top dresser drawer, with about sixty dollars. It's yours; I dasn't go in for it."

Charley blinked; sixty dollars was a lot of money.

"Max can drive me into Salem," Curtis went on, "and I'll take the train to Louisville. After you've finished milking, phone up Bob and ask if he knows where I'm at. He'll tell you I started home after supper. Liiset will figure something's fishy, but there'll be nothing she can do except hope I show up later."

Leaving his father staring after him, Curtis went to the horse shed on one end of the barn, saddled Blaze and rode away, keeping the barn between himself and the house. When he came to the lane along the fence line, he rode north through the beginning of dusk to the Maple Hill Road. He wasn't totally sure this was necessary. Perhaps he could just go in and talk to the clone, tell her he wasn't interested. But the two men with her? They'd kidnaped Varia that day in Macon County;

they might kidnap him. And if the men were tigers, burn the house to cover the kidnaping. The bones in it would be his parents' and Ferris's.

He wished, though, that he could have gone in and gotten his own money, and the heavy sheath knife Arbel had given him, that had saved his life in the Kullvordi Hills.

Well, he reminded himself, he at least had his memories and all the things he'd learned. He patted the wallet in his jacket pocket: It held six dollars, and the picture of Varia his mother had given him when he'd mentioned not having one.

And he had a destination, too. He and Varia had talked about maybe going there someday. And the clone—Liiset or whoever she was—had probably never even heard of Oregon.

2

The Jungle Outside Miles City, Montana

It was night. Curtis Macurdy stood amidst sparse brush, watching stew simmer in a gallon lard pail. Sitting or squatting around him were seven men as hungry as he. Other fires, more or less scattered, flickered in the darkness; it seemed to him that more men rode freight trains these days than rode passenger coaches. President Roosevelt talked about economic recovery, and people were halfway hopeful, but times were hard. Perhaps hardest on those men, some no longer young, who'd left families behind, dependent on kinfolk, while they rode freight trains to California's orange groves, Idaho's potato farms, Arizona's irrigated cotton fields, where rumor said jobs could be found.

In the hobo jungle, most were unemployed working men; around this fire, only the grizzled oldtimer who called himself Dutch was not; Dutch and possibly one other. Dutch had lived on the bum a dozen years—since his house had burned with his wife in it.

The other was a seemingly crazy man, whom the rest of them avoided. His eyes were strange, and his lips moved in swift and silent monolog. Usually silent; at times he muttered a monotone of obscenities, the words almost too rapid to recognize. The man's aura was small and murky, its colors indistinct, brownish, with tinges of what might have been indigo. On one side, close to the head, it was black. Focusing more sharply, Macurdy got a sense of apathy, self-destruction, dying.

Dutch put a stick under the pail's wire bail and lifted the stew carefully from the coals. Most of the others got to their feet, anticipating. "Okay," Dutch said, "don't crowd. You'll get yours." Only Macurdy and a burly Indian held back; they and the crazy man. The pail belonged to Dutch, but most of them had contributed to the contents—a tin of beef, one of beans, another of stewed tomatoes, a carrot, a couple of potatoes. . . . Macurdy's contribution had been a sausage, which Dutch had cut up small. Some of the men had only tin cans to eat from—soup or bean cans, mostly—their rough-cut openings hammered carefully smooth with rocks so a man could drink from them. Dutch, like Macurdy, had an army canteen cup.

"Go ahead," Macurdy said when their turn had come. The Indian looked at him a moment, then held his can out, and Dutch ladled it full with a spoon. Macurdy felt a twinge of guilt at taking any. He'd learned to draw energy from the Web of the World when he needed to, though Vulkan had told him he'd need to eat fairly regularly for other needs. But his stomach grumbled and complained when unfed. Besides, refusing food would make him seem too peculiar.

Macurdy too had a spoon. The stew wasn't bad, he decided, the serving small but thick. Dutch's bindle held salt and pepper. Dutch was looking at the crazy man now. "You better have some," he said at last. "When this is gone, there won't be no more till we rustle up the makings."

The crazy man's lips had stopped. Slowly he got to his feet, staring intently not at the pail but at Dutch, then limped over and stood empty handed, left shoulder hunched.

"Ain't you got no can?" Dutch asked.

The shaggy head shook a negative.

"Anybody got a can for this guy?"

No one answered.

"Where's that bean can we had? That'll work."

His canteen cup in one hand, Macurdy went to where the can lay, and brought it to the crazy man. Its inner rim was jagged with teeth of tinned steel, formed by opening it with a jack knife.

The man held it out to Dutch.

"No hurry," Dutch said. "Hammer down the edges first, or you'll cut yourself."

The can remained unmovingly extended, and shrugging, Dutch filled it; the others had paused in their eating to watch. The silent man drank off most of the liquid, then unflinchingly reached into the can, plucked out pieces and put them into his mouth, licking and sucking stew and blood from his fingers, heedless of ragged steel edges and staring men. When he was done, he retreated out of the firelight and squatted again, sucking his cuts. None of the watchers said a word; after a moment they continued eating.

When they were done, the men withdrew a little distance to sleep, Macurdy and the Indian lying down a few feet from each other. They'd been together since a jungle outside St. Cloud, Minnesota, where a confused and exasperated Macurdy had asked how to find Oregon. "From here," the Indian had answered, "take the Northern Pacific. Don't take the Union Pacific! Oregon's where I'm going, too. I live there. If you want, we can travel together." They hadn't talked a lot in the twenty-odd hours since then; Macurdy didn't even know the man's name. When he'd said his own, the Indian had answered "White people call me Chief," saying it without irony. They felt a mutual affinity, but the Indian seemed reticent by nature, and Macurdy left it at that.

Macurdy's only bedding was a horse blanket he'd gotten from Max, to make a bindle and for appearances. He could keep as warm as he liked by drawing on the Web of the World, with or without a blanket. Just now he wasn't sleepy—not a bit—but it seemed better to lie there and rest than wander around.

Briefly he thought of offering his blanket to the crazy man, who had nothing but the ragged filthy clothes he wore, then decided against it. God knew what bugs the man might harbor.

Somewhere not far off he heard angry voices, and wondered if there'd be a fight. His hand felt for the heavy skinning knife he'd bought in Dickinson, North Dakota earlier that day, sheathed now inside his pant leg against his left calf. In Indiana there'd been no need to go armed, but on the bum like this it seemed a good idea.

The noise was coming nearer, two men arguing drunkenly till they stood by Dutch's fire. Macurdy had raised himself on an elbow to watch. Some of the others had gotten up, wary of potential violence. Suddenly one of the two—seemingly the drunkest—drew a knife and slashed at the other, who staggered backward screaming. The first, off balance, fell on the fire. Then both were screaming, and Macurdy was there, jerking the one from the bed of coals, throwing him down, slapping the flames out with his bare hands. That done, he crouched over the other, who had dropped to his knees, holding his belly and keening.

"Shut up and lay down!" Macurdy ordered, and slapped him sharply. The man obeyed, and Macurdy examined the wound with eyes and hands. The belly had been slashed, the blade slicing fat and muscle, leaving a ten-inch gash that welled blood but had not cut through the abdominal wall. "Lay still!" he ordered calmly. "You're not going to die. I'm going to stop the blood now." The words, though not loud, were an imperative, beyond argument. Macurdy's fingers explored lines of energy, weaving some of them into a web of occlusion to halt the bleeding, and as an energy template for healing, the latter procedure learned not from Arbel, but from Omara, a healing Sister. Within half a minute Macurdy stood up. "Lay still now," he repeated. "You'll be all right if you lay still."

Then he turned to the burned man, who writhed and whimpered on the ground. After stilling him with a command, Macurdy turned him onto his belly and pulled up the charred sweater, the scorched shirt. The burn was less severe than he'd expected, the skin red but not charred, blisters rising. He'd never had great confidence with burns, but now, without Arbel to lean on, it seemed he'd learned his lessons better than he'd realized.

When he'd finished, he looked around. "Who'll help me with these guys?" he asked. The others stared, awed and a little fearful of him.

"I will," said the Indian. "What do we do?"

"We'll help them to the yard and ask the bulls to call an

ambulance. These burns can get infected, and that cut's deep enough, it might tear through. If it does, he'll likely die."

They helped both men to their feet, and through the jungle to the railyard. One of the bulls had heard the screaming and called the sheriff's office; a sheriff's car had arrived before Macurdy and the Indian. The car had a shortwave radio, something new in police equipment. The deputy used it to call for an ambulance, then questioned Macurdy and the others while they waited.

When he'd finished, he stared hard at Macurdy. "I should book you for vagrancy, but I won't. Just get out of here and don't let us see you again."

Macurdy nodded—Chief was being as inconspicuous as anyone can who stands six feet and weighs 230—and the two of them headed back to the jungle. "How are your hands?" Chief asked.

"My hands?"

"You used them to beat out the flames in that guy's clothes."

Macurdy peered at them. It was too dark to see whether they were burned or not. "Okay, I guess. They don't hurt." He contemplated the question as they walked. Maybe healing the others had healed his hands, or maybe somehow they'd never been burned. He was pretty sure he'd felt no pain.

Dutch had watched their goods while they were gone, and after asking a few questions, retired to his bedroll. Chief laid dry sticks on the coals and blew them into flame, then the two large men sat without talking, Macurdy examining his hands by the firelight. It was Chief who broke the silence. "I'm going to tell you my name," he murmured. "I don't tell it to a white man very often. Only when I have to, like to get a job. It's Roy. Roy Klaplanahoo."

Macurdy repeated it quietly. "Roy Klaplanahoo. Mine is Curtis Macurdy. You already knew the Curtis part."

Roy nodded. "I saw how you lit the fire. The others thought you used a match, but you didn't. Then when you stopped that guy's bleeding, I knew what you are: You're a shaman. I never heard of a white shaman before."

"Yeah. I apprenticed to a white shaman named Arbel. That was in another country. But then I got away from it."

"What are you going to do in Oregon?"

"I thought maybe I could get a job logging there."

"My brother and me log sometimes for the Severtson brothers. Swedes. They like us because we turn out lots of logs. They're pretty good to work for; don't cheat anyone, not even Indians. And they feed good. Maybe they'll hire you."

"Thanks. It should be easier where I know someone."

That was the end of their conversation for a while. They watched the fire die down again, then went back to where they'd bedded before. "You want to use my blanket?" Macurdy murmured.

"Your blanket? What will you use?"

"That's something else I learned from Arbel: how to keep myself warm."

Roy considered that remarkable statement for a minute, then nodded. "Thanks. I could use another blanket." He got up and laid the blankets on top of each other, then rolled up loosely in them. "When we get where I live," he said, "you can stay with my family as long as you want."

No more was said, and after a while, Roy's aura told Macurdy the Indian was asleep. In no hurry to sleep himself, Macurdy lay awake with his thoughts. At first they were of his ex-wives, Varia and Melody, but after a bit shifted to a giant wild boar named Vulkan, a four-legged sorcerer large enough that Macurdy could ride on its bristly shoulders.

Strange thoughts that soon blurred into stranger dreams.

3
Discovering Oregon

Near dawn, Roy shook Macurdy awake. "It's time to go," he said quietly, "before it starts to get daylight."

For a moment Macurdy lay there, his dream receding like a wave from a beach, leaving a brief wash of images and impressions. The principal image was of Vulkan, who in the dream had called himself a *bodhi sattva.* Macurdy had no idea what a bodhi sattva was.

Silently he rolled to hands and knees, got to his feet and looked around. A half moon had risen about midnight and begun its trip across the sky. Roy was rolling his bindle, and Macurdy rolled his. Then, bindles slung on shoulders, they entered the railyard, keeping to the shadows of freight cars. They could hear the chuffing of a yard engine, the clash of couplings in long chain reactions as a train was assembled. In the night it sounded spooky. The yard seemed a maze of tracks, and to move through it inconspicuously required crossing some of them. Often this meant climbing between cars, and a string of them could jerk into deadly motion without warning.

Others from the jungle had preceded the two, and at the far end, Roy and Macurdy waited with three of them in the shadow of a hopper car, watching the main line. Finally a tandem of line engines rolled slowly past, followed by freight cars gradually picking up speed. The men moved out of the shadows, trotting alongside. An empty boxcar pulled even with

Roy, and grasping the edge of the open door, the burly Indian pulled himself in, then rolled to hands and knees and helped Macurdy. A moment later they stood in shadowed darkness, their legs braced against the swaying. Macurdy sniffed a familiar aroma. Alfalfa. This car had hauled baled hay recently.

Dawn also traveled west, and soon overtook them. Roy had blocked the door open with a length of dunnage stashed in the car, and part of the time they stood watching the countryside roll by. And feeling their stomachs grumble, for they had eaten only twice in two days. From time to time they drank, barely, from their canteens, swallowing a short mouthful only after swishing it around for a few seconds.

Occasionally, at some high plains village, the train paused. Cars would be shunted onto a siding—empties to be filled or laden cars to be emptied. The men kept out of sight then, grateful when the train began moving once more without their car having been cut from it.

By midmorning, Macurdy had seen his first big mountains, bigger and more abrupt than any he'd seen in Yuulith. By noon they were hemmed in by them, and several large locomotives—"Mallies" Roy called them—had been added to drag the train over the continental divide. Macurdy got a look at the massive black engines, spouting gritty black smoke as they passed their own freight cars on a hairpin curve.

That evening their car was part of a string cut out in the yard at Missoula. By then they were glad to get out; they were out of water, and their stomachs complained constantly. Other 'boes were disembarking too, and Roy quickened his pace.

"We got to be first," he told Macurdy. "Find a restaurant or grocery store and see what they got in their garbage. You can always find something, but after other guys have picked through it, it's kind of bad." They were in the lead when they saw a cafe ahead. It was closed. "Let's find one open," Macurdy said. "I've got a little cash. We can eat a real meal."

They walked several blocks before they found one. Gilt letters on the window spelled "Sig's Cafe." A middle-aged couple sat at a table, and two working men sat side by side at the counter. The two hoboes went in, filthy with coal soot from locomotive smokestacks. The cafe's owner, a tall, rawboned, blond man, got instantly to his feet, scowling. Two steps took him to the revolver he kept on a shelf beneath the cash register. Macurdy read his aura. "Are you Sig?" he asked. The man nodded. "I've got money," Macurdy told him. "You got a place we can sit?"

He could almost see the man's mind considering. Business was poor, but two bums? They were so dirty he'd have to clean the chairs they sat on. "Let's see the money," he said in accented English.

From a shirt pocket, Macurdy removed a grubby one-dollar bill. The man pointed to a small round table in a back corner, two chairs beside it, and when they'd seated themselves, he brought a menu. Macurdy looked it over. "I'll take a pork chop with mashed potatoes," he said. "And buttermilk."

"The same for me," Roy added.

"The buttermilk's extra."

"We'll have it anyway," Macurdy answered. "We only ate twice in two days, and then not much." The man's aura still reflected distrust, so Macurdy handed him the dollar bill. "Take it out of this. Maybe we'll have something else when we're done."

The meal came with bread, butter, and rice pudding with canned milk, but before they were done, they'd each had another serving of potatoes. It used up the whole dollar. In Sig's eyes they were customers now, not bums, and pulling another chair over, he talked with them briefly. There was no work to be found in Missoula. The sawmills that were running at all were down to one shift a day, running on inventory; almost no logging camps were manned. "I heard it ain't no better in Spokane," Sig added. "Maybe on the coast."

Macurdy and Roy went back to the railyard with stomachs and canteens filled. They were not heartened by what they'd heard. Roy said if they needed to, they could stay with his family till something broke for them. But he didn't sound terribly confident; his family would be hard up at best, trawling salmon for a cannery that probably wasn't paying much at all.

Macurdy slept his way across the Idaho panhandle, waking when the train stopped at Spokane, Washington, and again to the clash and jerk of couplings as it started to leave. The next time he awoke, they were rolling across grassy hills and bare rock washes. After they left Pasco, they never stopped at all, rolling down the Columbia River Gorge through scenery that to Macurdy was beautiful almost beyond comprehension.

So this is Oregon, he thought. *God, Varia, if you could only see it!* As newlyweds, moving to Oregon had been a dream, nothing urgent, but something they'd do someday. Now she was in another world with another man, and he was here alone. That should, he thought, have spoiled it for him, but somehow the beauty overrode such considerations.

They spent a day at Portland, swimming in the river with their clothes on to get out most of the soot, then wearing them dry in the sunshine, eating on Macurdy's money, and walking around. They took the elevator to an upper floor of a bank building, where Macurdy stared in awe at distant snow peaks. The nearer, to the east, was Mount Hood, Roy told him, and the one off north, Mount Saint Helens. They spent that night with one of Roy's aunts, who treated Macurdy as a welcome guest. The next day they hiked to the railyard and caught another freight, this one on a branch line, headed for the sawmill town of Nehtaka, where Roy, not so confident as he'd been fifteen hundred miles east, hoped they'd find work.

4

Severtsons' Camp

They didn't go to the hiring hall. Instead they hiked a dusty road out of town, past yards of great dark logs, and acres of fragrant lumber stacked in the sun to dry. Past a sawmill, whose shrieking headrig and growling planers they could hear from the road four hundred yards away. Above the mill, a tall stack trailed a pennant of woodsmoke. A slab burner, like a fifty-foot sheet-iron teepee, leaked more of it, from the top and every seam. Like the visual scene, the resinous pungencies charmed Macurdy. Oregon!

Roy led him to a large, shed-like building covered with asphalt siding. At one end was an office, and it was there they entered. A tall, rawboned blond woman sat at a desk, with a typewriter, a phone, and a pint-sized mug of coffee. On a nearby table sat an electric burner—something Macurdy had never seen before—topped with a large enameled coffee pot, robin's egg blue with black chips. Within the woman's reach was a battered file cabinet, another novelty; Macurdy didn't even know what it was.

"We come to see Axel," Roy told her. "We're looking for work."

This was a self-deprecatory Roy Klaplanahoo, figuratively with hat in hand. White men had left Europe to avoid such servility for themselves. She looked them over, then turned toward an open door. "Axel!" she called, "there's a couple of jacks out here looking for work. One's a Klaplanahoo."

A moment later a tall, big-shouldered, middle-aged man came through the door. He was bald as an egg, but a thatch of flaxen chest hair bushed from his open collar. "Vhere you been?" he said to Roy. "I ain't seen you for a year or more."

"I been to Oklahoma. I'd heard it was real Indian country, and I wanted to see it."

"Vas it? Indian country?"

"Outside the cities it was. The cities were like Portland, only hotter in summer and colder in winter. I didn't like it very much."

Axel Severtson turned to Macurdy. "Vhere you from?"

"Indiana."

"Indiana." Severtson frowned. "You know anything about the voods?"

"Yeah. I've cut timber off and on all my life."

The Swede appraised him, checking the heavy shoulders, the large beefy hands. "Come vit' me," he said, and beckoning, led the two of them through another door into the shed end of the building. Mostly it was storage. Tools hung on the walls; large, well-greased spools of cable lay on skids; and there were chests presumably holding other equipment. "You a faller?" Axel asked Macurdy.

"When we cut, my uncle and me, we did everything: felled, bucked, and skidded."

"Vhat did you cut?"

"White oak, more than anything else. Barrel stock."

The Swede grunted, as if oaks were beneath the attention of real loggers, then took down an axe and tested the blade with a thumb. "C'mon," he said, and led them out the back of the building. A log perhaps three feet in diameter lay there on skids. Someone had already cut into it with an axe; there was a pair of cuts a few feet apart, one of them ragged and rough. Severtson handed Macurdy the axe.

"Let's see vhat you can do vit' it."

Macurdy hefted it—the handle was longer than he was used to—checked an edge for himself, then stepped onto the log, planted his feet and began, his strokes measured and powerful, precise. Chips as big as books began to fly. Halfway through, the Swede called a halt. "Okay," he said, "you'll do. I got some guys didn't come back from the Memorial Day veekend, and I ain't vun of those that goes to Portland to bail them out of yail."

✧ ✧ ✧

Axel sent him back into town to get boots and caulks—said it wasn't safe working without them—and tin pants and whatever else he needed. After giving him a note saying he was hired, in case he needed credit in the stores. Macurdy invested in a toothbrush, too, but not a razor. Like most Macurdy men, he grew little hair except on his skull—because of his ylvin genes, Varia had told him. He'd never grown more than a faint down on cheeks and jaw.

By noon they were on their way to camp, in a truck hauling rigging gear. They ate a late lunch of sandwiches in the messhall—the crew carried their lunches—then were taken into the woods. Macurdy wondered how it was possible to cut timber on such steep slopes. And the stumps! Most were between fifty and ninety inches across, maybe twenty inches high on the uphill and five feet on the downhill side. On this job, he would learn, most of the trees stood between two hundred and two hundred eighty feet tall. He'd never imagined such forest.

They had to wait a few minutes while the foreman—the youngest Severtson brother, Lars—finished marking out a new cutting strip for a pair of fallers. Then Lars assigned a bucker to fell trees with Roy. Finally Macurdy was given the ex-bucker's long one-man saw and steel tape measure, and told what to do. He realized now why buckers worked alone: Most of the prostrate trunks were too large for men to work together on opposite sides.

"You ever do this before?" Lars asked. His accent was slight; he'd come over as a child, and gone to school in Nehtaka.

"Not in trees like these," Macurdy answered.

"Let's see how you do."

The cut had been started, and the saw left in the kerf. Macurdy took hold of the handle, and after a few strokes got the feel of it. "Okay," Lars said. "Remember, I don't stand for nobody loafing, even if this is piece work. If you don't get the wood out, you go down the road."

He left then. As Macurdy drew and pushed the long saw, he decided he was going to like this job.

✧ ✧ ✧

In Severtson's camp, buckers slept in their own shack, and fallers in another. The choker setters and whistle punks shared still another, as did the cooks, the riggers and skinners and donkey engineers, the cookees and swampers and stable boys and bullcook, the filers and blacksmiths. They ate together though, at long tables bent beneath food, served by the several cookees—mostly boys, but with an old timer whose back couldn't stand the heavier work any longer, and a Finn with a stumpy foot, earned in the always dangerous woods.

For two weeks Macurdy bucked fir—two weeks in which he also learned to file a saw like a pro. The camp had filers, but the general attitude was that any real honest-to-god sawyer filed his own. Macurdy's dad had taught him as a boy, but he'd never been more than adequate before. Now he learned the fine points of swaging, and how to get the set so even, the cut surface was as smooth as if planed.

Then Roy's felling partner was afflicted with terminal thirst, and left for Portland to drink up his money. Roy suggested Macurdy for a replacement, and Lars agreed to give him a trial. Skill with the axe was the most demanding part of the faller's job, and axemanship Macurdy's best woods skill; they became not only a successful team, but by Macurdy's second week felling with Roy, they were in contention for the highest producing team, and the big monthly prize of twenty dollars each.

The previously dominant team included a man everyone stayed clear of, so far as possible. Even his partner was wary of him. Like Macurdy, Patsy Hannigan was new in the area, but already had a reputation as both a logger and a troublemaker. His aura reminded Macurdy of the late Lord Quaie's, in Yuulith, with cruelty smoldering at the surface, poorly concealed.

Hannigan was not a particularly large man—six-foot one and one hundred seventy pounds—but sinewy, and tough as a bullwhip. He'd gone to Nehtaka for Memorial Day, and fought twice; both his opponents were hospitalized. He fought dirty—not the usual thing among loggers. The only men in camp who didn't seem leery of him were Lars and Macurdy—and possibly Klaplanahoo; it was hard to be sure about the Indian. Lars's reputation as a fighter was well established; his older brother had made him woods boss at age eighteen, and several brawlers of reputation had quickly tested him. He'd never been whipped, and since then had seldom needed to fight.

Surprisingly, Hannigan had shown no inclination to call the foreman out, but the general belief in camp was that when "the Irishman" decided to hit the road, he'd try taking the boss before he left. Or possibly Macurdy, whom most felt could take him, though they'd never seen Macurdy fight.

It never happened. Hannigan discovered Hansi Sweiger instead. Hansi, seventeen years old, had come with his family from Germany at age eight, and in school had lost his accent entirely, though his family still spoke German at home. When he'd graduated from high school that spring, he'd come to work as a whistle punk. Now, belatedly, Hannigan had discovered the kid was German. It was the excuse he needed to abuse him verbally, as if Hansi had been personally responsible both for the World War and Germany's defeat in it. Macurdy had expected Lars to call Hannigan on it, but he never did. Roy said it wasn't done that way; in the camps, a man stood up for himself, though in Hansi's case, no one doubted that if he ever stood up to Hannigan, he'd be beaten half to death.

That never happened either. Because one morning the sheriff and a deputy came to camp, Axel with them, bearing a warrant from Coos County for Hannigan's arrest on charges of rape and murder. They came into the messhall to serve it.

The crew had finished breakfast, and the men were gathered at the lunch tables, packing their lunches. As soon as the sheriff identified his purpose, Hannigan's hand went inside his shirt and emerged with a flat .38 caliber pistol, firing even as he drew. The first shot tore through the sheriff's right bicep, spinning him around; the second hit the deputy in the middle of the forehead; the third struck Axel high in the chest. Then, for a reason that would never be known, Hannigan turned his pistol toward Hansi Sweiger, who stood big-eyed by the coffee tank, thermos in hand.

His fourth shot hit no one, however, because Macurdy threw his heavy sheath knife, taking Hannigan between the fourth and fifth ribs on the left, barely missing the breastbone and plunging into the heart. Hannigan shot into the floor as he fell.

Macurdy used an Ozian shaman's version of first aid to help Axel and the sheriff. The deputy and Hannigan were beyond help, though Macurdy wouldn't have helped Hannigan anyway.

He had no idea what Hannigan had done for him, nor had Hannigan.

5

Mary Preuss

Lars sent the crew to the woods anyway. Axel wasn't dead, he said, Hannigan was, and dead or alive, the sonofabitch wasn't going to shut down Severtson's camp.

Production wasn't up to standard that day, of course, except by Klaplanahoo and Macurdy. There was a lot of talking, much of it about Macurdy: how quickly he'd moved, how accurately and powerfully he'd thrown.

Two days later a deputy arrived with a court order: Macurdy was to come in for a hearing. Lars demanded to know why. Because, the deputy told him, anyone who willfully killed someone, even with good cause, had to have a court hearing, to establish in law that the act had been necessary. That way, he explained, no one could ever claim he'd done wrong by it.

Lars explained back that that was a lot of bullshit—that no one could ever say there was anything wrong with what Macurdy had done. But he took the deputy out to Roy's and Macurdy's cutting strip, and Macurdy left for town in the sheriff department's new 1933 Ford V-8, with a radio like the police car in Miles City. Macurdy wasn't worried; the deputy's aura reflected friendly admiration.

In town, the sheriff, Fritzi Preuss, sat behind his desk with his right arm and shoulder in a cast. His face was drawn, his aura marked by trauma and the strong analgesic he'd been given for pain. Hannigan's bullet had smashed through his humerus, an injury much more traumatic than a flesh wound or ordinary fracture. Nonetheless he got to his feet, shook left hands with Macurdy, and with a mild German accent, asked some routine questions. One was where he'd come from—county, state, and home address—Fritzi writing the answers slowly in careful, left-handed block letters.

Having come to Oregon to keep from being traced, the questions made Macurdy uncomfortable. "I'd rather my folks don't get word of this," he said. "They'd worry."

Fritzi grunted. "Your address I need only for the record. I'm not going to write to your family. But the law says I also have to contact the county there, to find out if you have a criminal record." He paused, fixing Macurdy with his eyes. "Do you have a criminal record?"

Macurdy shook his head. "No sir."

Fritzi smiled lopsidedly. "Good! I tell you what: We kill two birds with the same stone. I tell them I want the information because I'm considering hiring you as a deputy. I am, you know; to replace Marvin. You should make a good deputy. You are big; that helps when loggers are in town. You think quick; that's always good for a lawman. And after what you did, you will have a reputation. They will talk about you in camps all the way to Canada, to California."

Macurdy stared.

"It's a better job than logging," Fritzi continued calmly. "I know. I have done both. There won't be lay-offs, you won't have to live in a bachelor camp, the work isn't as hard, and you don't get rained on so much." He half smiled again. "It's safer, too."

"I don't know," Macurdy said. "I like logging."

The sheriff grunted. "Axel says you are new here. Do you know we get seventy inches of rain a year? Sixty of it between October and May. All you've seen is the dry season."

A phone rang. Fritzi ignored it; a deputy picked it up. "Well," Fritzi went on, "you don't have to decide right now. But I'll handle it that way with your county back east."

"Excuse me, sheriff," the deputy said, "it's Onni Hautala. That fire on Devils Creek has crowned and crossed the ridge; spotted all over the next drainage. He says he's got a bad blowup on his hands, and wants you to shut down all the logging in the county till we get some rain."

The sheriff stood and took the phone. "Onni," he said, "you

really think it's that bad? . . . That will make problems—hundreds more people not working. Hundreds more eating on credit or the county, or not eating at all. . . . All right, if it's that bad, we'll shut them down. Maybe the state will hire them to fight the fire. . . . Okay, I'll tell them you said it."

Fritzi hung up and turned to Macurdy. "So now the logging is shut down for a while, and you got to find something else. Probably fighting fire day and night. The deputy job is yours if you want it, unless we find something wrong. Now I've got a lot of phone calls to make. Come to my house at 6:30 for supper, and we talk."

Macurdy bought a watch, and it was 6:30 sharp when he knocked on the sheriff's door. A girl answered, in her late teens he thought, fair, blonde, and slender, not remarkably pretty, but nice-looking in a flowered print dress. Her eyes in particular took his attention. They were blue, with a tilt that reminded him of Varia's, though she'd hardly have Varia's pointy ears.

"I'm Curtis Macurdy," he said. "The sheriff told me to be here at 6:30."

She stepped aside, motioning him to enter. "Come in, Mr. Macurdy. I'm Mary Preuss. Dad just phoned. He'll be here in a few minutes." She was poised, her voice quiet, her aura reflecting—not self-deprecation, just modesty, he decided. *And maybe a little shyness around men she doesn't know.* An elderly woman stood in the living room, square-framed like Fritzi, wearing an apron, her gray-blond hair braided and coiled. She nodded, then exchanged words with Mary in a foreign language. His name was part of it.

"My grandmother doesn't speak English," Mary told him matter-of-factly. "Her name is Klara Preuss; she's dad's mom. She came from Germany—East Prussia, actually—after my mom died. To keep house and take care of me." She gestured toward an upholstered chair, straight-backed with wooden arms. "Won't you sit down?"

Macurdy sat. Mary took a similar chair opposite, while her grandmother chose a wooden chair close to the kitchen door, as if to keep an eye on the stove. For an awkward moment no one spoke, then Mary broke the silence.

"Dad told us what you did, the day before yesterday at Severtson's camp. That was pretty remarkable."

"So's your dad. Getting shot and his arm broken like that, and back at work again already."

The girl turned and spoke to her grandmother in quick German. The old woman grinned and spoke German back to her, then turned and looked at Macurdy, sharp-eyed but smiling. "She says," Mary told him, "that you're a bloodstopper—a kind of magician. That's something country people believe in where she comes from. Dad said when you touched his arm, the bleeding stopped, just like that. To her, that makes you a bloodstopper. And to him too, but he'd never put it that way."

Uncomfortable with the subject, Macurdy shifted away from it. "It's a good thing your dad's tough. He's had a lot to do today, with that big fire. I hiked out to Severtson's office; they've sent their whole crew to fight it. I'd have gone, too, except I'm supposed to talk with your dad this evening."

The two of them talked for nearly thirty minutes, with occasional brief pauses while Mary summarized in German for her grandmother. They talked about the Hard Times and Roosevelt, the PWA and the NRA. Macurdy knew little about government programs; his parents, to save money, had stopped subscribing to the Louisville paper. And of course, he'd been out of the country till four months earlier, though he said nothing of that.

He decided Mary was older than she seemed. Her looks suggested seventeen or eighteen, but her poise and maturity suggested several years more than that. "What do you do?" he found himself asking. "You sure know a lot about what's going on."

"We get the Portland paper, and my grandmother can't read it, so she has me read the major parts to her. In German that is, translating. She's really interested. She . . ."

There were footsteps on the porch, then the front door opened and Fritzi came in, slumped and gray-faced. "Hello, Macurdy. Hello Mary. *Heda, Mama.* I'm sorry to be so late. All hell has broke loose in the woods. It is already the worst fire since 1910, and no one knows how much bigger it will get."

Klara spoke curtly to him in German and disappeared into the kitchen, Mary following. Fritzi lowered himself painfully, awkwardly into a wingbacked chair. "It looks like Severtson's camp will get burned out."

Macurdy thought of those magnificent trees, that awesome volume of timber. Fritzi talked briefly of other fires he'd known or heard about, then Klara called them to supper. The food was plain but good, like his mother's, Macurdy thought. Now that Fritzi was home, Mary left the talking to him. Macurdy wondered if it was the custom in Germany that the man of the house did the talking to male guests. When they'd finished eating, Fritzi got down to business.

"One question I got to ask. I should have asked when we talked in my office. Do you get drunk sometimes?"

"No sir. Never."

"Good. Earl asked Lars this morning, and Lars said he didn't think so. At least you never went to town."

Briefly they talked about the deputy job, and Macurdy agreed to take it. As soon as Fritzi heard from Washington County, hopefully the next day, the hearing could be held. After that he'd begin his training, on probation. Meanwhile he was to find a place to live, and move in. One of Fritzi's sisters-in-law was looking for a boarder.

Fritzi closed the conversation then: "I'm sorry, but I got to take my pills and go to bed. I hurt like hell. Be at my office at one." They got up from the table, and the last thing anyone said to Macurdy, except goodbye, came from Klara. No one interpreted for him, but Mary blushed brightly.

Walking back to his room in the Nehtaka Hotel, he wondered what the old woman had said. Something about him, he was sure. Whatever it was, he had something to think about, something that shook him, because he was strongly attracted to Mary Preuss. She wasn't beautiful like Varia, or sexy like Melody, but there it was as close to love at first sight, he admitted to himself, as he was likely to experience. And it troubled him, worried him, because so far he'd had no luck with love. Or—actually he had, up to a point. Varia had been a wonderful wife, for the weeks they'd been together, but he'd lost her. And Melody had loved him passionately, until she'd drowned.

And there was his life expectancy to consider. And Mary's age: Fritzi had mentioned her high school graduation as having been that spring; she was as young as she looked. But in a dozen or so years she'd probably look older than he would.

Maybe, he told himself, he was making a mistake, staying in Nehtaka. Maybe he should go somewhere else. But he knew he wouldn't. He'd stay and see what developed.

6

A Strange Courtship

Depositions by Fritzi, Axel, and several of the jacks who'd witnessed the death of Patsy Hannigan, all supported Macurdy's testimony. Not that there'd been any doubt, but now the law was satisfied. No charges were filed against him, and for a few days he was a local celebrity. It would have been talked about more, had it not been for the giant Cedar River Fire, busily devouring some quarter million acres of prime timber.

The last embers had hardly cooled before salvage logging began, with crews at first living in tent camps. Macurdy didn't envy them. On Saturdays they came to town telling of work clothes hopelessly blackened from charred bark, and of clouds of ash that rose each time a tree was felled. It was, they swore, the worst kind of logging in the world, even worse than logging blowdown.

Meanwhile Macurdy was discovering there was more to learn than he'd anticipated. Each day he went with, or stayed in the office with Fritzi or one of his deputies, learning by watching and doing. And each day he spent at least a couple of hours reading manuals and other books, while from time to time, Fritzi grilled him, the questions mostly beginning: "What do you do if . . . ?"

He hardly had time to think about Mary, let alone talk with her, until, in his third week on the county payroll, he went with Deputy Lute Halvoy in the paddy wagon to the Moose

Hall, where a brawl was reported. He'd never seen anything like it. In the lot next door, a dozen or so loggers were punching, grappling, and rolling around grunting and swearing on the ground, while twice that many were cheering them on. Halvoy blew his whistle, but no one paid any attention at all, so he drew his nightstick and waded in, Macurdy a stride behind and to one side, whacking men on arms, shoulders, backs, to get their attention.

They did. Someone turned and punched Macurdy flush on the nose. It was the wrong thing to do. Macurdy dropped his nightstick, slugged the man in the gut, and delivered a crushing blow to the side of the jaw, dropping the logger like a sack of sand, then turned to the next man, and the next, doing essentially the same thing. This gained real attention. With a loud bellow in Norwegian, a man the crowd cheered as Big Erik squared off with Macurdy, and they began to fight. Big Erik might have been as strong—even stronger—but he lacked Macurdy's technique and quick hands, and when he went down, peace descended. The two deputies herded the crowd back into the club, then handcuffed those on the ground, locked them in the wagon, and started for jail. The idea was not to discover perpetrators or punish anyone, but to remind the loggers that public brawling was illegal in Nehtaka County, and to uphold the reputation of its sheriff's department.

Macurdy's nose had been bleeding freely, and while Halvoy drove, Macurdy silently exercised his bloodstopping skills. Meanwhile his nose and eyes were swelling, so Halvoy dropped him off at Sweiger's Cafe, where he could get ice to put on them.

Mary was there when he walked in. Mainly she worked there from 9 AM till 2 PM, but this evening she was covering for Ruth Sweiger. At the moment there were no customers. She stared wide-eyed at Macurdy, at his swollen, discolored face and bloody shirt front. "Curtis!" she cried, "what happened?"

"We stopped a brawl at the Moose Club," he said, talking like a man with a bad head cold.

Quickly she got a large dish towel from the kitchen, wrapped ice in it, and brought it to him. He'd seated himself in a back booth where he couldn't be seen by people coming in. Now he held the ice to his offended features. Mary sat across from him, facing the door.

"You're all bloody."

"I know."

She giggled in spite of herself. "I suppose you do. Did you hit anyone?"

He grunted. "Guess."

She laughed out loud, then sobered. "Is it broken? Your nose?"

"It's not the first time."

"I'd noticed."

He remembered what had happened after that first time: Melody and Jeramid had rescued him, taking him half conscious to Melody's cabin. He'd had a concussion, and she'd spent the night ministering to him in more ways than one. It occurred to him that he'd like Mary to do the same, and rejected the thought irritatedly. Mary and Melody were as different as Nehtaka was different from Oztown, and that was a lot of difference.

"Does it hurt much?" she asked.

"I wouldn't want someone to hit it again just now."

The towel was beginning to drip ice water, and Mary got another from the kitchen to wipe the table with. Then they sat and talked, their first real talk since the night they'd waited for her father.

"Mary," he said at last, "would you go to a movie with me? When my face looks better?" He'd lowered the ice-filled towel to look at her. Her face sobered instantly at his question.

"I'm sorry Curtis, but no. I like you, quite a lot, but I don't date."

"Have I said anything or done anything I shouldn't?"

"No no! Really you haven't. It's not you at all. But—I just don't date. I promised myself years ago that I'd never get married, so I just don't date. Especially someone I think I might like a lot."

He looked worriedly at her. "You can trust me. I wouldn't get rambunctious. Really. And I'm not someone that gets into fights ordinarily. This was in line of duty."

She reached for his hand, clasping his thick fingers. "Curtis, understand me. I do trust you. I can see more about people than most do, and I like what I see. It's me I don't trust, because I truly must not get married."

A couple entered the cafe. Mary took their orders, then went into the kitchen and made their burgers. Macurdy had the towel back on his face again. The ice had shrunk, but the towel was still cold. It seemed to him the swelling had gone down somewhat, though he supposed his face would be discolored for two or three weeks. It would look bad for a deputy to go around with a pair of black eyes like some drunk, at least it would in Washington County, Indiana. Probably, he told himself, there was a shamanic way to clear discoloration, though Arbel had never mentioned it. Maybe he could work something out from the treatment for fractures.

When the couple had their burgers, Mary came back to the booth and sat across from him again. "Let me see how it looks," she said, and when he showed her she nodded. "The swelling's already going down." She paused. "It's almost ten o'clock. I'm supposed to close then."

"Can I walk you home?"

She smiled, touching his hand again. "Of course. I'd appreciate it. It will save Dad coming after me."

He smiled wryly. "That's the only reason I asked. To save him the trouble."

She colored briefly, then phoned her father, telling him he needn't come and get her, that Curtis would walk her home. When her customers had finished eating and left, she closed the flue and draft in the big stove, put things in the refrigerator, the cash in a bag and the bag in the safe, then turned out the lights. Larry Sweiger would come in soon to clean up. After she'd locked the door behind them, they started east up Columbia Street. The whole downtown was dark now. After a block walked in silence, Macurdy spoke.

"I don't want to badger you or anything, but I really hope you'll tell me more about not wanting to date or marry."

She didn't answer at once, and when she did, it was stiffly. "There's nothing to tell."

Her aura reflected not so much irritation, though, as an unpleasant mix of emotions he couldn't sort out. For the next block and a half he thought about his old mentor Arbel, remembering how the shaman had questioned people who didn't know why, or wouldn't tell why, they felt or thought or did as they did. But mostly Arbel's patients were interested in freeing themselves of whatever devils or disorders troubled them, while seemingly Mary didn't. She might not even have any.

How might he apply what Arbel had shown him? It took him two more blocks to speak again. "Can I ask some questions? To help me understand?"

This time Mary's aura did show irritation, and she stopped, about to tell him "no" again, emphatically this time. Yet somehow the word "yes" came out. "But not here," she said. "We can sit on the porch at home and talk."

They turned south down a residential street lined and darkened by Norway maples and Douglas-firs, the air cool and damp off the nearby ocean, smelling of salt and kelp instead of the smoke that had made the air so pungent recently.

The sheriff's two-story frame house stood in a large lot, well back from the street, dark with the shadows of trees and hedges, and lit dimly by a single light somewhere inside. They turned up the walk, went up the steps and onto the porch, where they seated themselves in wicker chairs, facing each other. It was hard to begin. He wished he had a shaman drum or flute, but even if he had, he could hardly start thumping a drum on the sheriff's front porch in the middle of the night. Nor had Varia used one to spell him when they were newlyweds, and she'd wanted to activate his ylvin genes.

For a moment he turned inward, gathering shaman focus, then turned that focus on Mary and spoke quietly. "I got it that you don't want to date or marry, but tell me—tell me something you could like about marriage."

She frowned. "About marriage."

"Right. Tell me something you could like about marriage."

She might have told him it was none of his business—it occurred to her—or that she didn't want to talk about it. But there was something compelling in his question. She spoke even more quietly than he had. "Well—it would be nice to have someone to talk with, and go places with."

"Okay. Now tell me something you *wouldn't* like about being married."

There was a long lag before she answered. He wished he could see her eyes. Arbel had taught him that eye movements and color shifts could tell more about some things than auras could. "Children," Mary said at last. "I wouldn't like to have children."

That was it; that was the key. Her aura left no doubt. "All right. What is there about children that you don't want?"

She was facing him, looking past him. "I couldn't stand to have children."

"Fine. What specifically is there about children . . ." Then, in his mind, he saw the picture that was stuck in her own, hidden from her by trauma. "That's it," he said. "What *is* that?"

"Nothing. There's nothing." Her voice was little more than a whisper.

"Is that lady in bed your mother?"

He felt her rush of emotion, followed by a sense of brittleness, as if she'd turned to glass. Then the brittleness dissolved, and she began silently to cry. Briefly he let her, then said, "Tell me about it."

"She—she died—because of me."

"All right. How did that happen?"

She shook her head. "I don't know, don't remember. I was just a little child. A baby, really."

"Ah. Look earlier, and tell me what you see."

"I don't see anything. There's nothing there."

"Okay. A minute ago you could see a lady in bed. Your mother. What I want you to do now is see what happened before she was in bed."

That picture came through too, for him as for her. "I see—I see her flopping around on the floor. Jerking. Howling." Mary's voice remained little more than a whisper. "I run out of the house to Mrs. Nelsen's next door." Mary's focus left the scene she'd described, shifting to Macurdy. "Mrs. Nelsen called the doctor. Mama had cancer of the brain. She died a few weeks later, maybe a few months, and they wouldn't let me see her while she was dying. They thought it was too terrible for a child to see. She'd have convulsions, and scream, and say terrible things."

Macurdy took a deep breath. "All right." He paused. "Did you do something to make that happen?"

Mary grimaced through her tears. "Me? What could I have done?" Abruptly her voice intensified. "She had *cancer!* In her brain! Don't you understand?"

"How old were you?"

Her anger subsided. "I was three when she died. On my birthday. So, two-something when she—got sick."

"Okay." He continued quietly, with a calm learned from Arbel. "Look a little earlier, to before her convulsions started, and tell me what you see."

She frowned, peering inward, then her aura sparked and swelled like a threatened cat, while her face began to slacken as if entering a trance.

"What do you see?" he nudged.

"I—see—a little child. Me. I'm playing with a dish, a bowl, and drop it. It breaks in pieces. Mamma's bowl that her *isoäiti* gave her. I start to cry, and mamma hears and comes in, and cries hard, and scolds me because her grandma is dead, and spanks me *so hard! So hard!* And screams at me because I broke her grandma's beautiful bowl she gave her before she died, that I knew I wasn't supposed to touch. And I'm so scared, and she spanks me so hard, I pee on her lap when she spanks me, and she throws me on the bed and falls on the floor, and begins to jerk and scream!"

All through her description, Mary's whisper had tightened, tightened, her body writhing now, twisting with inner agony. "Then *cry!*" Macurdy ordered sharply. *"Cry! Let it out!"*, and she began to keen, dismally.

Seconds later he heard feet hammering down the stairs inside. A wild-eyed Fritzi stepped onto the porch in his nightshirt. "What in hell?!" he said, staring.

"She told me about her mother dying."

Fritzi gawped, bug-eyed. Mary's keening had turned to blubbering; it seemed to Macurdy she didn't even know her father was there. When she'd calmed a bit, he spoke once more. "Tell me again, from the beginning. See if there's something you missed before."

Basically she repeated, this time in the past tense but added something now. "And while she was spanking me, mama yelled, 'You terrible terrible child! I wish I'd never had you! How could you cause me such *pain?!'* Then she threw me on the bed and fell on the floor."

Mary's tears still flowed, but the terrible grief was gone. Both Macurdy and Fritzi stared. Klara too was peering out the door now, alarmed and bewildered. "And that's it," Mary said, then hiccuped, which made her giggle. Even Macurdy gawped at that. He'd seen Arbel's patients respond in more or less the same way, but he'd never caused such an effect himself.

"Sorry," she said. "Yes, Curtis, I'll go to a movie with you. What night?"

"I better find out for sure what night I can have off. I'll let you know."

She stared unseeingly past him toward the lilac bushes at the corner of the porch. "You know what? When they picked mamma off the floor and laid her on the bed, I told myself I would never ever have a child who would do such wicked things and make me die. Because I knew she was going to die. I knew it before any of the grownups. And I thought it was my fault. I was too little to understand that she'd already had the cancer, probably for months, and no one knew it; a kind the person is dying from before they show any symptoms. I remember Pappa telling Uncle Wiiri that."

Fritzi stared, shaken. "I remember. The doctor told me, and I told Wiiri. He called it *glioblastoma* something. I remember that. It is what killed my Aina."

Klara spoke sharply to Fritzi in German, and he gave her a brief summary. The old woman grumbled something more, then left, presumably returning to bed. Fritzi spoke gruffly to Mary: "Better you come in and go to bed. Rest. The whole neighborhood must be awake now."

"In a minute, Pappa. First I have to thank Curtis. Privately."

Fritzi backed through the door, no doubt to wait listening in the hallway. Macurdy wondered if Mary was going to kiss him. Instead she talked.

"You're a strange man, Curtis Macurdy, but a very nice one. How did you know what to do? To ask those questions? I feel like a new person, I can hardly believe how new."

"I had a friend once who did things like that," he answered.

"I'll tell you about him sometime; I'll tell you a lot of things you should know about me. But not tonight. Your dad's right. Wash your face and go to bed. Sleep on it. I'll see you tomorrow, and see how you feel."

She peered at him for a moment, seeing he didn't know what. Then, standing on tiptoes and holding his face in her hands, she did kiss him, gently. He left in a daze.

Back in his rented room, Macurdy again gave shamanic attention to his damaged face, then went to bed, where he reviewed the evening in his mind. He knew he'd ask Mary to marry him, probably soon, and he knew she'd say yes. It seemed strange but inevitable.

Mary lay looking at a shaft of moonlight through her window. If her mother hadn't had that cancer in her brain, she told herself, she wouldn't have gotten so mad about the dish. Wouldn't have hit her so hard and said those terrible things. Poor *äiti!* It must have been an awful death.

And if it hadn't been for Curtis and his questions, she'd never have remembered, never have known what festered in the back of her mind, hidden by her sense of childish guilt.

What kind of man was Curtis Macurdy? She'd find out, she told herself. Because she knew he'd ask her to marry him. And she would. She would. Perhaps he'd ask her after the movie. Perhaps in a week or a month. She would not, she resolved, disappoint him, with her answer or her love.

7

Disclosures. Proposal. Advices.

By Monday morning, Macurdy's efforts with shamanism, massage, and hot washcloths had reduced the discoloration to a faint greenish yellow, a remarkable accomplishment. He arrived at the courthouse a few minutes before eight. Fritzi was already there, as usual, and Macurdy peered into his office.

"Excuse me, sheriff," he said, "can I talk with you a minute?"

"Go ahead."

"I wonder if I could have a day shift today."

"That's what I planned for you. This morning you go to the courthouse and read some court proceedings. I have written a list.

"You were along when Earl arrested Arne Peterson, and he showed you how to do the paperwork. The trial is this afternoon, and Earl will be there as arresting officer. I want you there too. You got to have experience with these things."

He paused, eyeing Macurdy. "Now. Why did *you* want the day shift today?"

"I want the evening off, to take Mary to the movie. There's things I need to tell her about me, the sooner the better."

Fritzi nodded worriedly. "Macurdy," he said, "I like what I know about you, but I don't know very much. I don't know what happened last night, only that it seemed to end all right. But I love my daughter more than my life. Don't hurt her."

Instead of answering, Macurdy reached across the desk and

shook the sheriff's left hand. "Now," he said, "I'm ready for that list."

The movie was a western, *The Last Roundup*, starring Randolph Scott. They ate popcorn, and when the popcorn was gone, they held hands.

Afterward they strolled Nehtaka's tree-lined residential streets. In jackets; September had brought offshore breezes, and the evening was cool and humid. For the first fifteen minutes they hardly spoke at all, but Macurdy's mood was pregnant with things needing to be said. He'd lost totally the confidence he'd felt Saturday night.

Finally he broke the silence. "How old do you think I am?"

"I don't know. Twenty-five?"

"Twenty-eight."

"That's not old."

"Old enough to have been married. Twice."

There was a long moment's silence before Mary responded: "Tell me about it."

"My first wife's name was Varia. She'd always seemed kind of strange, but we were in love. We were married about six weeks when her family sent people to kidnap her, and I followed them. Out of the country. By the time I found her, she was married to someone else."

"But—that was bigamy! Couldn't you get her back?"

"Not under their laws. And her new husband was an important man. Later I married a girl there named—it translates to Melody—and I got a farm. But a few months later she drowned."

Her hand on his arm, Mary stopped him, looking earnestly into his eyes. "Those things were no fault of yours. Were they?"

"Not so far as I know. But that's just part of what I've got to tell. The easy part. I'm afraid you'll think I'm crazy when I tell you the rest of it, but it wouldn't be honest if I didn't."

When he said nothing more, she turned, and they began walking slowly again, still holding hands. "I have a secret, too," she said. "Not like the one I told you on Saturday, that I'd hidden from myself all those years. It's one that goes on every day of my life, and I've only ever told one person."

He didn't ask, but let her continue in her own time. "You've seen pictures of Jesus and Mary, with haloes around their heads."

"Yeah."

"I see haloes. Everyone has one, and not just around their heads. They're brightest there, but when I take the trouble to, I can see them around their whole body." She peered at him earnestly. "Does that sound crazy?"

This time it was Curtis who stopped. "You see them? I do too! Varia called them auras." He paused, his features vague in the darkness, but to Mary's eyes his aura had expanded: pastels of red, gold, violet—a kind of personal aurora. "That makes it easier for me," he said. "Easier to tell you what I need to."

They walked again, one street after another, Macurdy talking at length. He told her more about Varia, who'd married his Uncle Will when Curtis was four years old. Varia had seemed about twenty. Twenty years later, when Will was killed felling timber, she still looked twenty. Then she'd married Curtis.

The story grew stranger, Macurdy's voice becoming monotone as he told it, as if he'd lost hope again that Mary could possibly believe. Varia had come from another world, he said, then repeated it—another world, named Yuulith, with gates that from time to time opened into this one. In Yuulith she'd belonged to a Sisterhood that was like a tribe. Its women used magic—nothing all that amazing, but useful—and stayed physically young for nearly a century, then rapidly grew old, and died in just a few years. They had men in the tribe for breeding and soldiering, but the head Sister was the boss, like a queen. What she said was law.

A month later, when the gate had opened again, he'd gone to find Varia, and on the other side been made a slave by a tribe there, then a shaman's apprentice, then a soldier. Had been in a war, and found Varia, only to discover she'd remarried. Then he'd married and lost Melody, and returned home again.

They'd stopped on a low bluff overlooking the sparsely lit town, the Pacific stretching in the distance to a horizon seen only by inference, where the stars ended, the blackness becoming sea instead of sky. "And now," he finished, "you probably think I'm either crazy or the world's biggest liar."

She took both his hands. "Curtis," she said quietly, "I'm not even going to think about it. I'm glad you told me, but the smartest thing for me to do is just be me and let you be you, and see how things develop.

"I see haloes, or auras, and most people, if I told them, would think I was crazy or lying. Of course, another world, with gates to this one, sounds quite a lot stranger than that, and I might never quite *believe* in it. But I'll get used to the idea, and that's more important.

"I can generally tell when people are lying, by their haloes, and you're not. And you don't have bad intentions, either; I can tell that too.

"As for magical powers—what you did last night was magical enough for me, and that happened! It was real!"

She moved closer to him. "I want you to take me home now. But first I want you to kiss me, because I'm in love with you."

The kiss was soft and lingering, then they turned back down the hill, saying almost nothing at all until they reached her block, when Macurdy could delay no longer. "There's something I didn't tell you. Something more important."

"Yes?"

"Varia said I won't get old either, till I'm maybe ninety. And that's kind of how it seems. If she was right, then in fifty years I'll still look about twenty-five."

It was Mary's turn to introvert now. After a long moment she responded: "And I'll look about sixty-eight."

They walked on till they reached her front steps, then stopped. "I have a lot to sleep on tonight," she said. "Perhaps even more than on Saturday. Kiss me again, Curtis. It will help."

Again they kissed, a kiss cool but slow. "Thank you," she said. "Stop at Sweiger's tomorrow when I'm at work, and we'll make another date." They stood a couple of feet apart, holding hands between them. "And before you go to sleep tonight," she added, "remind yourself that I love you."

He did. He also told himself that each woman he'd loved had been very special—better, it seemed to him just then, than he deserved.

✧ ✧ ✧

The next day dawned drizzly. He arrived at Sweiger's just before 2 PM, and walked Mary home, both of them wearing raincoats. This time when they reached her porch, she didn't offer to kiss him. Instead she looked him in the eye and said, "Curtis, will you marry me?"

He stared. "Do you mean it?"

"Dammit, if I didn't, would I ask? Let's try it again. Will you marry me?"

It took him a moment to answer. "Yes, Mary, I'll marry you. I just—it's hard to believe this is happening. I'll be very happy to marry you, and I'll be a good husband." *As I was to Varia and Melody. Oh God, let this one last. Let it go on a long time.*

"When?" she asked. "When will you marry me?" Now she didn't seem like a determined young woman at all. She stood like a young girl, straight-backed, brave, hopeful, vulnerable.

"Soon," he said. "We need to get the license, the blood tests, a preacher . . . You need to decide whether you want a lot of people there, a big party—keeping the expense in mind. It could be in a week, I'd think, or maybe a month."

She nodded thoughtfully. "I'll meet you after I get off tomorrow. If you can get off, too."

Then, though it was daylight, she kissed him before turning and going inside.

Curtis went back to the courthouse and told Fritzi he thought he was coming down with something and wanted to go home to bed. He lied about feeling sick, but he did go straight home to bed, and slept for ten hours without waking.

He went to Doc Wesley for his blood test. They were already acquainted; Wesley had examined him before Macurdy had been signed on as a deputy. The doctor drew the necessary blood, then said, "You laid with a woman recently?"

"Not for quite a while."

"How long?"

Macurdy looked back to that night when Omara had come to his room at the palace in Teklapori. "Most of a year." Not really so long, he realized, but a world away.

"A prostitute?"

"Nothing like that. A good friend. A nurse."

The doctor grunted skeptically. "Drop your pants. You were a logger till recently, and even you might not know what you did in Tacoma or Portland or Medford, some Saturday when you'd been drinking."

Macurdy dropped them. The examination took only a minute. "Well, that looks all right," the doctor said. "Look. I won't beat around the bush. I suspect your blood tests will be clean, too. But this whole community knows Mary Preuss. And we like her. A lot. We want her to be happy. What do you know about ladies? Beyond your mother and sisters? I'm talking about ladies now. This girl is no floozie that hangs around drinking in blind pigs, waiting to be picked up. Odds are a thousand to one she's a virgin. She's hardly out of school! Does a roughneck like you know how to treat a girl like that?"

Macurdy bristled a bit. "I think so," he said.

"Well let me tell you some things, because I don't think you do. Your intentions may be good, but I don't trust your knowledge, and the instructions are free."

Then he gave the would-be bridegroom a lecture, with diagrams, on how to deflower a virgin gently. Macurdy left embarrassed and grateful.

Under "Announcements," the Nehtaka *Weekly Sentinel* reported that on October 5, 1933, a marriage license had been granted to "Miss Mary Preuss and Mr. Curtis Macurdy, both of Nehtaka. Miss Preuss is the daughter of Sheriff Fritzi Preuss. Mr. Macurdy is a deputy in the sheriff's department." Word had gotten around quickly, even among those who didn't read the announcements section, and since Macurdy was a local hero, the general response was more enthusiastic than Doc Wesley's had been.

Two days later, Macurdy went into Sweiger's Cafe for a late supper, his duties having precluded taking it at the boarding house. There was only a handful of customers drinking coffee and eating. Hansi Sweiger waited on him, and when he brought his food, sat down to visit.

The first thing he did was to thank Macurdy for saving his

life that early August day in Severtson's messhall. He had no doubt at all that Hannigan was about to shoot him.

Now he was in town for the winter. After the fire, Lars Severtson had promoted him to choker setter. It paid better than whistle punk, but setting chokers on a burn was the dirtiest job in the world. Usually he had to lie down in the ashes and dirt, to poke the cable knob under the logs, while to hook them up, he often had to lie on their charred bark.

So finally he'd quit—his father hadn't been happy about that—and come home to help out in his family's restaurant. He doubted he'd log again. With so much burned timber to salvage, it'd either be more of the same, or he'd have to go somewhere else.

"In fact," he said, "I'm thinking about going back to the old country. Things were really bad there for a while—a lot worse than here—but they've gotten a lot better recently. My cousin Karl's been writing me about it; a guy named Hitler got elected chancellor, and he's putting everyone to work. He's better than Roosevelt any day." Hansi paused. "Roosevelt's a Jew, you know. His real name is Rosenfeld.

"My old man really blew up when I told him what I might do. He says Hitler will ruin Germany—that he'll start another war. Geez! Hitler's not crazy; he doesn't want a war! I tried to reason with dad, but it's like arguing with a brick wall. He got wounded four different times in the last war, you know." Hansi's expression turned thoughtful. "I never thought I'd want to go back, but now—maybe I'll give it a try. I can do it. I put more than enough money away working for the Severtsons."

He changed the subject. "Maybe I shouldn't tell you this, because you're marrying her, but I had a crush on Mary since the eighth grade. In high school, a couple times, I asked her to go out with me, but she never would. She never went out with anyone. People thought she might end up in a convent, but I guess all she needed was to meet the right man."

The door opened, jingling the bell, and Hansi got up. "Sorry I talked your arm off," he said. "Congratulations on getting engaged." Then he went to the counter to wait on the new customer.

✧ ✧ ✧

Helmi Dambridge had come to Nehtaka from Finland at age five. By age seventeen she was an exceptional beauty who had scandalized her family and their Lutheran pastor, and titillated the rest of Nehtaka. The young men of the community found her particularly interesting, but she was interested only in those with "prospects."

Her first marriage was to the handsome young owner-skipper of a sealing ship, who arrived back from an expedition to the Aleutians to discover her gone. She was living with a sawmill owner in Longview, a man equally handsome and with even more money, who didn't sail away and leave her for months on end. Her husband promptly filed for divorce, and when the decree was final, his rival married her. But now, with a legal claim to her fidelity, he too became jealous, on one occasion to the point of blackening her eyes and loosening some teeth; she thanked him by plunging a letter opener into his abdomen.

Her lawyer provided more than legal services, and afterward they married. Twenty-five years older than she, he was totally devoted to her, while she had learned something from her first marriages. It helped, of course, that he had a very lucrative practice. Unfortunately he developed a heart condition, and at age thirty-six she found herself single again, a widow.

Still beautiful, accomplished in the bedroom arts, and with many friends in Portland society, the condition was temporary. She soon married Andrew Dambridge, a fifty-year-old *bon vivant* who had coveted her for years. Dambridge had built a considerable fortune through activities in railroads, lumber, and real estate. He'd also developed a reputation as a ladies' man, but with Helmi in his bed, his philandering dwindled almost to nothing. After a few years, problems of health reduced both his business and bedroom activities, and he died of an aortic aneurism on their ninth anniversary.

Most of his fortune he had willed to the children of his first marriage, but he'd established a very considerable trust fund for his second wife. He was not, however, a man who liked to lose possessions, so the trust fund carried the proviso that if she married again, she'd lose it.

She had no intention of losing it.

She'd continued her life in Portland's upper crust until the Great Depression eroded her trust fund rather severely. In the spring of 1931, she sold her Portland mansion and bought a nine-room home in Nehtaka. She had it modernized, then moved in, a storied and somewhat reclusive figure who lived alone with a housekeeper and custodian, traveled a lot, and largely ignored local doings. The townsfolk, who of course knew nothing of the trust-fund proviso, expected her to find another millionaire and leave again, but she failed to cooperate.

The Widow Dambridge was Mary Preuss's aunt, her mother's eldest sister. When Helmi had moved back to Nehtaka, she'd established limited connections with her family, including Mary, appearing occasionally at family events. But mostly she kept to herself. She was in her studio, painting an Aegean shorescape from a photograph, using memory for the colors, when her maid informed her that Mary was in the parlor.

Helmi sailed down to meet her. "Mary! This is a surprise!" she said. "Sit down, dear, and tell me why you're here."

"I'm going to be married. And—I thought you could advise me."

Helmi laughed. "Shouldn't you be talking with your Aunt Siiri? She's been married to the same man for twenty-five years, and very happily as far as I know."

"I have talked with her. But it seemed to me that . . ."

"Yes?"

"That there are things you could advise me on better than Siiri could."

"Hmm. Interesting. What kinds of things?"

"Well—I love him a *lot,* and I don't want him to be disappointed. You see."

Helmi was careful not to smile. "No I don't," she lied.

"I want to be good in bed for him."

"Ah. And you suppose I was good in bed."

"I think you must have been."

The aunt laughed again. "I was, my dear. I seem to have been born without inhibitions, and brought enthusiasm to bed with me. Those are the basic ingredients—those and imagination; if you lack them, you must develop them. And

I had experienced husbands who knew what they wanted, so I learned from them.

"This fiancé of yours—is he experienced?"

"He's been married before. To a very beautiful lady; he showed me a picture."

Helmi raised an eyebrow. "Really? I'd like to meet this young man. He is young, I suppose?"

Mary read her aunt's skepticism. "Twenty-eight," she said.

"Where is his first wife?"

Wanting to avoid strange and incredible explanations, Mary adjusted the truth. "She drowned. She was riding her horse across a river and the ice broke. The current swept her under it."

Helmi studied her niece for a moment. "Bring him to supper tonight," she said firmly. "At 6:30. I want to meet him."

Mary felt trapped by the invitation—order actually.

"I'll see if he can come," she said. "He works for Dad; he's a deputy. Sometimes he works at night."

"Call him. There's the phone." Helmi pointed. "I need to know now, so I can tell Lempi what to fix for supper."

Mary went to the phone and called. Three minutes later the invitation had been accepted, and the cook/housekeeper given instructions in a rattle of Finnish.

Helmi turned back to Mary, smiling again. "Now for your questions," she said. "Let's go up to my studio, where we have more privacy. Lempi is shy about using English, but she understands it somewhat; Eino's been teaching her. And visitors are so rare in this house, she might decide to eavesdrop."

Macurdy arrived with Mary, wearing his uniform and driving Fritzi's 1932 Desoto. He'd bought a suit, but didn't want to wear it before the wedding.

Helmi made him feel welcome, and the food, Macurdy thought, was as good as anything he'd ever eaten. After supper they stayed for over an hour, talking. Helmi's reason for inviting him, he realized, was to check him out, but at the same time she put him at ease. He answered her questions without creating complications, and increasingly her aura reflected liking and approval.

Before they left, he excused himself to use the bathroom,

and when he was out of the room, Helmi put a hand on Mary's arm.

"My dear," she said, "I'm truly happy for you. I believe you chose well."

Hansi Sweiger decided to go back to Germany, which made his father so angry, he refused to drive him to the depot. So Macurdy threw the youth's three suitcases in the back of a patrol car and hauled him to the train. Expecting never to see him again.

8

A Major Change in Plans

Mary and Curtis wanted an early date for the wedding, and no one tried to talk them out of it. Nor did anyone suggest a lavish ceremony. Nehtaka's Lutheran community, largely Scandinavian and Finnish sawmill workers, loggers, small farmers, and their families, would have frowned on that kind of display, especially in Hard Times.

Food, though, was another matter.

Fritzi was an important county official, and Macurdy something of a celebrity, while Mary's maternal family, the Saaris, were locally prominent. Wiiri Saari had talked with Fritzi about a buffet luncheon, a *voileipäpöytä,* with lots of invitations sent out. They agreed there would be no booze. Fritzi was, after all, the sheriff, and while Congress had passed an amendment to repeal prohibition, the necessary three-fourths of the states hadn't ratified it yet: Liquor was still illegal.

The wedding was held in Holy Redeemer Lutheran Church at 10:15 AM, on Saturday, October 28, 1933, and the buffet at 11:30 in the high school gymnasium. Axel Severtson had been sent an invitation for his loggers, and many had shown up, most of them a little oiled on bootleg liquor, but well behaved. The Saari and Severtson clans were on hand to see to it without the sheriff having to get involved.

The rowdy element was a major Pacific storm front that crashed the party about noon, led by skirmishers of rain and the rumble of approaching thunders, followed directly by the main assault force: a hard, cold, wind-driven deluge. By that time the bride and groom had sneaked out—been spirited to the depot by one of the numerous Saaris—and were on their way to Hood River for a five-night stay at the palatial Columbia Gorge Hotel. Transportation, lodging, meals, and money for tips were wedding gifts from Helmi, who held significant stock in the resort.

The storm overtook them on a train in the terminal yard at Portland, and they arrived at Hood River in a downpour. A redcap hustled their luggage to a hotel limo, and Curtis tipped him (he'd been coached by Helmi on tipping etiquette), then the grinning couple rode to the hotel.

A doorman met them under the entrance canopy, whistled for a bellman, and thanked Macurdy for the tip, making him feel like nobility. The bellman deposited their luggage in their room, and Curtis tipped him. By that time a maid arrived, and lit the gas fireplace. After Macurdy had tipped her, the couple found themselves alone.

First they explored the large room—big bed, fireplace, comfortable chairs, drop-leaf table, luxurious sofa, a bathroom with a very large tub, and french doors opening onto a (just then) rain-lashed balcony overlooking a dimly seen, rain-lashed Columbia River. Then they busied themselves briefly with unpacking their suitcases (also gifts from Helmi), and hanging up their clothes. When they'd finished, they went back to the French doors, and holding hands, watched the storm.

After a minute, Mary rested her head on Curtis's shoulder, and turning, he put his hands on her arms and kissed her, gently at first, then more passionately. She'd rehearsed this moment in her mind, but found herself abandoning the script, unbuttoning her husband's shirt, kissing his chest. Next she found herself cutting short the sofa scene before the fire.

"Curtis," she murmured, "let's take off our clothes."

"That's a wonderful idea."

That didn't take long either, even with frequent glances at each other. Pants, shirt, dress, undergarments, stockings were draped over the back of the sofa. Then, slowly, glowing, they went to each other and embraced, feeling the other's body against their own, lips meeting, tenderly now.

"You're beautiful, Curtis," she breathed.

He chuckled. "I'm the one supposed to say that."

"Am I really? Beautiful?"

"As beautiful as any man could hope for."

She stepped back and pulled the covers to the foot of the bed. "The beautiful Mrs. Curtis Macurdy wants her gorgeous husband to make love to her."

"Mr. Macurdy's been looking forward to this," he answered. Again they embraced, kissing, then lay down together.

Both had learned from their tutors, and Curtis from his previous wives. Both were also naturally talented, and each loved the other very much. They spent the rest of the afternoon in bed, or soaking in the tub, or petting on the sofa in front of the fire.

Finally they dressed again and went down to supper. Afterward they danced, something they'd learned during their brief engagement. On their way back to the elevator, the bell captain asked if they'd like a beverage in their room, compliments of the hotel, and Macurdy said yes.

It arrived almost as soon as they did—champagne, with an ice bucket and long-stemmed glasses. Mary had never drunk before; the bubbles went up her nose, and she got the giggles. It was late before they slept.

It was nearly 10 AM when they awoke, languorous and somewhat sore, their morning kisses soft and loving, but not passionate. They ate breakfast by a window in the hotel restaurant, overlooking a river mostly in sunlight, the storm having migrated east to Idaho. Curtis, feeling experimental as well as famished, discovered cheese blintzes, and told Mary he hoped she'd learn to make them. After helping him eat one, she promised she would.

Afterward they walked the pebbled paths through the hotel gardens, which were somewhat bedraggled from their rain-battering, though gardeners were already out transplanting. Next they took a long carriage ride along the river, ate a midafternoon lunch, then stopped at the gift shop, where they bought magazines and a copy of Sunday's Portland *Oregonian*. Finally they returned to their room, where they made slow love.

It was already night when he found a notice in the *Oregonian* that shook them both.

Woman Injured at Wedding

> Klara Preuss, mother of Nehtaka County sheriff Fritzi Preuss, was struck and seriously injured by a car outside the Nehtaka High School gymnasium, where she had been attending her granddaughter's wedding luncheon. Mrs. Preuss was seriously injured. Egil Nordby, of rural Nehtaka County, was arrested and charged with intoxication and reckless driving.

Curtis phoned the depot, made reservations on the early morning train, arranged an early wakeup, then phoned Fritzi to let him know they were coming. At 7:42 the next day, they were on their way back to Nehtaka.

Klara had a broken right hip and multiple fractures of the thigh—very severe injuries at age 72—and while her life seemed unthreatened (barring a thrombosis of course), Doctor Wesley said she wouldn't walk again.

Helmi had talked Fritzi out of telegraphing the newlyweds. "Call them on Wednesday," she'd said.

Now that they were back, they talked the situation over with Fritzi and Doctor Wesley. Because *Grossmutter* would be unable to shop, keep house, or cook, they'd move in—take the front upstairs bedroom—and Mary would handle the cooking and housekeeping.

Curtis had no idea how important this would be to him, how critical to what would be the defining experience in his life on Earth.

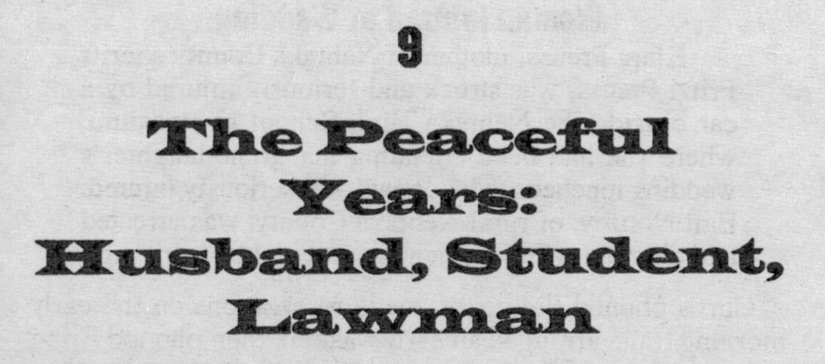

9

The Peaceful Years: Husband, Student, Lawman

When Klara Preuss arrived home from the hospital, a hospital bed had replaced her old one. It was Mary who looked after her, but it was Curtis the old woman asked for. "She says you can help her," Mary explained.

"But I can't talk German!"

"She says bloodstoppers can help bones knit."

Curtis blinked at that. Probably he could. Certainly he shouldn't have overlooked the possibility. He just didn't think like a shaman, he told himself. Between Arbel and Omara, he'd learned, if not always fully mastered, a number of healing techniques, procedures, and principles. And from those could infer others.

He started by examining the fine structure of Klara's aura, and as a basis for comparison, examined and imaged mentally the thread-like energy lines around his own body and Mary's. Then he adjusted—normalized—the energy lines around Klara's.

They didn't stay normalized long, but while they did, healing progressed at a much increased rate, and normalization persisted longer with each treatment. At the end of her first week at home, Dr. Wesley visited, and commented on her surprising progress. At the end of the second week, he said he'd never seen anything like it before. After the third, she spent much of her time in her new wheelchair, and ate in the dining room or kitchen with whoever else was home.

Meanwhile the auric field around his father-in-law's right arm was quite distorted. Fritzi admitted that it ached chronically, especially when he tried to sleep, and agreed readily to let Curtis treat it as he had Klara's. The results were excellent, and surprisingly quick.

Macurdy began to feel quite proud of his shamanic skills, especially when Klara began relying on her cane almost entirely, inside the house, taking to her wheelchair mainly for trips outside. He was doing with the help of analysis what Arbel had done largely by intuition.

Mary had anticipated problems with her *Grossmutter*—that having run the household for so long, she'd try to enforce her ways on her granddaughter. To Mary's surprise, however, Klara seemed pleased to let someone else run things. Not surprisingly, the old woman delighted in her grandson-in-law. His only shortcoming was that he spoke no German, so she set about to teach him. When they were in a room together, she'd point at or touch or slap an article and name it: *der Tisch!* the table. *Die Kaffeekanne!* the coffee pot. He was not only to repeat it, but pronounce it correctly, even if it took a dozen repetitions. Her repeated admonition was, *"Du musst das richtig sagen!"* (You must say it right!)

He enjoyed it, as a game and a challenge. It was easier than learning Yuultal had been. In fact, German grammar had parallels in Yuultal, and he discovered that quite a few German words were recognizably similar to English words meaning more or less the same thing.

Then Mary began working with him on verbs, while Fritzi taught him everyday phrases and simple sentences. Curtis began stopping at Sweiger's almost daily, for coffee and to exercise his expanding German on someone outside his own household. They teased him a bit about his *baltisches Deutsch* pronunciations, sometimes amusing word choices, and often clumsy grammar, but enjoyed and respected his interest and progress.

They never mentioned how Hansi was doing, or even if they heard from him, and diplomatically, Macurdy never asked.

By summer he understood quite a bit that was said at the supper table. Of course, the others spoke more slowly and carefully than they might have, but it seemed to him that before too long he'd be modestly competent with the language.

One of the first things Fritzi had done, when Macurdy came on the job, was introduce him to the .38 police special—show him *how* to use and care for it. And talk with him about *when*, and more importantly when *not* to use it.

Although Macurdy had never before held a side arm, he proved a natural marksman. On occasion, off-duty deputies would get together on the department's makeshift firing range in what had been the Nehtaka Livery Stable, and before long he was firing the best scores in the department.

One day the following spring, Fritzi sent him with his undersheriff, Earl Tyler, to take a prisoner to Portland. After they dropped the man off, Curtis bought a large picture postcard showing Mount Hood, then wrote on it:

Dear Mom and Dad,

I am traveling and today have stopped in Portland. I can see this mountain from the city. It is even more beautiful to the naked eye than in the picture.

I am feeling fine and doing well. I hope you are the same. Give my regards to Frank and Toodie, to Julie and Max, and to Ferris and Bob and Hattie. Also remember me to Trapjaw and Blaze.

I intend to get home someday for a visit, but it will likely be awhile. It is hard to get away from work long enough, and while I travel on the job, I never travel very far east.

Your loving son,
Curtis

He gave them no address. Actually he seldom thought about his parents, or Indiana or Yuulith, or even Varia. Though occasionally he dreamed of her, the dreams invariably including sex.

Mary never asked if he dreamed of his earlier wives. If she ever should, he told himself, he could truthfully say he dreamt more often of Vulkan than of Varia—of a half-ton great boar more often than of his beautiful first wife. He'd never told Mary about Vulkan; that would be a little much even for her, it seemed to him—a sorcerer in the body of a giant wild hog! He could never remember much about his dreams of Vulkan, but somehow they seemed meaningful.

His dreams of Varia, on the other hand, he remembered clearly. They were always in the same place, a kind of gazebo on a seashore. They'd talk—about what always escaped him within moments of wakening—and then they'd make love, and when they did, he loved her as much as when they'd married. Maybe more, because now he wasn't spooked by her powers.

He couldn't honestly say which of his three wives he'd loved most. When he'd been with Varia, he'd been a different person, ignorant and naive, while his marriage with Melody had been passionate, occasionally even tempestuous on her part. But his new marriage was the happiest, beyond any doubt.

No doubt Varia could say the same thing of hers. Cyncaidh was as good a man, or as good an ylf, as anyone. Along with being wealthy and powerful, he was honest and thoughtful, and had integrity.

He wondered if Varia ever dreamed of him—if perhaps they dreamed of each other at the same time. He rather thought they did.

The next March, Mary came up pregnant, but soon afterward miscarried. They were both disappointed, but not deeply so. There'd be other pregnancies; they made love often enough.

Macurdy had been reading auras for several years—since he'd learned to see them. With Arbel's help, he'd learned to read emotions, character, to a degree even intention from them.

Now, for the first time, he made a study of them, and his readings became more refined and precise, enabling him to avoid or deal with trouble as a law officer.

Fritzi was careful not to favor his son-in-law unfairly on the job, but with a year under his belt, Curtis was easily the best of his deputies, except perhaps for the undersheriff. So he promoted him to corporal.

The duties weren't often dangerous, or even particularly onerous. With the repeal of prohibition, several bars had opened in Nehtaka, and drunkenness became more common, or at least more open. The Moose Hall quickly got a liquor license, followed promptly by the Swedish Club, the Sons of Norway, and the Finnish Brotherhood.

Public drunkenness, fighting, and traffic violations made up most of the work load, and the brawlers in particular could be hard to handle. So in 1935, Fritzi sent Macurdy to Seattle for three weeks of intensive jujitsu training under a Japanese who advertised in law enforcement journals. Macurdy came back with a certificate of completion, another as "best student," and an excellent basic grasp of principles as well as very useful techniques. Fritzi then had him train the other deputies, and afterward, Macurdy claimed that teaching had been almost as helpful as taking the course in the first place.

More important, he had a definite talent for cajoling drunks and others out of violence, and when cajolery wasn't adequate, onlookers were invariably impressed with his new physical skills, which augmented his previous reputation nicely, and helped make cajolery effective.

At the jujitsu classes, Curtis Macurdy met a Jack McCurdy, a deputy sheriff from Lewis County, Washington. Jack McCurdy's uncle kept saddle horses on his place near Morton, Washington, and on three different summers, Curtis and Mary went with Jack and his wife on horseback trips into the wild high country of the Cascade Mountains. They'd pack in to a lake and make camp. It was the women who fished, while the men explored the craggy higher country on horseback and afoot. Jack asked Curtis where he'd learned to ride so skillfully.

Curtis didn't tell him it had been in a world called Yuulith. He thought it best not to.

He never imagined the experience gained in those Cascade outings would prove valuable, a few years later.

Traffic accidents increased with the constant increase in cars and speeds, and Macurdy had occasions to use his shamanic skills to save a life.

In addition he'd received valuable first-aid training as a deputy, but more interesting was the help he got from Doc Wesley. Fritzi had bragged to the doctor about his son-in-law's work on his arm and Klara's leg and hip. The doctor loaned Macurdy basic texts on anatomy and physiology, with the comment: "If you're going to mess around with healing, you'd better know something about bodies."

Much of the physiological material was over Macurdy's head. His only actual instruction in science had been in the eighth grade, in the one-room Maple Crossing School, which was innocent of a laboratory. But he found the anatomy text, and the more general physiological discussions both understandable and interesting. Particularly since on several evenings, Doc Wesley took the time to answer and even discuss his questions.

In 1937, Mary got pregnant again, and again miscarried. Macurdy wondered if perhaps he was snake-bit on the subject of fatherhood. Or if the ylvin strain in his ancestry might have something to do with his family tendency not to beget many children, at least with regular humans.

By that time he was reading a German language weekly paper, the *California Demokrat* from San Francisco. Reading it aloud, because Klara could no longer see well enough to read newspaper print. He'd read all of it that interested her, with only occasional corrections of pronunciation. Fritzi told him he had a talent for German, that if he ever went to Germany, he'd get along just fine.

In the fall of 1937 they got a new young preacher at Holy Redeemer, Pastor Jacob Huseby. Pastor Huseby's wife, Margaret, was said to have an eye for men. It was even rumored that in

Huseby's last church, she'd seduced a teenaged parishioner, who'd become so guilt-stricken, he'd run away. Macurdy was skeptical; wishful thinking, he told himself. Margaret Huseby was well-built and sexy, and he'd heard men say they wished she'd seduce them.

In the summer of '38 she swam too far out in the river, and went under before she could make it back to shore. Her husband swam out to rescue her, while someone drove to a phone and called an ambulance. Macurdy, hearing the siren, sped after it in his patrol car.

When he arrived, the trauma of Melody's drowning kicked in, and he brushed aside the ambulance driver, who was about to begin artificial respiration. After Curtis's futile efforts to revive Melody, not so many years before, he'd talked with Arbel about how to revive drowning victims. He'd never before had an opportunity to test Arbel's advice, but he soon had Margaret Huseby conscious, and she was taken to the hospital for observation.

And that, Macurdy thought, was the end of that, because he seldom went to church. But seeing him in his '35 Chevy one day, getting gas at the Sinclair station, she asked him for a lift home—she'd just left her car for a major tuneup—and he said sure. Before he got her home, she was groping him. She wanted to repay him for saving her life, she told him, and her husband was out of town.

What really shook him was how tempted he'd been. He told himself he wouldn't go to church again till after Pastor Huseby was transferred to another parish. Something else would happen first, however, that made his resolution irrelevant.

10

War!

Macurdy awoke one Friday—September 1, 1939—to a kid shouting in the street: "Extra! Extra Paper!" The only time he could recall the *Oregonian* distributing an extra edition in Nehtaka was when Bruno Richard Hauptman was executed for the Lindbergh kidnaping. Pulling on his pants, he hurried outside, called to the boy, and bought a paper.

The Germans had bombed Warsaw and invaded Poland. There was war in Europe! Not civil war in Spain, or Italians fighting somewhere in Africa, but an invasion of one European country by another, with France and England almost sure to get involved. It was the war people had feared might happen and spread, maybe even to involve the United States.

That noon he read it to Klara, translating into German. Her thin old lips were a grim slit. Like Hansi Sweiger's dad, she'd disapproved early and emphatically of Hitler and his policies. Two of her four brothers had been killed fighting for Germany in World War One. A quarter of the village's men of military age had died, and others had been maimed. All because of war, she said, war and crazy rulers!

At first the war in Europe didn't greatly affect life in Nehtaka. The depression had already eased a lot; local men had left to work on dam construction in Washington state and Montana, and projects of other sorts. Now shipbuilding boomed all along the coast, and logging increased. Jobs were easy to find. People listened more to the news on radio, read the papers with greater interest, and talked about the war. In the logging country there was particular interest in the Nazi invasion of Norway and the Soviet invasion of Finland.

But the changes were neither deep nor difficult, let alone painful. America was at peace.

The war became more troubling when the Nazi *Wehrmacht* ground its way through the Netherlands, Belgium, France, and the Balkan peninsula. The British army, badly mauled in the defense of northern France, was driven from the continent at Dunkirk, leaving behind its armor and heavy weapons. Afterward came night after night of German bombing attacks on English cities. And Britain, an island nation dependent on shipping for many of its needs, had more than three million tons of merchant vessels sunk by German submarines in 1940 alone.

But though some people believed that America would be in the war before it was over, so far it was foreign, and not fully real.

In September 1940 that reality level jumped. With passage of the Selective Service Act—America's first ever peacetime conscription law—millions of American men registered for potential military service. Curtis wrote to Indiana and got a birth certificate. His birth year was given as 1904, which startled Fritzi but not Mary. Curtis had written 1914 on the employment form, by accident, he said. He still looked 25, give or take a couple.

Now great military training camps had to be built, and the demand for lumber really boomed. Within weeks, the first drafts of young men were loaded onto trains and hauled away. But at age 36, and as Nehtaka County's undersheriff (Earl had left to be police chief in Manders, California), Macurdy was marginal as far as the draft was concerned.

Meanwhile times got better as the defense industries grew. In Nehtaka, the Saari Brothers greatly expanded their machine shop, retooling it to build bomber parts for the Army Air Corps. There were so many jobs, they had to hire women!

And in the summer of 1941, Mary, now 25 years old, was visited again by morning sickness.

By then the Germans had invaded the Soviet Union, and

advanced so rapidly, it seemed they'd defeat the Russians before winter. Meanwhile there were major diplomatic differences with the Japanese, but most Americans paid much less attention to those. Asia was farther off than Europe, geographically and culturally, and anyway, diplomatic problems seemed a long way from warfare.

Of more immediate importance was the basketball game between Nehtaka and Saint Helens high schools, on Friday evening, December 5. Nehtaka won in overtime, 36 to 34.

Two days later, at about 10:30 AM, Curtis was in the kitchen drinking coffee, reading the funnies, and listening to the Mormon Tabernacle Choir on the radio. The music was interrupted by an announcement: Japanese bombers had just attacked Pearl Harbor.

The war was no longer someone else's.

A lot of Nehtaka County's young men enlisted. The Severtson Brothers lost quite a few of their loggers, and advertised for men. On the Monday after New Year's Day, 1942, two of Fritzi's deputies enlisted, one in the Marines, one in the Maritime Service. That evening after supper, Fritzi commented (in German, of course) that he was glad Curtis was 37 years old. "Otherwise the draft would be after you for sure."

Curtis looked thoughtfully at him. "I've been talking with Mary about whether I should enlist."

Fritzi, alarmed, looked at Mary. "What did you tell him?"

She met her father's gaze. "That it's up to him."

"What about the little one?"

"It will be all right. And so will Curtis."

Her father grunted. "Bullets and shells do not select their victims. If someone is in their way, the person is dead." He turned to Klara. "Talk sense to them, Mama!"

The old woman's jaw clenched. She too met her son's gaze. "If Curtis wants to go, he should. If Hitler and those Japaner win the war, we will learn how bad things can be, even here."

Snorting, Fritzi put down his knife and fork. "They can never win. We are too much for them here."

Klara sat taller, straighter, more stern. "They will win if we do not do what we can. And if Mary wants to go to work at

Saari's, making—whatever it is they make there, I can cook. I can even keep house; a little dust never hurt anything."

Curtis grinned in spite of himself. For years Klara had made war on dust, even when she had to wage it by proxy. So much for the unchangeable.

Fritzi subsided. It hadn't occurred to him that his mother would side against him. Now it seemed to him that if Curtis hadn't already made up his mind, Klara's declaration might well make the difference.

That night Curtis and Mary lay in bed listening to a cold winter rain beat on the porch roof beneath their window. They'd just agreed—Curtis would go. Not in the Maritime Service or Navy—he'd said that in battle he'd feel trapped on a ship at sea—but in the Army. Now she reached, took his hand in her's.

"But you'll wait till the baby's born? It will only be a couple of months."

He raised himself on an elbow and kissed her. "Of course I will. Unless the draft takes me."

"And long enough afterward that you can make love to me again. I know it's selfish of me, but I'm going to miss you terribly, especially lying here alone when you're far away."

He kissed her again, then they both lay staring at the ceiling, each with their own thoughts. The last time he'd seen Axel Severtson, the logger had reminisced on their first meeting, then added, "You know, you ain't changed any at all. Vhen you first come here, you looked like a big kid, a big strong kid vhat had got his nose broke somevhere, and vhen I stop to really look, you look yust as young now." He'd laughed. "Maybe you been drinking from that fountain of youth. Vhat vill you charge to get me a bottle?"

And at work, Lute Halvoy had commented, "Macurdy, you better start showing your age, or people will think you're a draft dodger."

How long, he wondered, did they have, he and Mary, before they had to go somewhere else? Before people really began to wonder? Mary understood, of course. Sometimes when she looked thoughtfully and a bit wistfully at him, it seemed to him she was thinking about a future when she was old and he was "still young." Eight years ago it hadn't seemed fully real. Now it had begun to.

Sometimes he wondered if he'd done her wrong by marrying her. Once he'd even wondered out loud. "If you'll remember," she'd answered, "I was the one who proposed. And if you're still young when I'm old and dried up, it's you who's likely to regret." She'd paused. "I read that in China, a wife who's gotten old will sometimes select a ripe young girl and bring her home, to help around the house and keep her husband company in bed. I might not want one in the house with me, but if you were seeing a girlfriend now and then, I'd understand. When I'm old."

He'd closed her lips with a kiss. "Don't say such things," he'd whispered.

The love behind her saying it should have touched him, warmed him. Instead, her words had been like a large stone on his chest, and when he remembered them, they still were.

Three days later, Mary miscarried.

Dr. Wesley didn't show the seven-month fetus to the parents, though he would have if they'd insisted. He told Curtis it would never have been remotely normal; that they, and it, were lucky it was stillborn. "I'm surprised she hadn't miscarried a lot earlier," he said. "I suspect it lived as long as it did because your wife was so determined to have a child."

She'd probably have three or four of them by now, Macurdy thought, *if she had a normal husband.*

That night, for the first time since he'd returned home to Farside, to the United States of America, he dreamed of Melody. The details were as clear and normal as in his recurring dreams with Varia, but the setting was different. Instead of a gazebo beside a sea, they met in something that reminded him of pictures he'd seen of the Jefferson Monument, though much smaller, and she wore a flowing robe of what seemed to be silk.

Afterward he didn't remember much she'd said in the dream, but he remembered her last words the rest of his life. "Curtis, your Mary loves you deeply and selflessly. Accept her love as offered, and don't ever imagine you're not deserving. She's much happier for having married you."

He wished afterward that he'd made love with Melody before he awoke, as he did in his dreams with Varia. Probably, he decided, the souls in heaven didn't have sex, even in dreams.

In mid-February, Macurdy enlisted. He told himself it wasn't a matter of wanting to, but of patriotism. But in fact, once he'd signed up, he felt a focus he hadn't felt since the end of his war with the Ylver.

Three weeks later he was on a train, enroute to infantry training at Camp Joseph T. Robinson, Arkansas.

He knew this would change his life, but he hadn't a notion how greatly, how powerfully. Or how well he'd prepared for it.

PART TWO
Airborne!

11

Infantry Training

The Camp Robinson military reservation seemed big as a county. Its red-clay hills were covered mostly with scrub oak. The more moderate terrain had mixed woods of larger trees, laced with creeks and interspersed with abandoned fields. Part of the camp itself had new, cream-colored frame buildings, but most of the trainees lived in squad tents boasting wooden floors and a small round sheet metal stove. It was the second week in March, and winter had launched a counteroffensive against encroaching spring. The tent sides were tightly secured to keep out the wind, rain, sleet and snow.

At the end of each row of tents was a coal bin from which they took their fuel. The real problem was lighting it. Even with the draft and damper closed, fire in the little knee-high stove burned out in a few hours and had to be restarted, which was hard to do without wood for kindling. And usually there was no wood. The men did the best they could, using cookie cartons, newspapers, and lighter fluid. A few of the more adventurous foraged in the night, hunting for kindling in the bins of other companies. On the third night, four men from Company B were caught stealing wood from the fuel bin at D Company's messhall, and the resulting fight sent three of them to the dispensary with minor injuries, notably split lips.

In the nine years since returning from Yuulith, Macurdy had mostly avoided showing his powers. Except for that night in the jungle outside Miles City, he'd let no one but Mary see him use magic to light a fire. On Macurdy's fourth morning in 2nd Squad, 2nd Platoon of Company B, and with the grass crisp and white with frost, the stove was out as usual. While several other trainees looked on, he knelt before it. Poking a finger through the opened draft, he drew on the Web of the World and directed a thin stream of white hot plasma into the coal. None of them could see what he did, but within seconds they could hear the fire, and stood variously gawping or frowning. Then one asked, "How the hell did you do that?"

Macurdy had learned in Yuulith that a poor explanation often works better than a good one. "It's something my Aunt Varia taught me years ago," he said.

Actually it was Arbel, not Varia, who'd taught him to start fires, but "Aunt Varia" sounded more innocuous and required no elaboration. Besides, Arbel had done it differently; Arbel's technique, though fine for wood, seemed to Macurdy not intense enough to ignite coal. Later, also in Yuulith, Macurdy had learned by sheer chance to create and cast small balls of plasma, but he'd wanted to provide more intense and prolonged heat. So improvising, he'd created a plasma jet.

Of course it got talked about, and that evening, men from other squads were asking him, hopefully but skeptically, to show them how to start fires. His solution was to start a small coal fire on the ground behind the company shower room, from which they could take coals with a shovel; the latrine orderly could keep it burning. The company officers were soon aware of the fire and whose idea it had been, but assumed he'd started it from the firebox in the big water heater. They credited him with resourcefulness, rather than magic, a resourcefulness that went into his personnel record.

They became aware of Macurdy in other respects, as well, for in his new circumstances, he showed leadership qualities he'd mostly subdued after leaving Yuulith. After the first week, he was made trainee leader of 2nd Platoon. He excelled at everything—the obstacle course, the rifle range, boxing matches . . . even foot races! The company clerk noticed his birth date, and certain it was a typo, called him in. "Macurdy," he said, "your birthdate is listed as 1904, but you're obviously not 38 years old. Assuming that only one digit was typed in wrong, it's got to be 1914, right?"

Here, it seemed to Macurdy, was a chance to bring his official age more in line with his appearance. "Right," he answered, "1914."

There was one minor awkward incident. In the showers, his virtual lack of body hair, even pubic hair, impelled someone to say, "Jesus Christ, Macurdy! Whataya do? Shave your body?"

"Nobody in my family's got enough body hair to notice," he answered mildly. "I don't even shave my face. Probably never will." Then his gaze and voice turned cold. "Is there anything about it you don't like?"

And that was the end of that.

Training had started mildly but built rapidly. At the end of the first two weeks, an ordinary training day might start with an hour in the exercise pits and on the obstacle course, followed by hiking four or five miles with full field pack (usually routed over Drag-Ass Hill) to some field training area, for a lecture followed by hands-on training of some sort, capped by a four or five-mile march back. And it continued to get tougher. Commonly, lunch was served from a truck, about as close to a vehicle as the trainees ever got. More often than not they trained in the evening, too, perhaps with an hour's speed march—again with full field pack—or a night combat problem. Captain Reid was especially strong on filling open hours with speed marches and bayonet drill.

Normally, after an indeterminate number of weeks at infantry camp—as few as seven to as many as seventeen—the trainees were shipped off to one or another of the new divisions constantly being formed. After six weeks, Macurdy was ordered to report to the company's executive officer after breakfast. The XO, a 1st lieutenant, smiled genially.

"Macurdy," he said, "I've heard good things about you from Lieutenant Bosler and Sergeant Hogan—among other things that you're an outstanding soldier, and someone the men in your platoon look up to. So I looked over your personnel papers. No high school, but your alpha score is high. And you have experience in law enforcement; obviously you're accustomed to exercising authority. In other words—" He paused, looking meaningfully at Macurdy. "You'd make a fine officer, the kind the army's looking for. I want to recommend you go to Officer Candidate School when you've finished here."

Macurdy's response lag was about one second. "No disrespect, sir," he said, "but I'm not at all sure I want to be an officer."

The XO's eyebrows rose. "Well, you don't need to decide now. But being an officer is a lot more agreeable than being an enlisted man. Think about it. If you change your mind, let me know. But don't take too long. Training here can be cut short any time, and you could be shipped off to a new division somewhere. At which point it may be too late.

"Incidentally, you might like to know that Sergeant Samuels caught an error in your birthdate—someone had typed in 1904! The correction's been passed up lines."

He dismissed Macurdy then, and the once self-made warlord of Yuulith's Rude Lands, now a buck private, left wondering why he'd declined to volunteer for OCS.

But over the next several weeks, he wasn't even tempted to change his mind. He'd learned long ago to trust his intuitions. Someday they might lead him into something he'd regret, but so far . . . He paused to review a few of them: marrying Varia, following the old conjure woman up Injun Knob, beating up Zassfel and his bullies in the House of Heroes, invading the Ylvin marches. . . . He'd felt regret a few times—a time or two almost more than he could handle—but things had worked out. He wasn't going to change the way he operated now.

In their tenth week, at the end of a training day, an unfamiliar officer addressed the company before they were dismissed. On his blouse he wore a stylized silver parachute with wings, and on his overseas cap, a large patch with a parachute symbol. Instead of an officer's neat oxford shoes, or rough G.I. clodhoppers and lace-up canvas leggings, he wore boots that gleamed like polished teak.

The officer told them that parachute regiments were being formed. The requirements for joining were stringent, but if you were accepted, and if you made it through the training, you'd be in one of the toughest outfits in the world, outfits that would be given the most difficult assignments. And in addition to the regular pay for your rank, you'd earn fifty dollars a month jump pay. "Any of you who are interested," he concluded, "be at the orderly room at 2000 hours."

Macurdy's guts had tightened like a fiddle string, and he felt a powerful, inexplicable, even shocking desire to volunteer. *My God!* he told himself, *this isn't something for you! You're a married man!*

The announcement dominated conversation in the showers and mess line that evening. Mostly the talk was of the supposed near certainty of getting killed, and the fifty dollar a month bonus—a bonus twice the base pay of an ordinary buck private: "Talk about sitting ducks! The fucking krauts (or japs) will be shooting at you all the way down. Anyone who'd volunteer for that kind of bullshit is out of their fucking mind." And "the extra money's for your funeral."

At 2000 hours, Macurdy and twelve others were at B Company's orderly room. He was, he told himself, just there to hear more about it. From there they were marched to a nearby lecture shed, where some thirty-five candidates from the battalion's other companies also were gathered. There the parachute officer described the training; it made infantry training sound leisurely. When he'd finished his description, he asked how many were still interested. Some thirty held up their hands.

"All right," he said, "the men who raised their hands remain seated. The rest of you fall in outside and wait at ease." When the others had left, the men who'd raised their hands were lined up in front and ordered to "drop down and prepare to do twenty-five pushups. GOOD pushups! Airborne pushups! None of that halfway crap! Your sergeants will be watching. Anyone who cheats will be on company punishment. Now! By the numbers!" And he began to count, pausing now and then to shout "Touch those chins to the floor! All the way! All the way! Straighten those arms! Get those butts in line! Sergeant, take that man's name! The one with his ass in the air like a goddamn tent ridge!"

In spite of getting little serious exercise during his years as a deputy, Macurdy hadn't lost much strength. What he had lost was condition, endurance. But during nine weeks of infantry training, he'd gotten a great deal of exercise, and his endurance was at least as good as it had ever been. After reaching twenty-five, the officer had continued to count, for those who were still pumping. Macurdy, despite his two hundred seventeen pounds, had lasted through fifty-eight. Only two had surpassed him. The seemingly tireless Shorty Lyle, from Macurdy's squad, was still grinding them out when the officer stopped counting at one hundred.

When Shorty was on his feet again, the officer put his hand on the trainee's shoulder. "This," he said, "is the kind of man we're looking for." But obviously didn't require, because all nineteen who'd done twenty-five had their names taken down; they were accepted. Seven were from B Company.

They were all pleased with themselves. Shorty Lyle was a bit miffed, though, that the officer hadn't kept counting, so he could show how many he could do.

12

Jump School

The airborne volunteers left for Fort Benning on June 6, 1942. Though they didn't know it, 2nd Battalion of the 503rd Parachute Infantry Regiment had just shipped to England, the first airborne outfit to go overseas. Several other parachute regiments were in training, and in mid-August, the 82nd and 101st Airborne Divisions would officially be formed, and begin theirs. The armed forces were shifting out of military conservatism, trying new methods.

At Fort Benning, as at Camp Robinson, assignment to squads was alphabetical. Thus Macurdy and Shorty Lyle were in the same squad again. Even more than Macurdy, the flamboyant Shorty—five feet four and one hundred forty extremely muscular pounds—caught the attention of the airborne training cadre because he was tough, cocky, and seemingly fearless. He was twenty years old, had been a high school track and field star, a member of a local gymnastics club since age ten, and a sometime Golden Gloves boxer who'd spent two years in the CCC. They were an odd pair: Macurdy large, mild-mannered, and seemingly deliberate, Lyle small, flamboyant, and impulsive.

The first week of training was the most grueling; fewer than forty percent got through it, the rest being shipped back to whatever command they'd come from. And the daily four hours in the physical training pits weren't the end of it. They ran everywhere they went—would as long as they were there—

pausing on command to drop down and pump out twenty-five pushups. Even in the packing hangar, where they learned to pack their own chutes, they were stopped frequently to "give me twenty-five." The man who, on leaving the messhall, wasn't running on his first stride out the door, regardless how full his stomach, might be ordered to "give me fifty," an order few could meet, though a clean thirty-five might avoid a training gig. All in all, that first week, the trainees probably averaged at least 700 pushups a day.

Friday was make or break day: The trainees did 1400 side-straddle hops, by which time a lot of gigs had been recorded. (A gig—a penalty point—was given for failing to complete an exercise; three gigs and you were washed out, eliminated.) Then they lay on their backs, legs straight, booted feet some twenty inches above the ground—and were left like that. Soon little grunts of pain and effort could be heard, with occasional and increasing thuds as heels dropped to the ground. When about half had failed, the order was given to lower their feet.

During the final hour they ran. Running gigs were especially potent; each one got double value. And while the trainees were used to fifty-minute runs, this day's was different, with spurts of sprinting—a sort of gruesome interval training in boots—and for the first time, their trainers cycled in and out, taking turns. Well before the fifty minutes were up, men were peeling off to heave their guts, or falling headlong, until the sixty percent wash-out was attained.

In every training exercise, Shorty Lyle excelled, even at running, short-legged though he was. Once, for doing his pushups more rapidly than the count (to get in extras), he was ordered onto the demonstration platform and told to "give me twenty-five."

"Which arm?" he asked.

The captain's gaze turned to steel. "Right arm." So he did. That was followed by "now the left," and he did twenty-five of those, too. By that time the captain was grinning like a wolf. Without giving Shorty time to recover, he ordered, "Now fifty with both." Shorty gave him fifty without a struggle, then bounced to his feet. The captain put a hand on Shorty's shoulder and turned him to face the other trainees. "Men, take a good look. This is the kind of soldier we want here." Then he sent Shorty back to his place among the others without a word about having mouthed off. The trainees knew for sure now that this was a truly different kind of outfit, and for most of them, the only kind to be part of.

Shorty reveled in the training—until the third week, and the tower drops. Then he turned morose. Because though he allowed himself to be hooked up, when he was raised from the ground, he froze, paralyzed, filled with dread, and his limbs turned to jelly. Cut loose at 250 feet, he rode his chute down like a sack of potatoes, his mind numb, non-functional. Nor did he feel better with repetition.

The next week they'd make their qualifying jumps from planes—four by daylight, one at night—and he *knew* he couldn't do it, not even if his life depended on it. Yet he couldn't bear the thought of returning to an ordinary ground unit. So he took his problem to the 1st sergeant. It wasn't exactly fear, he insisted, but being hauled up on the towers paralyzed him.

Several of the training cadre were due to jump that Saturday, to retain their jump status, and they decided to take Shorty with them. They'd jump singly, rather than as an entire "stick" of men. They assumed that by encouragement and cajolery they could get their star recruit to jump too, and that once he'd jumped, he'd be all right. Jumping him without authorization would be a serious breach of regulations, but that didn't bother them in the least: They were going to save a good man and his pride.

They failed: He remained frozen in his seat.

Shorty returned to the barracks in despair. The company was to make its first training jumps on Monday morning, and he *knew* he'd fail, wash out.

When Macurdy saw him, he set his paperback aside. "What's the matter?" he asked. Asked quietly, though only a few men were there, on their bunks writing letters or reading. Shorty just shook his head.

"Come on," Macurdy said. "Let's sit on the back stoop."

They went out and sat in the shade of the building. "I'm your buddy," Macurdy told him, "and you've been holding out on me. Now give!"

Miserably, Shorty described the whole wretched situation, while Macurdy watched intently—*watched an image take shape in Shorty's subconscious, of a steelworker on a bridge girder, leaning back, clutching at air, eyes wide with horror.*

"Okay, look at me!" Macurdy ordered. Shorty's gaze raised to his, and for a moment Macurdy held it. "Now," he said, "who is it that's scared?"—and without warning clapped his hands like a gunshot! Shorty jumped as if slapped, and suddenly the image was visible to him, live now, for both of them, the figure hurtling down, down.

For a moment neither man said anything. Then Shorty spoke. "I—I— Hell, I don't know. Not me though. It's not—it wasn't me." He stared at Macurdy, dumbfounded.

"Good. What did he look like?"

"Kind of dark complected . . . Wiry hair . . . Wore work gloves. Hell, I never saw him before." He shook his head, astounded. "I never saw anything like that in my life!"

"And that's who was scared? Not you?"

"Uh . . ." Shorty stared at Macurdy, then nodded decisively. "Yep. Not me."

"Good. So that's handled. You want to go to town tonight? Celebrate? We don't need to get drunk, just have a few beers and relax."

They did. After a couple of beers, Shorty wanted to walk, so they left the bar and went to Promenade Park, where they strolled on a path beside the Chatahoochee River. "Macurdy," Shorty asked, "what happened back at the barracks? When you said what you said. I mean—I saw that guy, saw him fall, and then— All of a sudden, I knew I could jump."

"What did I ask you?"

"You asked me—" Shorty frowned. "You asked me who it was that's scared to jump."

"And you told me it wasn't you."

"Right." Shorty's head bobbed a brief affirmation. "But who was it?"

"Some poor sonofabitch working on a high bridge, and fell off. You saw it when I clapped my hands."

Shorty nodded, still frowning, then asked, "Was it real?"

Macurdy looked sternly down at him. "Absolutely," he said, wondering if it really had been. "Would I lie to you?"

"No . . . No, you're one guy I trust completely."

"Good. You see, I've got the sight. I see things other people don't. It wasn't Shorty Lyle that was scared."

They kept walking, a thoughtful Shorty looking at the path in front of his boots. Finally he looked up at Macurdy. "You're a strange guy, you know?"

"Yep, I am. For me it's the only way to be. But we won't tell anyone what happened."

Shorty put a hand on Macurdy's arm, and they stopped. "You're not only a helluva man, Macurdy," he said, "you're one helluva friend. Sure as shit, though, someone's going to ask what happened that I can jump now—Sergeant Bryant for sure—and I'd like to tell him it was talking to you that did it. Okay? But I won't tell him what happened."

Macurdy grinned. "Okay. But now you owe me a beer, for services rendered."

They arrived back at the barracks not actually drunk, but Shorty was a bit oiled. They'd obviously been in a scuffle somewhere, but weren't much the worse for it.

And on Monday, Shorty jumped next in the stick behind Macurdy. Without difficulty, and found himself hooked on parachuting.

After qualifying as jumpers, they were sent to the expansion area in Alabama for advanced training. On completion, Macurdy was one of a handful promoted to private first class. Afterward the troopers were assigned to various new regiments in training, except for a few, including Macurdy, who were assigned to 2nd Battalion, 503rd Parachute Infantry Regiment, in England, as replacements for men injured in training, or lost for other reasons.

13

Leave

Because they were headed overseas, the men assigned to the 503rd were given leave—two weeks plus travel time. Macurdy gave his destination as Nehtaka, Oregon, but went first to Salem, Indiana, where Charley and Edna met him at the depot.

They hadn't seen their youngest son for more than nine years, and Edna hugged him, weeping, a remarkable display of emotion for a Macurdy. Charley simply stared. "Good God," he breathed when Curtis was able to give him his attention. "You're another one. You haven't aged a day." Then he too embraced their son.

Curtis spent two days with them, and his parents told him some old family lore, stories he hadn't heard before—that very few had in his generation. His great great grampa was said not to have aged. He'd disappeared when his oldest boy reached seventeen, only to turn up again, briefly, on one leg and two crutches, at the end of the Civil War. Even then he'd looked young, though scar-faced and short a limb like so many who *were* young. To learn that his wife had died sixteen years earlier. His two sons recognized him when he told them who he was, but at his request referred to him as "Cousin Martin from back east."

But after "Cousin Martin" was gone again, one of them told his wife who their visitor had been, and the story leaked to others in the family. But not all, and mostly it stopped there. Until one of the "old man's" grandchildren—one of Edna's uncles, who was also a second cousin of Charley's—had left his wife and children when he was thirty-six and looked about twenty-five. Left without warning, but semi-regularly had wired money from California until about 1915.

"You can probably understand how we felt when Varia didn't age," Charley said. "We thought she might be one of my cousin's kids by some second wife out west. Although from what you told us before, I guess she couldn't have been."

Edna took Curtis's hand. "And now here you are, thirty-eight years old and still so young looking, no older than Frank's oldest boy. And married, you say."

Curtis nodded. "Mary knows about me. About how I don't age. I told her before we got engaged, and she married me anyway. I guess it wasn't all that real to her then; even I wasn't entirely sure. And of course, she's still not quite twenty-six. We'll probably leave Nehtaka when the war's over." *If I'm still alive,* he added silently.

Liiset, or whichever of Varia's clones it had been, had returned just once, a few months after Curtis had left. After that it was as if the Sisterhood had given up on him. So Curtis gave his parents his Nehtaka address.

His reception in Nehtaka was also marked by hugs and tears. The next day he got hold of some black market gas, and in their '35 Chevy, he and Mary drove south down the coast, where they rented a cabin and spent three days alone, walking the beach, hiking the old spruce forest, watching the surf beat on massive black boulders and ledges . . . and loving each other. It seemed to both of them they were more in love than ever.

His leave melted like snow on the stove, but when Mary delivered him to the train, she didn't cry. She waited till she got home. And Klara, the tough old Prussian peasant widow, half blind now and three-quarters crippled, comforted her granddaughter. The old woman's tears were for the young wife, not the soldier. Soldiers were expected to die.

14

England

England's southern ports were often visited by German bombers, thus the 503rd replacements disembarked in Greenock, Scotland. There they were put on a train and taken south, almost the length of Britain, to rural Berkshire County, where 2nd Battalion 503rd was camped in Nissen Huts on a sprawling manorial estate called Chilton Foliat.

Only the 2nd Battalion was in England; the rest of the regiment remained in the States. 2nd Battalion was proud, cocky, and close-knit, and replacements like Macurdy were looked upon at first as outsiders. Especially in his squad, where he'd replaced a happy-go-lucky sort of wildman named Joe Potenza. Private Potenza was currently in the stockade, and would be for another five months, for starting a fight while on a weekend pass in London, a brawl that had seriously embarrassed the Army. Previously in trouble for starting a fight with British servicemen, he'd been treated as an example by the American high command.

In his squad, several resented Potenza's replacement, and one morning Macurdy awakened to find his boot laces cut from the bottom up. That evening he went to each member of the squad and asked if he'd done it, at the same time observing the man's auric reaction. When he found the culprit, a private named Carlson, he hit him without warning—*whop!* in the forehead with the heel of his hand. Carlson dropped like a stone.

Unfortunately, Carlson was about five feet eight inches and

one hundred fifty pounds, so this did not commend Macurdy to the rest of the squad. The next night a trooper named Cargill, who'd been Potenza's closest friend, came into the hut and saw Macurdy asleep with no cover. Carefully he slipped a safety match head-first between Macurdy's toes, then lit the other end and gave him a barefooted hotfoot. Macurdy awoke with a yell, then looked around and found Cargill glaring at him, jaw set. "I did it, asshole," Cargill said. "Now let's see if you've got the guts to tackle someone your own size."

Actually Cargill, though about as tall, was twenty pounds lighter than Macurdy. Macurdy didn't quibble though; he went outside with Cargill and beat the snot out of him. After that, the majority, who'd accepted him in the first place, were Macurdy's buddies; he was their kind of man.

Meanwhile, though he had a nasty burn between his toes, Macurdy didn't report the injury or go on sick call. He handled it himself, with a shamanic technique.

The next morning in the Nissen, Cargill apologized through swollen lips. "Macurdy, I was an asshole to burn your foot yesterday. I know it's not your fault that Potenza's in the stockade. All I can say is, I loved him like a brother. We all did. You'd have to know him."

"I've got no argument with that," Macurdy answered. "People ought to stand up for their buddies. But if I'm not willing to stand up for myself, I've got no business being here."

"Amen to that," said their squad sergeant, who wore the name Rinaldi above his pocket. "You're a good man, Macurdy, in more ways than one." He shook Macurdy's hand, and one by one the others followed, only Carlson abstaining. Rinaldi scowled. "What's the matter, Carlson. You short on brains? Or just can't admit you acted like dog shit?"

Carlson stalked out, but in the supper line spoke quietly to Macurdy: "I shouldn't have cut your laces. I know it and everyone else knows it. But goddamn I was pissed when they railroaded Potenza! Six months for chrissake, for one lousy brawl! I've seen guys do lots worse in Phenix City and not even draw company punishment. And you couldn't ask for a better trooper than he was."

Macurdy didn't point out the differences between Phenix

City and London. He simply smiled slightly, as much as he thought Carlson was up to having just then. "It's an imperfect world," he said, "but Potenza will be back. If not to the 503rd, then to one of the other outfits forming up. And whoever gets him, they'll have themselves a real fighting man."

Carlson nodded soberly. "You got that right," he said, then put out his hand and they shook on it.

Colonel Raff was a fanatic on endurance and toughness, and pushed his battalion mercilessly. In June, soon after landing, it had undergone intensive combat training by officers of the British 1st Airborne Division, and in July they underwent sixteen tough but valuable days at the Mortehoe Commando School. They became skilled in night operations, learned the proper way to silence sentries, became competent demolitionists, and could fire and field-strip German, Italian, and British weapons as readily as their own.

And the lessons they learned were passed on to replacements like Macurdy by the battalion's own officers and noncoms.

What they didn't do for two months was jump out of airplanes. Transport planes were in short supply, and none were available to the battalion till after Macurdy had joined it. Then they jumped frequently, from altitudes as low as 350 feet. Once they jumped in Northern Ireland as part of joint English and American maneuvers.

Meanwhile Macurdy transferred his marksmanship with the S&W Model 10 .38 caliber police revolver to the army's heavy M1911A1 Colt .45 automatic.

It seemed to Macurdy that Varia's invisibility spell would be very useful, even though it was less than completely reliable. But he didn't know how she did it, except in a very general way. However, he'd had further input on invisibility spells later, from a tomttu named Maikel. Among other things, Maikel had said that intention was a key element. And Maikel's spell, at least, had only to be cast once. It could then be activated and deactivated by consciously willing it.

Working from this basis of limited knowledge, Macurdy experimented when he could, until wearing his American uniform with its airborne insignia, he walked one evening through a well-lit pub full of British servicemen (engaged with their beer, girls, and conversations), and wasn't noticed.

Obviously it was at least somewhat effective, but its parameters of protection were uncertain. Maikel's could be seen through, at least by some, if a person knew where to look, and Varia's wasn't reliable in full sunlight. But almost certainly, his wasn't the same as either of theirs.

Those were things he'd keep in mind. Meanwhile he soon had a reputation for his stealth at night. He avoided testing it by day. At night his skill could be written off as "natural"—an ability to move silently and skillfully in darkness and shadow. But by day? To explain his talent as sorcery didn't seem wise.

In his fifth week in the 503rd, Macurdy was called into the office of Captain Grady, the company commander. Grady wasn't the only officer waiting for him: a Lieutenant Netzloff was there. "Macurdy," Grady said, "we've been looking through your service record. Everywhere you've been, your folder has accumulated favorable comments and commendations. Lieutenant D'Emilio and Sergeant Boileau agree with them. So although you haven't been with us long, I'm promoting you to corporal, to take over for a man we lost this morning." He turned to Netzloff. "Lieutenant, he's yours. Tell him what he needs to know."

Macurdy and Netzloff left then. Beyond telling him what squad he'd be in, the lieutenant didn't say much except: "There's two or three in the squad who might be a little sour about you ranking them without having the training and experience they have. But Lieutenant D'Emilio says you've got a knack for handling things, and his men like and respect you. So the captain and I are trusting you to handle any objections your new squad might have. Now, let's go find Sergeant Ruiz. He's your platoon sergeant."

Staff Sergeant Ramon Ruiz was as large as Macurdy, and looked as strong, a calm direct man who neither in words, face, or aura showed any resentment toward this relative greenhorn coming into his platoon as a noncom. "Where you from, Macurdy?" he asked.

"Nehtaka, Oregon."

"A westerner! I'm from a ranch near Peñasco, New Mexico. What'd you do before you joined up?"

"I was a deputy sheriff." Then, in case this sergeant had reservations about lawmen, Macurdy added, "Before that I logged."

"A deputy sheriff? How come the army didn' put you in the MPs?"

Macurdy grinned. "I sure don't know. I speak pretty good German, too; I'm surprised they didn't send me to the Pacific."

The sergeant grunted. "Speak German? You don' have a German name."

"I married into a German family, and my wife and I lived with them. The grandmother didn't speak any English, so they all talked German in the house, and I had to learn it."

This sharpened Ruiz's interest. "What do they think of you fighting the Germans?"

"They think of it as fighting Nazis. The whole family hates Hitler, especially the old lady. She says he'll be the ruin of Germany."

"She got that right. Well, it's a good thing to have another guy in the platoon that speaks German. A guy named Mueller speaks it, too; he's from North Dakota." Ruiz got to his feet. "Come on. I'll introduce you to Sergeant Powers. He's your squad leader."

As it turned out, Macurdy had no problems at all in his new squad. It already knew of him by reputation; he was a man people noticed.

As summer waned into autumn, their officers were briefed on what was to be the battalion's—and the Army's—first airborne operation. And although for some weeks the troopers were not told what was up, training intensified, carrying now a sense of urgency.

They were made familiar with French arms and equipment, which to some suggested a raid into German-occupied France.

The battalion had read and heard about the disastrous cross-channel Dieppe raid by seven thousand commandos, a few weeks earlier. And eager though they were to see action, the debacle at Dieppe was sobering. Even elite units could come to grief in an operation sufficiently ill-conceived.

One day they were visited and inspected in ranks by the First Lady, Eleanor Roosevelt, who paused to ask questions of the men. Macurdy was as impressed by her aura as by her height, and she was taller than most of the troopers.

Meanwhile Mary had written that she was pregnant. Curtis didn't much fret about it; he was remarkably focused on where he was and what he was doing. Which helped him get another quick promotion to buck sergeant, replacing a squad leader who'd broken a collarbone.

Shortly afterward, the men were put on restriction and briefed on their upcoming operation, until they knew their drop zone and missions about as well as they could, considering they still didn't know where in the world that drop zone was.

Not that they'd drop there, or carry out that mission—a remarkable set of snafus would intervene—but they'd make themselves valuable regardless, on the ground and in the evolution of new warfare.

Finally they were loaded onto trains and taken to Land's End, in the extreme southwest of England.

15

Snafu in the Desert

On November 4, 1942, 2nd Battalion of the 503 Parachute Infantry Regiment was put on a train. They'd removed their unit patches. Their equipment, even their jump boots and jump suits, was sent separately; no one was to know they were paratroopers.

Their route was indirect, and of course they spent a lot of time waiting. On November 7 they arrived at two small airfields in the southwesternmost corner of England, Lands End. There they learned what their mission actually was, and what the circumstances were. In small groups, again to be inconspicuous, thirty-nine twin-engined C47 transports arrived, to fly them to French-ruled Algeria, in North Africa.

At that stage of the war, there could be no adequate fighter escort for slow, unarmed transports flying over Nazi-occupied France. So the small armada was to fly well out over the Atlantic, and then, without Spanish approval, cross neutral Spain and the western Mediterranean, to capture two key airfields in Algeria, to keep them out of German hands. Meanwhile seaborne attacks would take place at the city of Oran and elsewhere.

There were complications of course: the French defense forces. "Free France" was ruled by a Nazi puppet dictatorship under 86-year-old Marshal Henri Pétain, who'd sworn allegiance to Hitler. An American general, Mark Clark, had been landed covertly at Oran by submarine, to negotiate a secret agreement with the French commander there, allowing allied forces to land unopposed. But considering Pétain's attitude, it wasn't certain the French commander would be obeyed.

If it seemed the French would fight after all, the planes would leave England early enough to jump their troopers while it was dark in Algeria. If it seemed the French would not fight, the planes would leave later, and land with their troopers by daylight. In either case, the battalion was to secure the airfields from possible German takeover.

There was also the problem of the planes finding the drop zone, 1,600 miles away over water and across Spain, without benefit of beacons enroute, or familiarity with Spanish geography. The pilots hadn't been trained for that sort of navigation. Most wouldn't even be given a map; they were to follow the leader. On the plus side, compass bearings should keep them approximately on course (unless it was windy), and the British would have a beacon ship some miles off the port of Oran, near the targeted airbases; the planes should pick up its signal as they crossed the southeastern coast of Spain. It would also notify the planes if the French changed their minds. (Unfortunately its radioman was given the wrong frequency, and its signals were never received.)

The drop zone itself was to be marked by a spy-placed radar beacon to be activated shortly before the troop planes arrived. (However, the intelligence officer who placed and activated it was given the wrong expected arrival time. When the planes didn't appear, he blew up his top-secret device, as he was supposed to, and slipped away dressed as an Arab.)

At almost the last hour, word came that the French would cooperate. Thus the planes waited an extra four hours before taking off, in order to arrive at the landing site in daylight.

It was not a joyride. The troopers sat shoulder to shoulder on metal bucket seats, the only upholstery their packed chutes. At the head of the troop compartment were two strapped-down barrels of aviation gasoline, backing up the fuel tanks and reminding the troopers that this would be a long flight.

The November night was chilly, and not only was the compartment unheated, the doorways held no doors; the propwash sucked out and blew away whatever body heat they produced. Furthermore they were flying at an altitude of nearly two miles.

Despite the cold, they dozed, Macurdy better than most because he drew heat from the Web of the World. From time to time he'd waken, to peer through the small windows behind him. The only lights were one or two glowing cigarette tips marking wakeful troopers. On almost none of those occasions did he hear a word from anyone, and for the first several hours, all the window showed him were ocean and stars, and the blue lights of other planes in the formation.

After some hours, his dreams became restless, and he awoke to bouncing and swaying. Turning to the window again, his eyes found darkness, rain, and cloud. What he couldn't see was the thirty-knot east wind. They'd run out of their good weather. If there were other planes nearby, he couldn't see them, either.

At 4 AM the compartment lights came on and field rations were passed around—crackers, canned meat, and candy. Then the lights were turned out again. Macurdy was wakeful now, waiting for a dawn that seemed slow in coming. When it did, they were over water—not the Bay of Biscay this time, but the Mediterranean.

They'd flown out of the storm; the sky was merely overcast. Men turned in their seats to peer out the small windows. As the light strengthened, Macurdy could see brown hills ahead. The others saw them too; what they couldn't see were the other thirty-eight planes. Four others, yes, but not thirty-eight. Had they gotten lost in the storm? The talk picked up. Oran was supposed to be up ahead somewhere. Had the pilot gotten the signal from the beacon ship? Where was the invasion fleet? Dead ahead maybe, someone suggested, where only the pilot could see it.

Lieutenant Warner was the senior trooper on board, and getting to his feet, he went to the cockpit. A few minutes later he came back out. "At ease!" he shouted, and the talking stopped. "The pilot doesn't know exactly where we are, or where the other thirty-four planes are. The storm winds blew from the east, which means we blew off course to the west. When we get closer to shore, he and this group are going to fly east for a while, till they see some landmark they recognize from the map."

There were groans and a few oaths. "What about the beacon ship?" someone asked.

"They haven't heard a peep from it. They'll know Oran for sure though, when they see it." Then he moved on to his seat. The Pratt & Whitney engines continued their reassuring roar, smooth and constant, as if they could go on forever.

With land close ahead, the five planes veered eastward, continuing on a line of flight that allowed the troopers to make out Arab villages on the shore. Half an hour later, the Lieutenant disappeared into the cockpit again, and this time stayed a while. Finally he stuck his head out, grinning.

"They know where they are now. They're going inland, and get to La Sénia from the west." This didn't bring actual cheers, but Macurdy felt the tension ease. The airfield at La Sénia was their primary target. Engines droning steadily, they flew inland over barren rugged hills.

Soon he could see a large flat area with a whitish look, that he thought might be a salt flat, a dry desert lake. He'd never seen one before, but it fitted the description. Warner came out of the cockpit again. "They've spotted more 47s ahead," he said, "sitting on the ground with guys around them, and our gas gauge reads empty. We're going to land."

There were no cheers, and not much was said, except the wry comment that, if that was La Sénia Airfield below, or any other goddamned airfield, they'd sure as hell camouflaged the hangars well.

Other groups of C47s arrived after they did. The lakebed, which their pilot said was 35 miles long and 7 wide, consisted of a salty crust beneath which was the stickiest mud Macurdy had ever experienced. Walk fifty feet, and each boot had ten pounds of it stuck on like glue. None of the pilots had heard a sound from the beacon ship, or picked up the radar beacon that was supposed to mark the drop zone.

Some of the planes that had crossed the coast near Oran had been fired on from the ground; the French had decided to fight after all. When Colonel Raff arrived with six planeloads of troopers, and spotted the planes on the lakebed, the non-jumping Air Corps officer in overall command of the operation radioed him that they were taking sniper fire, and were threatened by enemy armor. So Raff and the six planeloads jumped to attack the armor with small arms, grenades, and anti-tank mines. (Bazookas were still unknown.) The colonel hit a large rock when he landed, broke a couple of ribs and was spitting blood. The sniping, it turned out, was at such long range, it had failed to hit anyone, while the "enemy armor" turned out to be an American armored reconnaissance patrol that had gotten through the French defenses earlier that morning.

Before long, most of the 39-plane armada was there in the mud, with too little gas to fly anywhere, and the nearest target was not La Sénia, but the military airfield at Tafaraoui, 38 miles away, much of that distance on the lakebed. Part of the battalion was left with the stranded planes. The rest started hiking through the gumbo toward Tafaraoui. Macurdy had thought that any exertion they'd experience in the field couldn't be worse than they'd survived in training. Now, trudging through the gumbo, he changed his mind. A trooper named Hennessy, a Wyoming cowboy, called it "goddamn 'dobe clay, the worst fucking shit in the world," and no one argued with him.

They hiked all night, arriving at the airfield not long after dawn, utterly bushed, to find it in the hands of an American armored force. The field was beautiful in a way: Rows of willow trees along the road, a tall pink water tower, pink barracks . . . but Macurdy was too tired to appreciate it.

Some of 2nd Battalion's troopers were already there, some of them dead. While Macurdy and the others had been slogging through the mud, the afternoon before, the force left behind had gotten a radio call. American armor had just taken Tafaraoui, and needed infantry to guard five hundred French prisoners, so Raff ordered the remaining dregs of gas drained from the other planes, until they had enough for three of them to fly there. Then he'd loaded the three with troopers—as many as they'd hold—and the planes had taken off. Partway there, they'd been shot up by three French Dewoitine fighter planes, killing or wounding twenty Americans, and forcing the transports to land on the lakebed again.

Most of the troopers they'd carried, including some of the wounded, marched much of the night to reach Tafaraoui. There, with more than a little satisfaction, they heard that a flight of British Spitfires had jumped the Dewoitines and shot all of them down.

The next day, transportation was sent to the 47s on the dry lake, and the rest of the battalion was trucked north to the airfield. The American armor there was needed for the assault on Oran, so its commander turned the airfield over to 2nd Battalion to defend, and left. In the hills, a lone French howitzer kept lobbing in 75mm shells, and the Spitfires couldn't find the well-camouflaged gun. The battalion took more casualties from the shelling. Meanwhile, the men who'd made the long march took advantage of the barracks there, and slept.

Macurdy dreamed, half-wakened, and dreamed again, dreamed of beaches and monsters and death. Then the platoon was rousted out for muster in the morning, leaving brief dregs of dream, baleful and menacing.

But roll call, the mess line, and rumors banished them. At breakfast it occurred to him that sixty hours earlier he'd eaten supper in England, in what seemed like a different world. Not as different as Yuulith, where he'd fought his last war, but different enough.

16

Dancing in a Vacuum

Oran surrendered on the second day—Algiers, farther east, had already surrendered to the British—and all of Algeria was nominally in allied hands. Mostly the French had not fought very hard; they'd had their orders and a Gallic sense of honor, but their hearts weren't in it. Surrendering may have hurt their pride, but most of them disliked or even hated being allied with the Nazis.

Meanwhile, the Allied high command was concerned that the Germans would move to occupy the airfields in eastern Algeria and neighboring Tunisia, where there was a power vacuum. The Allies had only a few divisions in all of Algeria, concentrated in the north. On the other hand, though nominally Field Marshal Erwin Rommel's Afrika Korps occupied neighboring Tunisia, his forces there were concentrated near the east coast, where they were engaged with the British 8th Army near the Libyan border.

So on November 15th, most of 2nd Battalion jumped on Youks les Bains Airfield, half expecting to be met by German paratroopers. Instead there was a small number of poorly equipped French infantry, who preferred Americans to Nazis. With no fighting necessary there, Colonel Raff sent a company on foot to take and hold Tebessa Airfield nine miles away, near the Tunisian border. They found no Germans there either.

Raff's assigned responsibility was the defense of Youks les

Bains and Tebessa airfields, which stretched his battalion thin, but he phoned Allied headquarters in Algiers, asking permission to occupy the central Tunisian town of Gafsa, which controlled key mountain roads. The French told him there still were no Germans there. General Clark approved only a reconnaissance, however, and "not one step farther" than Gafsa. Then the British General Anderson, in charge of allied ground forces in Algeria, countermanded even that limited permission.

Raff pretended he hadn't gotten the countermand, and his idea of a reconnaissance was more than liberal. It seemed to him that Gafsa and its airfield were a prize the Germans would grab if he didn't. Besides, he was looking for a fight.

As Gafsa was eighty miles southeast of Tebessa via a mountain road, the French commander at Tebessa provided him with two dilapidated, green and white civilian buses, so covered with dirt as to be nearly camouflaged by it. Raff, his broken ribs taped and padded, loaded twenty men in each bus, and started off with them down the road. Macurdy was included because he spoke fluent German. Being within easy range of German fighter planes, Raff had a machine gun mounted atop each bus, with gunners to man them. He had no artillery and no air support.

As reported, there were no Germans in Gafsa, just a French unit of thirty *chasseurs*, light reconnaissance cavalry stationed there to keep a finger on the local pulse. The French commander really did have his finger on that pulse—in fact on the pulse of all Tunisia—and knew the country intimately. So the two commanders set about to do as much with their tiny forces as they could.

Meanwhile the distant generals decided it had been a good idea after all, and the paratroopers in Gafsa were increased to all of eighty-five.

Back in England, British airborne officers had told Raff that the Germans didn't like operating at night. So Raff sent men by jeep, civilian car, even a hitchhiker on a train, on small nocturnal demolition raids and reconnaissance patrols. Sometimes troopers went out on their own. Macurdy tried his hand at that, with a sergeant named Cavalieri, whose Italian was as good as Macurdy's German.

Then Macurdy got transferred to Kasserine, just in time to miss a sharp fight—the "Battle of Gafsa"—with German paratroops and Italian light tanks. Fortunately Raff's tiny army had just been reinforced by a company from the 1st Infantry Division, and a platoon from the 701st Antitank Battalion.

Meanwhile the troopers had just learned that their battalion was no longer part of the 503rd Parachute Infantry Regiment, and hadn't been for weeks. The 503rd, with a new 2nd Battalion, was being shipped to Australia, halfway around the world; Raff's Ruffians had been redesignated the 509th Parachute Infantry Battalion. The plan was to expand it to a full regiment, when enough qualified troopers were available.

It was at Kasserine that Macurdy's mail caught up with him. He got seven letters from Mary, and realized he'd written her only once since leaving England. Her most recent letter said she'd miscarried again, and he sensed her deep disappointment. That night he wrote her a three-page letter—long by his standards. It would have been longer, but as he pointed out, there wasn't that much to say that the censors wouldn't delete.

Then, having written Mary, he wrote his parents for only the third time in his life.

Rommel began taking more interest in western Tunisia, and in the first week in December, German and Italian troops occupied the strategic but undefended Faid Pass. The further enlarged Gafsa garrison was sent to take it from them. The troopers at Kasserine were also sent, and arrived in time for the second (and final) day of fighting, which ended with the surrender of the surviving Axis troops. It was Macurdy's first taste of real combat since he'd left Yuulith—his first ever that involved firearms instead of swords, bows, and pikes.

Soon afterward, the paratroopers at Gafsa were replaced by straight infantry. Macurdy's company was moved to the airfield at Thelepte, to protect it and carry out patrols. It was the only company of 509ers left in Tunisia. The rest of the battalion had been sent to Boufarik on standby, several hundred miles northwest, near Algiers.

17

Von Lutzow

It was evening when it happened. Macurdy, who now wore staff sergeant's chevrons on his sleeves, was settling down to read awhile before hitting the sack, when Lieutenant Shuler came into the barracks. "Macurdy, get your boots on."

As Macurdy reached for his boots, Shuler elaborated. "Captain Buckman's got a job for you and me. He's waiting to brief us."

In the orderly room, the captain filled them in. Operating by night, a light British plane had picked up two spies—one British, the other American—wearing German uniforms, and been hit by small arms fire during takeoff. Later it had crash-landed on a mountain road. The pilot was badly injured, but he'd gotten off a Mayday call, giving their approximate location. Both spies were injured too. Algiers wanted them picked up; they were supposed to be very important.

The Germans would also have gotten the signal, and would undoubtedly send men to capture them. Probably by truck; it would be a long drive, but feasible. However, it was possible they'd jump paratroops in.

Captain Buckman told Macurdy to pick eighteen men and get them ready: He and Shuler would go over the quick and dirty operations plan. Macurdy and his men were to be at the taxi strip in twenty minutes, with three stretchers, and K rations for three days. Major Marden would be their pilot.

Macurdy left wondering if three stretchers would be enough: Twenty men jumping at night in the mountains could easily result in two or three of them getting busted up on landing.

It wasn't windy, and the moon had just risen, something more than half full, but even so . . .

He supposed the spies had confidential information, and wearing German uniforms, they'd be executed if caught—pumped of what they knew, then shot. While if the Germans caught him on the mountain with a broken leg, he'd probably, hopefully, just end up in a POW camp. Still, he took five stretchers. They could always leave what they didn't need.

And they had one thing going for them besides themselves: Their pilot had a reputation. Major Rollie Marden didn't have to *find* places. He just sort of *went* to them, like some of the mountaineers in Yuulith. It was like an instinct. There was no way he'd miss the drop spot.

Macurdy knew without thought what men he'd take, and not one of them bitched at foregoing his night's sleep. He told them to bring no weapons heavier than M1s, and no more grenades than they could take in their thigh pockets. This was a rescue operation, not a combat mission; they needed to travel light.

Ten minutes after he'd given them their instructions, they trotted to the C47s warming up on the taxi strip, leaving the rest of the platoon jealous.

Shuler arrived a few minutes later. Two minutes after that, they were on board, taxiing to the runway. Shuler handed out French army topographic maps, and briefed the troopers as they flew. They'd take the rescued spies and pilot to a road, where they'd be met by trucks and troops of the 26th Infantry and taken to Gafsa. From there they could get air cover if needed—some of Major Cochran's P40s would be standing by, ready to take off on a moment's notice.

It seemed like no time at all before they were over the jump spot, hooked up and ready. Shuler was jump master. The green light came on and the lieutenant jumped, the rest of the stick following almost in lockstep, Macurdy last, the cleanup man, shouting the battalion's jump cry: "San Antone!"

He looked up, checking his canopy, then down, orienting himself. The landscape was a mosaic of moon-wash and black shadow. He could see the primitive road, even the plane lying on it, almost at the summit of a grade. *Right on target,* he thought. *I need to look up Marden, when I have a chance, and tell him how much that means to us. And so damned quick! It'll take a hell of a lot longer getting out than it did in.*

He hit the ground about two hundred yards beyond the broken plane. Shuler almost slammed into it when he landed. Almost. What he actually hit was a boulder, or more likely two of them. The result was a broken leg, and despite his steel helmet, a severe concussion. Two blasts on Macurdy's whistle oriented any troopers who might have missed seeing the plane. Except for Shuler, none had injuries severe enough to hamper them seriously. All in all, Macurdy thought, they'd been damned lucky. They even found their equipment package, in this case the stretchers, with no trouble at all.

Two of the crash victims were still in the plane. The mission medic checked them first. One of them, the pilot, had bled to death, the radio mike in his lap. The other, in a German uniform, was unconscious, his breathing shallow. Macurdy had a man take the pilot's dogtags, go through his pockets, and look the cabin over for envelopes, papers—anything like that. Others gathered up any chutes visible from the road and stashed them out of sight.

The second spy, an American, had gotten out of the plane and seen the drop. He was walking, which meant they wouldn't have to carry him—at least not all the time—but he was also groggy, and his scalp was peeled half off. After cleaning both flap and skull, the medic laid the flap back where it belonged, and fastened it in place with a bandage. Strongly built and about six feet tall, his patient wore a German officer's field uniform, sharply tailored, with a captain's insignia.

Macurdy, trying to get him into the here and now, asked him his name. "Vonnie," the man muttered, then, in a monotone, "Captain William Von Lutzow."

That he could give his name was encouraging. Macurdy shook Von Lutzow's hand. "Mine's Macurdy. Sergeant Curtis Macurdy. Can you remember what happened?"

Von Lutzow stood a moment without answering, and when he did, it was in the same monotone: "We got shot at, taking off. Bullet hit the gas tank; we could smell the gas. Another one hit the pilot, but he said he was all right."

Concussion, Macurdy told himself, *but not really bad, or he wouldn't remember so much.* "We're going to get you out of here," he said. Then, because the winter night was near freezing, and Von Lutzow shivering, he put his hands on him and flowed warmth, drawing on the Web of the World, while the medic got the unconscious spy and Lieutenant Shuler strapped onto stretchers. Macurdy would have taken the dead pilot, too, but that would mean carrying a third burden more than twenty miles through mountains, with the prospect of enemy fighter planes hunting them by day, and perhaps troops by night. He'd settle for taking out the dead man's dogtags and wallet. Von Lutzow would hike out.

Macurdy checked once again; everyone was there. "All right," he said, "let's get going," and led off. They'd follow the road as long as it was safe.

They'd gone about half a mile when they heard distant trucks grinding up a steep grade on the other side of the crest behind them. Germans, Macurdy realized. They'd reach the plane soon, and have to stop until they could drag the wreckage off the road. Meanwhile they'd search the plane, and look around for the missing spies. It wouldn't take a genius to realize they'd been rescued, especially if the stashed chutes and stretchers were found.

The road took the troopers downward across the long slope, and when they reached the bottom, Macurdy halted them. Up on top, the trucks had stopped. Meanwhile the road turned southwestward, down the ravine. Macurdy took a topographic map from a tunic pocket and turned to the next ranking noncom. "Cavalieri," he said, "I'm taking Williams, Montague, Cherbajian and Luoma with me. And Captain Von Lutzow. The rest of them are yours. I want to make sure we get at least one of these two guys out of here safely for debriefing.

"I'll keep going west down the road as long as the krauts let me." He had one of the others hold a pen light on the map, and traced a route with his finger. "You head northeast up the ravine; they won't expect that. In about half a mile, a draw enters it from the northwest. Take it; the grade looks pretty moderate, and it tops out in a saddle. Cross the saddle and follow down the draw on the other side. It opens into a wide ravine that runs west. The map shows a camel road down it, so it ought to be decent hiking. Eventually it'll hit Road 163; you'll see it on your map. By then it ought to be daylight, or close to it; you'll probably want to hole up and rest."

Cavalieri nodded, awed. It was, he thought, as if Macurdy had memorized the topographic map on the plane, and things fell into place for him as needed.

"Stay with 163 to the Gafsa-Tebessa Road," Macurdy continued, "then use your own judgment. If we get out first, we'll tell them to look for you there." He took some of the extra K rations from his musette bag. "Turn around," he said. Cavalieri turned, and Macurdy shoved the rations into the man's musette bag. "For the limey," he added, "in case he wakes up hungry." Then he shook Cavalieri's hand. "Good luck, partner. See you at Thelepte."

Cavalieri grinned. "Good luck yourself. And don't do anything I wouldn't." Then he led his men off the road into shadowed darkness.

Macurdy didn't stay to watch them disappear. Up on the ridge, the trucks had started again; the Germans had gotten the plane out of the road. Presumably whoever was in charge would send part of his force in pursuit. No doubt others would continue searching above. On Macurdy's order, his people, even Von Lutzow, quickened their pace. Two minutes and a sixth of a mile farther, he turned off the road, crossing the ravine bottom to lead them angling up the ridge on their right.

With a little elevation, they could see three trucks coming down the road from the crash site, headlamp beams broad and bright in the night, light security ignored. Spotlights played over the roadsides as they growled down the grade in third gear. There wasn't effective cover, only thin spiny shrubs, rock outcrops, and minor terrain irregularities. "Come on, you guys," Macurdy ordered, "kick her out of neutral! We'll need to be farther up the hill than this, or we're dog meat. They'll have machine guns and lots of Schmeissers on those trucks."

They hunkered down, digging for uphill speed. Von Lutzow's concussion hadn't lessened his will to survive; he hustled with the rest of them. The trucks reached the bottom of the ravine and never paused, just rolled on down the road in a thick cloud of dust. Their spotlights swept the bordering slopes, but never reached high enough to find the gasping, puffing troopers. The Americans stopped to rest, watching.

"We lucked out, sarge," someone said quietly.

"That wasn't luck, Monty," Macurdy growled, "that was legs." There were still two trucks by the wreck, spotlights playing in the distance. There'd be a whole damned platoon up there searching; they'd find the chutes for sure, if they hadn't already. *Not that it'll do them any good,* he told himself, then added, *they really do want these guys.* He looked speculatively at Von Lutzow, who seemed about ready to puke, whether from exhaustion or concussion, Macurdy didn't know. Maybe both.

When they'd gotten their wind, he moved them on again toward the crest, now at an easier pace. It seemed to Macurdy they had the situation whipped, even if they did have a long way left to hike. When they reached the top, he stopped again. "Take a break," he said, and the men flopped down, lying back on their musette bags. Macurdy sat on the ground beside a prostrate Von Lutzow. The man's aura was shrunken, and there was a black hole in it above the forehead.

"How are you doing?" Macurdy asked. In German.

The spy looked up at him and answered in English. "My head hurts." He paused. "And my scalp burns." Another pause. "I'm worried about Morrill."

The words were still somewhat monotone; his mind was functioning at maybe fifty percent, Macurdy thought. He switched to English, too. "Morrill's your partner?"

Von Lutzow barely nodded, probably because his head hurt.

"Cavalieri will get him out; I'd bet a month's pay on it. And he's got the medic with him." Macurdy stood. "Sit up, captain," he said. "Let's see if I can do anything for your headache."

Von Lutzow sat up and Macurdy knelt behind him, putting a hand on each side of the spy's head, holding them there for long seconds, frowning slightly, then moved one to the forehead and the other opposite. After another ten seconds he asked, "How's that feel?"

Von Lutzow's jaw had sagged slightly. "The headache's not half what it was!"

"Good." Macurdy removed one hand, while the fingers of

the other traced lines in the space immediately above Von Lutzow's bandaged scalp. This continued for perhaps half a minute, then he worked his fingers gently down the spine, pausing here and there while his fingertips wove patterns, shifting threads of energy. Von Lutzow only blinked. Finally Macurdy sat back.

"How's the scalp?"

"Tingles like a son of a bitch, but the burning's gone. The headache too, now." Von Lutzow's monotone had been replaced by thoughtfulness.

A nearby voice commented, with an accent that reminded Macurdy of the Saari brothers. "My mother would love to watch you, sarge," Luoma said. "She's always talking about stuff her grandma did like that, back in the old country."

Other eyes had watched, too, and other ears had listened. They'd known and liked the fact that their sergeant was different, peculiar, but this healing business was new to them. Macurdy stood up. "Time to move," he said. "On your feet."

They got up, Von Lutzow rising without help, and Macurdy led off, westward along the broad crest.

Over the next three hours, Macurdy pretty much observed the standard breaks—ten minutes on the hour. On that basis, troopers with full field gear could push fifty miles in twelve hours, on a road. But these guys had been on patrol all afternoon before coming out on this mission. And the German trucks had returned up the ravine and up the hill; the danger seemed over. At least until daylight, when Messerschmitts might come hunting them. Besides, the moon had climbed higher, shortening the shadows. So Macurdy had set no watch on this break. Men dozed, and his own lids too slipped shut. The ground was hard and stony, and like the night, cold. At worst he wouldn't sleep longer than a few minutes.

The same sound wakened them all, a quiet voice perhaps 120, 150 feet away, speaking German, ordering, *"Take a break. Pass it on."* Other voices repeated it at intervals in both directions.

None of the six Americans moved. They occupied an area not twenty feet across. "Come to me," Macurdy murmured softly. "On your bellies. Now." They did, wondering, until all of them would have fitted under an eight-foot-square tarp. But it wasn't a tarp Macurdy planned to cover them with. This time his voice was scarcely more than a whisper. "Take out your .45s, but no one move or shoot unless I say so, or I'll see your ass on a fence post. Just lay still. They won't see us as long as you keep quiet." He chuckled softly, deliberately. "Trust me; me and my Aunt Varia. If you pray, do it under your breath. God'll hear you."

Then he spread his cloaking spell to cover them, using his hands because he'd never spread it over an area before.

How long had he dozed? he wondered. Surely not more than ten minutes. And what were Germans doing up there? Looking for them, obviously; but why there?

It seemed to him he knew: The *feldgrau*, the Germans, had found the chutes; obviously American paratroopers had taken the spies. And where would they have gone with them? Unless they were hiding near the plane, they'd have gone in a westerly direction, toward the American outposts, probably following the road. So the German commander had sent three truckloads of men after them, commanded by a junior officer.

But after a few miles, having found no one, they'd look at other options. The Americans might have left the road and followed the crest, which after the road gave the best hiking. So the trucks had returned empty, and the *feldgrau* were working their way back on foot. It was a low percentage sort of action, done so they could say they'd covered all the prospects. They didn't really expect to find anyone.

Apparently the German breaks were ten minutes long, too; that's how long it was before a voice said in German, "On your feet," then after a moment, "move out. And stay alert!"

Macurdy lay on his side, the heavy Colt in his fist, thumb on the half-cocked hammer. His M1 lay on the ground beside him. If it came down to it, he'd empty the Colt at whatever targets offered themselves, then pick up the rifle. The Germans approached, more than half a dozen he could see. By their helmets and coveralls, they were *Fallschirmjäger*—German paratroops. With submachine guns.

One of the Germans was coming directly toward them, scanning from side to side. Unless he changed course, he'd walk right into them. Macurdy stared as the man approached, to 20 feet, 10, 5. As he passed, the German's toe struck

Macurdy's booted foot, and he stumbled. *"Verdammter Felsen!"* he muttered, cursing the outcrop he imagined had tripped him, and continued walking, peering about.

You could have cut the tension with a knife; Macurdy wondered the German hadn't sensed it. No one spoke or got up until, supported by an elbow, Macurdy could no longer see the Germans. "All right," he murmured, "sit up if you want, but stay quiet."

"Jesus Christ, sarge!" Williams murmured, "that was the goddamnedest thing I ever heard of. Scared me out of five years growth! I don't know which was the spookiest, you or the damned krauts. And *fallschirmjäger,* for chrissake! That would have been a fight!"

"Thank your ass it wasn't," Macurdy growled.

Luoma chuckled. "With you around, sarge," he said quietly, "I don't worry too much."

Macurdy grunted. If the Germans had spotted them, all the magic he'd ever seen or heard of wouldn't have meant a thing when the Schmeissers started spewing 9mm slugs at seven or eight per second each.

With the pale light of dawn, Macurdy led them into a side draw, where there was cover—coarse brush and some small trees. There they ate a K ration each, then most lit up cigarettes, Macurdy lighting Von Lutzow's with a finger. After that they made themselves as comfortable as they could, and settled down for a few hours of restless sleep. Only Macurdy slept warm. He awoke once to the sound of a plane, flying fast and fairly low, to pass without showing itself, hidden by a ridge. One of Cochran's P40s, he decided. Not a Messerschmitt or the twin-engined P38s, or the Junkers they saw and heard from time to time. He could hear the difference.

Toward noon, with so little air activity, he led them down to the road. They could travel faster, and there was intermittent tree cover along its edge. Several more times during the day they heard fighters, and once a P40 streaked overhead. An overcast developed, then thickened. Toward evening it began to drizzle, and they paused to put on their ponchos. Macurdy offered his to Von Lutzow, who refused it.

"Take it," Macurdy ordered. "It's my fault I didn't bring an extra, and anyway, I don't get cold."

Von Lutzow peered at him with interest. "What do you mean, you don't get cold?"

"Remember how I warmed you before we left the plane last night? I stay as warm as I want. My Aunt Varia's a witch; she taught me."

Von Lutzow half grinned, uncertain whether he was being put on, and accepted the poncho.

Dusk was thickening when the road reached a larger ravine, this one with trees numerous along the roadsides. Macurdy turned left and they kept hiking. The drizzle had changed to a light but steady rain. With no poncho, he was wet to the skin, and water trickled down the ponchos of the others. Von Lutzow had held up well—his conditioning was obviously excellent—but they were due for more than a ten-minute rest. At the next break, he told himself, they'd stop for a couple of hours.

It didn't happen, because half an hour later they heard a vehicle coming ahead. Macurdy sent the others off the road to cover, M1s ready, while he crouched beside a tree, pen light in one hand, .45 in the other. A minute later the vehicle came into sight, headlamps hooded—a jeep! As it approached, he stood up and waved the pen light. "Hey!" he shouted. "Going my way?"

The driver braked, tires grabbing wet dirt. "Macurdy!"

The voice was Cavalieri's. His party had met a patrol of French infantry in jeeps with machine guns. The French had radioed Gafsa for him, and the 26th Infantry sent a truck, along with an ambulance for the injured. Morrill was alive, but hadn't regained consciousness. When Cavalieri got to Gafsa, he'd reported to battalion by phone, then grabbed a jeep and come looking for his buddies.

He picked up his mike and radioed Gafsa. Then, at Macurdy's urging, Von Lutzow got in the jeep and headed for Gafsa with Cavalieri. Macurdy and his four troopers took an hour's break in the rain, until a weapons carrier arrived to pick them up.

He never expected to see Von Lutzow again. Their very different paths had crossed, then diverged. It was so common in wartime, he never gave it a thought. Wouldn't for months.

18

A Very Strange AWOL

Under heavy pressure by the British 8th Army, Rommel pulled his Afrika Korps entirely out of Libya that winter, but it was a strategic retreat. The Desert Fox saw possibilities in the west: Drive through Tunisia into Algeria, take the city of Algiers, and the situation would become much more favorable.

Thus in mid-February 1943, the Afrika Korps brushed aside the small American and French units and rumbled through Gafsa toward Tebessa, which Rommel considered strategically vital. Between Gafsa and Tebessa lay the Kasserine Pass, which the Allied Command raced to defend. There the Afrika Korps savaged the green U.S. 1st and 34th Divisions. But it never quite reached Tebessa, because the fighting had taken a toll of Nazi men and armor, and Allied air forces had established dominance.

The 509th Parachute Infantry (nee 2nd Battalion, 503rd) played no part in any of this. The whole battalion was quartered in Boufarik. The Allied Command had decided that employing lightly armed parachute units in regular ground operations was to misuse a special tool.

Then, in early March, the battalion was put on trains and moved 380 miles west to Oujda, in French Morocco, where it was bivouacked outside the city. There it received replacements, and returned to intensive training.

But even in French Morocco, battles were fought. In early

May, the new, highly trained but unblooded 82nd Airborne Division arrived, eager to prove itself, and was bivouacked near the 509th. Whose men took umbrage at the newcomers' cockiness, particularly when, in early June, the Allied command attached the previously independent 509th to the green 82nd as just another constituent battalion.

It might not have been so bad, had living conditions not been so lousy, both for the old hands and the newcomers. The training was brutal and unrelenting, humping equipment up and down the rugged hills, running, and especially training at night: They were to become the masters of darkness.

Which meant sleep time was not only short, but often came during the day. And they slept in pup tents—crawl-in shelters that by day were like ovens.

Nor were there mess-halls, or even mess tents. They took their mess tins to the kitchen, got their food (which was poor and monotonous), and sat on the ground to fight for it with swarms of flies. They soon gave up trying to shoo them away, or even brush them off effectively. They simply cursed, chewed, and swallowed.

On the occasional day off, there was little to do except go into Oujda, where keepers of cheap bars dispensed bad whiskey. And arriving in a less than Christian mood, the troopers were inclined to truculence. In fact, the battles of French Morocco were fought in the bars of Oujda, notably between troopers of the 509th and those of the 82nd. In these, any reluctance to trade blows tended to be lost.

Not all troopers took part, of course. Bar brawls are not vital experience for young warriors, but for many at that stage they were inevitable, indeed for many a joy.

Macurdy, however, preferred to avoid brawls, and found quieter, more out-of-the-way bars, frequented by those who preferred friendliness to fist fights. He'd learned to drink in Phenix City, Alabama, and did it more gracefully than most. Having a rare ability to control his physiological processes, and being neither obsessive nor addictive, he didn't get drunk. Largely he drank wine—he hadn't learned to like hard liquor—allowing himself at most a certain mellowness. Of course, he'd recently had his 39th birthday, but he'd have handled his trips to Oujda more or less similarly had he been ten years younger.

In fact, he would probably have come through his Oujda months unscathed, except for a two-and-a-half-ton truck.

He was with Cavalieri and Luoma, headed back to camp, not drunk or even tight. Over-relaxed perhaps, and less alert than might be. The truck was heavily laden, hauling ordnance from the docks at Mellilla. The driver said he never saw them, that a donkey cart had turned in front of him, and he'd swerved. Also, he'd been continuously on duty for seventeen hours. At any rate he knocked down a G.I. and ran over him.

MPs appeared as if by magic, filling out forms, taking names, ranks, serial numbers, units. . . . The driver they hauled off in an MP jeep. The victim, who was taken away in an ambulance, was Staff Sergeant Curtis E. Macurdy, serial number 36 928 450.

Macurdy awoke in the base hospital, remembering nothing of the day. The heavy truck had run over his right leg, doing extreme soft tissue damage, breaking the femur, patella, tibia and fibula, but somehow missing foot, hip, and left leg. He didn't know this, of course. All he knew, vaguely, was that his right leg was in a cast and elevated, its shrunken aura a chaotic mess, and that he was doped to the gills.

He thought of doing something about it, but it seemed like too much trouble, so he fell asleep again, drifting in and out for an indeterminate period that seemed quite long.

The next day he awoke more or less alert. The ward was less than half full, but he had a neighbor in the bed on his left, his right leg also elevated and in a cast. The man was reading a paperback.

Macurdy lay quiet for a while, searching his mind for what had happened, and finding nothing. So he interrupted the reader. "Where am I?" he asked.

The man looked at him. "The base hospital in Oujda."

"What happened to me?"

"Damned if I know. A medic can probably tell you. How's your leg feel?"

Macurdy gathered focus and looked again at the aura around

it, more clearly than before. It was still shrunken, but a little less chaotic. "Busier" now; the leg was trying to heal. It was also dark with pain, more pain than the hard-edged ache he felt. He was still doped up, he decided, but not nearly as much as he had been.

"Not too bad. I'd like to know what happened though. What happened to you?"

"I'm in the 505th Parachute Infantry. We jumped on an exercise in the hills east of Jerada, five days ago. It was pretty windy, and I came down in a ravine full of rocks." He paused. "What outfit are you with?"

"The 509th."

"Ah! One of those! See any combat, did you?"

"Not much. We took some shelling at Tafaraoui, and swapped shots on a night patrol I was on out of Gafsa, but the only real fighting I saw was when we drove the Germans off Faid Pass."

He paused. "Not all that much—some companies got more—but enough to get the feel of things. We had almost as many casualties jumping and training as we did fighting." He chuckled. "And barroom casualties here in Oujda. I stay clear of those. I'm basically a peaceful man."

The 505er laughed. "Me too. I'm thirty years old; I leave those bullshit brawls to the kids. My name's Keith. Staff Sergeant Fred Keith, from Gwynn, Michigan."

"Mine's Curtis Macurdy, from Washington County, Indiana by way of Nehtaka, Oregon. I'm a staff sergeant too."

They were interrupted by a nurse. "How are we doing, Sergeant Macurdy?"

"Could be better. What happened to me?"

"You were run over by a loaded truck. The surgeons spent several hours putting your bones back together. You have enough pins in your leg to make a magnet spin."

"Huh! How long do they figure I'll be in here?"

"Two months if you're lucky—if healing progresses the way we hope. Then another month or two in rehab."

Her aura told him she was withholding from him. "Then what?" he asked.

"You should be able to walk normally."

"What about jumping? Parachuting."

Her eyes evaded his. "The doctor can tell you more about that than I can." She sensed his awareness, and added: "I expect you'll get a non-combat assignment."

Inwardly Macurdy smiled. *I'll give them something to think about,* he told himself as she left, and decided that complete recovery in ten days would be about right.

Meanwhile his neighbor stared at him. *Two months!* Keith thought. He didn't commiserate though; didn't know how Macurdy felt about it. At any rate, his neighbor from the 509th seemed to have his attention elsewhere.

Actually, Macurdy was examining the aura around his good leg, imaging it mentally as a basis for working on the damaged one. If need be, he could heal by the feel, but he preferred having a base line. He couldn't get at it very well with his hands, but he could do a good enough job using his eyes and mind. And this project, he told himself, would improve that skill.

The next day, when a visitor arrived to see Keith, Macurdy was reading, and paid no attention till the man spoke. "How you doing, sarge? The guys said to tell you they want you back before we get shipped somewhere." It was the voice that grabbed Macurdy's attention, jerking his gaze from the page.

"Any rumors?" Keith asked.

"Nothing different than usual: Greece, Italy, Sicily, southern France . . . But one thing is real: Division sent a team of officers somewhere to set things up. Probably the place we'll invade from."

Macurdy stared. The man's broad back was to him, but it was a back he knew, and the bull neck was familiar. Both went with the voice.

"Anybody else hurt since I left?" Keith asked.

"Not bad. What does the doc say about getting out of here?"

"Four more weeks, then rehab. I'll be as good as new."

Macurdy interrupted. "Damn it, Keith! I wish you'd get a pretty girl visitor, instead of a big mean Indian logger from Oregon."

Roy Klaplanahoo spun and stared. "Macurdy!" he said. "What are you doing here?"

The next twenty minutes was a three-way conversation that ended with Keith and Macurdy knowing one another much better than they might have without Klaplanahoo's presence. All three had been loggers, Keith mainly a pulper and tie hack from Upper Michigan; it added a bond between the two patients.

"Macurdy is a healer," Klaplanahoo told him. "I seen him heal a bad cut a guy got in a knife fight. In a hobo jungle outside Miles City, Montana. And a couple guys that got shot in a logging camp. He does it like a shaman, except he don't use a drum." He turned to Macurdy. "I'll bet you been working on that leg."

Macurdy grinned, and lowered his voice for privacy. "They told me I'd be here at least two months. I gave myself ten days at most."

Keith looked intensely at him, and lowered his voice too. "They'll never believe it. They'll keep you two months regardless."

"Maybe I'll get a little help from my friends. Maybe a hacksaw."

"There's no bars on the windows here."

"To get this cast off. A saw will go through it like nothing. Then I can break it off."

Keith's gaze went out of focus; he was thinking. "You serious?" he asked.

"Damn right."

"I could get a hacksaw," Klaplanahoo murmured.

And that just about finished the conversation. All three men had something to think about. Macurdy decided to give more time to his leg. Ten days had been a guess. Maybe he could shorten that a few days.

Later that day Keith murmured to him: "Macurdy, I'm worried my outfit will leave me behind. Can you really heal people? Broken legs?"

"I guarantee it."

"Guarantee is a pretty strong word."

Macurdy nodded.

"How about healing me?"

"As long as you're willing."

"How do you go about it?"

"If I can't reach it with my hands, I do it with my eyes."

Keith looked doubtfully at him. "Show me."

Macurdy put his attention on the aura around the elevated leg, then the good one, then the broken one again, and began to manipulate the thread-like energy lines, working on them for several minutes with eyes and intention. The lines tended to slip back the way they'd been, but when they did, he simply readjusted them. After ten minutes they were behaving pretty well, and he could sense Keith's body cooperating.

It's as if, he told himself, *the energy threads make a kind of template, an energy skeleton for the body—flesh, bones, guts and all. Fix the template, and the rest of it goes along.* At least it acted that way. He wasn't going to ask the doctors what they thought of the idea though.

"That's enough for now," he said. "I'll work more on it after a while."

Keith regarded the leg uncertainly. It seemed to him he could feel a difference. *By God,* he told himself hopefully, *maybe this'll work. It just might.*

A number of times on each of the next several days, Macurdy worked both on his own leg and Keith's for about ten minutes each. Already on the second day, Keith felt enthused, certain he could feel it working. At the end of a week, Macurdy felt sure that either of them could get up and walk, but he knew the medics wouldn't hear of it.

Meanwhile all he had for clothes was a ridiculous little green hospital gown with his bare ass hanging out. By then he'd had visitors himself—the battalion didn't train all the time—and when Cavalieri and Luoma showed up that evening, he asked them to smuggle a set of his class A khakis to him.

Their expressions changed from cheerful to unhappy. It was Cavalieri who answered him. "Jesus, Macurdy, I'd sure as hell like to, but—"

"But what?"

"They—they took your clothes. This morning."

"*What!* Who took them?"

"We weren't going to tell you, but you've been transferred."

"Transferred! Where?"

Cavalieri could hardly bring himself to say the words. "To the MPs. It's in your records that you were a deputy sheriff, and the sawbones said you won't be able to jump anymore, or anything like that, so . . ." He shrugged. "They latched onto you. Your khakis went to your new outfit, your jumpsuit and boots to supply. Maybe I could get your boots back though, and bring them to you."

Macurdy seemed to collapse for a moment. "Shit." He paused. "I've got to think about this." Then he changed the subject, asking what the battalion had been doing, and didn't mention the matter again, except to take up Cavalieri's offer on the boots. He'd like to have them for old times sake, he said.

The best thing he could do now, it seemed to him, was act resigned to it.

After Cavalieri and Luoma left, he wondered briefly if maybe he *should* resign himself to it. MP duty was unpopular—at least MPs were—but someone had to do it, and it was relatively safe. As an MP, he'd likely return alive to his wife, while as a paratrooper, his prospects were doubtful.

On the other hand, he wondered, not for the first time, if Mary might not be better off if he didn't come home. Their future as a couple held decades of relocations, while she grew old and he remained young.

But his decision didn't grow out of that. It simply seemed to him he was supposed to be airborne. For better or worse, he'd spent most of his life heeding his deeper feelings, and for better or worse, he'd follow them now.

So he had a serious discussion with Keith, their voices scarcely louder than whispers. When it was over, he gave some attention to Keith's leg again. The thread-like lines of energy around it looked pretty much normal, so he concentrated on increased blood flow. He didn't pay much attention to his own leg anymore. It seemed to him he didn't need to.

The next day the company supply clerk sent out Macurdy's boots, by a guy pulling fatigue duty; Cavalieri was off on a training problem. After checking the boots for a bottle, the duty nurse told him to put them under Macurdy's bed.

Roy Klaplanahoo stopped by that evening as early as he could. The three troopers plotted briefly in undertones, then he left. Two hours later he was back. He could never get away with bringing in a package; the nurses and orderlies would suspect booze, and search it. But inside his Class A khaki shirt—required wear on pass—he wore a second, both tucked into the outer of the two pairs of khaki trousers he had on. He carried the hacksaw blade in two belt loops of the inner pair; Macurdy would have to make do without a frame for it. All in all, Roy felt both conspicuous and uncomfortable, but it was twilight out, and no one paid much attention to him. After looking around nervously, he took off the outer pants, then the outer shirt, and put them under a sheet. The blade he tucked under the edge of Macurdy's mattress.

"Can you cut off the cast yourself?" he murmured worriedly.

"I'll manage. Later, when it's darker."

Both Macurdy and Keith shook hands with Roy then, and the Indian left.

It was after midnight when Macurdy did it. The leg didn't look as bad as he thought it might. His healing actions had done more than repair bone, muscle, and connective tissue; they'd reduced the discoloration to a pale greenish yellow, and atrophy was minor.

In the small ward, he was the only man fully awake. Roy's pants and sleeves were a little short, but beyond that, the fit was decent. After cloaking himself with his invisibility spell, Macurdy left carrying his boots. The saw blade he'd left with Keith. No one looked up as he padded barefoot down the corridor and past the nurses' station.

Getting out of the building was not so straightforward. The exit had a screen door, and a sentry was posted by it. If the door were suddenly to open beside him, it seemed to Macurdy the sentry would surely see through the spell. For just a moment he considered using a choke hold on him, but slipped instead into a quiet ward, unhooked a window screen, let himself out, and pushed the screen shut behind him.

Leaving behind a round-eyed patient, who despite seeing the screen open, then close, had failed to see anyone doing it. The spell was better than Macurdy realized, better than Varia's had been, or Maikel's.

Once away from the hospital, he deactivated his cloak, and following Roy's instructions, found the road to camp without any trouble. He didn't even need to walk far before an airborne lieutenant in a jeep picked him up. "What regiment, sergeant?" the lieutenant asked.

"The 509th, sir."

"Ah. Them." The officer shifted out of neutral and started down the road. "I don't smell any booze on you, sergeant. What's the story?"

"I've got a girlfriend, sir. She doesn't drink."

"Did you use a pro kit? We don't want men hospitalized with VD."

"She's the daughter of a French major, sir. We hope to be married." The lieutenant's eyebrows raised, and Macurdy felt pleased with himself. It wasn't the sort of lie he'd think of, ordinarily. He felt as if he could do anything that night.

At the company area, he walked into the orderly room—a tent—and wakened the CQ, who stared at him as if he were a ghost. "Manny," Macurdy said, "I'm back. Got my transfer cancelled. Can you get me into Supply? I need my jumpsuit and gear."

"Jesus, sarge, you took me by surprise! I can get you into Supply, but I don't know where anything is there."

"That's all right. Let me in and I'll find it."

He did. He'd been prepared to take anything that fitted, but there was his own jumpsuit and helmet, with his own name on them. After putting them on, he folded Roy's khakis, put them in a pillow case and left with it. Stopping at the orderly room tent, he thanked the CQ before leaving him mystified and unsure. He hadn't asked Macurdy about his leg, but Doc Alden had supposedly said it looked like a blood sausage the size of a duffel bag. And that had been only—how long? A week ago? Week and a half?

✧ ✧ ✧

Macurdy then went to the 505th's bivouac—it wasn't far—went to the regimental CQ, learned where he could find Roy Klaplanahoo, then went there and woke him. As planned, Roy had gotten Keith's boots and a set of his khakis, which he gave to Macurdy. Macurdy gave Roy his khakis back, put Keith's in the pillow case, then shook hands with his old friend and started back to Oujda and the hospital.

It was a fairly long hike, with time to think. He preferred that Keith not know about the cloak; it might spook him, and the ward in the middle of the night was no place for explanations. Then he remembered Varia that first night: They'd walked hand in hand, and he could see her just fine despite the spell; they'd both been inside the cloak. So hopefully physical contact would do it; contact and his own intention.

By the time he got there, his right leg was tired, and it was getting daylight. He'd have to wait till the next night to spring Keith. Finding a place to hide out promised to be tricky, because he wasn't sure the spell would persist if he slept. He waited by the door until the morning shift came in, and went in half a stride behind an army surgeon.

Then he snooped some rooms that were not wards. One held big bags of clean linens, and on top of one, a surgeon was having sex with a nurse; they never noticed the door quietly open and close. When they were done, they tidied themselves, then quickly dressed, kissed, and departed. Watching them had stimulated Macurdy. He wished he was back in Nehtaka, in bed with Mary.

Apparently this room was reasonably private. He made a place for himself between a wall and big bags of linens, and went to sleep there. It was chancy, but he couldn't think of a better place. And there was a window not four feet away. If he was discovered, he'd leave through it.

Several hours later he awoke hungry, and drew energy from the Web of the World. It didn't help his grumpy stomach, but at least he wouldn't get wobbly from hunger. While he'd slept, someone had dragged out the bag of linens he'd been behind. Obviously his cloak had persisted in his sleep.

Meanwhile he wasn't sleepy any longer, so he meditated—it was the first time in years—and after a while, slept again.

Even so, it was a long day and evening. No more lovers came in, only orderlies a couple of times for linens. After 2200, everything was quiet, and he slipped down the corridor to the ward, where he wakened his friend and freed his leg from its cast. When Keith had dressed, Macurdy murmured to him not to worry about being seen. "Just hold on to the back of my shirt, walk softly and say nothing. I've got everything taken care of." Keith frowned. *Hold on to the back of your shirt?* But he did, and Macurdy activated his cloak. There was no reaction from Keith; apparently the man still saw him as before. They walked together down the corridor, then left by the same window Macurdy had used the night previous.

As Macurdy went through the window, he deactivated his cloak, and Keith followed him. Then they walked together to the road. They'd gone a hundred yards or so before it really struck Keith that he was walking. When it did, he just stood there and laughed, guffawed, for about a minute.

After that, they talked while they walked. There'd been a big flap that morning when a nurse discovered Macurdy was missing. "The MPs arrived quicker than you'd ever imagine, and before lunch a guy from the CID showed up, with lots of questions. I told him I'd assumed the medics had moved you, but that I wasn't surprised; those cocky bastards in the 509th would do anything." Keith laughed again. "He told me you'd gone back to the 509th and gotten your jumpsuit, or someone had gotten it for you. The guy who'd been on CQ there said you'd walked in as if you'd never been hurt. The docs here said you couldn't have walked anywhere, in or out, for three or four months. The CID guy thinks there was a conspiracy by your buddies to spring you, but where the hell they stashed you was a mystery. They're probably checking all the whorehouses in Oujda. That's where guys would hide somebody."

Macurdy didn't laugh. Keith had given him food for thought. He hoped no one got into serious trouble over this.

On the road back to camp, they'd thumbed a ride, in a jeep with two officers from the 504th, heading back to camp from a bout in a presumably better class of brothel. They'd drunk enough they weren't worried about anything, and if they heard any strange stories the next morning, weren't likely to remember the two sergeants, or at least wouldn't volunteer it. They didn't even ask Macurdy why he was in his jumpsuit, which in town was "out of uniform."

Meanwhile Macurdy and Keith learned something from the officers: the 504th's 1st Battalion was to ship out that morning—the officers didn't say where to—and the rest of the division was sure to follow shortly.

They were let out at the 505th's area, and went to Keith's pup tent. Keith crawled inside, but Macurdy sat outside briefly, and with his pocket stiletto picked away at his 509th "Gingerbread Man" unit patch until he got it off. Then both lay waiting for sleep, each silently considering the morning to come. Belatedly, both felt ill at ease about it. Getting out of the hospital had been the easy part; if the MPs had been at the 509th so quickly after Macurdy's disappearance, they'd be at the 505th by breakfast.

They should, Keith thought, have holed up somewhere for a day or two before coming here. Maybe they still should. But then he thought to hell with it; he'd stay and see what happened. Shit! Here he was, walking around. They wouldn't hardly take him back to the hospital and put another cast on him, for chrissake. Even the army wasn't that stupid. They might take him away, but he'd be back before the day was out.

Hell, he told himself, *something like this is so weird, they won't even put it in my service record. They'll be afraid to.*

Macurdy wakened at dawn, and went to Roy's tent to see if he could get hold of some mess gear. A guy in Roy's squad had gotten arrested in Oujda two nights earlier for slugging an MP officer, so Roy loaned Macurdy his.

They were sitting on the ground eating breakfast when the MPs arrived with the company commander, who spotted Keith and took the MPs to him. The three sergeants got to their feet as the C.O. approached, Macurdy wishing he dared cloak himself. As it was, there he stood, less than four feet from

Keith, with the name Macurdy above his left breast pocket, and stenciled on his helmet. It seemed to him he might as well be wearing neon lights and an alarm bell.

But when the MPs took Staff Sergeant Fred Keith away with them, Macurdy was still there, ignored.

Except by the C.O. "Sergeant," he said ominously, "I don't believe I know you." He peered at the name on Macurdy's helmet. "What's your outfit, trooper?"

The name on the C.O.'s helmet was Szczpura, and he had a trace of accent. The scars on his face, and the broken nose, suggested years in the prize ring; probably, Macurdy thought, as a middleweight. And almost certainly he'd never seen West Point. OCS probably. His mien as well as his aura reflected not only competence but integrity, a man who acted according to his convictions.

So Macurdy sketched out the whole story for him, except for the invisibility spell, with Roy Klaplanahoo supporting the parts on healing. "It looks like the 505th could be leaving here without one of its platoon sergeants," Macurdy finished, "and I'm a good one. I jumped at Youks les Bains, and was in on the capture of Tebessa and Gafsa." He neglected to say there'd been no Germans at either of them. "I've done recon patrols of German and Italian outposts in Tunisia, fought at Faid Pass, and commanded a jump in German territory to rescue a couple of our people. And got them out alive." He paused, then added in German, *"Ferner spreche ich ganz gut Deutsch"*—(Also I speak rather good German)—hoping it would make him more attractive.

Szczpura laughed drily. *"Das ist nicht gutes Deutsch. Das ist baltisches Deutsch,"* he answered. ("That's not good German. That's Baltic German.") The captain's German was a little rough but easily understood. "I was born in Poland, in Olsztyn. There are a lot of Germans around Olsztyn; I had a German grandmother that lived with us."

His gray eyes appraised Macurdy coolly, then Klaplanahoo spoke again. "Captain, Macurdy and I are friends from way back. We logged together in Oregon, on opposite ends of a saw, and got bonuses for cutting more than anyone else in camp. And I saw him kill a guy with a knife throw, a guy that had just killed a deputy sheriff and shot the logging boss. He's not afraid of anyone, and he's even stronger than me. He's somebody guys like and respect, and . . ."

Szczpura cut short the plaudits. "Where did you get that nose, Macurdy?"

"A couple of places, sir. Before I joined the army. I'm not a drinking man or troublemaker, sir."

"You're AWOL from the hospital and the MPs."

"Yessir, I am sir."

The captain pursed his lips thoughtfully, then said, "Come with me, Macurdy," and led him to the orderly room. Inside, the captain spoke to the 1st sergeant, who sat at a desk with his breakfast in front of him. "Sergeant Barker, this is Sergeant Macurdy; he just arrived as Keith's replacement. His transfer papers are delayed or lost, but they'll turn up sooner or later. Have someone take him to Lieutenant Murray, then post him on the roster."

He turned to Macurdy. "Glad to have you with us, sergeant." Then added softly: "I hope you don't make me regret this."

"Thank you, sir. Glad to be here, sir."

Almost the last thing Macurdy wanted to do was disappoint this man. As he followed the company clerk to meet his new platoon leader, it seemed to him that in the Army, this miraculous salvation could have happened only in the airborne, and even there, the odds against it had been heavy.

Though neither Macurdy nor Captain Szczpura realized it, Fred Keith might soon have returned, not that day as he'd hoped, but within three or four, and at worst with only a reprimand on his record. But it didn't work that way, not because of the MPs, who in his case didn't really care much one way or the other. But because of the surgeon in charge of his case, who insisted he be assigned to a month in a rehab company. As a physician with the rank of lieutenant colonel, he felt wronged and insulted that the trooper had made him look bad.

19

Sicily

A few days later, the 505th loaded onto trains and rolled out of Oujda eastward, with twenty men and their duffel bags to a small boxcar. It could have been worse—the official capacity stenciled on the cars was forty men or eight horses—but they had eight hundred miles to go, and given the traffic, and the state of the equipment, tracks and bridges, it would probably take them four days or more. Twenty to a car was more than enough.

The trip ended in eastern Tunisia, where they camped near the holy Muslim city of Kairouan. The countryside wasn't as desolate as that around Oujda. It actually had trees, even if some of them did resemble cactus.

Training continued, but they weren't there long. Long enough to learn that their objective was Sicily, and to be briefed on their units' missions, drilling them on sand tables. Remembering the confusion on the flight from Land's End to Algeria, Macurdy wondered how meaningful those drills were. And this drop would be at night.

There was a shortage of troop planes for the division. Thus it would have to be flown on consecutive days, the 505th jumping on the first day, along with one battalion of the 504th. The heavily loaded C47s would take three and a half hours to fly the 420-mile dogleg course, using the island of Malta as a checkpoint. Then they'd return to Kairouan and bring the rest of the 504th the next day.

The veteran 509th would remain in Tunisia as a reserve. Macurdy could guess how pissed off they'd be.

✧ ✧ ✧

Appropriately it was Melody, his spear-maiden second wife, of whom Macurdy dreamed that last night in Africa. Daylight and shrilling whistles woke him, and the dream slipped away, leaving behind only that it had been of Melody. After an early breakfast, the 505th lined up to draw ammunition and field rations, along with atabrine pills to prevent malaria, pills to purify water, and antifatigue pills.

They were scheduled to take off at dusk; it would, Macurdy thought, be a long day of hurry up and wait.

The men sat and stood around until shortly after noon, when the shouted order, "Load on the trucks," echoed down the line from the battalion commander to the company commanders. The trucks took them to various small airfields in the vicinity, where they waited again, now in the shadows of their planes. Macurdy field-stripped his BAR—so far as he knew, he was the only platoon sergeant who carried one of the 18-pound automatic weapons—then checked and reassembled it, less from concern than for something to do. He did the same with his .45. One big thigh pocket bulged with fragmentation grenades, and the Fairbairn knife he'd traded for in England was on his belt; he preferred the double-edged British weapon to the GI trench knife with its brass knuckles. His folding stiletto was in its concealed inner pocket, available to cut himself free if his chute hung up, or slit a throat and escape if captured. There were bandoleers of magazines for the BAR, and a canvas bag with additional grenades. Along with boots, steel helmet, trenching tool, first-aid kit, musette bag, map case . . . and of course his two chutes—main and reserve. He told himself wryly that with all of that, he'd weigh well over three hundred pounds, but there was none of it he'd willingly leave behind.

A mess truck rolled up to the company, with aproned men in back, and Macurdy got to his feet. "What the hell is that all about?" someone asked. "It's only half past four."

It was an early supper, suggesting they'd take off before too long. They got out their mess kits and lined up by squads, while a cook lowered the tailgate. It was far the best meal they'd eaten in Africa—roast turkey, dressing, mashed potatoes, gravy . . . even ice cream.

"The Army's version of the Last Supper," someone quipped. It didn't get many laughs; a lot of men only picked at their food. Macurdy ate all of his; God only knew when they'd have time to eat again. He wondered what Mary would serve tonight. His mail hadn't followed him to the 505th; maybe it never would. But he'd written to Mary about his new outfit, so her future letters should find him. Thus far he hadn't gotten on the 505th payroll, either—that would probably take a legal transfer—but there'd be time enough to worry about that when he'd left Africa and the provost marshal behind.

After supper they lay around digesting as best they could, when a jeep rolled up, and Macurdy saw Captain Alden get out, one of the 509th's battalion surgeons. Briefly Alden spoke with Colonel Gavin, the regimental commander, then walked around among the troops, pausing to speak to some of the company officers. Macurdy felt concern. Had the 509th learned where he was? Was Alden looking for him? The officer came nearer, then recognized him and walked over, peering as if he couldn't believe it.

"Is that you, Macurdy? What the devil are you doing here? The last time I saw you—hell, it wasn't a month ago!—you were in the hospital with one of the goddamnedest sorriest-looking legs I'd want to see. Bigger than a melon! What are you doing in the 505th? Hell! How are you even walking?"

The comments from the 509th officer caused nearby heads to swivel.

Macurdy grinned, reassured: Doc wasn't there to pick him up. Of course not. It wasn't something they'd send a battalion surgeon to do, and if they did, Doc would carefully not see him.

"At the hospital," Macurdy answered, "they said I'd never be fit for combat again, so someone in base command transferred me to the MPs. But I'm the fastest healing sonofabitch in the army, so after about a week, a guy smuggled me a hacksaw blade to cut off the cast, and a guy in the next bed—from the 505th—got me in here."

Alden laughed, shaking his head. "You're not very strong on regulations, are you Macurdy? I won't tell your buddies till after you've taken off. They'll be jealous as hell." He gestured with his head at the C47 beside them. "That's why I'm here; thought I might get a seat in one of these gooney birds, and go along, but your CO wouldn't have it." He reached, shook Macurdy's hand. "Fast healing? That took more than fast healing; it took a damn miracle." He paused, frowning, as it struck him how miraculous Macurdy's recovery really was; he'd seen the x-rays. "Well," he said, "good luck. I'll see you when we catch up to you."

"Uh, sir?"

"Yes Macurdy?"

"Will you do me a favor? Get my mail forwarded to me, to B Company, 505th?"

"B Company, 505th. Sure." They shook on that too, then Alden left.

When he'd gone, one of Macurdy's troopers asked, "Who the hell was that, sarge? He's got medical insignia on his collar, a slung carbine, and a .45 on his belt. You don't see that combination very often."

"The limies have had medics picked off by snipers, so Doc had his men take off their arm bands and carry guns."

Someone laughed. "Medics carrying guns? And he said *you* weren't too strong on regulations. Where'd he get that red beret? That sure as hell ain't regulation."

"General Browning gave it to him. The limey airborne general. I guess he likes guys a little crazy."

"What happened to your leg he talked about?"

"It got run over by a loaded truck. Looked worse than it was, though."

"Jesus! A fucking truck?! When was that? He said it wasn't a month ago, and you've been with us three weeks, I'll bet."

"I heal fast."

His men stared at him with new respect, a couple of them with awe. He removed his attention from them, and after a minute they returned to their thoughts. Macurdy had one of his own now: If his mail could catch up with him, might the provost marshal as well? Provost marshals had long arms.

The sun was nearly down when the word came to buckle their chutes. They'd put them on earlier, leaving them unbuckled. It won't be long now, Macurdy thought; so did 3,400 others.

It had been breezy all afternoon. Now it was downright windy, enough that the plane shuddered from it. *If this were a training jump,* he told himself, *they'd have cancelled it hours ago.* Thirty miles an hour, he guessed. The order came to load, and bent by the snug parachute harnesses, the troopers waddled to the ladders and hauled themselves aboard, to sit in two rows, facing each other. Shortly the engines started, the bird taking life. No one said a word. The abrupt engine acceleration of the final warm-up check made her quiver, then she calmed. After a couple of minutes, Macurdy heard and felt the power swell, and gradually the plane began to move, taxiing. Briefly it stood still again, then rolled into line. Plane after plane surged down the runway, taking off. His own began to roll, vibrating, accelerating, quivering. The tail rose, and they lifted. He looked around at the other troopers. Without exception their faces were serious.

Across from him, one of them spoke, more to himself than to anyone else. "Three and a half hours to drop time. I wonder what I'll be doing four hours from now?"

It would be a long three and a half hours. The plane bobbed and swayed in the wind, and a few men lost their turkey supper. "It's that damn ice cream," one of them said, drawing scattered laughs.

Macurdy was seated across from the door, an opening snarling in the slipstream. Through it he watched twilight thicken, become moonlit night. After a long time, he spotted a fleet in the moonlight. Not the assault fleet, he thought; probably supply ships. Nonetheless the sight troubled him. Their planned flight course was to keep them well clear of the fleets, so they wouldn't be fired on. *Shit!* he thought, *I suppose we're lost, like we were on the way to Algeria. But surely the damned airplane jockeys must see them down there!*

The ships were soon left behind, and the planes hadn't drawn their fire. Then there was nothing, until someone saw land ahead in the night. Minutes later, tracers rose past the plane, seeming to float upward almost lazily. White tracers; American and British were red. On this plane he was senior, and jump master, so he got up and waddled to the door. There were flashes as well as tracers, antiaircraft shells exploding, and he realized how thin were the aircraft's aluminum sides. He could feel the plane climb. Nearby, another exploded in a ball of orange flame; tracer hit a gas tank, he supposed.

Beside the door, the red light flashed on. Four minutes, supposedly. "Stand up!" Macurdy bellowed, and the men stood. "Hook up!" Each man snapped his static line hook onto the jump cable that ran the length of the troop compartment, tugging on it to make sure it was secure. Then they checked each other's chute packs.

"Stand in the door!" he shouted, then positioned himself with his toes over the edge, a hand on each side, and the line of men shuffled forward, nearly touching, guts churning. The plane rocked, bobbed, shook in the wind.

It should be losing altitude, not climbing, he thought, and the sound of the engines told him they were going too fast; the pilot was supposed to slow to one hundred miles an hour. Spooked by the flak, Macurdy decided. *I hope to hell the sonofabitch remembers to raise the tail, or he'll kill half of us.*

Next to the door, the green light flashed on. *Too soon! Too soon!* Macurdy thought as he launched himself. The prop blast flung him backward: The plane was going close to top speed, he realized, and felt brief anger. The men were going to be scattered all over hell.

His chute opened, the shock slamming him, then the gale swung him like a pendulum. *If this is a thirty-mile wind,* he told himself, *we'll hit at thirty miles an hour horizontally and maybe twenty-five feet per second downward—plus or minus the pendulum speed. There'll be injuries tonight for damn sure.*

Miles away he could see the constant strobing of artillery, probably coastal guns and naval vessels. Hopefully the enemy was getting pounded.

At least the sky was clear. The terrain below was a wash of pale moonlight and dense shadow. It did not look difficult. When he hit, luck was with him: he was oscillating upward, forward, his risers didn't twist, and he got his chute collapsed almost at once. He hit the harness release, then lay listening for a moment, hearing nothing except the rumble of distant artillery. The planes had already passed beyond hearing.

Getting to his feet, he scanned around. About two hundred yards away was an aura, dimly visible—another trooper shedding his chute—and in another direction a second. The pilot had jumped them from well above the 600 feet specified; more like 1,500, he decided. It had taken far too long to get down, more than a minute. God only knew where the rest of his men were.

He shouted to bring them, then unlimbered his BAR and scanned around again, finding none of the landmarks he'd hoped for. All he knew for sure was, he was on mildly rolling upland. *Somewhere in southern Sicily,* he told himself wryly. Now he could see a third trooper hiking in his direction, and while waiting, considered what to do. If he was anywhere near where he should be, which he doubted, then the Ponte Corvo airfield should be southwest.

The first two men reached him, one of them limping a little, and together they waited for the third, who was approaching slowly, apparently also injured. While they waited, they heard machine gun fire, and Macurdy registered the direction. In the absence of anything to the contrary, they'd head there, along with any others they found. When the third trooper arrived, Macurdy asked how he was. "I hit like a load of bricks," he answered. "I think my fucking ankle's broke; something grates in there when I walk. Hurts like hell."

"You got your compass?"

The man felt for it. "Yup."

The machine gun fire repeated. "Good. Stay here. We'll head for the shooting; take an azimuth on it now, in case it quits. If you see any of the others, send them after us. If a machine gun or mortar crew shows up without their weapon, tell them to find the sonofabitch. Same with demolitions."

They left. Shortly the firing stopped, and it occurred to Macurdy that he hadn't heard any return fire, just the one heavy machine gun, its cyclic rate too fast to be American. After about ten minutes of walking, they came to a dirt road that ran roughly in the right direction. It had been graded, presumably by the military, and bore the light tread marks of what Macurdy guessed were tracked German weapons carriers. He angled off, paralleling it at about a hundred yards. Bordered by scattered small trees, it was easy to keep in sight.

In something like another mile he saw more trees ahead. When he reached them, he found they marked the rim of a shallow, sparsely wooded ravine, so he turned right, toward the road. When the road reached the rim, it turned sharply left, angling down the slope to ease the grade. Near it, the trees had been cut as if to clear a field of fire, and he could see a bridge below. Near its far end, the west end, were the overlapping auras of three men, who seemed to man a machine gun. The bridge was concrete, not what he'd expect on a country road in Sicily, where the word was the locals used only mules and horses. So then, built by the military. There'd no doubt be a low-profile, dug-in pillbox on the west side, probably on the rim, not visible at night from where he was.

The central question was, what should he do about the bridge? Destroy it—assuming someone came up with explosives—so the enemy couldn't use it? Or prevent it from being blown, so that seaborne forces *could* use it? All the briefing in the world didn't help when the goddamned airplane jockeys dropped you in the wrong county.

"Anderson," he murmured, "you're in charge. Take cover here where you can watch the road. More guys should be coming. I'm going to check the bridge for explosives; I'll be back before long. If any krauts or eye-ties come along, lay low and let them pass."

With that he left, the other two following him with their eyes. When he reached the first trees, he disappeared seemingly swallowed by shadow.

Cloaked, Macurdy worked his way down the side of the ravine as quietly as possible. The bottom was sand, with occasional large rocks too heavy to be carried away by the torrents of the rainy season. A man sat dozing at the base of a bridge piling. His uniform was Italian, and a submachine gun lay across his lap. He smelled of wine. Carefully Macurdy lifted the man's gun, sprinkled dirt in the action and barrel, then laid it down beside him.

The bridge had been mined, the caps wired for electrical detonation; obviously the Italians would rather blow the bridge than let the invaders take it, but wanted it available as long as it was in their hands. After removing the wires, he drew his trench knife and cut them far too short to be reattached. Then he buried the caps in sand—he hated the touchy damned things—and moved back down the ravine again before climbing out.

As he climbed, heavy machine gun fire began again, one gun, then another; not from the bridge, but from the rim above the ravine, repeating sporadically as if at scattered targets briefly glimpsed. From where they were, the gunners could no doubt see the road approaching the ravine from either direction; probably they'd spotted more troopers coming. He speeded up. Now he heard the hammering of an American machine gun; obviously more guys had arrived, hopefully quite a few of them. Almost at once there was more enemy machine gun fire. German, he thought. They favored the 7.62, its high cyclic rate unmistakable.

Back on top he found quite a few more troopers, but they were pinned down, less by the pillbox across the ravine than by two armored half-tracks with the German military cross, black edged with white. Remaining invisible, he slunk along just below the rim, counting men and assessing the situation. The troopers were under the command of an officer now, and still invisible, Macurdy approached him from behind, then dropped his cloak. "Lieutenant," he said. The man started in surprise.

He didn't know Macurdy, but he did know the bridge. His company's mission was to take and hold it. Unfortunately he had no idea where most of the company was, except that a plane carrying fifteen of his platoon had been shot down. With only a dozen of his own men, some with landing injuries, he was glad to have Macurdy's troopers, most of whom had shown up.

Just now it was a standoff, he said. Some of the troopers had grenade launchers for their M1s, though the supply of grenades was limited, and when a trooper had launched one almost into the rear of a half-track, the Germans had backed away. They seemed satisfied to pin the Americans down, as if expecting reinforcements. He'd send men to take out the machine gun at the bridge, which so far hadn't fired on his positions, though the pillboxes—there seemed to be two of them—had fired sporadically at them. Italians, he thought. Germans would be more wholehearted about it.

There'd been flurries of rifle and submachine gun fire from *feldgrau* who'd dismounted from the half-tracks, probably at troopers he'd sent to scout them.

Macurdy reported what he'd found and done, then without asking for orders, crept away, cloaking in the nearest shadow, the lieutenant frowning after him. And continued as rapidly as he could, hampered by his BAR, a clumsy weapon to crawl with. When he was well out on the flank, out of the American field of fire, he rose to a crouch and trotted toward the half-tracks.

He dropped to all fours again as he approached them from the side. The troopers' fire would be directed at the vehicles, seeking the firing slots to suppress German fire, but the half-tracks' real vulnerability was the lack of a roof, which was why they'd backed away from the grenade launchers.

At ten yards from the nearest, Macurdy paused, drew a grenade, pulled its pin and lobbed it. It landed in the half-track, flashed and roared. No one exited the back door, but from the offside, a man emerged from the cab. Macurdy, on all fours again, scrambled forward. The German, sheltered by the half-track, climbed onto the track's mud-fender to peer over the side. Sheltered himself now from American fire, Macurdy shot him pointblank in the back, then stepped to the open door, shot the driver, and slammed the door shut.

He dealt with the other half-track in much the same way, then dragged two dead Germans from the cab and clambered in.

Although the outlying *feldgrau* would have had their attention firmly elsewhere, some must have noticed the explosions in the rear of the half-tracks, and be feeling serious concern. Almost surely one or more were crawling toward him on elbows and knees, Mauser or Schmeisser in hand.

He started the engine. His own people would have seen

the grenade flashes and know that something was going on. Hurriedly he opened his first-aid kit, drew out the white triangular bandage, tied it to the muzzle of his BAR, slid back out of the cab and waved his flag of truce above the engine hood. Almost at once the American fire decreased, and he yelled at the top of his lungs: "YEEE-HAAA! SAN ANTONE! HOLD YOUR FIRE! IT'S MACURDY, COMING IN!"

Then he scrambled back into the cab, German bullets striking the inside of the door as he pulled it shut. The German gearshift worked more smoothly than that in American half-tracks. He turned the vehicle toward the American line, while bullets banged the armor. Within a minute he had a trooper on the seat beside him and four in back, while others sprinted to take the other half-track, still others providing covering fire.

He put on the late driver's coalscuttle helmet, raised the cab's steel shutter to see and be seen, and started down the road to the bridge, which he crossed without being fired on. The Italian machine gunners were gone, dead or fled.

At the top of the slope were two low pillboxes, eighty yards apart on opposite sides of the road. Getting out, he spoke to the men in back. "Cover me," he said, then to assure the Italians, shouted in German: *"Ich bin gleich wieder da, warte auf die Amerikaner!"* and without activating his cloak, trotted toward a pillbox, depending on the German helmet to fool the Italians. One large hand concealed a grenade, its pin pulled. Almost at the pillbox, he released the charging lever, counted silently to three, and tossed it through a gunport, then dropped. The grenade exploded, and someone inside began screaming, so he tossed in another, then cloaked himself and ran toward the halftrack. From the other pillbox, a heavy machine gun began to hammer. A terrific blow on his right arm spun Macurdy around and dropped him.

He almost blacked out, then rolled onto his back, fumbling for his knife. Lefthandedly, and shaking from shock, he cut and tore his right sleeve off. The wound was massive, bleeding heavily, and gathering himself as best he could, he wove and willed its occlusion. At once the bleeding slowed, then stopped. He was aware that the other pillbox had stopped firing. Forcing himself to stand, he staggered toward the half-track. A trooper hopped out of the rear, rifle in hand, and Macurdy dropped his cloak. The trooper's head jerked toward him.

"Jesus, sarge! You startled me." Then his eyes widened. "You're hit!"

"You got that right," Macurdy said, and feeling his knees giving way, sat down on the ground.

The trooper knelt by him. "Oh shit! That's a bad one." Taking the large airborne aid-kit from his belt, he pulled out sulfanilamide, bandage, and tape. Within a minute the wound was medicated and wrapped, then using the big triangular bandage, he immobilized the arm against Macurdy's body. Shakily and with the trooper's help, Macurdy got to his feet, climbed into the cab on the off side, and collapsed again. He could hear the trooper outside, shouting to the others. "Let's go! Let's go! We're done here. The sarge got hit; a bad one."

Someone else told off others to hold the pillboxes, then the man who'd bandaged him climbed in behind the wheel. Another got in on Macurdy's side and sat him up to make room. The driver turned the half-track and they headed back to the American position.

When they got there, the troopers still lay more or less dug in along the rim of the ravine. Most of them weren't his; there had to be forty or fifty now. The driver stopped, and the lieutenant called to them. "More krauts have arrived. Don't get careless."

The driver wheeled over to him and opened the door. "The sarge got shot," he said, "a bad one, one of those big 50s in the arm. But we cleaned out the pillboxes; he cleaned one out by himself. I left guys to hold them."

Macurdy got out without help, crowding past the steering wheel, wearing his own helmet now. "Medic!" the officer shouted, then turned to Macurdy. "Take it easy, sergeant. More men have come in; the shooting drew them. I sent your other half-track through to meet them, and it brought back a radio, so I let the beach commander know we've got the bridge but don't have many men to hold it. He said he'd get armor here as soon as he can, but when that'll be is anyone's guess."

The lieutenant sounded as casual as if talking about the

price of gas. Then he sent a half-track back to the pillboxes, with more men to man them.

A medic arrived, wearing his armband, and in the shelter of the rim, carefully but quickly removed Macurdy's bandage to examine the wound. "Whoever took care of this did a good job," he said, and began rebandaging it. "Sarge, you earned yourself a nice hospital vacation." When he'd finished, he took out a syrette of morphine and injected it into the other arm.

Macurdy watched him crawl over to the lieutenant and speak in an undertone, something about "tough sonofabitch," and "could have bled to death," and "sleep."

He had no intention of sleeping. Almost certainly more Germans would arrive before seaborne reinforcements could, and the troopers would be in serious trouble. Meanwhile someone had taken his BAR, along with his bandoliers. Which made sense; he couldn't handle it one-handed. But, he told himself, he was the only one here who could make himself invisible. And even left-handed, he ought to be able to hit something close up with his .45, and toss a grenade far enough to do some good.

But first he'd gather his strength for a minute—and fell asleep in spite of himself. He didn't even waken when the racket of fighting intensified, until a mortar round landed nearby.

Regaining his wits, Macurdy crawled to the rim and peered over it, looking toward the enemy positions. The Germans had been reinforced, and were laying down a lot of rifle and machine gun fire. Presumably quite a few troopers had been wounded or killed. The captured half-tracks had attacked the Germans and been disabled, presumably by a *Panzerfaust*, and the Germans were keeping flares in the air almost constantly, to foil sneak attacks.

On the other hand, the troopers' aimed fire, and the cover afforded by the rim, had discouraged the Germans from rushing them. The German strategy seemed to be to wear the Americans down with casualties—the mortars would do that—and wait for reinforcements, maybe panzers.

Someone had lifted Macurdy's bag of grenades, too. Except for his knife, all he had left was his holstered .45, and two grenades in a tunic pocket. So he crept out toward a flank, to a trooper he didn't know, whose M1 had gotten hot enough, Macurdy could smell char from the forepiece. The Germans must have pressed things at some point. "Let me have some grenades," Macurdy said. "Someone took mine."

Eyeing Macurdy's immobilized arm, the trooper frowned, then rolled half over and fished out two.

"That all you got?" Macurdy asked.

The man started to reply, then instead, took three from his grenade bag for himself and gave Macurdy the rest. For just a moment he watched as Macurdy crept over the rim, toward the Germans, and seemed to disappear.

Bullets did not respect invisibility spells, so Macurdy crawled along on his good side, directly toward the Germans, pushing mainly with his left leg, chagrined at how tired he felt, though he drew on the Web of the World. Once a bullet clanged against his helmet, a glancing blow that made his head swim and his heart race. Eventually he reached the German positions. Now the bullets that threatened him were American, but mostly aimed fire, and not nearly as numerous as the Germans were pumping out.

Approaching a machine gun nest, he rolled onto his back, left-handedly dug out a grenade, and pulled the pin with his teeth. Then, ignoring the American fire, he rolled to his knees, released the charging lever, paused, raised his body, side-armed the grenade into the machine gun nest, and dropped onto his left side again.

The grenade roared, then he crept to the next machine gun nest and repeated the action.

While tossing a third, a mortar round landed close behind him, this one American; an airborne mortar crew had arrived and was attacking the Germans from behind. Concussion shredded the back of his blouse, at the same time that a fragment struck him in the back, breaking his shoulder blade, another punctured a lung, and a third mangled a buttock. Then he lay unconscious, unaware that his final grenade toss had been successful.

He was lucky the shock had disrupted his invisibility spell. Even so, he very nearly died.

✧ ✧ ✧

Three days later he awoke in a base hospital. In the dream he'd awakened from, Varia and Melody and Mary and Vulkan all had been caring for him. A day later, General Ridgeway, 82nd Airborne commander, came through the ward with an aide and a surgeon, stopping to talk briefly with the airborne patients who were awake. At Macurdy's bed he looked at a clipboard and smiled. "How are you feeling, Sergeant?" he asked.

"Getting by," Macurdy murmured.

"Colonel Massey here"—the general indicated the doctor—"says he's sending you to England to get your shoulder blade reconstructed. Meanwhile I have a brief report written and signed by a Lieutenant Maye, describing what you did. You're as lucky as you are brave. When things get a little more organized, I expect you'll hear more about it.

"You'll be glad to know your people held the bridge, but it was touch and go for a while. The Germans got panzers there ahead of our Shermans."

Macurdy's eyes had closed before the general finished.

PART THREE
Actor Without A Script

20

Das Weutische Projekt

The hospital's sitting room for convalescents held about twenty men just then, some in summer khakis, most in pajamas, playing cards, checkers, or chess, reading, or just listening to the BBC. When the visitor crossed the room toward him, Macurdy knew him at once. The last time he'd seen him, the man had worn a German uniform and cropped hair, and been half scalped. Now he was dressed as an army officer, his hair longer than regulation, and he looked fit.

The man grinned. "Remember me, Macurdy?"

"Tunisia, last winter. 'Vonnie,' you said. Captain William Von Lutzow."

Von Lutzow laughed. "You lit my cigarette with your finger, warmed me, healed me, and made us—what? Invisible? On top of all that, you hunted *feldgrau* with a trench knife; at least that's what your men claimed. I talked with some of them before I left Gafsa."

Macurdy shrugged. "I went off with Cavalieri a couple times, trying to be useful. There was a kind of thrill in it. But I never knifed a *feldgrau*. I suppose someone said, 'I wonder what he's doing out there?', someone else made a guess, and a reputation was born." He paused. "That was a good platoon. Like brothers."

"Your new platoon must have been pretty damned good, too, considering what it did."

"How do you know what it did?"

"I researched you." Von Lutzow looked like the cat that got the cream. "I also know that Ike draped a Distinguished Service Cross around your neck for that night on Sicily. That's one hell of an honor."

Researched you. The words did not reassure Macurdy. His green-hazel eyes studied the captain. "How did you find me? And why? You connected with the provost marshal?"

Von Lutzow laughed. "Don't worry about that; it's already taken care of. We need to talk, you and I. Privately." He gestured, indicating the other convalescents in the room, some of them listening. "How'd you like to get out of here? Take a ride; eat in a restaurant. I've cleared it with your doctor."

Macurdy stood up, curious about where this was leading. "I could stand a change. Is this going to be your treat? I'm broke. My pay status is screwed up."

"That's taken care of too. Your back pay will catch up with you next payday."

"Huh!"

After he'd changed his slippers for shoes, Macurdy followed the captain outside and got into a jeep with him. Von Lutzow started it, then drove out the long driveway to the road. A country road; four years earlier, the hospital had been the palatial residence of a British earl. "You're walking well, Macurdy," he said, "for someone who had a chunk torn out of his ass by a piece of steel." He turned an intent eye on his passenger. "And that was about a month after a truck drove over your leg. According to Doc Alden, your leg looked like a giant purple watermelon."

Von Lutzow was enjoying himself; he grinned at Macurdy. "The doc here tells me I arrived just in time. Says if I'd come a week later, I'd have missed you—you'd have been off to rehab. He says your recovery has been nothing short of miraculous." He laughed. "Why is it I'm not surprised? Your right arm even healed to the same length as the left; that impressed him as much as anything. When they brought you in, they figured you might be ready to leave in four months. It's been less than one.

"How did you do that?"

Macurdy shrugged, a bit uncomfortable. "With mirrors," he said, then added, "honest to God." Quick-healing the shattered shoulder blade, after surgery, had involved holding a shaving mirror in his good hand, to look at his back in a bathroom mirror. Then he'd manipulated the lines of force with his eyes and mind.

Von Lutzow gazed at him appraisingly. "I thought maybe it was your Aunt Varia. The guys in your platoon told me more about her than you did. They half believe in her, you know? And me? I believe in her all the way. Three-fourths at least."

Macurdy sidestepped the subject. "You were going to tell me how you found me," he said, "and why. I can kind of see the how—you knew I was with the 509th, they told you the outfit my mail had been forwarded to, and someone referred you to Doc Alden . . . That still leaves why."

Von Lutzow replied in German. "Because my outfit wants to recruit you."

Macurdy answered in Klara's *baltisches Deutsch*. "Have you cleared this with Division?"

Still in German, Von Lutzow replied, "You're not in the 82nd anymore. You've been assigned to ETOUSA—headquarters for the European Theater of Operations U.S. Army. The whole shebang. It's also known as the paperwork capital of England and the chickenshit capital of the world. Which it needs to be."

Macurdy frowned. ETOUSA didn't sound like anyplace he'd like to be. "And that's your outfit? I thought you were in G-2, some kind of spy."

"We're entirely separate from G-2. We're the OSS—the Office of Strategic Services. You'd like it; it's a good outfit, even more unconventional than the airborne." Von Lutzow cocked an eye at his passenger. "And it has an absolute minimum of chickenshit."

Macurdy introverted. It seemed to him he was being railroaded. The choice was the OSS or ETOUSA, and ETOUSA sounded worse than the MPs by a big margin.

They drove some beautiful country roads, Von Lutzow describing in general terms what the OSS did, which went far beyond spying. One of its principal jobs was to work with partisans in Nazi-occupied countries, training them in guerrilla warfare. Macurdy's impression was, that's what they'd have him doing.

By that time, evening was settling. In a town named Tonbridge, they went to a small Italian restaurant. The food and wine both were excellent, but the conversation—now in English, of course—was innocuous. Then Von Lutzow took him back to the hospital, not pressing for a decision.

Nor did Macurdy volunteer one. It seemed to him his only choice was the OSS, but there were questions he needed answered before he'd commit himself.

When Von Lutzow showed up again the next day, Macurdy suggested a walk in the estate's woodland park, and while they walked, they talked. "You've gone to a lot of work to recruit me," Macurdy said. "Why? Why not just order me to report?"

"The OSS is like the airborne: volunteers."

"Volunteers? Sounds like the only other choice I've got is ETOUSA."

Von Lutzow ignored the comment. "We have a mission that so far as I know, you're the only person suited for. In the whole damned world. In fact, you're ideal for it: intelligent, resourceful, you speak German . . ." He paused meaningfully. "And you have psychic talents."

"Psychic talents? If that means magic, about all I can do is light fires and heal. What good is that to the Office of Strategic Services? You're not part of the Medical Corps."

"There's one other thing." Von Lutzow paused. "Apparently you can make yourself invisible, and others around you if they're close enough. How else did that German patrol miss seeing us in Tunisia? One of them actually stumbled over your leg, for chrissake!"

"Foot," Macurdy corrected.

"Foot, leg, whatever. He even cussed the rock he thought he'd tripped on. And in Oran, how did you get out of the hospital without being seen? And get Sergeant Keith out the next night? With him holding on to your shirttail, for chrissake." Von Lutzow paused. "Invisibility's one talent I didn't mention at headquarters."

Macurdy grinned. "They'd think you'd gone over the edge."

Von Lutzow shook his head. "Most of them would, but that's

not the reason; not a decisive reason. Because turning invisible is strange enough, weird enough, it might get talked about. We're supposed to be smart enough to keep our mouths shut, but it might get talked about, and word could get to the Germans that we have someone like you. So it's between you and me. In our work, a talent like that, especially unsuspected, could make the difference between success and failure."

The path they'd been walking had come full circle. Now Von Lutzow changed the subject. "Let me take you out to supper again. I can charge it to my expense account, and it gets me away from army chow."

This time they ate Chinese. Macurdy didn't talk much, and guessing his thoughts, Von Lutzow didn't either. When they'd finished eating and were sipping their tea, Macurdy made his decision. "Captain," he said, "I hate to see someone go to so much trouble for nothing. Get me out of the hospital, and you've got a volunteer."

It wasn't at all like volunteering for the airborne; even as he said it, he felt serious misgivings.

That night he had a long disjointed dream, which after he woke up, remained with him in the form of impressions. There were Germans in black SS uniforms, and 50-foot monsters that strode through a battlefield crushing GIs under their feet; it seemed to him he'd dreamed about them before. And Varia was in it, not in the usual gazebo, but riding on Vulkan, with Blue Wing perched on her shoulder. That seemed strange to Macurdy; Melody had been the spear maiden, and Blue Wing had been her buddy, not Varia's.

After breakfast, waiting for Von Lutzow, he found his misgivings had flattened. *Why not?* he asked himself. *It'll be interesting, and if Von Lutzow is any kind of sample, I'll like the OSS.*

He wasn't sent to an ordinary rehab company. His new bosses wanted him trained as quickly as possible, and sent him to an OSS school on a rural estate in the Midlands. There, while going through rehab, he worked intensively on his German.

OSS headquarters in London had sent an ex-professor to tutor him, a refugee from Königsberg, in East Prussia. From listening to Macurdy, the man actually pinpointed the rural district from which Klara and Fritzi had come. But while Macurdy might at first pass as a native Baltic German, the tutor explained, in Germany people would soon realize he was foreign. He had usages distinctively German-American—artifacts of a foreign environment. In the States, they were used even by Germans who spoke no English, and were common in German-language newspapers there. Meanwhile in Germany, particularly under the Nazis, new usages had developed that few German-Americans had ever heard.

The tutor's job was to have Macurdy sounding like an East Prussian who'd never been out of Germany, and writing German cursive as it might be written and spelled by a poorly educated East Prussian peasant.

"That will also help in the development of a personal history for you, with documents," he explained. "To a German from München or Frankfurt or Berlin or Hamburg, all Baltic Germans sound alike. Like your southerners sound to someone from New York. But we need to do better than that, you and I. When I've finished with you, you can pass even in Königsberg as a rural East Prussian, and pass very well. And it will not take so long; your wife's grandmother was a good teacher."

After two weeks, his therapist reported him fit enough that he could complete his rehab by exercising with the other students. Meanwhile Macurdy began training in covert operations: Among other things he learned the use and maintenance of various communications devices, and more refined techniques in demolitions than had been needed in the airborne. He drilled Morse code intensively, learned to pick locks of various kinds, practiced finding his way crosscountry by the stars and sun, and became thoroughly familiar with German geography. He learned how to conduct himself in German homes, restaurants, railroad depots . . . and how to deal with German government bureaus, especially at local levels.

Then he was sent to the therapist again. The man grinned at him. "Macurdy, your recovery's been too damned complete.

Headquarters says you need a limp, a good consistent limp, and I'm supposed to coach you on it. Along with your scars, it'll help explain why you're not in the German army." He laughed, then spoke in a burlesque German accent: "You vill be a goot, patriotic Cherman poy vhat hass sacrificed his body for his Führer, but can still vork on de docks."

Along with his demolitions training, this led Macurdy to suspect he'd be sent to Germany as a saboteur, instead of training partisans.

He was wrong about that, too.

In late autumn he was sent to London, to OSS headquarters in Grosvenor Square. There he was promoted to warrant officer—a W-2—which paid much better than staff sergeant.

Then he was briefed. He'd been told that Von Lutzow would be his briefing officer, but Vonnie was in the south of France, in the maquis, working with French partisans. Besides, this was only a preliminary briefing, sketching out his mission.

What it boiled down to was that *Reichsführer* Heinrich Himmler was very interested in the occult. And Himmler, who now ranked second only to *der Führer* himself, commanded not only the Gestapo—the German secret police—but the *Schützstaffel*—the elite guard. Within the SS he'd established a small de facto office called the Occult Bureau. At one point, the Gestapo had been ordered to investigate all reputed Aryan psychics, some of whom were then conscripted into the Bureau. This was not a roundup of astrologers, as in *Aktion Hess.* It was on a much smaller scale, and not punitive.

The Occult Bureau had lost credibility with the Reichs Chancellery over the past several years, had even been reported cancelled. But what seemed to be an Occult Bureau project was housed in rural southern Bavaria, near a lake known as *der Kiefersee.* Not a lot was known about the project except its name: *das Weutische Projekt,* and even that was mysterious, because in German there was no such name or word as *Weut* (phonetically, *Voit*). The OSS wanted to know what that project was—its mission and its methods—and Macurdy's job was to find out.

In the neighborhood of the Kiefersee, local tradition held

that in early centuries, on the night of the full moon, witches gathered on the crest of *dem Hexenkamm*—"The Witches' Ridge"—to sacrifice, and hold orgies with demons. Among the local peasants, some still took those stories at least semi-seriously. Some said that even today, in the vicinity of the ridge, dogs howled and cats refused to go out when the moon was full. The Occult Bureau project was housed in what was called locally *Schloss Tannenberg*—Tannenberg Castle—after the most prominent local hill. It wasn't actually a castle, but a 19th century baronial manor, built on the site of an old ruin. And *Schloss Tannenberg* stood at the foot of *dem Hexenkamm.*

It occurred to Macurdy that the briefing officer might be pulling his leg, but the man kept talking. Supposedly a number of psychics were held at the schloss in some sort of training, and the rumor was that the trainers were foreigners, which might be the source of the word *Weutische.* It was definite that an SS guard platoon was quartered there. It was from a local "party girl" agent, who'd drank and slept with some of the SS, that they'd learned most of what was known about the project. Which wasn't much, if one allowed for the inevitable exaggerations of troops sporting with girls.

The project commander and his executive officer were subject matter specialists. Lt. Col. Karl Gustaf Richard Landgraf was a Prussian aristocrat, a decorated veteran of horse cavalry on the Eastern Front during World War One. During the 1920s and early '30s, he'd published a journal of occult studies. His managing editor, a Wilhelm Kupfer, was now his XO.

Macurdy would be provided an identity, suitable papers, and a German wife; it hadn't been determined yet who she'd be. And no, he wasn't expected to actually marry her. He and his "wife" would then travel to Bavaria, where they were to get him recruited by the Weutische Project.

He was to find out the nature and goals of the project, and as many of the details as he could.

At one point, Macurdy had interrupted to clarify what "occult" meant. The question had startled the briefing officer. Macurdy had been recruited, the man told him, because supposedly he had occult powers, yet he didn't even know what occult meant!

Before they left the briefing room, Macurdy set the man's mind at rest: he lit his cigarette with a finger.

Among other things, for the next four weeks he worked with a drama coach on his role as an East Prussian peasant. He was to seem marginally retarded, providing an apparency of harmlessness. That would also help explain why, limp and all, he had not been drafted by the military. And of course, he was familiarized with the SS table of organization, including the SS titles of rank, which differed from those of the German army.

He was also given some old Swiss parapsychology journals to read, to get a sense of the field.

He proved a quick study; by the fourth week, the role was second nature to him.

During those four weeks, he was also put through intensive, personalized short courses in Bavarian geography, and the advantages and disadvantages of possible escape routes to Switzerland. He studied contour maps of those routes, even made rough clay table models of the likelier.

His limp had been well perfected: Repetition had programmed it thoroughly into his motor system. It was not severe, but worsened when he was tired.

Meanwhile he was given a further briefing. He'd been provided an identity: He would be Kurt Montag. And a landing site: He'd be taken to the Baltic on a British submarine, and landed by rubber boat on the Mecklenburg coast. There he'd be met by an agent who would take him to Lübeck, to his wife, a woman named Gerda Montag, *nee* Schwabe. She in turn would take him to Bavaria, her home state.

When he'd finished his training, he was commissioned a 2nd lieutenant.

Meanwhile he'd written to Mary several times, and again to his parents, telling them nothing meaningful; if he had, the censors would have deleted it. He was, he wrote, on staff in London. Let them think the dangers were over.

21

Kurt Montag

For the Bavarian town of Kempten, it was a lovely January day, sunny, with a mid-morning temperature of 5 degrees C—41 degrees F. A young couple, the woman seeming older than the man, walked across the square to the *Rathaus*—the town hall—the man limping slightly, more so on the stairs.

A guard stopped them in the foyer. "What is your business here?" he asked.

It was the young woman who answered. "We are newly arrived from Lübeck. We have come to register."

The guard looked them over thoroughly, then pointed. "At the top of those stairs, turn right. You will see a door with *Polizei* on it. Go inside. They will tell you what to do."

They climbed the stairs and went into the police office. A middle-aged desk sergeant looked at them with his one eye, squinting as if near-sighted, although he wore no glasses. "What is your business here?" he asked.

The woman gave him the papers, and frowning, he looked them over, muttering to himself in places, then looked up at her. "Why have you come here from Lübeck?"

"My grandparents live here. My grandfather was a farmer, but has severe arthritis and can no longer work. My grandmother is partly blind. I am the only one of the family who was able to move here and care for them."

He glanced at the young man, then returned his frown to the woman. "It says your husband is 'brain damaged.' In what way?"

"It is not severe. He is not crazy, but he thinks slowly. His head was injured in a logging accident in Ost-Preussen, when he was still a boy. His other injuries are from an air raid on Lübeck." She gestured at the papers. "He has been working as a longshoreman there. He is no longer agile, but he is very strong. And—" she paused "—he can do other things."

The sergeant's eyebrows rose slightly. "Other things?" He turned back to the husband. "What other things, Herr Montag?"

Montag looked uncertainly at his wife, who put a cigarette between her lips. "Light it for me please, Kurt," she said. He raised his finger, and at its tip a small light appeared, round and bright; he moved it to the cigarette. She drew on the cigarette, and smoke appeared; its tip grew red.

Briefly the squinting eye widened. "One moment," said the desk sergeant, and spoke to someone through the door behind him, then left the room. Another policeman came in and sat down behind the desk. Gerda Montag reached over and patted her husband's knee. "It will be all right, Kurt. Do not worry."

In a few minutes the sergeant returned. "Come with me," he said, and led them to a wing on the third floor. On its entry door was written *Geheime Staatspolizei.* Inside he left them with a uniformed female receptionist, who told them to sit, then pressed an intercom button: "Herr and Frau Montag are here, sir," she said.

A moment later a man appeared, a lieutenant's insignia on his black uniform, and took them into his office. Before seating them, he put a cigarette between his lips and spoke to the man: "Herr Montag, light my cigarette."

Montag repeated his earlier performance.

"Sit down." When the Montags were seated, he also sat. "Do you do anything else unusual?" he asked.

Montag answered proudly. *"Jawohl, Herr Kapitän.* I can carry four bags of cement in my arms!"

The lieutenant frowned slightly. "I meant anything else as unusual as lighting cigarettes with your finger."

Montag nodded emphatically. "Yes, captain. I can keep warm in the coldest weather, without any coat or cap or gloves. I even go barefoot in the snow sometimes." Without being asked, he got up, stepped to the lieutenant's desk, and held out his hand. "Feel it," he said. "I can make it warm whenever I want."

The lieutenant touched Montag's palm. It felt distinctly hot. For just a moment he peered up at the man as if trying to see how he did it, then called in a young aide, who took them to reception and left them under the suspicious eye of a sergeant. Some minutes later he returned, to take them back to the lieutenant.

"Frau Montag," the lieutenant said affably, "I have arranged very good employment for your husband. As it happens, he must live on the estate where he will be employed. You do not need to know where it is, but I can tell you that, despite his injuries, he will be serving his *Führer.* A part of his wages will be mailed to you, and it may be that he will be permitted to visit you from time to time.

"Meanwhile he will remain here until transportation arrives for him." He gestured at the young aide. "Corporal Hochdorf will conduct you to the lunchroom, here in the building, where you can eat. No doubt you will want to talk before you are separated. Afterward you can bring some of his clothing and other necessaries. They will be forwarded to him."

While they ate, Corporal Hochdorf sat watchfully nearby. The meal was adequate. The sausage was probably eighty percent oatmeal, Macurdy thought, and there was something peculiar about the bread, but the cheese was good. The so-called "coffee" was wretched, even compared to what they served in England these days, but he supposed he'd get used to it. He'd be glad to leave Gerda; she'd propositioned him in Lübeck, and several times had stroked his thigh on the train. He wasn't sure he could keep refusing, and to give in would be disloyal to Mary.

22

Schloss Tannenberg

The country road had not been graded for months—fuel, equipment, and drivers were all in short supply—so the staff car's driver kept the speed below 50 kph, 31 mph, on the washboard surface. Beside him in the front seat sat a young SS 2nd lieutenant—an *Untersturmführer* in the SS terminology. "Lipanov," the Gestapo officer had called him. In back, wearing civilian clothes, rode Kurt Montag, with an SS lance corporal beside him. The rear side-windows had plush curtains, and Montag's big fingers spread them slightly. He turned to the corporal.

"Is it all right that I look out?"

"If you wish," the corporal replied, then said more quietly, "what do you think you will see?"

"Bavaria," Montag answered. "I have never seen Bavaria before."

"Where do you think you were this morning? Where we picked you up?"

"In Kempten," Montag answered.

"And where do you think Kempten is? In what state?"

Montag shook his head.

"Kempten is in Bavaria!"

Montag looked puzzled.

The lieutenant had overheard, and glanced back over his shoulder. "Herr Montag," he said, "where are you from?" He suspected his passenger was *Volksdeutsch*, ethnic German from one of the Baltic countries. He'd known a *Volksdeutscher* from Latvia; his German had sounded much like this man's.

"I am from Hermans Acker, *Herr Kapitän.*"

The lieutenant ignored the unexpected promotion. "I don't mean what farm! What *country* are you from?"

"From Germany, Herr Kapitän."

"Lieber Gott," the lieutenant muttered under his breath. "Another idiot." Some of these psychics, it seemed to him, were candidates for eugenic cleansing. "What state!?" he said aloud.

"Ost-Preussen, captain, from Kleines Torfland Gebiet."

Macurdy had kept part of his attention out the window. They were passing a longish lake that had to be *der Kiefersee;* he knew it well on maps. He wondered idly what kind of fish they caught there. A forested ridge backed the far shore, while the near shore was fields and pasture, with woods here and there. They'd be at Schloss Tannenberg very soon.

They passed the lake's upper end, where a lane ran down through pasture to a small wooden dock locked in ice. Briefly the road burrowed through woods, mostly of beech and fir, the latter shading patches of old gray snow. The car slowed, then turned onto a horseshoe drive that led to a preposterous-looking building: a large stone manor house three stories high, built in the shape of a U, its courtyard to the rear. Providing some pretense to the title *Schloss*—castle—its ridged, red-tiled roof was bordered by battlements, embellished at intervals with drain spouts in the form of gargoyles, and by a tower that stood like an afterthought at the end of the farther wing. Macurdy wondered what sort of man had designed the place.

The car unloaded its passengers in front of the entrance, and the driver pulled away. With the lance corporal's hand on Montag's sleeve, they followed Lieutenant Lipanov up several steps to a roofed porch with concrete pillars, and through the main entrance with its black-uniformed guard. Behind Montag's oafish gawp, Macurdy's eyes sized things up. The foyer, also with a guard, was as oddly laid out as the building, forming a U around a broad central flight of stairs leading to the second floor. The carpet was well-worn, both on floor and stairs. Pale rectangles on the walls showed where art had been removed. A front corner held the only furniture, a banquette and three club chairs, all of them threadbare. In a side wall toward the back was a door which might access a cellar stairway.

The lieutenant took Montag to the broad cross corridor that passed beneath the staircase, and turned left to the first door. Its polished brass plate read PROJECT OFFICE. He opened it, and they entered a small reception room partitioned off from the office behind it. A corporal rose abruptly from behind a desk, his right arm snapping forward sharply. "Heil Hitler!" he barked.

"Heil Hitler! I am here to see Hauptsturmführer Kupfer."

The corporal opened the door behind him, spoke to someone, then sent Lipanov through, Montag following. Inside, Lipanov stopped at attention with a sharp clack of heels, and again his right hand shot out. "Heil Hitler!"

The man he'd saluted outranked Lipanov, his insignia marking him as a Hauptsturmführer, a captain. "Heil Hitler!" he answered, but though his words were as loud, his salute as stiff, from him they seemed awkward, a required formality. From Lipanov, the words had reflected fervor, or at least well-drilled false fervor.

"I am here to deliver your new psychic, Herr Hauptsturmführer," Lipanov snapped, then stepped to the desk and handed over the papers given him by the Gestapo.

The captain—Kupfer, from the name plate on his desk—scanned them, then laid them on his blotter. "Thank you, Lipanov. I will require Corporal Karlsbach's services for a bit. You are dismissed."

"Thank you, Herr Hauptsturmführer!" Again Lipanov's heels clopped, and his arm shot out again. "Heil Hitler!" Then he about-faced and left.

After giving Lance Corporal Karlsbach brief instructions, Kupfer sent him off to show Montag what he needed to know about the building. This would use time, allowing Kupfer to finish his paperwork before Colonel Landgraf returned from Munich.

First the corporal took Montag back to the foyer, to the door leading to the cellar. "Do not go down there," he said pointing. "If you do, you will be shot."

He didn't elaborate, and his aura gave Macurdy no clear

indication that he was or was not exaggerating. Macurdy was also to avoid the north and south wings totally, except if escorted, for the same compelling reason.

"Either that," Karlsbach added, "or the colonel will give you to the foreigners for punishment." His aura indicated now that he was lying—no doubt playing with the newcomer.

"Foreigners? What will they do to me?"

The answer was a shrug and smirk.

Then Montag was taken to the second floor main, to the men's quarters—the room where the male psychics were quartered. It held eight steel-framed army cots with mattresses, pillows, and blankets. Several had linens, and were made up for use. Connected to the sleeping room was a latrine, with commodes, urinals, washbasins, and an attached shower room with eight showerheads. He was also shown a door, diagonally across the corridor, which the corporal identified as quartering the female psychics. "I think they are very lonely in there," he said. "Perhaps they will invite you to visit them some night." Again he smirked. From there, Montag was shown the psychics' messroom, also on second-floor main, to which their food was delivered from the enlisted men's kitchen. An unoccupied classroom, on third-floor main, was equipped with tables, chairs, a blackboard, and large cabinet, but nothing else. There wasn't a clue as to what might be taught there.

The tour finished, Montag was returned to Captain Kupfer's office. The most interesting things he'd learned were the off-limits rules. Enforced rules: The foyer guard would see anyone attempting to visit the cellar, while a sentry stood at each corridor ell to each wing.

Kupfer was a *Schwabe*, a Swabian, gangling, nervous, forty-six years old, with large eyes suggesting hyperthyroidism—certainly not in the SS image. At first his *Schwäbisch* speech was difficult for Montag to follow, nor was Montag's Baltic German much easier for Kupfer. Nonetheless, Kupfer gave him the standard interview for psychic newcomers to the project, typing Montag's responses with quick index fingers. The interview required that if possible, the newcomer demonstrate his talents. Montag lit the captain's cigarette of course, but his invisibility spell, and ability to cast plasma charges, he kept carefully to himself. The written tests took longer. Kupfer hadn't been sure Montag could read well enough, but he managed, though laboriously. Or so it seemed. His most conspicuous difficulty was inserting the carbon paper right side up.

He is more ignorant than innately stupid, Kupfer decided; *perhaps the Voitar will find him teachable*. What Kupfer didn't consciously articulate in his mind was an underlying hope—that this unlikely seeming young man, who had surely been more at home manhandling cargo on the Lübeck docks, might actually prove to be what they'd been striving for, thus validating Reichsführer Himmler's hopes for the project.

At the same time validating his own hopes for psychic phenomena, for Kupfer, though lacking psychic talent, was a true believer. Just having his cigarette lit had given him a considerable boost.

By the time Montag had plodded through the written tests, classes had let out for the psychics in the third-floor classrooms. Kupfer pressed a button on his desk, and a minute later a private arrived from the duty room. He took Montag to the men's quarters, delivering him, along with a carbon copy of the interview form, to the civilian in charge—the psychic who was senior to the others.

Briefly the guardsman waited until the senior psychic had scanned the form and handed it back. Then, fixing Kurt Montag with a hard gaze, he said, "You will do as the Herr Doktor Professor orders, or it will go badly for you here." With that admonition, he turned and left.

Herr Doktor Professor Edouard Friederich Schurz had taught psychology at the Jesuit University in Karlsruhe. Here he was a trainee, not a teacher, his titles honorific. Forty-one years old, he was rather tall and still somewhat spare, a bachelor who, as a student, had been the star of his university's tennis club. As a graduate student, he'd been suspected by a professor of influencing the minds of others psychically, an ability more common than generally realized. Schurz himself hadn't realized he did it, but when included in a study of psychic dynamics, his ability had been superior at the 0.001 probability level.

That is, there was almost no chance that the results were accidental—coincidences. It was through that study he'd come to Landgraf's attention, years before there'd been an Occult Bureau, or even an SS. Hindenburg had been president, and Hitler an obscure radical not long out of prison.

Schurz also read auras. Not in much detail, but enough to indicate somewhat about a person and their frame of mind, and he used it more or less automatically. In no more time than it had taken for the guardsman to introduce them, Schurz knew that Montag was not dull-witted, or even slow-witted, regardless of his facade, or anything his personnel form might say.

The simple fact of pretense was interesting. And worrisome. He needed time and observations to evaluate this newcomer. As he introduced the other male psychics—Herr Jensen, Herr Steinbach, Herr Eich—his mind worked on the problem. What might motivate Montag's pretense? Two possibilities occurred to him. It might be simply a means of staying out of the military, or he might be a spy from Berlin, sent to gather evidence that *das Weutische Projekt* was a useless waste of men and resources.

He hoped it was the former. Although he himself no longer had faith in the project, he'd hate to see it shut down. That would leave him vulnerable to military service, a gruesome thing to contemplate.

From Schurz's aura, Macurdy quickly realized the man saw through him. Was he telepathic? If so, this was a deadly situation. But by the time the introductions were completed—thirty seconds at most—Macurdy had rejected the thought: A telepath would have reacted more strongly. Perhaps Schurz simply read auras.

Then Schurz took him to the SS orderly room for an issue of bed and bath linens, and two suits of cheap, ill-fitting civilian clothes. On the way back, he showed him the psychics' recreation room. It was a bit like an army dayroom—a place where the psychics could spend their off hours reading, playing cards, talking, perhaps writing a letter. Just now, no one else was there. Schurz gestured toward a chair. "Sit down, Herr Montag," he said, and when Macurdy was seated, took a chair facing him, pulling it close.

"It might be well," Schurz said quietly, "if you knew something about your roommates. Otto Jensen is a sixty-year-old peasant smallholder from Schleswig, who developed a local reputation as a blood-stopper. And for healing in general, both of farm animals and humans. Reportedly he also sets bones without traction, simply by stroking the limb. Unfortunately the Project is not interested in healing powers, and drills have not elicited the sort of abilities hoped for.

"Philipp Steinbach, as perhaps you have guessed, is mentally retarded—what is called an 'idiot savant.' He is thirty-one years old, but his intellectual age is about six, and he is, of course, emotionally crippled. On the other hand, he can compute complex mathematical problems in his head, particularly of calendar dates, and on occasion produces poltergeist phenomena. It is the latter which brought him to Colonel Landgraf's attention. Unfortunately for the project, he has so far been unteachable. He simply does what he does."

Schurz grunted, a sort of humorless half chuckle. "As for Manfred— Herr Eich is a compulsive bully. He would bully physically if allowed to—I can imagine what life must have been like for his more susceptible school mates—but here that is forbidden him, so he bullies Otto and Philipp psychologically when he can. But not in front of me, because I have authority and do not put up with it. And remarkably, he is afraid of me physically; I can read it in . . ." Schurz waved a hand as if to cancel what he'd started to say. "He outweighs me by at least twenty kilos, but he fears physical strength, even strength no more than mine. Of course, he has only recently passed his eighteenth birthday; in time his confidence may increase, making him a more serious menace."

Eich's principal psychic power, Schurz went on to say, was an ability to beam confusion and fear in their raw form. This had come to light in secondary school, when the severity of his bullying, and an unwise choice of targets, had earned him the serious attention of school authorities. And through them the attention of psychological researchers at the University of Leipzig. They in turn had uncovered his talent. One of them, aware of Colonel Landgraf's needs, had written to him about this unusual and unpleasant youth.

Eich had been brought to the schloss the preceding summer. Fortunately, psychics, even Philipp, had at least some innate resistance to psychic coercion.

Schurz had a covert motive in telling all this to Montag: He wanted to see his reactions. And though the newcomer looked confused by it, his aura reflected alert interest.

They went from the recreation room to the dining room. By then Macurdy had no doubt at all that Schurz had seen through his pretense. But there was no hint of hostility or distrust, simply interest. This might, Macurdy decided, work out after all.

The meal was boiled potatoes, sauerkraut, bread, margarine, and cheese, and the decoction masquerading as coffee. All in all it was adequate. Macurdy wondered, though, if perhaps the SS troops got oatmeal-loaded sausage with theirs.

It was at supper he first saw the female psychics, who ate at their own table somewhat apart from the men. There were four of them: two more or less young, one middle-aged, and one whom Macurdy thought might well be in her seventies. He was aware that one of the two younger—the larger—had given him evaluative looks, her aura reflecting more than curiosity and sexual interest. Also there was a knowingness, as if, like Schurz, she saw through his facade.

He first got to know one of them, a little, in the recreation room after supper. There the women more or less segregated themselves—perhaps in response to Manfred Eich's unpleasant vibrations—but after a bit, one of them came over to Kurt Montag, bringing with her one of the folding chairs, and sat down facing him. Her aura marked her as a basically dominant person, but not innately aggressive. Simply bold and impulsive. Physically she was in her early or mid-thirties, and rather tall, about five-feet-eight or nine. And pretty, with lovely coloring despite an indoor life and marginal nutrition. If they served seconds in the dining room, Macurdy thought, she might be heavy.

"You are new here," she said. "My name is Berta Stark. What is yours?"

"Kurt. Kurt Montag."

"Where are you from, Herr Montag?"

"Kleines Torfland Gebiet. It is in East Prussia. Where are you from?"

"I am from Kassel."

Macurdy had no doubt at all now that Berta Stark realized he was not what he seemed. But judging from her lack of reaction to his lie—that he was from East Prussia—she didn't read minds. Auras then, but not in much detail.

Her own aura suggested no threat. She was hoping for something from him, not primarily sexual. Could she be a spy for the British? He was already aware, from London, that the SIS and the OSS withheld things from each other.

"What did you do in Kassel?" he found himself asking.

"I was a nurse. A healer, actually; I heal with my hands. Most doctors would have nothing to do with me, but some did. I worked for them." According to her aura, she spoke truthfully, with a trace of irony.

She took Montag's right hand in hers, and while regarding him calmly, traced a pattern on his palm with a finger that raised goose bumps. That definitely felt sexual, but still Macurdy read something more immediate in her aura: some interest other than sex. What it was, he had no idea, nor was it anything he could ask about, certainly not there.

He would let it be for now. Let her find a way to talk privately, if she wanted to. When she left, she had something on her mind. Perhaps just that: how they could be alone.

Montag stayed in the recreation room till 9:20, when Schurz told him to come with him. Lights out, Schurz said, was at 10 o'clock; Montag needed to put the sheets on his bed before that.

They left Otto, Manfred, and Philipp behind, the old farmer reading a well-worn bible, and Manfred an old journal on parapsychology, of which there was a sizeable stack on a table. Philipp sat alone, playing with a deck of cards, a seemingly aimless, repetitive activity whose purpose, if any, was known only to him. It was how he spent his evenings.

As they walked to their quarters, Schurz told Montag that

to be in the corridor at all, after lights out, was against the rules and would be punished.

It seemed to Macurdy that the curfew simply reflected the Nazi impulse to control, but the other restrictions might protect important information. The corridors were not well lit, but how much light might it take for an attentive guard to see through his invisibility spell? And how attentive might the guards be?

After he'd had made his bed—without any difficulty—he and Schurz sat down facing each other. "Berta found you interesting," Schurz commented.

"She is a nice lady. Friendly." Macurdy would maintain his Montag persona, even though Schurz saw through it.

Schurz grunted. "She is rather interested in men. If circumstances permitted, I believe she would try us out. And I believe she finds you more interesting than she does the rest of us. She sees something in you that most do not—something more than your large and powerful physique." He raised a knowing eyebrow at Macurdy.

It seemed to Macurdy that Schurz had said this to read his response. "I would like to try *her* out," Montag answered. "I like ladies."

Schurz's smile flicked on, then off. Macurdy realized that the Herr Doktor Professor would like to try her out too.

"Why is she here?" Montag asked. "Why are any of us here?"

"According to her folder, she sometimes exhibits poltergeist phenomena when she drinks. Colonel Landgraf finds that promising."

Montag looked confused, and Schurz, instead of explaining *poltergeist*, changed the subject. "Did you pay any attention to the other women?" Macurdy's lack of auric response told him he hadn't. "The small, younger woman is Anna Hofstetter. I believe she must have an interesting history, but Colonel Landgraf has not told me what it is. Nor do I know why she is here. Her talent is listed as broad-band telepathy, but so far as I know, telepathy does not contribute to the purpose of this project."

He smiled. "Incidentally, do not be alarmed by her. Such telepathy is not continually operative. At least under ordinary circumstances it must be consciously turned on, otherwise the constant mental noise becomes intolerable. Also, persons like ourselves seem to have a built-in shield against telepathic snooping; she is unlikely to discern your thoughts. Your secrets. It would be interesting to know hers however.

"The round-shouldered, graying red-haired woman is a gypsy. She . . ."

That was as far as Schurz got, because Otto and Philipp came in. Macurdy took toothbrush and paste from the small kit issued to him and went into the latrine. When he was done, he came back.

"What is our job here?" he asked Schurz. "No one has told me what I am to do."

Manfred Eich had returned by then, and it was he who answered, before Schurz had time to. "Each of us has his own work, according to his intelligence," Eich said. "In the morning you will report to the stable, to clean up behind the colonel's horses."

"Oh," said Montag, "that will be easy for me. It was part of my work at home when I was a boy."

Manfred sneered, disappointed that his victim showed no hurt. Schurz simply looked at Montag quizzically.

At 9:55, Schurz blinked the lights. By that time Macurdy was already in bed, eyes closed, reviewing the day. Somehow neither he nor the OSS people who'd prepared him had foreseen the risk of psychic detection, an oversight that seemed to him a major bit of stupidity on their part and his. Kupfer hadn't noticed anything, but what might Colonel Landgraf see? Landgraf or someone else. He wasn't convinced that a persistent and perceptive telepath couldn't learn something dangerous from his mind; his aura had already compromised him. And if Landgraf lacked the talent, what of the instructors here? Almost certainly they were psychics, and presumably more powerful, even much more powerful, than Edouard Schurz or Berta Stark.

They were foreigners, according to rumor; he should soon know.

He wondered what tomorrow would be like.

23

The Voitar

Shortly after breakfast the next morning, Schurz took Montag to Kupfer's office, and Kupfer, through a connecting door, delivered him to Landgraf's, saluting as he entered. "Heil Hitler," he barked; it was their first meeting of the day, and the formality required.

"Heil Hitler." Lieutenant Colonel Karl Gustaf Richard Landgraf neglected to stand. If necessary, he could claim exemption on the basis of a war wound received as a young cavalry officer on the Vistula. That had been in August 1915; the German army had fought on an eastern front before.

It was an injury that hampered him only when convenient.

"Herr Obersturmbannführer," Kupfer said, "this is Herr Montag, a psychic turned over to us at the Gestapo office in Kempten yesterday. His papers are on your desk."

"I have looked at them. Thank you, Kupfer, you may leave. I will speak with Herr Montag."

He looked calmly at this newcomer he thought of as young. "I see you are married, Herr Montag. Are you worried about your wife? How she will get by in your absence? Do not be concerned. Here you will have no expenses. We will take good care of you; even your cigarette ration costs you nothing. And being restricted to the grounds, you will need no money for visits to town. Your pay will be that of a lance corporal, and all but five marks a month will be sent to your wife."

Montag stood as if all this was incomprehensible. Reading auras while looking dull and confused had taken practice, but he did it well. Landgraf looked like the stereotypic Prussian aristocrat, erect, in charge, autocratic—and in fact he was. He wore black riding breeches, and glossy black riding boots that reached his knees; Macurdy wondered how he got them off.

But his aura reflected a mildness, a humanity that might make him one of a kind in the SS.

And he was a lieutenant colonel. The officer in charge of the Occult Bureau, Colonel von Sievers, was only one rank higher. Perhaps Landgraf had brought his rank with him from some earlier command. Or did an aristocratic family still count for something in the Third Reich?

"Yessir, Herr General sir!" Montag barked.

General? thought Landgraf. *When Schmidt wrote "retarded" on the form, he was at least marginally correct.* "I am not a general," Landgraf replied mildly. "Call me—" He paused. *Keep it simple,* he cautioned himself. "Call me colonel."

"Yessir, colonel sir!"

You must work with what God sends you, Karl, the colonel thought. "Tell me, Herr Montag, do you ever get angry?"

"No sir, colonel sir!"

"Never?"

"Hardly ever."

"Ah. If someone does something to you that is very unjust, what do you do about it?"

"I try to keep away from him, colonel sir."

"Um. And if you want something very much, what are you willing to do to get it?"

"I would work very very hard, sir."

"When you are very angry at someone, is there something you sometimes do about it?"

"Sometimes I beat them up. After that they left me alone."

"I see. Now—" He paused meaningfully. "If there were some very bad people who wanted to destroy your country and your Führer, would you want to do something to prevent that?"

"Yessir, colonel sir!"

"Would you be willing to destroy them?"

"Yessir, colonel sir!"

"Good. Because there are such people, and we want to teach you to do something that *will* destroy them."

Landgraf took a cigarette holder from his desk and put a cigarette in it. "I am told you can light my cigarette with your finger. Show me how you do that."

He put the holder between his teeth, and Montag lit the cigarette, Landgraf watching with interest.

"Very good, Herr Montag. That was well done. Now suppose I am on one side of the room and you are on the other, and I want you to light my cigarette. How would you do that?"

"I would walk over to you."

"And if you were unable to walk over to me?"

"I—" Montag stopped.

"Well . . . Can you get the *idea* of lighting my cigarette from across the room?"

Montag's features reflected confusion. "Yessir, colonel sir!"

"How might you do that?"

Montag stared blankly.

"No matter. Now I want you to imagine someone very bad. Can you imagine shouting angrily at him?"

"Yessir, colonel sir!"

"What is the worst thing you can imagine shouting at him?"

There was a long pause. "Pig."

"Nothing worse than that?"

Montag swallowed, seeming visibly troubled. "Cow turd?"

"Very good, Herr Montag. If you could shout something at them that would make them roll on the ground screaming, would you do that? For your Führer?"

"Yessir, colonel sir!"

"Good. We will give you a chance to do that."

Kupfer had left the door open between the two offices, the usual procedure, and Landgraf raised his voice instead of pushing the intercom button. "Hauptsturmführer Kupfer, come in here please."

Kupfer stepped in, and Landgraf told him to take Montag to "Baron Greszak." They'd left then, Kupfer steering Montag with a hand on the arm. When they were gone, Landgraf shook his head tiredly. *Here we have someone who tries hard to be civilized, and it is my duty to de-civilize him. What kind of world are we trying to make?*

⟡ ⟡ ⟡

Kupfer led Montag up to third-floor main. As they went, Macurdy considered what he'd read in Landgraf's aura. The colonel was a discouraged man, and Montag's demonstration had not noticeably changed that. Perhaps some of the others had also given good demonstrations, then failed to improve sufficiently.

They stopped at an unmarked door, and the captain knocked. "*Kommen Sie rein,*" called a voice, and they went in. Inside stood easily the tallest man Macurdy had ever seen, intimidating not only by his height, but by presence and strangeness. He wore a semi-fitted black coverall that emphasized his raw-boned slenderness. A tall, bag-like black cap with red splints and a knit, dark-green band covered his forehead, accentuating an almost albino-white face. His piercing eyes were as green as Varia's, but their resemblance ended with their color. These eyes were cold, impersonal. Macurdy felt like a bug on a pin.

"Good Morning, Baron Greszak," Kupfer said. There was no Heil Hitler. "We have a new student for you. This is Herr Montag, from East Prussia."

This giant was one of the reported foreigners, that was obvious. A German might conceivably have that build, those features, perhaps even that name, but the aura was distinctive; different than any human aura Macurdy had seen before, ever.

Different in kind.

Greszak didn't trouble to acknowledge Kupfer's greeting. Instead he examined Macurdy thoroughly. "And what is it, Herr Montag, that causes you to be considered psychic?"

"I can start fires. I can light your cigarette. With my finger!"

"Hmm. Show me. Light Captain Kupfer's cigarette."

Grimacing sourly, Kupfer took out a cigarette and placed it between his lips. Then Montag created a brilliant bead of glowing plasma an inch from his fingertip, and a minute later the cigarette was smoking.

The *Voitu* did not change expression. "What else can you do?"

"If someone is cold, I can warm him with my hands."

Greszak stepped around his table and reached out a very long hand. "Warm it," he ordered, and Montag did. Greszak regarded him for a moment, then without speaking, turned and went into a connecting room, closing the door behind him.

"Arrogant swine!" Kupfer muttered. Macurdy wasn't sure how much of Greszak's attitude was arrogance, and how much simply foreignness. He looked toward the two stacks of books on the table—from their spines, all were in German—and wondered if Greszak intended actually to read them. And if he did, how far he'd gotten. Certainly his German seemed fluent, what little he'd heard.

The door opened again in half a minute, and Greszak gestured him in, closing it after him, leaving Montag alone with a man almost a head taller than Greszak, more than seven and a half feet, Macurdy guessed. He had the same pale skin and green eyes, the same black coverall that might be a uniform. The same slender build, the same peculiarities of aura.

"Kurt Montag," he said, "I am *Kronprinz* Kurqôsz. Baron Greszak told me what you showed him. What else can you do?"

Montag simply stared. Suddenly Kurqôsz pulled off his strange cap, tossing it on the table—the move uncovering his ears, like two goat's ears, perhaps six inches long and pointed, covered with the same copper-red hair that, stiffened, covered his skull and formed a sort of crest on its meridian. "Now perhaps you have something to say."

Montag stared, his awe more genuine than pretended. *"Jawohl, Herr Kronprinz,"* he answered. "What planet is the *Herr Kronprinz* from?"

For just a moment Kurqôsz stared, then laughed a single loud whoop. *"Der rote Planet,"* he answered. The Red Planet. He knew the German for Mars, but had translated literally from his own language. Macurdy might have taken him seriously, except for his laugh, and an auric reaction that in a human coincided with amusement.

"If you do not satisfy me, I will give you ears like mine. Now, show me how large a fireball you can make."

Montag made one perhaps an inch in diameter, which floated a couple of inches from his fingertip. Kurqôsz stepped toward him, and reaching, tested it for heat, seeming surprised when, at several inches distance, it was uncomfortably hot, though Montag showed no indication of discomfort.

"Does it not burn?" he asked.

The question took Macurdy by surprise; he hadn't thought about it before. "No, *Herr Kronprinz*. It is *my* fire. It cannot burn *me*."

Kurqôsz pursed his lips. "Interesting, interesting. Make it be thirty centimeters away."

"I—cannot, *Herr Kronprinz*. I—don't know how."

Kurqôsz turned, gestured, and above a table, a hawk-like bird materialized, hovering on loudly thrumming wings that scattered papers from a table. Its head was like a great bat's, eyes glowing red, gaping mouth showing needle-teeth. "It can be killed by casting your fireball at it," Kurqôsz said. "I will count to five, and if you have not killed it by then, I will have it attack you! One, two . . ."

At five, the thing darted forward. Montag's large right hand snatched, caught its head and crushed it. He felt its weight, its blood in his fist, its briefly flailing wings. "I'm sorry, *Herr Kronprinz*!" he cried, "I'm sorry! It was going to do something bad to me!"

Kurqôsz stared, then grinned, cocking a quizzical eye. "Do not be concerned, Herr Montag. I can make as many of them as I wish." Without raising his voice, he spoke to the closed door: "Greszak, come and take Herr Montag back to his keeper. I am done with him for now. Tell the *Hauptsturmführer* we may be able to do something worthwhile with this one."

When the bird had appeared, Macurdy assumed it was an illusion. But when it was launched toward him, or launched itself, his gut reaction was to defend himself. And it seemed well that he had, considering how real—how physical!—it had proven. Sorcery like Kurqôsz's exceeded by far anything he'd witnessed in Yuulith. What were these Voitar? Could they really have come from Mars?

And like Landgraf, Kurqôsz had realized at once his ability—or at any rate his potential—to throw plasma balls. So much for secrecy.

Going down the stairs to Landgraf's office, a notion struck Macurdy. Opening his hand, he looked at it, willing the blood gone. And abruptly it was. Apparently Kurqôsz's fierce bird was only conditionally real after all.

✧ ✧ ✧

Landgraf buzzed the duty room. Two minutes later a guardsman arrived, and took Kurt Montag to the recreation room, where he ordered him to wait. Being alone, Macurdy picked up a seventeen-year-old copy of *Mitteilungen der Gesellschaft für Parapsychologie.* The articles looked interesting, but most interesting was the masthead: the publisher and managing editor had been K.G.R. Landgraf, Phil. Doc. Landgraf might have no psychic talent at all, Macurdy told himself. He might simply know a lot, and have lots of contacts who knew and worked with psychics.

Meanwhile, sitting there half reading, half contemplating, he realized something about the two Voitar: While their auras were like those of humans in important respects, they resembled even more those of the great ravens of Yuulith. And the great ravens shared minds—had what Blue Wing had termed a "hive mind." He wondered if perhaps the Voitar did too.

If they did, then what one knew, the others knew, at least if they troubled to look.

After a while the corporal returned, and Macurdy, slack-jawed, pretended he was simply leafing the journal idly. He was taken back to Greszak's office, where a man stood waiting. He wore a coverall like those of the Voitar, but no cap. About Macurdy's height and width, he looked as strong, perhaps stronger, and somehow dangerous. But his hair approached Voitik red, his skin was almost Voitik-fair, and his eyes were Voitik green. His ears weren't nearly as long, but they were prominent and pointed.

He scowled at Montag as if disliking him on sight. Macurdy guessed he was from wherever the Voitar were from, although his aura was essentially human.

"Tsûlgâx," Greszak said in German, "take Herr Montag to Nargosz." Then he turned his attention to the book he held open, and they left. As they walked together down the corridor—not more than fifty feet—Tsûlgâx's hostility was almost palpable, and Macurdy wondered why. He also wondered why Greszak hadn't taken him there himself, or simply sent him. Was it something to do with rank and status? Intimidation?

Macurdy found himself in a classroom. Nargosz was about Greszak's height but seemed older, and had less presence. He didn't *dominate* a room as Greszak did, let alone the Crown Prince. The students—Otto, Anna Hofstetter, and the elderly female psychic—were on break, Otto and the old woman sitting quietly, doing nothing. Anna, on the other hand, walked briskly around the room swinging her arms, perhaps the only physical activity she got, Macurdy thought.

Nargosz assigned Montag a seat, and after two or three minutes had Anna sit down. Then he had them all do a drill, in which they sat with closed eyes, visualizing. At varying intervals he had them visualize something different. They continued this for two hours without a break, then were released for lunch. After lunch, Macurdy thought of faking it—the drill seemed useless—but didn't. Clearly these Voitar were powerful magicians; perhaps the drills would take. He'd never thought of monotony as particularly instructive though.

By 2:00 PM he'd turned on a peculiar mental phenomenon: He was groggy, felt desperately sleepy—but did not doze off! His head lolled as if his neck were a string, he slobbered, felt an intense, an *excruciating* longing to curl up on the floor. If only he could nap, just for a minute, he'd sit back up and continue the drill. Somehow he continued anyway, struggling, almost whimpering—then the condition faded, the longing passed, and the drill went easier. A little later, Nargosz gave them a ten-minute break, requiring all of them to get up and move around.

Afterward they sat in a row, facing a blank wall, imagining scenes with their eyes open and unfocused: a pleasant scene, then an unpleasant scene, on command. This continued without a break until 4:30. By that time, Macurdy had thrown in a "pleasant" scene of himself strangling Nargosz, which elicited no response from the instructor. Apparently the Voitu wasn't telepathic, or wasn't monitoring him, or just didn't care. The great ravens, sharing a hive mind, had a sort of racial telepathy, with free access to each others' minds and experiences, but not to those of any other species. He recalled Blue Wing's caustic comment that he was glad he didn't have to share minds with humans. Perhaps these Voitar felt that way.

All in all, his first day in class had been difficult, but after it was over, rather interesting. Hopefully something worthwhile would develop. If nothing else, he thought wryly, he might at least develop a tolerance of monotony.

That evening in the rec room, Macurdy avoided Berta Stark's glances. Perhaps later. Just then he could see nothing useful in that direction. Briefly he thumbed through magazines, but to simply sit and read, he felt, would be at odds with his persona as marginally retarded. So he picked up a pack of cards and began to play a disinterested solitaire, thinking that his spare time threatened to be as boring as class had been.

It wasn't, because solitaire permitted his mind to wander, albeit unproductively for the most part. Among other things, he thought about Tsûlgâx, and wondered if the creature was a hybrid between a Voitu and a human. If he was, then where the Voitar were from, presumably there were humans, too.

For the rest of the week, classes were more of the same. Sieges of desperate sleepiness recurred, but briefer and less intensely, and Macurdy found his visual images growing stronger, sharper, more detailed. By the end of class on Saturday he was experimenting with color, both bright and pastels, and had increased image complexity without loss of resolution.

Perhaps, he thought, the Voitar knew what they were doing after all, though how it would benefit his psychic talents, he had no idea. Meanwhile he was concerned that he was getting out of shape physically, which under the circumstances seemed dangerous. So he began doing pushups, situps, and knee-bends during class breaks. When Nargosz asked why, he replied that in school at home they had always done that. "So we would be strong for Germany," he added.

For whatever reason, apparently the Voitar considered the notion favorably. Sundays were off-days, and previously the psychics had simply loafed around. On the next Sunday, however, they were mustered at 9 AM and issued army field jackets, ankle-length SS boots, heavy knit caps with earflaps, and mittens with trigger fingers. At 10 AM, with Schurz in command, they went for a walk outside, accompanied by two disgusted-looking guardsmen. The weather had turned wintry again, with snow on the ground and in the air, so they walked fast to keep warm.

While the psychics walked, Colonel Landgraf and Captain Kupfer passed, wearing greatcoats and riding a pair of beautiful saddle horses. Both belonged to the colonel, Macurdy supposed. Landgraf rode like someone born to it. No doubt he had been; even his name was aristocratic.

An hour later the psychics were back in the schloss, and most of them napped after lunch. After his own nap, Macurdy went to the rec room and sat with his thoughts. So far he'd learned nothing very useful about the project, beyond the strange physical appearance of the Voitar. He needed to learn a lot more than that.

As for the stringent "off-limits" status of parts of the building: The north wing he could understand. It held the quarters, storage, and administrative activities of the SS platoon. And the south wing seemed to be Voitik country, though why so few needed so much room was not clear. So far as he knew, there were only six of them, plus Tsûlgâx, but even if there were twice that many . . . Perhaps it simply reflected the status of Kurqôsz and Greszak—a crown prince and a baron, if that's what they really were.

But the cellar?

Even invisible, investigating would be dangerous. A case could be made for playing it safe, of simply pursuing the training, and seeing what it would teach him about the project's purpose. But by not snooping, he might be missing something very important.

That night, when Schurz and the others were asleep, Macurdy cloaked himself and went to the door, which opened inward. Leaning into the corridor, he peered at the guards, one at each ell. They stood more or less at order arms, looking reasonably military, but by his aura, the nearest, at least, was daydreaming. He'd been spoiled by such routinely peaceful duty.

24

The Party Room

On Monday, all but the old woman were mustered in the corridor before breakfast, for twenty minutes of light calisthenics led by Schurz. This too was new. The Herr Doktor Professor was not a severe master; his purpose was to maintain their health, not build strength. The movements were hardly enough to benefit Macurdy, but he continued his independent exercises during class breaks, doing his pushups in sets of forty.

One evening after supper, when Schurz was in the washroom, Manfred came into the sleeping quarters. Otto had just lit a cigarette. Manfred smoked more heavily than the others, thus his cigarette ration invariably ran out early, so he stepped up to the old farmer and demanded a smoke. As usual when spoken to, Otto didn't answer.

"Jensen!" Eich snarled, "I told you to give me a cigarette!" When Otto looked away, Manfred grabbed him by the shirt and jerked him close. The old peasant's reaction took them all by surprise: His big farmer fingers sunk like talons into Manfred's chubby arm, and with a cry of pain, Manfred struck him, knocking him against a wardrobe. Then Montag grabbed Manfred and threw him violently to the floor.

"Achtung!" Schurz had come out of the washroom, and for the first time in Macurdy's experience had spoken loudly, commandingly. All of them except Manfred snapped to something more or less resembling attention, which in Philipp's case meant getting from his bed onto his feet. Manfred, on the floor, propped himself on an elbow, slack-faced and pale

with fright at Montag's overwhelming strength. He realized with shock that this man could kill him if sufficiently provoked.

"He struck me!" Manfred whined. "The *Schwachsinniger* struck me!"

"I saw what happened," Schurz answered testily. Actually the first part he'd only heard. "You tried to coerce a cigarette from Herr Jensen, and when he refused, you struck him. And Herr Montag did not strike you, he only threw you down."

Manfred got slowly up, resentment already replacing fear on his features. "I will get even with you, feeble-minded pig."

Swelling, Montag leaned his face toward Manfred and retorted. "I will break you in two, cow turd!"

"Shut up, both of you! And stand at attention! I am in charge here. If I report you, the SS will see to your correction." He paused to let the threat sink in. "Herr Eich, I will not report your misbehavior to the *Hauptsturmführer* this time, on the assumption that you have learned a lesson. But if you undertake to bully anyone again, it will go hard with you. There will be no further leniency. The *Obersturmbannführer* is already unhappy with your lack of progress, and the Voitar have told him you do not sufficiently apply yourself. You could very easily end up in the army in Russia, staggering through snow with a frostbitten face, a pack on your back, and a thirty-kilo mortar barrel on your shoulder, while angry Russians shoot at you. They would like so large a target."

He turned to Montag, who stood stiffly at attention. "Herr Montag, do not harm Herr Eich! That is an order! Do you understand me? You do not realize how strong you are."

"Yessir, Herr Doktor Professor sir!"

"At ease then, all of you. It is time to wash for supper."

Schurz's demeanor had seemed to show anger, but his aura showed satisfaction, as if he was pleased at Manfred's comeuppance. As for Macurdy—he was irritated with himself. He now had a dedicated enemy here, and in his position that was dangerous. But damned if he was going to let that tub of shit abuse the old man, whom he outweighed by seventy pounds.

Meanwhile he was impressed with Schurz.

✧ ✧ ✧

Two evenings later, Macurdy spoke quietly to Berta as they left the rec room. "Fräulein Stark," he murmured, "you are very pretty."

Her eyebrows raised. "Thank you, Herr Montag. You are a fine-looking man. You may call me Berta, if you'd like." Her glance was frankly appraising, with no trace of coyness.

"You may call me Kurt. How could we get to know each other better? Without alarming Herr Schurz?"

He realized he was on the edge of acting out of character, but it seemed necessary, and at any rate, Berta had already seen through him.

"I will think about that," she answered. "To be alone here is difficult." She gestured at the south wing ell. At that distance Macurdy couldn't read the guard's aura, but it was a safe bet he was bored, and probably inattentive. "If we met in my room," she went on, "the other women would be upset, and perhaps tell. Also, the *Schwarzrücken* patrol the corridors from time to time."

Schwarzrücken. Blackbacks; a disdainful term. So Berta was no admirer of the SS, the personification of the Nazis. That fitted the sense of—not rebelliousness but disdain that tinged her aura.

They stopped in front of the men's door, and she lay a light hand on his arm. "You are an interesting man, Kurt, as well as an attractive one. There is much more to you than meets most eyes, and I am very curious." Then, after a quick look around, she kissed him, her full lips pressing his briefly. "I will find a way," she said. "I am told—one of the blackbacks propositioned me once—I am told there's a room in the cellar where we can find privacy. If we can get there."

She left it at that, and Macurdy went thoughtfully into the men's quarters. This was developing faster than he'd expected. Now he needed to decide what he wanted to accomplish with this contact.

He only wished her kiss hadn't given him an erection.

After lights out, he examined what he might hope to accomplish, and at what risk. The basic risk was that Berta would give him away, but her aura belied that. And the scope of her disdain extended beyond the SS to the government, he had no doubt.

As for getting caught: If they moved together under his cloak, the odds seemed good that they wouldn't be seen, not at night in these indifferently lit corridors. Unless of course they triggered an alarm system. Jangling alarm bells would sharpen attention drastically, probably enough that his cloak would be seen through.

And if they were caught, they could say they were simply looking for somewhere to be alone together. A claim that would probably not be questioned, and would very likely keep them from being executed, though they'd no doubt be punished. It seemed highly unlikely that an invisibility spell would be suspected. Inattentive guards would be blamed for whatever progress they'd made through the halls.

Most troublesome, Berta would know about the spell. Would she keep it secret? It was his bottom-line escape mechanism. What restrictions would be put on him if the SS learned of it?

Risks could be lived with, if the potential payoffs made them worth taking. But what were the payoffs?

His only answer was, he had to start somewhere. And if he was alone and his spell failed him, he might well be executed. If he was with Berta, on the other hand, they had a convincing alibi that very likely would save their lives.

In class they'd begun practicing with other senses than sight alone, giving their images sounds and odors, trying to actually hear and smell them. It went slowly, like starting over.

Seeing Tsûlgâx in the corridor reminded Macurdy of Sarkia's people, especially her tiger troops. Most tiger clones had reddish hair and greenish eyes—certainly greener than his own. Tsûlgâx's ears were considerably larger though.

On their group walk, the following Sunday, the psychics got strung out a bit, and Macurdy dropped back beside Berta, murmuring that he'd listened at the hall door on two separate nights. The corridor was patrolled at intervals of thirty minutes, give or take 5 or 6, the guardsmen making no effort to walk softly. That night, he said, he would come to her door about ten minutes after the first patrol had passed. If she'd come out barefoot, they'd go to the room she'd mentioned.

He didn't wait for questions, just moved on ahead of her. Let her think about it. She'd either do it or not. He wasn't sure which he preferred.

The covert message had excited Berta, and not just sexually, hungry though she was for a man. That Montag had carried out such observations and planning verified her reading of his aura. Perhaps together they could figure a way to reach the Swiss border and get out of this rotten prison Germany had become.

She could not, however, see a way of getting past the guards. Did he have one? What could it be? Or was he acting on faith? If the latter, they were in trouble.

Actually she didn't know for certain there was such a room, but the blackback who'd told her of it had stuck his neck out dangerously by propositioning her. Nor, assuming it was real, did she know which room it was; somewhere beneath the SS wing, she presumed.

Her impulsiveness had gotten her in trouble before. She hoped it wouldn't this time.

The windows of the schloss wore heavy blackout curtains, which in the absence of artificial light provided utter darkness in its rooms. However, in the men's quarters, one small bulb was left on at night in the latrine, along with the light in the shower room, and the latrine door was left slightly ajar. Thus one could see dimly in the sleeping room.

Some minutes after lights out, Macurdy activated his cloak, then got up and went to the door, where he listened intently. After a bit he heard two men walking down the corridor, one murmuring, the other chuckling.

He scanned the auras in his room. Only Philipp was awake, and he seemed on the edge of sleep. Presumably, hopefully, it was safe to open the door, despite the light it would let in. After a few minutes of hearing nothing outside, Macurdy pulled it open and stepped out, closing it softly behind him.

He glanced toward the guard at the south ell, which was much the nearest. The man had noticed nothing. But the risk would be greater when the women's door opened; it would be more visible to him.

Macurdy scratched at it anyway, and it opened at once. Berta peered out, failing to see him. "It's me," he whispered, barely breathing the words, and touched her wrist. Starting, she saw him. "I can make myself hard to see," he breathed, "as if I'm invisible. You will be too, if you hold onto me."

After staring for a moment, she took his sleeve and stepped out, closing the door softly behind her.

Macurdy held a finger to his lips and glanced toward the guard again. The man was looking toward them, frowning. He'd noticed the door open, then close, but seemingly nothing else. Berta's eyes followed Macurdy's, and she froze, but the guard turned away.

Macurdy nodded reassurance, and they started down the corridor hand in hand, Berta's aura and sweaty palm reflecting extreme nervousness. The guard at the farther ell never even glanced their way.

"To the cellar, you said," Macurdy whispered.

She nodded. They walked down the staircase—the foyer guard was almost asleep on his feet—and from the foyer slipped into the cellar stairway, and down. The cellar corridor was more poorly lit than those on the other floors, and they saw no sign of guards.

"Which way?" Macurdy whispered.

Berta had recovered from her fright. "Beneath the north wing, I suppose," she whispered back. "It's a room the guards use when they smuggle in girls from town. They call it the 'party room.' I don't think they use it during the week. They have no way to bring girls then."

Starting north from the stairs, they tried doors. Most were unlocked, the rooms empty. Macurdy could have opened those that were locked—their lever locks would be easy—but it wasn't the time for that. Then, beneath the north wing, he opened a door to a large room with a hodge-podge of furnishings. The thin light from the corridor showed sofas, a love seat, chairs, and on the floor, several large mattresses pushed together.

There were even paintings on two walls. Macurdy decided that furnishings must be stored in some of the rooms, and the guardsmen had plundered them. They stepped inside, and he tried the light switch; a table lamp turned on, and he closed the door behind them. On the inside, the door had a 5 x 10 cm oak bar that pivoted on a lag screw, and screwed to the door frame was a hand-carved wooden bracket. Macurdy seated the bar.

They examined the room more closely. At one side stood a table, with cards, bottle opener, and a box that held a bottle of brandy, two of schnapps, and several liters of beer. By one wall were two sets of large laundry tubs; over their rims hung several military-issue towels.

Berta put a hand on his arm, and they kissed, lingeringly, then passionately, his hands stroking the small of her back. Within a minute they'd begun undressing each other, and within another were naked on a mattress, fondling, kissing. Soon Berta was on her back, knees drawn high, Macurdy on top, rocking slowly. When they'd finished, they lay tangled for a bit, then cleaned up, and opening two bottles of warm beer, sat naked together on the love seat, drinking and touching.

"Why do you think the cellar is off limits?" he asked. "Could there be valuables stored here?"

"I don't know. At first I wondered if there were people locked up down here, but I'm sure there aren't. There are plenty of prison and labor camps for that."

She changed the subject. "Where did you learn to make yourself invisible? That's a valuable talent."

"From my first wife." It wasn't strictly true, but close enough.

"Do you ever think of escaping this place and going to Switzerland?"

"Sometimes. But while I'm here, I'd like to see what this place is about. Perhaps learn new skills; something to help me make a living."

She made a face. "I just want to be away from here. The Swiss know how to live: peacefully and democratically! I could get clients from doctors there, help their patients recover from surgeries." She shrugged. "Many I could heal without surgery, but doctors don't like that, so I compromise."

She cocked an eye at Macurdy. "What would you do, if you were in Switzerland? A man who can make himself invisible could surely find people he'd be willing to rob."

"In a decent country like Switzerland, I wouldn't care to be a robber. I've been a healer, too, though I don't have the experience you have."

"Why do you pretend to be feeble-minded?"

"It helps keep me out of the army. Even with my leg, they might take me for clerical work or a flak battery, but since I seem so stupid, they consider me unsuitable. So I worked on the docks at Lübeck, and got married there. For mutual convenience; there was no love involved."

Berta told herself it would be easy to love a man who could screw like this one. "Lübeck is a long way from here," she said. "Why did you come so far?"

"My wife is from Kempten. We came here so she could care for her grandparents."

"I suppose you want to get back to her."

"Not necessarily. As I said, it was a marriage of convenience. She was a barmaid and party girl. There were men who threatened her, for part of the money she made. I protected her, and we shared a place to live."

Berta traced the large scars on his leg with a finger. "And this?"

"An air raid on Lübeck, the same as my other scars. I would be much more crippled than I am, if I weren't a healer."

Her aura indicated acceptance of his lies. Her reading of auras seemed less acute than his. And that was a dozen years past, a dozen years of observing people.

"If we go to Switzerland together," Berta said, "we can do very well as healers. We can rent a nice apartment and live like real people."

Her fingers had moved from his knee upward. Now she fondled him, felt him swell. After a little loveplay, they went back to the mattress.

Later they dressed, and returned to their rooms without incident. For a bit, Macurdy lay in bed contemplating. What had he accomplished, beyond adultery? He'd learned something, he answered, learned he could move around the building at night. The next time he'd go alone and find out what the locked rooms had in them.

Meanwhile he'd avoid further trysts with Berta, so far as possible. He'd enjoyed it too much. Adultery as an espionage tool was bad enough; pleasure made it worse.

That night he dreamed of Mary. They were in Fritzi's get-away shack in the mountains, although in the dream, the shack wasn't really the shack. He told her about Berta, and they'd wept together. Then her lips moved, but there was no longer any sound, and he wanted so terribly to hear her words. Then Sarkia was there from his past, seeming ancient, and told him he was deaf from syphilis he'd gotten in his adultery.

Mary wasn't there any longer, and he was looking for her in the cellar of the schloss—heard sounds from the party room and was afraid to look in—when he was wakened by a hand on his shoulder. "Montag! Montag! Wake up!" The whisper was Schurz's. Macurdy raised himself on an elbow, shaking the cobwebs from his mind. "Come to the washroom with me!" Schurz's aura glittered with vivid anger.

In the latrine, the man gripped Macurdy's shoulders and tried to shake him. "You were talking in your sleep!"

Macurdy stared, confused.

"In English!" The words, though little more than a whisper, were almost hissed. "If you must talk in your sleep, do it in *German!* Do you understand? It can mean your life!"

Then Schurz left the latrine, an astonished Macurdy staring after him. After a minute he followed, but it was a couple of hours before he slept again.

25

Sorcery

The next time Berta and Macurdy managed to speak privately was on Sunday, during the group walk. The air was thick with snowflakes, blurring vision and muffling sounds.

"Kurt," she said, "let's go to the party room tonight. You are good, darling, the best ever. I ache to have you again."

He touched her mittened hand. "It is too dangerous now. Schurz discovered me gone. He was angry, demanding to know where I'd been. I told him to your room, and that you'd rejected me. I'm sure he didn't believe me though. He said if it happens again, he'll report me."

He peered earnestly at her; again her aura reflected—not belief, but not disbelief. His story had a major element of truth, he told himself: he had been discovered. "Maybe in a week or two," he added, "the Herr Doktor Professor won't be so alert."

The next night he sneaked to the cellar alone, this time with his "pocket knife"—in reality a small set of lock picks. The locks were old-fashioned lever locks, no challenge at all. He supposed they'd been there since the doors were hung.

He began his snoop in the main, central section, where he found the furnace, as large, if not as tall, as a small ship's boiler, in an unlocked room loud with the sound of screw feed, grinder, blower, fire, and forced draft. He backed out and continued working north, finding nothing interesting until, beneath the north wing, halfway past the ell, he found a powder magazine—a room with a large and tidy stack of TNT in half-kilo blocks.

He had no idea why they'd be stored there, but it could easily account for the cellar being so strongly forbidden.

He was more surprised to find a similar stack in the next room. Beyond that, none of the rooms were locked, and none had anything of interest.

The other major discovery was at the end of the corridor: the heavy exit door was locked only by a stout oak bar. This, he realized, was how the guardsmen brought girls in. Opening it, he found an entryway with a dozen steps. It seemed once to have had a covering door; now it was open to the sky. Snow had blown in, and been tracked by booted feet.

This was a far safer way to get out of the building than opening the front door in the face of a guard.

In class he continued to improve. He developed the ability to make visualized movement smooth and realistic, like a movie in three dimensions. When he'd learned to create images he could hear, smell, and feel—images that seemed entirely real—he learned to judge their weight by mentally hefting the images! That phase went quickly, and apparently well enough to satisfy Nargosz, for he graduated to another classroom, joining Schurz and Manfred. How, he wondered, had the Voitar decided he was ready? Seemingly they read neither minds nor auras. The only explanation he could think of was not very convincing, but perhaps—while they might not read thoughts—perhaps they saw and otherwise perceived his created images.

In his new classroom, the Voitu in charge—a gangling giant named Horszath—had them create images of monsters large and small, in three dimensions and fine detail. Monsters that stank. Monsters ugly, dangerous, indestructible—and as frightening as possible. Preferably terrifying.

It seemed to him that all of this could have only one purpose: He and the others were to create such monsters in reality, monsters as real as Kurqôsz's hawk-bat, only more frightening. But a mental image couldn't move around and kill people. At least not en masse. And it seemed to Macurdy that even if they succeeded, all the monsters they might make would be less dangerous than a battery of flak-wagons from the Krupp Works. Certainly far less dangerous than a panzer battalion.

And harder to create. Macurdy found himself unable to get the essence of raw horror that Horszath wanted. Which saved him from having to fake failure, for he had no intention of producing what Horszath wanted.

On his way to the rec room, one evening after supper, Macurdy met Berta in the corridor. "Kurt," she murmured, "I have learned why the cellar is forbidden us. If you'd like, I will tell you tonight. Privately somewhere."

That evening he browsed *Der Stürmer* awhile—it reminded him what the war was about—then played two games of solitaire and went to bed early, trusting the arrival of the others to waken him. After lights out he lay there until the auras around him indicated sleep. Then he cloaked himself and crouched by the door. After the first hall patrol passed, he went to the latrine, relieved himself, checked auras again, and left. When he scratched at the women's door, Berta was prompt and saucy. He let himself appear nervous, whispering "I am in serious trouble if Schurz discovers I've snuck out again." Then they slipped quietly to the cellar without incident.

This time there was no schnapps or brandy there, only beer. Macurdy wondered aloud whether there'd been any discussion among the blackbacks over who had been into the goods.

But he set his concern aside when Berta wrapped her arms around his neck and began eating his face. This time there was more foreplay, and after sex, he suggested they skip the beer, to avoid advertising that the place was being used during the week.

Berta laughed. "Let them think it was Robert and I, or Reinholdt and I." Macurdy looked surprised. "That's how I learned what I have learned," she said. "I came down here with Robert while Reinholdt was the foyer guard. The next night was Reini's turn. That also allowed me to ask each of them the same questions, to see if they gave the same answers."

She smirked. "Neither of them is the man you are, Kurt, in any respect. But when someone has a deep thirst and there is no beer, water will do. They told me why the cellar is forbidden us: Dynamite is stored in two of the rooms. In this wing! Enough to level the building and leave a hole in its place.

They said it was brought here for the Voitar a year ago, but neither of them knows why."

She fingered his nipple, then they kissed, and she began to fondle him. "Do not be jealous, dear Kurt. Next to you they are boys. You are the man. And I do not plan to come here again with them." They were sitting on the sofa, and now she pushed him down, straddling him. "I learned something else, too. The Voitar have women from time to time." She leaned over him, her hard-nippled breasts brushing his chest, and kissed him again.

"Women?" he said. "The Voitar?"

"That is more interesting than dynamite, is it not? There were three Jewesses last summer, or six if you believe Robert. They were brought here from a labor camp. Then, supposedly, the Voitar had them taken to the top of *der Hexenkamm*, where they were raped and sacrificed to the Devil at the full moon."

She slid down onto Macurdy's thighs and began kissing his chest, then paused.

"Two months later, or maybe only one, it was two German girls—Robert said two nuns—and a gypsy. And last Sunday night, they both told me, it was a German woman, tall and blond, a real aristocrat according to Reini, the sort of woman that might marry a general or a *Reichsminister*." She grinned. "Maybe *der Kronprinz* is screwing her this minute, having his fun before the moon is full. Although cooped in this rock pile, I don't know what phase the moon is in." She chuckled, her voice husky. "Have you seen the Voitar's ears? They remind me of goats, and you know what goats can do in their season." She slid down further, and purred: "But I prefer a German man with meat on his bones. And between his legs!"

When they'd finished, they cleaned up and went back to their rooms. Before going to bed, Macurdy went to the window and parted the heavy curtains. The clouds were broken, scattered. Through the gaps he saw stars but no moonlight.

He knew the story about the explosives was true, or mostly true. The explosive wasn't dynamite, but that was a detail. The story about the women might also be true, he supposed.

But sacrifices on the Witches' Ridge? How would the guardsmen know that?

He decided it was time to snoop the south wing. Tomorrow night.

Then, on an impulse and despite the risk, he slipped into the corridor again, to the rec room, and looked at the calendar. It was past midnight, a new day so to speak, and below its date was the symbol not of the full moon, but of its exact opposite, the new moon.

Nonetheless it gave him chill bumps.

The next evening he slipped into the corridor and went to the sorcerers' wing. On his own floor, the second. Third floor main was where classes were held, and he assumed that third floor south was where the Voitar were quartered. He'd never seen or heard of them being on any other floor. Nor was he prepared to snoop their living space. He was more interested in the other south-wing floors. If they lived on third, what use, if any, did they make of the first and second?

As always, the ell was guarded. Beyond it no bulb burned. The only light encroached from the main corridor.

Barefoot as usual in his nocturnal trips, Macurdy slipped past the sentry, wondering if the Voitar had an alarm system. It seemed to him they did; he could feel an energy. In the dimness three meters past the ell, he perceived a faint rose field, like barely visible pink cellophane blocking the corridor. He might well have missed it, had he not been looking for something like it.

Stopping, he examined it, and as he looked, it became more visible, emanating from what seemed to be a gray line in the ceiling, as vague as the screen itself.

How to get past? How might the sorcerers do it? On an impulse, he told it mentally to move aside—and it retreated upward into the gray line! Tentatively he walked through, then stopped and looked back. The screen was in place again, faint as before. The sentry, who faced away, had noticed nothing.

Macurdy went on, pausing to listen at doors; there was no sound. Nor any light beneath them, except for the door at the end of the hall, which seemed to be an exit. Cautiously he turned its heavy handle and pushed. It opened soundlessly into the cylindrical tower that rose above the building's roof, with a helical stairwell lit only by a weak bulb at each landing.

Something raised chill bumps again—an energy like that from the security screen in the corridor, intensifying as he proceeded downward. The stairwell continued below the first-floor landing and its weak bulb, and so did he.

At the bottom was a final door, of heavy oak, and carefully he opened it, enough to peer inside. Opening it had doubled the energy he felt, making his skin crawl, his hair stand on end. Inside was a small, thickly shadowed mezzanine, stone-paved and with no parapet, overlooking a stone-walled pit. Firelight danced on walls, as if from flames below, and the place smelled of charcoal smoke. There seemed to be no other light. On his belly, Macurdy crawled to the edge and looked down.

The cellar floor was perhaps four meters lower, the flames in a large brazier near one end. In the center was a stone altar, with a naked, long-limbed blond woman lying on it, clearly the aristocrat the guardsmen had told of. She was not physically restrained, but motionless, as if waiting, hands folded on her abdomen. Her eyes were open, her limbs and features composed as if for burial. Her aura suggested a hypnotic trance, her torso and head resting on what seemed to be a silver tray. Kurqôsz stood at the head of the altar. To one side were seven tall Voitar, not robed now, but wearing blood-red breeches and tunics, blood-red slippers.

Though the altar was centered in the room, the focus of the ritual was an intricately wrought tripod of what appeared to be black iron, topped with a shallow bowl, the seven Voitar forming a circle around it. The bowl held a round gem the size of an egg, surrounded by a soft pure glow that seemed more than light.

It gripped his attention, and with an effort, Macurdy pulled his gaze from it. A feeling of suffocation alarmed him; he'd been holding his breath. Cautiously he inhaled.

Kurqôsz held a slender knife in one hand, and in the other a silver shield, which he positioned over the woman's head and chest. Reflexively Macurdy closed his eyes. After a long blurred minute, the energy swelled, then surged powerfully. Macurdy's eyes sprang wide, and he lost consciousness.

When he awoke and looked down again, the sorcerers had left and the flames had burned out, the coals sullen red. The woman was slack, throat cut, torso bloody, with only the residual body aura of a corpse. The stand and jewel were gone. These things registered on his mind without conscious thought. Groggily he stood and backed away from the edge, failing to hear the bolt turn behind him. The door opened, almost hitting him, leaving him partly shielded by it. Someone, seemingly Tsûlgâx, stepped inside, leaving it open. Too groggy to wonder if his cloak had survived his unconsciousness, Macurdy watched broad shoulders and erect head disappear down stairs he hadn't noticed before. Only in hindsight would he wonder what the half-Voitu had arrived to do: clean up perhaps, and carry off the corpse.

Shivering, Macurdy left, plodding zombie-like up the stairs, not stopping at any of the levels, but continuing past the third, up a last flight to a gable door. It opened on a minuscule balcony, a tiny standing place at the eaves of the steep and circular tower roof.

The sky was clear, a great vault spangled with stars. Only then did he realize, vaguely, that the psychic energy he'd felt earlier was gone; had been since before he'd wakened. For several more minutes he thought not at all, until, shivering, he realized how cold the night was. Without checking to see if things were clear, he went back in, down to the second level and into the corridor. He didn't notice whether there was light beneath the doors. Gathering his wits, he cleared the alarm or barrier—whatever it was—and stepped through.

The sentry lay comatose on the floor. It registered, but Macurdy didn't wonder at it. Thinking only of bed, he returned to his room, where the auras would have told him, if he'd noticed, that the psychics were as comatose as the guard.

When he lay down, he had wits enough to deactivate his cloak, and as he pulled the covers over himself, thought blurrily that Tsûlgâx, or whoever had gone to clean up, was either enormously durable, or remarkably insensitive to psychic shock.

26

A Peculiar Gate

The next morning the psychics weren't taken to their instructors. They weren't even wakened for breakfast, but instead rousted out for an early lunch. It seemed to Macurdy that the psychic "power surge" of the night before must have left everyone, except Tsûlgâx and probably the Voitar, in a state of collapse.

About the time they'd finished lunch—rye bread, margarine, cheese and sausage—Macurdy became aware of a hum of energy; a different energy than he'd felt the night before. The others felt it too; he could read it in their auras, and by the way they looked around.

Not long afterward, a haggard Lieutenant Lipanov and an entire squad of equally haggard guardsmen took the psychics for a walk; all but the old woman. And if that wasn't remarkable enough, Greszak went with them, long legs like swift scissor blades. The Voitu's vigor startled Macurdy.

This time they didn't stay on the country road, with its mild ups and downs, but in just a short distance turned off on a truck trail that angled up the side of the Witches' Ridge. Built by the military for four-wheel-drive vehicles, Macurdy decided. He wondered why.

The day was sunny and mild, somewhat above freezing, and the upgrade unrelenting, so that despite frequent short breaks to catch their breath, most were soon sweating. The middle-aged gypsy complained of chest pain, and a guardsman took her back to the schloss, but everyone else kept hiking up the stony road until, two-thirds of the way to the top, they stopped. By that time the energy field was considerably stronger, oppressing all of them except himself—himself and Greszak—who'd been scanning the psychics continually.

On the way back down it suddenly cut off. By then Macurdy knew what kind of energy field it was, knew it well from Injun Knob: *Somewhere on the Witches' Ridge was a gate, if not to Yuulith, then to some place like it—an activated gate, though the hour was far from midnight.* The realization, when it hit him, had given him chills.

And the Voitar? The Voitar were definitely not from Mars. *They were—they had to be—from the other side of the gate.*

Neither Landgraf nor Kupfer nor the Voitar explained the unusual walk. Nor Schurz, who almost surely didn't know. It was not a coincidence though, Macurdy felt sure. Perhaps a test, to see which of them were affected, and how much.

The next day the psychics returned to their class routine, but something had changed. The gate field turned on for something approaching an hour, but at roughly an hour later. It repeated the next day, an hour or so later than on the day before.

Later that day, the glowering Tsûlgâx took Montag from the classroom to Kurqôsz's office. "Herr Montag," said Kurqôsz, "have you felt anything unusual in the air, lately? In the afternoons?"

"Yessir, *Herr Kronprinz!*"

"How would you describe what you feel?"

Montag frowned as if trying to think. "There is a—feeling to it. It made my skin buzz at first."

The red eyebrows arched. "Indeed! Do you find it unpleasant?"

"No sir, *Herr Kronprinz!*"

"Hmm." It seemed clear to Macurdy that his answer was no surprise to Kurqôsz, yet the intense green eyes looked as if they were trying to bore into his skull. Abruptly they disengaged, turning to Tsûlgâx, and the crown prince nodded dismissively without speaking.

And that was all there was to that. Tsûlgâx gripped his arm

and returned him to class. Something, Macurdy told himself, was up, but he had no idea what.

After class that day, Schurz delivered him to Kupfer's office, and Kupfer delivered him next door to Landgraf. The colonel looked him over with a gaze serious but mild.

"Herr Montag, Crown Prince Kurqôsz tells me you have done well here. I am proud of you. You are a good German psychic."

"Thank you, Colonel sir!"

"Herr Doktor Professor Schurz tells me that even your intelligence has improved, an entirely unexpected effect. Do you understand what I'm telling you?"

"Yessir, Colonel sir!"

Landgraf looked as if he wasn't fully convinced. "The Crown Prince," he said, "believes you might progress further if you trained somewhere else. He will take you to his homeland, a place called Hithmearc, and work with you himself. You will like that. You will be well treated, a guest of the Imperial Family. When you come back, you will perform very important services for your *Führer* and Fatherland, and be well rewarded." He got to his feet then, and Macurdy expected the Nazi salute, with a sharp "Heil Hitler!" Instead the colonel shook his hand. "Congratulations," he said.

He looked tired.

By that time Macurdy had a theory about this gate. Presumably, like the Ozark Gate, it had turned on once a month, at local midnight nearest the full moon. That's why he hadn't felt its field: he'd been asleep. Now it was activating daily, at whatever hour the moon crossed the local meridian. That would explain the daily shift in time.

As to why: It seemed to him the Voitar had caused it with their midnight ritual at the new moon. How that could be was hard to imagine, but certainly the timing fitted.

The next day Montag went to class in the morning as usual. After lunch, Schurz had him pack his few things in a military rucksack, then they went to class again. Macurdy had realized for some time that he excelled the others in creating monsters, but still they were no more than three-dimensional, solid-seeming images. Horszath seemed to see them well enough, but when he'd asked the others, they didn't see them at all. Macurdy, on the other hand, could see theirs clearly, and felt confident his were better—more "real," so to speak, more convincing. Manfred's lacked a sense of solidity and mass, and the evil with which he imbued them was more perversion and cruelty than the raw essence that Horszath wanted—and that none of them succeeded in giving him.

Montag's version departed even further; it held grief, despair, loss. Horszath found it unacceptable.

At breaktime, Montag, with his rucksack, was delivered to Greszak's office. Moments later, Kurqôsz, with Tsûlgâx in tow, took him outside with them to a waiting military VW, and its SS driver. Almost as soon as they left, Kurqôsz began to look ill, though the gate had not yet turned on. When it did, partway up the ridge, the Voitu looked no worse, while Tsûlgâx seemed unaffected. Nearing the crest, the crown prince stopped the driver and they got out, to walk the rest of the way. Whatever had been wrong with him, it eased quickly as they hiked. On the crest, the road became rougher, more rocky, and they followed it north a short distance.

Macurdy could feel the gate powerfully now, and wondered what the experience would be like. When he'd gated through on Injun Knob, he'd been in place before it turned on. Here he'd have to walk into it. Soon he could feel it *pull* on him as if by suction, more strongly as they approached, so that it was hard not to run toward it. For one alarming moment, it threatened to suck him from his body, then darkness swallowed him—indigo-tinged nothingness with a bass resonance more felt than heard. For a gut-wrenching instant it was as if his body disassembled, then he was somehow spit out, arms flailing for balance, and sprawled into—straw! After a moment he got up and looked around, unsteady, shaking a bit. Kurqôsz and Tsûlgâx were still down. Here darkness was simply night, a night much colder than the evening he'd just left. They were in a steep-roofed, ceilingless structure—a sort of pavilion perhaps a hundred feet long, open beneath the eaves to air and moonlight. Several Voitar had been waiting with spears and lantern, and one of them called in a language Macurdy didn't know.

Kurqôsz answered, then rose unsteadily to his feet, Tsûlgâx rising with him, and gave orders. The Voitik men-at-arms wore bulky fur cloaks and carried others, putting them over the shoulders of the arrivals. Hands, non-threatening, helped them from the shelter, on a path shoveled through snow too deep for Macurdy to see over.

Ahead was a building, two-storied and steep-roofed, with walls of broad overlapping planks. Its entrance was marked by something like the kerosene lamps he'd grown up with—an oil lamp with an open-topped globe of glass that shielded its flame from the wind. One of their escort raised a bar and held the door open. They went into warmth, and it was closed behind them.

Kurqôsz gave more orders. Two guards, these without spears but carrying scabbarded swords, took Macurdy down a lamp-lit corridor, a smell of fragrant smoke overlying the smell of wood—cedar of some kind, he thought. They stopped at a door. One of the guards opened it and gestured him in, the motion brusque but not hostile. The room was lit by another oil lamp, this one open: in one wall was a window tightly shuttered, in a corner a built-in ceramic stove, flames visible through a window that might have been isinglass. A long low bed stood by one wall. The guard, whom Macurdy judged at about seven feet, said something unintelligible—a single word—then stepped back into the corridor and closed the door, leaving him alone.

Macurdy checked the bed. The sheets resembled flannel; the covers were fur. A small table held a washbasin, a bowl of soft soap, a large pitcher of water and a mug. A towel hung by it.

He wondered if they always had quarters ready like this, or if someone had come through from the schloss the day before, with instructions. Meanwhile he wasn't sleepy, but it seemed he was to stay there. Someone, he hoped, was seeing to supper for him, though here it was probably nearer breakfast time. He decided he might as well wait lying down.

He did, atop one fur blanket and beneath the other, and before he realized what was happening, fell asleep.

27

Rillissa

Macurdy awoke spontaneously, feeling as if he'd slept for hours. Swinging his legs out of bed, he got up, went to the door and peered out. Two guards stood there. He pantomined his hunger, and one of them led him down the corridor to a room with a 12 foot long table, and a floor covered with thinly spread straw. There he was seated, the guard standing behind him, Macurdy wondering how long it would be.

Ten minutes later a female came in, her appearance almost human, more handsome than beautiful, but with Voitik hair and eyes. Macurdy wondered if that was normal for female Voitar, or if she was a mixed-blood. Sending the guard away, she sat down across from him. "You are Kurt Montag," she said carefully. "Excuse my halting German. I have practiced it only two days."

He stared.

"My name is Rillissa. The Crown Prince has assigned me as your companion. I am told you are hungry. Food will soon be brought for you."

She recited her sentences as if doing a drill, but her pronunciations were quite good, and her grammar, if stiff, was correct.

"You began to learn German only two days ago?"

"Learn?" She frowned, then seemed to realize something. "Ah. Of course. You are not used to us. It is not necessary that I learn it, you see, only that I practice it to gain facility. Skill." She paused, then smiled. "I shall ask that you speak slowly, until I am more practiced. The Crown Prince warned me that you speak an atrocious dialect."

She smiled as if totally unaware that her comment might offend. Macurdy realized now that the Voitik species did in fact share a hive mind, as he'd speculated, that she tapped it to speak German, and that access alone was not sufficient for fluency. "You speak German well," he said. "I will try to speak slowly. I am glad the Crown Prince sent you."

A human servant came in, set the table for two, and left. Almost at once another entered with a tray. Breakfast was a kind of omelet, heavy on onions and what Macurdy guessed was barley, with a coarse dark molasses bread. On the side was butter, a kind of pickled fish, two large mugs, and a large pot of buttered tea with honey. While they ate, they talked hardly at all, lacking grounds for easy conversation; they'd need to concentrate to talk together.

Over tea he said, "I do not understand why the Crown Prince sent you."

"To help you learn well. Also, you have none of your own people here, and need a companion so you will not be lonely. Loneliness is a problem for you because you do not share mind."

It occurred to Macurdy that he'd rarely felt lonely in his life, but he let it pass. She smiled again, and changed the subject. "When you are ready, I have something to show you."

He swallowed the last of his tea, and she led him upstairs to a balcony. The sun had risen, and she pointed out the pavilion that housed the gate on this side. "That is where you arrived," she said. "And that"—she pointed past it, up the valley—"is the *Gletscher* that covered this location for a very long time, so that no one knew what was here."

Macurdy judged the glacier's foot as about a hundred yards above the gate.

"Seven years ago," she went on, "when the snow melted in May, a woman was found frozen, farther down the valley. No one knew who she was, but her clothing and shoes were strange. Though it was not known then, she had pushed her way more than three kilometers through snow, which could not have been nearly so deep as now."

Rillissa began to shiver, and they went back inside. Macurdy wondered if she lacked the talent to draw on the Web of the World, or just didn't know how.

"And of course," she went on, "no one could guess where the woman had come from, or how. To the local authorities, who are human, she was simply a strange discovery, a mystery, and soon no one thought about her anymore.

"Two months later, a cattle herder reported a strange couple at the site where the gate is. The woman was—" Rillissa paused, briefly uncertain of the word "—was in a coma, and the man who crouched beside her was raving. The woman soon died, and the man, who never recovered his sanity, died a few weeks later. It was supposed they were connected to the woman who had frozen—their clothing and shoes had similar peculiarities—but the mystery remained a local matter.

"Until a month later, when the same herdgirl found three dead men just where the couple had been found. They wore strange uniforms, and what were thought might be weapons, though how they worked was unknown. This brought the mystery to the attention of the imperial police."

The two events that could be dated had occurred when the moon was full, Rillissa went on, so a month later the imperial police had officers waiting, just in case. At midday they'd felt a physical pressure—somewhat like a strong wind—and three more strange humans had appeared suddenly, flailing and sprawling. The two in uniform soon died. The other recovered, after suffering what seemed to be the flu. He was a German psychic, who identified the frozen woman as a reputed witch, based on a reported disappearance, false teeth, and her clothing.

"Meanwhile, one of the imperial police had pushed against the repelling pressure, and after a brief darkness found himself in a strange place on top of a ridge. And not in midday sunlight, but the middle of night! Afraid he might not find the place again, and demoralized by isolation from the hive mind, he'd stayed there till daylight. Then men in uniform arrived, and arrested him." Rillissa shrugged. "And from that unintended exchange, a German psychic for an imperial police sergeant, has grown a relationship between our government and yours, and further exchanges."

"Then there are other Germans here besides me?"

"Others have been sent, partly to learn more about it. Only three survived, psychics, young women, who arrived early this winter. They were sick only briefly. We are trying to teach them to share mind, but unsuccessfully so far." She shrugged. "You are the first to arrive without at least being ill."

"Is that why I was brought through? To learn to share mind?"

"No. You are to be taught other skills. My father says you show more promise than others of your people."

"Your father? Who is he?"

"Crown Prince Kurqôsz."

"You are a princess then?"

She laughed. "Me? A princess? To be a princess, my mother would have to be Voitik as well." Taking him by surprise, she leaned forward and kissed him. "No, I am a slave. But of royal blood; I have slaves of my own."

They donned furs and skis then, to explore the neighborhood, explorations that proved quite limited. Macurdy had never been on skis before, and floundered at first, Rillissa laughing and helping him. Afterward she took him to a hot tub, and began to undress. When he didn't at once follow her example, she ordered him to, then helped him. Before they left, she'd had him on a bench. What would the Crown Prince do if he found out? Montag asked her. She told him her father had instructed her to lie with him; he suspected Montag might have traits useful to the bloodline.

That confused as much as clarified. If Rillissa was a slave, how would her offspring by a foreigner become part of the royal bloodline? Or—perhaps the bloodline Kurqôsz referred to was more like that of the family livestock.

28

The Palace

They left the next morning in four horse-drawn sleighs: Kurqôsz and Montag with Tsûlgâx and Rillissa, plus guards and personal slaves. Macurdy didn't know it, but sleighs were almost the only land conveyance that the Voitik species, the "Voitusotar," rode in. Meanwhile they'd dressed him as prosperous humans dressed in Hithmearc, his cloak and cap of dark lustrous fur. He strutted a little in them, as a peasant boy might.

Dusk was settling when they reached a town, on the shore of a sizeable river, the Jugnal. There the snow was much less, and the river unfrozen. One wing of an inn had been prepared for the crown prince and his entourage—Montag and Rillissa shared a large feather bed—and in the morning the whole party started downstream on a pair of luxurious barges.

For four days and four nights they floated, the first day on the Jugnal, then on the mighty Rovenstarn, through sunshine, drizzle, and snow showers, carried by the current and the slow strong strokes of burly human oarsmen, past bluffs, towns, the mouths of tributaries, and the overlooking ruins of castles. Castles knocked down, according to Rillissa, by Kurqôsz's barbarian ancestors after they'd conquered these lands. Of other traffic there was little, beyond barges piled high with fuelwood, but of those there were plenty, for long peace had brought burgeoning populations. The fuelwood cutters had stripped the country increasingly bare of woods, and fuel was brought from farther and farther away, from rugged hills and mountains.

Late each day the royal barges stopped, just long enough to take on provisions and new oarsmen, then pull away again.

Rillissa's appetite for sex was remarkable. Fortunately she was aware of male limitations, and between bouts in bed, they spent breaks bundled on deck, watching the banks pass, and talking. Her German flowed more and more easily, and she recounted for Macurdy the history of the Voitusotar. They'd originated far to the north, in a land of plateaus, mountains, ice fields and fjords, a murky country wet with rain and snow, mists and fogs. The valley dwellers had herded goats and sheep, the highlanders reindeer.

Then an epizootic had nearly wiped out their reindeer, and the highland clans had migrated eastward across a vast, near-arctic wilderness they called "the neck." In all other directions the sea had blocked them, and on the sea the Voitusotar were so gripped by violent nausea, they died. River boats were the extent of their travel on water.

Nor did this tall and slender people ride animals or carriages. They became ill from the motion, though not so badly as on ships. Mostly they traveled afoot, and no human could begin to run with them. This people who'd long herded goats and reindeer in moccasins and on skis, who'd hiked a thousand leagues in their migrations, could run for days on end if need be. An ordinary Voitik male could easily outsprint a human champion. Running was bred into them, and pride in it instilled from infancy. In war they were cavalry without horses.

Compared to those they'd conquered, the Voitusotar were not a numerous people, despite intrinsically long lifespans and an indisposition to illness. For they were not very fertile, even among themselves, and they culled their offspring. But they were shrewd and ruthless warriors and potent sorcerers, whose hive mind enabled them to plan and coordinate in battle to a degree inconceivable to humans.

She also began to teach him the language of the land, Hithmearcisc. It was not, she said, the language the Voitusotar had brought with them, but in time it became the one they used. Voitik was used primarily for naming and spells.

He found himself recognizing occasional words he'd learned

in Yuulith. Hithmearcisc and Yuultal seemed to be of the same world, sister tongues, apparently with an ocean somehow in between. This sparked his interest, and as he began to develop an ear for Hithmearcish, he recognized more and more cognates.

He avoided mentioning Yuultal, and Rillissa commented on how rapidly he learned. Probably she mentioned it to Kurqôsz as well.

Just after daybreak on the fifth day, the barges came to a city known as Voitazosz, gray with old and dirty snow, and murky with drizzle. By that time, to Rillissa's annoyance, her sexual demands had debilitated Macurdy. Fortunately he'd gotten her pregnant; that was clear to him from her aura. And to her from the hive mind: The embryo was already plugged into it, so to speak, a minute and primitive animal presence that shared life force with all her father's race, and with some mixed-bloods like herself.

The only person Macurdy wanted to sire children on was Mary, who was in another world. Meanwhile, Rillissa's pregnancy had taken the pressure off him.

At Voitazosz, the River Quarm flowed into the Rovenstarn, and their steersmen turned up it. Two miles above the city was the imperial palace, extensive as a town—mighty fortress walls with towers and domes looming above them. As a farmboy from Washington County, Indiana, warlord of Yuulith's Rude Lands, undersheriff of Nehtaka County, and an American G.I. in England, nothing he'd ever seen had struck him as so impressive or so foreign.

There were stone docks outside the walls, and a slip for landing important people. It was there they tied up and disembarked. Human dockers handled the lines and unloaded the baggage. Without being conspicuous about it, they eyed Macurdy curiously, a human of seeming consequence in the Crown Prince's entourage.

He discovered that inside the walls, buildings occupied less than half the ground. As a group they were not attractive. Individually some were, but they went together poorly, like

Tudor and Bauhaus. Not that Macurdy analyzed the situation, but he sensed it. Of the ground unbuilt upon, much was paved with flagstone, while such gardens and lawns as there were, were drab with winter. The overall impact was aesthetically poor, as if the Voitusotar, or at least the imperial family, were imperceptive or didn't care.

The interiors were far better, with statuary, precious metals, stained glass, tiles, parquet, richly figured woods, paintings, tapestries, and gems. And quality construction. The designs were seldom inspired, but neither were they hodgepodges. And the buildings were centrally heated, their fireplaces supplemental or simply decorative. The small bedroom assigned to Macurdy—not shared with Rillissa—had a warm-air vent in one corner, while a closet contained a snug-lidded commode, emptied twice a day by some luckless servant, through a back panel that opened into a utility space.

All in all, Macurdy was impressed.

A Voitu named Zhilnasz was his trainer, and for a time the emphasis was not on monsters, but on creating and casting plasmas, and occasionally Kurqôsz tested his "German" protege. This casting of plasmas did not go well, partly because Macurdy deliberately withheld himself; he'd done better years before in Yuulith. It seemed to him that if he succeeded, Kurqôsz might keep him in Hithmearc. For why would the Nazis be interested in someone who could cast a two or three-inch plasma a hundred meters—or even a few hundred meters!—when they had thousands on thousands of 88mm artillery pieces and assorted larger guns, each with far greater power? Nor had he forgotten Arbel's warning on the personal dangers in creating large magicks, dangers to which it seemed the Voitusotar were immune.

He also discovered that casting plasma charges was tiring, took something out of him. Casting one or two wasn't bad; that's why he hadn't noticed it before. But to cast ten or a dozen in just a few minutes left him exhausted, and the energy wasn't made up by tapping the Web of the World. Apparently it was a different energy.

After a futile and exhausting week, the nature of his training changed again, with Kurqôsz showing less interest in him. Now he was to cast not plasmas but images.

These were not quasi-physical monsters, but holo-images pure and simple, images that frightened partly from their horror content and partly by breaking the victim's confidence in his own sanity. Within days, Montag could stand on a balcony, target a slave in the courtyard, and create in the man's mind the sight of headless corpses walking; bony scrabbling hands digging their way out of the ground; decaying bodies with worm-eaten faces moving as if to embrace and kiss the victim. Invariably the target collapsed or stood paralyzed, fell unconscious or broke and ran.

The first time, Macurdy had been pleased with himself. Then he'd realized the cruelty of the act, and the pleasure of accomplishment died.

More difficult, he learned to target people he couldn't see, at first in rooms whose locations he knew precisely, then rooms known only approximately. In these cases, he needed to have seen the person before, and be able to visualize them. He'd already become superb at visualizing.

To the extent practical—which was very limited—Macurdy had used Hithmearcisc around the palace, including with Zhilnasz. Zhilnasz, of course, answered in German—his function was not language instruction—but most of the palace staff were humans, who of necessity answered Macurdy in Hithmearcisc, keeping it as simple as they could. So his small knowledge of the language improved, and meanwhile it gave him a form of recreation.

Finally the Crown Prince tested his progress in image casting, providing himself as a target in a building halfway across the palace grounds. The results validated Montag's skill; his training there was finished.

The next day, instead of being sent to Zhilnasz, Macurdy was ordered to Rillissa's suite, and as usual her demands were imperious, not to be refused. That evening before he left, she astonished him by weeping. Her father had kept them apart, she said, and the next morning Macurdy would be leaving, unlikely ever to return.

"And I love you so!" she cried.

He'd known she was fond of him, in her way, but love? *Like a pet,* Macurdy realized as he walked down the hall, *like a favorite dog.* Which at that was better than some people loved their spouse. He could feel for her—she did the best she could—but to love her was beyond him.

The next day, with Kurqôsz and a surly Tsûlgâx, he left the palace on a barge again. The trip up the Rovenstarn and Jugnal was much slower than the trip down had been; there was the current to fight, and the beginning of spring had worsened it. He practiced his Hithmearcisc on servants and crew, and once tried it on Tsûlgâx, who simply glowered at him.

He saw Kurqôsz only occasionally, and wondered what the crown prince did with his time. *Perhaps,* he thought, *he spends it browsing the hive mind.*

On the eleventh day they arrived at the gate hostel, and on the twelfth passed through it into Bavaria again. Bavaria and spring.

29

Assignment

Back at the schloss, they returned Macurdy to drills on beaming emotions. He hadn't had much success with them before, and didn't improve. He doubted they expected him to. It felt more like keeping him occupied, though while waiting for what, he hadn't a clue.

Several days after his return, a guardsman arrived at the men's quarters after breakfast and took him to the colonel's office. The telepath, Anna Hofstetter, was there, but neither Anna's aura nor the colonel's showed cause for alarm.

"Stand at ease, Herr Montag," Landgraf said genially. "I hope you found Hithmearc interesting. The Crown Prince tells me you did quite well in your drills there."

"Yessir, colonel sir!"

Landgraf gazed quizzically at Montag, who stood stiffly at attention despite the order to stand at ease. Perhaps he was intimidated. He would phrase the next question so the man couldn't answer it with a simple yes or no, and see how he did.

"It is time to exercise your skill on the enemy—the Americans and British. What do you think of that?"

"I am glad, sir. At the palace I made slaves scream and run, or freeze, or fall on the ground. I can do the same to the British and American swine."

"Good." The colonel grimaced slightly, then turned his glance to Anna, fingers drumming briefly on his desk. "I am going to tell you both some things which you will discuss with no one except each other. Absolutely no one."

He looked sternly at Montag before continuing. "I have a mission for you. The details have not been worked out yet, but I will describe the main features. The Americans and British are expected to assault the north coast of France, in May or possibly June. The *Wehrmacht* has prepared powerful defenses to repulse allied landings. Your task is to disrupt Allied headquarters in England by projecting psychotic images into the minds of key personnel, especially General Eisenhower and his staff."

He examined Montag. "Do you know what *psychotic* means, Herr Montag?"

"No sir, colonel sir!"

At least the man could recognize and admit when he didn't know something; many brighter men could not do that. Landgraf turned to Anna. "Fräulein Hofstetter, explain psychotic to Herr Montag."

"Psychotic," she answered wryly, "means insane. Crazy."

The simplicity of her answer startled Landgraf, whose degrees were in psychology. "Good," he said after a moment. "Now, Herr Montag, Fräulein Hofstetter will go with you to England, where she will get you safely into the hands of the *Abwehr*—people who will help you. They will get you near enough to the enemy high command that with binoculars you will be able to see their supreme commander and other high-ranking officers. See them well enough that afterward you can attack them with images. The *Abwehr* will have a building diagram of their headquarters, with offices and conference rooms marked on it.

"Do you understand?"

"Yessir, colonel sir. The—those men . . . Our people . . ."

"The *Abwehr*," Landgraf said helpfully. "The intelligence service. Our spies in England."

"Our spies will take me to a place, some building, and show me who the enemy commander is. Then I will make him crazy, even if he is in a room I can't see. Our spies will have a paper that shows where the different rooms are."

Again Landgraf's eyebrows raised. He hadn't expected that much understanding so quickly. "You are going to do well, Herr Montag. I have great confidence in you. Fräulein Hofstetter will tell you more when we know more."

✧ ✧ ✧

It happened sooner than Macurdy expected. The next morning, Anna Hofstetter took him to an unused classroom, equipped only with a table and some chairs, and they sat down.

They would, she told him, travel by train to the submarine base at Saint-Nazaire, in France. From there they'd be taken by submarine to a beach on the east coast of England, put ashore by rubber boat, picked up by German agents, and taken to an *Abwehr* safehouse in London. From that point they'd be briefed further by the *Abwehr* station chief.

"Meanwhile," she went on, "it will be well for you to know a little about me. My father is German and my mother is English, a member of a fascist family. I lived in England until 1932, when I was thirteen years old, and for several years afterward we took our holidays there, so my English is excellent. I know English geography, much of it first hand, and I'm familiar with London. I am to be in full charge of the mission, and my function is to provide you with whatever you need to carry it out.

"I am not subject to the *Abwehr* station chief. On the contrary, I can command him, within limits. His function in this is to do whatever is necessary to support you."

She caught his gaze and held it. "I do not doubt that you understand me. You are considerably more intelligent than Colonel Landgraf imagines. You have been concealing your intelligence, pretending to be dull-witted. Herr Doktor Professor Schurz agrees with me on that. If I am to work with you in dangerous situations, I will have to know why you pretend to be otherwise."

"It is nothing very complicated," Macurdy said. "Even with my crippled leg, I could be called into the army in a clerical role, or manning some flak battery. But if I am thought to be feeble-minded, there is much less risk. Also, fewer demands are made on me."

Her aura reflected skepticism. "Is your limp as bogus as your feeble-mindedness?"

In answer, he pulled his left trouser leg above the knee. She grimaced at the scarring.

"It appears to be genuine," she said, and ended the briefing.

As Macurdy walked the few yards to Greszak's office, he

examined the morning and what he'd learned, both about the mission and Anna Hofstetter.

She'd talked with Schurz about him. Schurz knew he spoke English—dreamed in it!—but apparently hadn't told her. Meanwhile, Anna's aura showed that she mistrusted him, had for some time, yet she hadn't blown the whistle.

Schurz, Berta, and now Anna had covered for him. He would never have imagined such a thing. Strange, very strange.

For several more days, Macurdy continued his training under Greszak. On one of them, Anna took him to the room he thought of now as their private conference room. On their way, they passed Tsûlgâx in the corridor. As usual, Tsûlgâx scowled at him.

"I wonder why Herr Tsûlgâx dislikes me so?" he murmured. "I have never said or done anything to him."

"He doesn't simply dislike you," Anna said drily. "He hates you. He considers you a threat to his father."

Macurdy's buzz-cut crawled. "His father? Who is his father?"

"The Crown Prince. To whom he is thoroughly devoted."

"But—how am I a threat to the Crown Prince?"

"I don't know. Nor does Tsûlgâx. It is simply something he feels. He believes that he senses the future. Not sees it, but senses it."

Macurdy turned her answer over in his mind without saying anything. A threat to Kurqôsz? He didn't even dislike Kurqôsz, really.

They entered the room. "So you read their minds," he murmured.

"Not the Voitar's minds. They are totally opaque to me. But Tsûlgâx has no more shielding than he has compassion."

"Do you read mine?" Montag asked.

"I think you know the answer to that. No, not yours. Some people, and most psychics, have a shield which, if they feel sufficient trust, they lower, knowingly or not. But even if they do not lower it, I can sense their emotions and attitudes, and learn much from those. I have learned much about you."

Macurdy met her gaze mildly. "I know what people feel sometimes."

"I am sure you do. Herr Schurz thinks you read auras, and I believe he is right."

Macurdy neither verified nor denied it. "You do not show very much what you feel," he said, "even to me. But I don't mind. It is not necessary that I know."

Her aura and face both reflected wry irritation. "Do not be coy with me, Herr Montag. If we are to work together, please show me some respect."

"My apologies. I do respect you, and I am ready to listen."

She looked away, gathering her thoughts, then returned her gaze to him. "There is serious risk in what they have planned for us," she said, "but considering everything, I believe we can succeed." She paused. "Of course, if we are captured, we may be executed."

He ignored the comment. "Can you read the Colonel's thoughts?"

"As necessary."

"Does he know that?"

"He knows I am a telepath, but has decided not to be troubled by it."

"What have you learned from him?" He asked the question as much for her reaction as for information.

Her gaze was direct, calm but intent. "He has considerable confidence in both of us. Remarkably, he trusts us."

"Have you learned anything from him about the Voitar?"

"Quite a bit. It seems they came here through some 'opening' on the Witches' Ridge. But you know more about that than I. Apparently in their country, explosives are useless, but they are interested in steam engines and water pumps. Also in ship building."

Ship building? That definitely seemed false.

"In return they train us, mostly without useful results, probably because of our shortcomings as psychics, rather than theirs as teachers. Also, eight of them will travel to northern France, to help fight the invasion when it comes. To do what it seems we cannot—create terror monsters that are real, physical, and set them against the enemy."

Macurdy tried to imagine what those monsters would be like. Physical, she'd said. Vaguely he remembered nightmares, and a chill ran over him.

"When do they leave?"

"In May. On the tenth, unless it's been changed again."

"How will they get there?"

Anna seemed unhappy with the question, as if she'd struggled with it before, to no good conclusion. "Not by rail," she said. "They will travel on rivers and canals. There was also something about walking. Or"—she shrugged uncomfortably—"running, actually. Accompanied by a motorized escort. It makes no sense."

To Macurdy it did. Certainly more sense than an interest in shipbuilding. "When do we leave?"

"I don't know. But soon, obviously." Anna got up. "It is time you returned to your drills."

Montag nodded. The drills were definitely a waste of time now, but orders were orders, and anyway there was nothing else to do. If he had his way, they'd leave the next day.

That evening, leaving the dining room, Anna's aura reflected repressed excitement, though physically she seemed her usual calm self. She paused outside the door, and as he passed, she murmured, "Very soon now. *Very* soon."

Tomorrow? he wondered. The next day? She should have been explicit. Or maybe she didn't know explicitly.

Afterward, in the reading room, Berta sat down beside Montag while he played solitaire. "You've been back for a week now," she murmured.

He nodded, then got up. "Let's talk in the corridor," he replied, and they went out.

"The rumor," Berta said, "was that you went somewhere with the Voitar. To wherever they came from." She put light fingers on his arm. "You and I should go to the party room. I've missed you. And I am curious."

"I'd have invited *you,*" Montag said, "but while I was gone, I had more sex than I could handle. For the first time in my life. I'm not sure I've recovered yet."

"I've seen you with that scrawny little Hofstetter lately. Perhaps you have enough energy to take her downstairs."

"You live in the same room with her. You should know whether she slips out at night."

"Perhaps you screw her during the day. You are known to go into an empty classroom together. Apparently with permission."

"You might ask Schurz why we do that. Or Colonel Landgraf. They know. We are under orders, she and I."

Berta sulked. "Orders! She is a Jewess. That sharp face, scrawny body . . ."

"If she was sent here by the Gestapo, as I was, that is hardly possible."

Berta deflated. "Shit, Kurt, I know that. And I have nothing against Anna. I'm just jealous. She has the hots for you, and you're allowed to spend time together. Can we go downstairs tonight? I want you badly."

He considered. This was no time to get caught out after hours. The mission with Anna was his chance to report what he'd learned to Grosvenor Square. Or— If he was caught with Berta tonight, with the mission so close, what would they do to him? He had an assignment, and there seemed to be no one else they could send. He'd simply say it had been his last chance to go to bed with Berta. Besides, there was that old saw about Hell having no fury like a woman scorned.

"And I want you," he told her. "Who knows if I will have another chance. The usual time?"

Berta nodded, her excitement not primarily sexual. *What is that about?* he wondered.

He found out. After having sex, they talked, as usual. She thought perhaps he was getting ready to run away, escape to Switzerland, and wanted to go with him. That wasn't it, he told her. He'd gone with Kurqôsz through a sort of gate on the Witches' Ridge, "a hole in space," realizing how preposterous it must sound, even given the outlandish appearance of the Voitar. And on the other side, he added, they'd trained him to do a special job.

To his surprise, she merely raised a skeptical eyebrow. "Hmm. And who was it there," she asked, "who gave you more ass than you could handle?"

"Kurqôsz assigned a slave to keep me company, and to tell me things."

"A slave? She must have been something, if you couldn't bring yourself to say 'no more.' "

"She was not an ordinary slave. She was Kurqôsz's daughter."

"Kurqôsz's daughter? A slave?"

"She's a half-blood, like Tsûlgâx. She's a slave, but has slaves of her own. In a way I was one of them."

Berta laughed. "I wish you were my slave! I'd wear you down to a *Vogelscheuche!"* She leaned against him then, kissed his lips, his shoulders, his chest, her right hand fondling him until he was ready.

When they were done, they went back upstairs, both of them quiet.

30

Surprise in Albion

The next morning he was told to pack, that they'd leave at 1000 hours. Packing took only a few minutes, then both he and Anna were called to Landgraf's office for a final briefing. Afterward they were driven to the military transportation office at the railyard in Kempten, where they were met by an SS 1st lieutenant. His orders identified them as an intelligence team enroute to England; he was to accompany them, get them to the submarine base at Saint-Nazaire through any difficulties that might arise. In these times one could expect difficulties.

Theirs was an army train, mostly freight cars, but with a flak car, three troopcars, and a sleeper car for officers. Macurdy, Anna, and the lieutenant were assigned to the sleeper, along with the several officers of coast artillery replacements.

In peacetime the 650-mile trip would have taken a day. It took them nearly four, partly because other, strategically more urgent trains were given the right of way, leaving them on sidings for as long as an hour at a time. Mostly, however, the problem was bomb damage. The bridge at Breisach had been knocked out the night before, so they'd detoured south, and crossed the Rhine on the newly repaired bridge at Müllheim. At numerous locations, railyards had been heavily bombed, and damage, debris, and ongoing repairwork seriously reduced the rate at which traffic could be moved through, causing long delays. In other places, temporary bypasses and hasty repairs meant reduced speeds.

The first day, Macurdy wondered what night would bring. Berta had said Anna had the hots for him, but he'd brushed it off as petulance. Certainly he'd seen no indication of it, even auric. He was interested despite himself, and that troubled him. In the army he'd had opportunities for sex from Little Rock to England, and had avoided it because he was married. Then there'd been Berta, and a great deal of Rillissa, and having sex with them seemed to have weakened his resistance. He vowed not to have sex with Anna.

The railroad car had blackout curtains, of course, and at twilight they were drawn. At nine o'clock the corridor lights were dimmed. The lieutenant appraised Anna. "Fräulein, for security it is necessary that you share a compartment with one of us." He gestured at Kurt Montag. "Which one do you prefer?" He had no doubt, of course. Her companion looked like a peasant, limped, and wore a suit of ill-fitting tweed that looked distinctly British.

She saw through him of course. "I will share this one with Herr Montag," she said. "We are old friends."

The lieutenant locked his jaw without answering, telling himself she was thinner than he liked anyway, and nodding curtly, went to the next compartment.

Anna set the bolt, drew the compartment curtains, and took pajamas and a robe from her bag. Her aura showed only light sexuality: awareness, not desire. In fact, she put on her robe, turned her back to him, changed clothes beneath it, removed the robe and went to bed, pulling the cover over her. Physically he felt disappointed; mentally relieved.

"Anna," he said, "I have no robe. But if you would turn your back . . ."

She did, and he removed his outer garments. Then, after opening the compartment curtain just a bit to let in some of the corridor light, he turned off the night light and went to bed. Anna watched him in the dimness.

"I had wondered if there would be a problem between us," she said. "Thank you for your good behavior."

He focused on her aura. Her sexual energy had increased but was still unfocused. "I have a wife," he answered. "A very good wife, whom I love. I owe her my loyalty."

Her auric response equated to raised eyebrows. "Oh? And what about Berta? She would wait for you very much aroused, and return sated." She paused. "But then, Berta is much sexier than me, much more tempting."

"That wasn't it. I wanted to snoop around the schloss, but I was afraid I'd be caught and perhaps shot. With Berta, I had a good excuse: If we were caught, I could say we were looking for a place to make love. We would have been punished, but hardly executed."

"Ah. And how many nights did it take to complete your snooping?"

"One. But by then she had learned things about me. So when she asked me to be with her again, it seemed best not to offend her."

Anna smiled, not cynically. "And besides, it was such fun, *nicht wahr?*"

"She was good. I can't deny it."

"And what was it she learned about you that you wanted to safeguard?"

"You already know: that I am not a *Schwachsinniger.*"

"All right. And how did you manage to move around in the building without being caught? Even slipping down the corridor to the reading room or dining room would have been dangerous."

He said nothing. Undoubtedly she was reading his feelings, analyzing them.

"I must tell you," she said, "that for a time I supposed you were a spy, put here by some office that disapproved of the Bureau. I could see no other explanation for your ability to move around at night."

It seemed to him he could sense her mind perching at the edge of his, watching for a crack, a chink. Still he said nothing.

"Well, I can understand your silence, and I will let these questions lie for now. You have shown me respect; I will do the same for you. Good night, Kurt Montag, and pleasant dreams."

Saint-Nazaire had been a small city; now it was an expanse of rubble. But the submarine pens—heavily reinforced tunnels—still operated. The railyard was closed, had been heavily bombed again, and the two psychics rode the 35 miles from Nantes in a command car, over a road heavily and hastily patched.

After leaving their SS lieutenant at the harbormaster's office, they were taken aboard a submarine in midafternoon, and assigned quarters. Though his was in a crowded crew compartment, Macurdy was privileged: He didn't alternate in his narrow fold-down bunk with someone on a different watch, as the seamen did; it was his full-time. Anna was even more privileged: She occupied the tiny cabin normally used by the 1st officer, who would double up with the captain while she was aboard.

The craft stayed in its cavern till after dark; a submarine moving down the channel in daylight was at serious risk. One never knew when American or British planes might visit.

Eventually the vessel began to move, its throbbing diesels pushing it out of the pen, into the estuary. Despite himself, Macurdy sweated a bit, and raised a brief prayer, less to God than to allied destroyers and planes, that he might arrive safely in England. *Not that I wish you guys bad luck or anything,* he murmured inwardly, *but my mother didn't raise me to drown in some Nazi* Unterseeboot.

The seamen were calm enough though, and before long he slept, despite the strange sounds and smells.

For the sake of speed and the batteries, the vessel ran on the surface till dawn, then the humming electrics were cut in, and the diesels shut off. Then bells jangled. Without pausing, the submarine tilted downward slightly and submerged.

The rubber boat was low enough that any chop would have soaked and any real seas upended them. But the sea was relatively calm, its low smooth swells the aftereffect of some distant storm, perhaps off the west coast of Jutland. Neither Montag nor Anna spoke, even in a whisper. They'd been warned not to, before they'd climbed out the conning tower.

Now he could see the beach ahead, low and sandy in the starlight, the swooshing of the low surf as regular as a heartbeat. The sub was well out of sight behind them, and Macurdy wondered if crewmen, off in a rubber boat, ever had trouble finding it at night.

Then the surf gripped them, drove the boat onto the beach and left it grounded. Anna's mobility was hampered by the heavy wool, knee-length coat she wore, and hoisting her over a shoulder, Macurdy stepped out, a petty officer leading, hurrying a few paces to avoid the next wave. Once on dry sand, he put her down. They had no baggage, only Anna's purse and Macurdy's wallet, neither with anything incriminating except their skillfully counterfeited papers and English money.

"Everything is all right?" the petty officer asked Anna. He'd been told she was in charge.

"Yes."

"Well then, good luck." The man took time to shake their hands, then with the other seamen, pushed the boat back into the cold surf, and paddled out of sight in the darkness. Macurdy felt faintly guilty watching them leave, for wishing them a safe arrival, to their ship if not their port. This war, he told himself, needs to be over, and wished he could make it so.

Then the two spies crossed the sand to the thick bank of heath shrubs behind it. Beach contact, they knew, was the most uncertain point in such landings. The beaches were patrolled, or said to be, and their would-be pickup team might have to lay back, might even have been captured. Another possibility was that the captain had miscalculated, and put them ashore on the wrong beach.

Anna looked at her English watch. "It is about two hours till dawn," she said. "You might as well sleep. I'll stay awake and watch for our contacts. If I get too sleepy, I'll wake you and we will change places."

Macurdy lay down on the sand, protected from the damp chill by the Web of the World, and a heavy sweater with a Scottish label.

He fell asleep almost at once, and in that sleep dreamed: He was aboard the liner Queen Elizabeth, with the men he'd served with at Camp Robinson, at Benning, in the 509th, the 505th. Shuddering, he remembered dreaming this before, and had let it get away. The liner became a landing craft, one of many, but he was the only man on his, as if it were some derelict caught up unintended in the assault. Shells rumbled, warbled, roared. The craft staggered in the surf, then grounded. The ramp dropped, and he rushed off into chest-deep water; waves lifted him, set him down, and he was on the beach, no longer alone, one of thousands that packed the sand.

From between two dunes came giants, 50-foot redheaded monsters carrying great chains, anchor chains, wielding them like fly swatters, beating the beach with them. With each blow, dozens of men died. There were shrieks. A chain smashed the sand in front of him, jerked upward thick with blood and flesh, started back down . . . and he awoke, panting.

The beach had no crushed bodies. There was only Anna standing watch a few yards away, looking at him. He wondered if he'd cried out in his sleep. Shivering not with cold, he got to his feet, thinking of the Voitik sorcerers scheduled to meet the invasion army with spells and monsters. To the east, a band of faint silver lay on the horizon, and already he could see farther than before. Soon it would be daylight, and they had not been picked up. Anna had a decision to make.

Anna still watching, he began to do side-straddle hops to activate his body. When he'd finished, she said "let's go," and they began walking along the beach until they came to a path leading inland through the heath. They took it.

Macurdy's attention was not on where they were. It was on the dream beach where monsters tramped among G.I.s, crushing them beneath great clawed feet, smashing them with bloody chains. He hadn't dreamt it idly, he told himself. It was a reminder of duty, a duty he'd only now recognized.

They hiked through heath for much of a mile, while the dawnlight strengthened. Then the heath ended. Ahead was what had been a farm cottage, now a home guard outpost, with two jeeps parked outside and a uniformed sentry by the door. Anna headed straight for it, Macurdy following, wondering.

At fifteen yards, the middle-aged sentry pointed his rifle at them. "Stop right there," he said, and they did. "Who are you, and what's your business here?"

"My name is Anna Hofstetter," Anna replied in upper-class English. "We were just put ashore by a German submarine, and wish to report our mission to the authorities."

For a moment both the sentry and Macurdy gawped, then Macurdy added, "I'm Lieutenant Curtis Macurdy. We're an OSS mission—the Office of Strategic Services, U.S. Army. I need to get in touch with our superiors, at once."

The sentry gathered his wits. "Sergeant!" he shouted, forgetting protocol. "Come out here right away!"

Anna's stunned gaze didn't leave Macurdy till the sergeant arrived. They repeated their identities for him, then he ushered them inside and phoned his superiors. That done, he gave the phone to Macurdy, who reached Grosvenor Square by the confidential number he'd memorized. Afterward the home guard fed them porridge, bread and jam, cheese, coffee—even bacon!

A jeep from MI5 arrived from London in about an hour, in the charge of a green 2nd lieutenant, to take them into custody. Macurdy fended them off with obstinacy and lies, insisting that he was a 1st lieutenant, and not about to be ordered by a junior officer. Minutes later an OSS jeep arrived with an American captain, and took them away, leaving the unhappy lieutenant behind.

What stuck in Macurdy's mind, though, riding off down the road to London, wasn't his small victory over MI5, or even how quickly things had developed. It was that he'd never suspected Anna's disloyalty to the Nazis. Apparently she'd lived so long in secrecy that her aura had adjusted!

31

"Should Auld Acquaintance . . ."

Before the day was over they'd both been debriefed, which took until evening because the OSS wanted everything. Among other things, he emphasized that it was Anna who led them to the British Home Guard station and turned them in.

Normally his mission officer would have debriefed him, but the man was away, and a young lieutenant did it. Handling it quite professionally, even the description of the Voitar and their ears, and the drills Macurdy had done—until Macurdy told about his visit to Hithmearc. The lieutenant got nervous then; it showed in his eyes, and conspicuously in his aura. *He's afraid of me*, Macurdy realized. *He thinks I'm crazy.*

Awakening spontaneously the next morning, Macurdy went to breakfast and found Anna there. Someone had arranged for MI5, the British counter-espionage service, to pick her up. "And Curtis, I'm afraid," she said. "I feel threatened by them. I was, after all, born here to an English mother, and they may consider me a traitor."

Her aura told him she really did feel threatened, though he couldn't imagine the threat being real.

"I'll see if I can do something about it," he said.

When the MI5 man arrived—a lieutenant less green—Macurdy was with her, and explained that she was a German national, working with him. "We've got a mission," he lied. "We'll be leaving before noon."

"Sorry, chap," the Englishman said, "but I'm afraid you'll have to find someone else. She's our responsibility now."

Scowling, Macurdy stepped close, pushing his broken nose in the man's startled face. "Look, shit-for-brains, she and I have been working together for months. She may have been born in England, but you people never even heard of her until yesterday. So hear this, and hear it well. The only way you take her with you is to whip my ass first, and you don't have a chance in hell of doing that."

The man didn't flinch, only grimaced, as if he found such language and behavior offensive. "Your superiors shall hear of this," he said stiffly, and turning, stalked away.

They probably will, Macurdy thought ruefully, then turned and grinned at Anna. "Let's you and me go get a mission officer assigned to us right away," he said. "We need to find our *Abwehr* contacts and get them rounded up. Okay?"

She cocked her head at him. "Lieutenant Macurdy, you are a never-ending source of surprises. And yes I think we should." She paused thoughtfully. "Right now you're the only friend I have here, actually. The only friend I have anywhere."

That sobered Macurdy. With Anna in tow, he went to Personnel to see if Vonnie Von Lutzow was around; Vonnie knew the ropes there a lot better than he did.

He was around, now wearing a major's oak leaves on his collar. Macurdy got through to him by feeding a WAC secretary a cock-and-bull story. Von Lutzow had just returned from France again, and had spent the day before at Bushy Park, Eisenhower's new headquarters, reporting to the commander's G-2 on a mission he'd carried out in France. He seemed to have enjoyed his day with the high brass, as if the experience had been invigorating.

Macurdy sketched out his and Anna's situation, and Von Lutzow promised to get back to them that morning if possible, but just then he had a meeting to run to. He left them in his office, ordering his secretary to forget they were there. While waiting, Macurdy asked Anna if she knew anyone or anything that might be useful.

She smiled ruefully. "My spinster aunt Agnes," she said, "a rather dear soul, in her way, but an intransigent fascist." Anna explained that when she'd been a little girl in England, her mother's older sister, Agnes, had been her favorite aunt. Agnes had always been kind to her, and after they'd moved to Germany, their English vacations had been based on Agnes's flat.

When the war began, of course, all that had ended. Agnes had promptly and publicly renounced her fascist loyalties, and denounced those who didn't, including Anna's mother for abandoning England and taking German citizenship. But that had been a cover. Dear Aunt Agnes still did things for the *Abwehr* from time to time, unless she'd been found out since then.

When Anna had finished her story, Macurdy knew what he wanted to try.

When Von Lutzow returned, General Donovan's office had already called him, but he delayed calling back. When Macurdy told him what he had in mind, the major said he'd set it up. Then he took the two into an office whose occupant was on mission, and left them there. An hour later he was back with hastily drafted mission orders for Macurdy, and a temporary appointment for Anna as an agent, described as a German national. Which legally she was. As mission orders went, these were sketchy. They had to be; MI5 had already complained to Donovan's office, insisting that Anna was a British subject accused of treason. They also wanted Macurdy disciplined. Donovan's deputy had agreed to drag his feet, but the general was trying to cool the usual friction with MI5, so it was important that Anna be gotten out of sight.

The mission was risky, Von Lutzow pointed out. The local *Abwehr* apparatus would have known they were expected, and where, because on the night before the landing, the *Abwehr* would have been contacted by the submarine via radio. The message would have been no more than a code word, but when related to a previous and much more detailed message, it would have indicated when they'd land—namely the night after the code word was received—and on which of several candidate beaches.

That much Anna and Macurdy already knew. But now they'd

show up two days late, which by itself was grounds for suspicion. And the *Abwehr*, of necessity, was not only paranoid, but ruthless with those they considered traitors.

On the other hand there were grounds for optimism, Von Lutzow went on. Spy missions were notorious for screwups. The *Abwehr* was well aware of that, expected it, and to some degree allowed for it. And a few days earlier, the *Abwehr* station chief and two of his key people had been picked up by MI5, undoubtedly leaving the local apparatus confused and temporarily leaderless. In fact, it was possible they'd never received the radio signal.

Presumably a new station chief was in place by now, but in an apparatus organized into cells, with restricted communication between cells, a lot of information could have been lost. And Anna could make their connection through Aunt Agnes, who almost certainly wouldn't know when or if a code-word had been received. Nor, presumably, would she have any reason to question Anna's story.

Finally, Anna read minds and Macurdy auras, and Anna would carry a 6.35mm Beretta pistol.

Meanwhile MI5 just might have a tap on her aunt's phone. Anna should keep the possibility in mind when she called.

All in all it didn't look too sticky.

The next morning before daylight, a sergeant drove the two to a village in Essex, where shortly after dawn, Anna dialed her aunt on a public phone. After several rings, a voice answered: "This is Agnes Henderson."

"Aunt Agnes, I realize this is terribly early, and I hope it isn't too great a shock, but I'm your niece, Anna."

"Anna? Really! What a nice surprise to hear from you! How is your dear mother?"

"I'm afraid I haven't seen her for months. I've been away on confidential business, to do with the war effort actually, and been hard to reach. The reason I'm calling is that I'm stranded here in Essex, in East Dunsford, and desperately need transportation to London. For myself and my husband. It's quite urgent, I'm afraid. We have important business to transact there for our employer, and I do hope you can help me."

"I see. Well." Anna could imagine the wheels turning in her Aunt's mind, and wished she could tune in telepathically at distances like that. "Let's see. It is now—6:12. Where can you be picked up?"

"I'm in the lobby of the Dunsford Inn. It's in the center of the village, easily found."

"I won't be able to pick you up myself, my dear, but someone will be along later today. I'm not sure when. How are they to recognize you? I haven't seen you for years, you know."

"I'm still small, which doesn't surprise you, I'm sure. My husband is large—he looks rather like a docker, actually—and limps from a war wound. Both of us are unkempt just now—almost as if we'd spent the night walking about the heath—but we'll take the opportunity to tidy up a bit.

"How may we recognize the person you're sending?"

"I don't know yet who it will be. I need to phone around. But he'll wear—let's see. Something in his cap. A small flag perhaps, or a sprig of something."

She paused. "This call is costing you or your employer money, my dear, so unless there is something else that must be said, I'll hang up."

"No, I think not. It was so nice speaking with you, and so good of you to help. We're registered here as Mr. and Mrs. Monday. And thank you again."

Anna hung up and turned to Macurdy. "And now, Mr. Monday, it is time to register. I hope they have a room with a private bath. I could use one, and then a nap." She lowered her voice. "Can I trust you?"

Macurdy laughed, and answered softly: "Colonel Landgraf trusted me, and you know how that turned out. But yes, you can trust me, and I'll trust you."

Macurdy was still napping when their pickup arrived. Anna had been waiting in the lobby with the *Times*, and leaving the man there, went up to get her "husband."

She wakened him with a shake. "He's here," she said quietly. "Our ride. He's Irish. He even has a sprig of shamrock in his cap! With his connections that's idiotic during wartime! Let's go before he draws attention."

Macurdy got up and put on his sweater, the only outer garment he had. "And remember not to talk," she reminded him. "It's best if he thinks you speak only German—I'm sure the station chief does—but the innkeeper knows you're a Yank."

He'd do better than simply not talk, he decided. Once out of the inn, he'd reinstate fully his persona of Montag the retarded, Montag the handicapped.

In the lobby, the Irishman hardly glanced at him. His aura reflected a low level of curiosity and a simmering discontent. He'd taken the shamrock from his cap though, as if he'd only worn it for Anna's recognition.

Also, he'd brought along a small bag from Alice, with travel odds and ends for Anna. Seemingly she suspected her niece had arrived by submarine, a reasonable supposition.

Despite his dourness, the Irishman drove wisely, observing the speed limits all the way to London. It was dusk when they got there. Macurdy had wondered if they'd be delivered to Agnes, but instead they were taken to a tenement in a working class neighborhood, where their driver led them up two flights of stairs and knocked at an apartment door.

"Who is it?"

Macurdy couldn't identify the accent.

"It's Wicklow, come to ask after my spectacles."

The door was thin; Macurdy could hear someone moving around inside. Then it opened, and a smallish balding man looked out at them questioningly through thick glasses. The Irishman fished a small-folded paper from his watch pocket and handed it to him. The baldheaded man unfolded it and read, then looked up. "Come in. Come in."

"Not I," the Irishman muttered, "I've things to do," then turning, slouched toward the stairs.

Anna stepped inside, Macurdy following, the bald man closing the door behind them. He looked them up and down without speaking, then led them into the kitchen, and after gesturing them to sit, sat down himself. "What language shall we use?" he asked in English.

"Deutsch," Anna answered in German. "You were no doubt given erroneous names for us. I am Anna Hofstetter, and he is Kurt Montag. He speaks only German."

The man's eyebrows arched. "Only German?" he said. "It is strange to send someone here who speaks only German." He turned to Macurdy. "How did you come here? Under the circumstances."

"We came in an *Unterseeboot!*" Macurdy's pride and pleasure sounded childish. "All the way from"—he paused as if groping for the place name—"Saint-Nazaire. That is in France."

Their host's eyebrows had jumped again, not at what Montag had said, but at his dialect. "You are Baltic German!"

"*Jawohl.*"

"It is good to hear *baltisches Deutsch* after so long. Where are you from? East Prussia I think."

Their host proved talkative, soon addressing himself more to Anna than to Montag, because she seemed much the more intelligent. He was an ethnic German from Lithuania, from Memel, where his father had worked in a shipyard, when there was work to be had. Times had been hard. As a child, he himself had gotten involved in the underworld, and later in political issues. "Here," he said, "I pass as a Litvak, a Jew," and chuckled sourly. "I am known as Israel Geltman. At ten I was a runner for a criminal syndicate, and the fences to whom I carried messages were mostly Jews. I got on their good side by learning Yiddish. In Memel were enough Germans, the Yiddish wasn't too different from German anyway."

Then he asked more about Kurt Montag—where he'd grown up, what he'd done. Not primarily out of curiosity; he was examining the two, watching for signs of deceit. Macurdy was considerably protected by his mentally dull persona, and at length Geltman asked, "Fräulein Hofstetter, what is it that Herr Montag does, that he has been sent here?"

"He has certain—abilities, Herr Geltman, which I am not free to talk about, and you are better off not to know. Be content that he is not here to handle cargo on the docks, as he did before he was—discovered."

Geltman looked at Macurdy thoughtfully; he had no idea what she was talking about. "Excuse me, Fräulein. I did not realize . . ."

"Of course. One would not realize. That is another virtue of Herr Montag's: People look at him and do not realize."

She paused. "I presume you will be notifying someone that we are here?"

He nodded and stood up. "Please excuse me. I must make a phone call." He went into his living room, and they could hear him speaking Yiddish on the phone. When he was done, he came back in. "It will be awhile before someone arrives. When did you last eat?"

"At noon."

"Ah. I suppose I must offer you supper." He took boiled potatoes and boiled beef from the icebox, heated them, and put out unleavened bread and margarine. "I eat and live like a real Jew," he said. "Ironic, is it not? I have even been circumcised! But I do not go to the synagogue. Fortunately, it is enough to be a secular Jew. Otherwise I'd have had to spend years learning all their *verdammte* rules." He shrugged, then smiled. "Actually it is not a bad life. I make eyeglasses. Not very many; enough to serve as cover."

When they'd eaten, he took two narrow mattresses from a cupboard. To Macurdy they looked like those on army cots, right down to the blue stripes. "You might as well sleep," Geltman said. "We can't know when you'll be sent for, and I must leave. I have contacts of my own to see to."

Macurdy awoke to dawnlight filtering through sooty unwashed windows. Anna still slept. His watch read 6:14, Greenwich Daylight Time; he wondered when they'd be picked up, or whether someone would come there to examine them. Geltman hadn't returned, so he poked among the man's books. Most were in English, but some were in Hebrew script, Yiddish, Macurdy supposed, and wondered if Geltman could actually read them. If in fact Geltman read any of them; his life history didn't suggest someone who read much. After a while, Macurdy settled on one, a stout volume entitled—*History of England from the Accession of James the Second,* by Thomas Babington Macaulay. He didn't, he realized, know much about English history, so sitting on a sooty windowsill beside the bookcase, he browsed the book for quite a while, returning it to the shelf whenever he heard feet in the hall.

While he browsed, Anna got up and disappeared into the

bathroom, to emerge muttering that the tub wasn't fit for swine. She was poking around the small kitchen when Macurdy heard voices in the corridor and popped the book into its slot again. One of the voices was Geltman's, followed a moment later by a key rattling in the lock. While donning his Montag persona, Macurdy made a mental note to check Macaulay out of the Nehtaka County Library someday. Fritzi would like it too.

Geltman brought with him a long, rawboned man with quick nervous movements and a Cockney accent. Dispensing with introductions, which was understandable, Geltman told his guests they were leaving right away. "To breakfast," he added.

A taxi was parked at the curb. The Cockney got in behind the wheel, Geltman beside him, Anna and Montag in back, and drove off. The two men in front talked the whole trip in Yiddish, which surprised Macurdy: It hadn't occurred to him there were Jewish cockneys. He understood snatches of it from its kinship to German and its sprinkling of English. They were talking about the war, and rationing.

About two miles from Geltman's, the driver let them out. Geltman paid him—presumably the cabby had to account for his gas if not his time—and led them into a Chinese restaurant. It was nearly empty of customers at that hour, and so quiet, it seemed to Macurdy that sound was somehow suppressed there. The Chinese host even walked soundlessly. Geltman asked for a private room, "Just large enough for four or five." Nodding, the Chinese led them to one, smiled, presented them with small, dog-eared menus, and left.

Geltman spoke quietly to Anna in English. "We will meet someone here," he said, then gave his attention to the menu. Shortly a waitress arrived with tea, and following Geltman's lead, Anna and Montag ordered the "Assorted Chinese Favorites." They had no idea whether Geltman was familiar with the plate or not.

Before the food arrived, the man they were waiting for came in, sitting down without asking, his cool gaze appraising Anna and Montag. Macurdy evaded it, while Anna returned it calmly, no doubt reading the man's thoughts. Finally their visitor spoke to her, quietly and in very proper, public school English, with a hint of accent that Macurdy guessed was Scandinavian.

"Are you familiar with Professor Gebhardt? Personally or by reputation?"

"I've never heard of him," Anna replied.

"What of Friedrich Krohn?"

"He's well enough known. He publishes the *Volkischer Beobachter,* or did at one time."

"Anything else?"

"Not insofar as I'm aware."

"Colonel Sanne?"

"I'm not free to speak of Colonel Sanne; I was assigned elsewhere, previous to my present activity."

The man paused to digest that for a few seconds. "And what of *Aktion Hess*?"

She snorted, as if impatient with the questions. "Many people knew of that, though most not by name. It was talked about openly where I was previously assigned."

Her answers opened Macurdy's eyes; Anna was more than simply a psychic recruited for the Voitik Project. He began to see why MI5, and perhaps more, the SIS would be interested in her.

The visitor nodded as if satisfied, and stood up. "Thank you for an interesting conversation, Miss Hofstetter," he said, and nodding, left.

Macurdy would have liked to ask her questions of his own, but there sat Geltman, so they simply waited till their meal was brought to them. Then they ate and left.

A different cab sat at the curb, its flag down. When the driver saw them come out, he reached over and raised it. "Cab!" Geltman called, and the driver, getting out, opened the back. They climbed in, and a moment later the driver pulled away from the curb without asking their destination or being given one. Geltman said nothing; obviously their transportation had been prearranged, perhaps with the help of the Yiddish-speaking Cockney or Anna's Scandinavian questioner.

For several minutes the cabby followed a seemingly random course, as if watching for a possible tail, then drove west for a mile or more toward the city's heart, as always passing through or around bomb-shattered blocks and burned-out neighborhoods, the damage put to order, but awaiting less demanding times to be rebuilt.

Turning north, they entered a residential district and stopped in front of a flat, then went to the entrance, where the driver, not Geltman, pressed one of the buttons by the door. A round speaker grid sounded, the voice electronic, female, and British.

"Who is it?"

"Miss Henderson," the driver said, an obvious reference to Aunt Agnes. If there'd been any doubt before, Macurdy told himself, this killed it: Theirs was not an ordinary cabby.

"Just a moment. Someone will be down."

They waited. In perhaps two minutes the door was opened by an oriental male. This one had curly hair: part Chinese and part something else. The man also reminded him a bit of Roy Klaplanahoo—shorter, perhaps five feet nine, and even burlier, but giving a similar sense of physical strength.

The eyes were different though—slanted, hooded, suspicious. "Come in," he said after a moment, his voice surly. Macurdy found himself surprised the man had actually spoken. Geltman and the cabby stayed behind, no doubt to leave in the cab, and Anna and Montag followed the oriental up flights of stairs, through the smell of old carpet, mildew and disinfectant, to the third floor flat, where he let them into a small foyer, then a sitting room. There they were met by an attractive young woman with wire-rimmed glasses.

"You are Anna Hofstetter?" she asked.

"I am. Though the cabby announced me as Miss Henderson."

The woman ignored the comment, and did not give her own name. Without looking at him she asked, "I take it then that this is Mr. Monday."

"That's right."

"When did you arrive?"

Macurdy's guts grabbed. This was a moment of threat.

"I might better ask why you didn't," Anna replied. "We were put ashore three nights back, and spent several hours freezing on the beach while we waited. When dawn came and your people hadn't, we walked to a road, caught a ride, took a room and slept."

She paused, staring critically at her questioner. "The next

night we walked back to the beach, which was not an easy task for Mr. Monday, with his war wounds. Hopefully you can appreciate the risk, going about like that so near the coast, with Mr. Monday speaking only German! No one came that night, either, so we returned to East Dunsford and called my Aunt. We'd have been quite stranded if it weren't for her."

The young woman had stiffened. "You must recognize the strain on operations here," she countered. "Captain Streicher and two others were arrested last Wednesday, and operations were totally disrupted. We'd expected you some time, but didn't know on what night. We never received the signal."

Anna nodded. "Quite understandable. And I suppose one never knows if the—transportation—will get through the naval and aerial patrols."

"Of course."

It felt to Macurdy as if the two women had worked out a needed basis of mutual respect. For a moment he'd been prepared to cast a shock wave at the Oriental, if there were trouble. For at that moment he realized what had been missing in his lessons at the schloss: To cast an emotion effectively, he, at least, needed to *feel* emotion.

"You've eaten, I presume," the woman said.

"Within the hour. After your Scandinavian questioned us."

"Well then. You'll have another bit of a wait, but it shouldn't be extreme. Meanwhile I've work to do." She gestured at the oriental. "Bahn will look after you. You'll find magazines and newspapers. Don't believe the news from the war fronts. It's all lies."

"Naturally."

The woman turned away, then paused and looked back. "By the way," she said, "my name is Alice," then left the room.

Anna caught Macurdy's displeasure at the prospect of sitting around for an indeterminate time with nothing he could safely do, so she translated aloud to him from the paper, from articles on the war. Pausing several times to repeat in German, "You see now, Kurt, why it is so important to the Fatherland that you are here. When it is all over, you will be a very great hero."

The wait was shorter than he'd expected. The buzzer sounded three short blasts in rapid succession, startlingly loud and harsh.

There'd been no call from the front entrance—this was someone with access to the building—but Bahn got quickly to his feet, stepped to the door, and opened it.

The new station chief stepped inside and spoke in pure American English. "Hello, Bahn. Have we had visitors yet?" Stepping into view, he looked toward Anna and Montag, and Macurdy's blood froze. He made a flash self-review: His hair had been lank then, now it was bur-cut. And he'd known no German.

Anna was getting to her feet. Slowly, clumsily, Montag followed suit, standing round-shouldered, gaze fixed on the floor, looking as small as he could, *creating* an image of a different him, while opening his mind to Anna.

The man switched to German. "Ah! Fräulein Hofstetter I presume. And this must be Herr Montag." Abruptly he stiffened, and his right hand shot out in the Nazi salute. *"Heil Hitler!"* he barked, but not too loudly, then relaxed and smiled. "You will excuse my slowness in greeting you properly. It is a practice I've had to repress since I've been here."

He stepped toward them and shook first Anna's hand, then Montag's, showing no suspicion. Macurdy had regained his composure, but did not relax his exaggerated Montag persona. Apparently since they'd passed the preliminary vetting by the Irishman, Geltman, and the Swede or whatever he was, Hansi was accepting them at face value.

"I am Oberleutnant Hans Dietrich Schweiger, and as you have realized, I am the station chief here. I am also known as John Sweiger, of Portland, Oregon, USA. I report on the war for the Associated Press, and on occasion have spoken to the American public via NBC radio." He smiled wryly. "Journalists are the only contact Americans have with what, to Europeans and the English, are the realities of war."

He examined Montag more closely now, looking not for falsenesses, but at a claim he found hard to accept, even from Berlin—that this creature, this refugee from the eugenics authorities, was an actual, functioning psychic who could cast confusion and panic through SHAEF, and disrupt the invasion.

Or had the eugenicists already had him? The fellow certainly seemed cowed; he could almost smell his timidity. He'd heard rumors that thousands of the feeble-minded had been sterilized, and assumed it meant castration.

"Well," he said, "we have work to do, you and I. Fräulein Hofstetter, if you and Herr Montag will come with me to my office . . ." He turned and led them down a hall to the study: a fairly large room with a desk, file cabinets, supply cabinets, work table, and a gas fireplace. "I'm afraid I'm not fully operational here yet," he told them, "though Fräulein Gwynne has made major headway. We've had to move some of my things out to make room, and assemble, move in and organize a good deal of material for my new responsibilities. All having to be done very carefully, you understand. I have also been obtaining the materials which Herr Montag must have to carry out his mission here. And of course, I must continue my duties as a journalist, which not only provide my cover identity, but provide important contacts and information."

From the supply cabinet he took a map tube and laid it on the work table, then from a file cabinet, several large envelopes, meanwhile continuing to talk. "I've arranged locations from which Herr Montag can see both the Bushy Park headquarters and Norfolk House. I have even—" he paused to flash a grin at them "—have even obtained floor plans of both buildings, marked with the departments assigned to different areas.

"There may be difficulty getting near enough to recognize individual personnel, but perhaps we can work around that." From one envelope he took photo prints of uniformed men. "Here are enlarged photos of all the major ones: Eisenhower, Tedder, Montgomery, Smith, Leigh-Mallory . . . all of them. The names are on the bottom. And here are photos of some of the lesser fish, with their names and what they do. Can he work from photos?"

"I don't know that he's ever tried," Anna said. "And I must tell you, being in a strange country has affected him. He has always been shy; now he's become somewhat depressed. He will be happier when he has things to do. In training he was sometimes like a happy child."

She paused, frowning thoughtfully. "Do you have a photo of someone we can test him on? They'd need to be in a building he can see—in a known part of the building—and we'd need some way of knowing whether he's had an effect or not. We should look into that before we go further."

Hansi nodded. "I believe you are right. But first we should eat."

He took them back into the sitting room, where Bahn was already fixing lunch. They had open-faced sandwiches with cheese paste, a kind of fish Macurdy wasn't familiar with, potato, rice pudding, and tea—not a lot of any of it. Macurdy decided that in countries where civilian rationing was tight, he'd been fortunate in eating military meals.

After lunch, Hansi showed Anna and Montag a picture of a man, obese and middle-aged. After having Montag study it, he took them by cab to a small park not far away, where he pointed out a building across the street and down half a block. Speaking English, he directed Anna's attention to a 3rd-floor window. "That's his office. He's probably there right now. I know him well, and his secretary even better. He's an underworld associate of mine, a barrister who sometimes provides me with useful connections. Have Mr. Monday give it a try, then I'll drop in on him."

In an undertone, Anna briefed Montag as if he'd understood none of it, then showed him the man's picture again. "I want you to frighten this man, Kurt. Frighten him very badly."

Macurdy stared at the picture, then at the window, then closed his eyes. After two or three minutes, he nodded without speaking. Hansi crossed the street and walked briskly down the block to the building. Some minutes later they saw him returning; as he approached, he looked almost gleeful.

"It worked!" he said in English, and clapped Montag on the shoulder. "I asked to see him, and when his secretary buzzed, he didn't answer. She hesitated before she went to his door, as if she'd heard something peculiar. When she looked in, she backed away for a moment before stepping inside and closing the door.

When she came out, she was pale as a ghost, and said he couldn't see me just then. I pretended to be upset. 'When did Chas start giving me the cold shoulder?' I asked her. 'We're supposed to be buddies!' She told me he was sick, and to 'please go now.'

"So I left, but stopped outside the door and listened. I could hear her on the phone, urgent and upset—something about a doctor."

Hansi turned again to Montag, shook his hand, and congratulated him softly in German. "You did well! If *der Führer* were here, he'd shake your hand himself!"

Montag's lips moved as if mumbling silently, never looking at Hansi's face.

Hansi shook Anna's hand too, and spoke in English again: "I admit I had my doubts, but he did it, and without you, he'd never have gotten here. This mission will be a major coup, I'm sure of it, and you're as vital to it as he is. You are a remarkable woman!"

While Hansi was speaking to Anna, Macurdy had looked up, and what he saw startled him—Hansi's aura reflected a sexual intention toward her. He found himself offended by it.

Hansi took them back to his apartment then. He had arrangements to make, he said. Meanwhile they would sleep in his spare bedroom. Then he left, and to kill time for both of them, Anna read to Montag again.

Bahn prepared much the same meal for tea and supper as for lunch, leaving Macurdy wondering whether it was his larder or his skills that were limited. Hansi returned late and said little, as if preoccupied, and disappeared into the room he shared with Alice Gwynne. By then Anna had tired of reading aloud, and there being little else to do, she and Macurdy went to their room and also got ready for bed. From Bahn, Anna had gotten a pallet, sheets, and blanket for Montag. As usual, he would sleep in his underwear, which now at least were clean, while Anna had a nightgown sent by Alice.

She had turned on a tiny night light, installed because of the blackout curtains, turned off the table lamp and sat down on one of the two chairs. Macurdy took the other, and they talked quietly. In German; if anyone was listening at the door, they wouldn't catch words, but they'd probably recognize the language. Anna asked what Macurdy had beamed to his test target, and grimaced when he told her: an image of the man's face, an image that would not be banished, with worms coming first from the nostrils, then the mouth, then the eyes.

Then she told what she'd learned with her telepathy. Some he'd observed for himself, in demeanors and auras: Bahn had changed from hostile—probably his normal state in new situations—to bored and indifferent. Alice Gwynne had changed from suspicious to friendly. And Hansi had designs on Anna's body. He was no longer an uncertain adolescent; now he considered any attractive female a sexual target.

"Despite sleeping with Alice Gwynne," Anna added, somewhat bemused. "And Alice is exceptionally attractive, wouldn't you say?" She paused. "Of course, Lieutenant Schweiger is, too. They make a handsome couple."

Macurdy said nothing. Hansi had been a good-looking kid, but gawky. Maturity had filled him out, and increased his self-esteem. And his sexual ambitions.

"When do we notify Grosvenor Square?" Anna asked. "Schweiger intends to keep us here, keep close control of us. He's afraid we will do something foolish. Also, something may happen that he will recognize you."

For a moment, Macurdy didn't answer. There was still another consideration, more important than rounding up this Abwehr ring, and time was limited.

"Does he know the invasion date?"

"He was thinking about that on our way back from your little demonstration. There had been a specific target date—May 1st—but it was abandoned some time ago. Now they expect it at the beginning of June. Apparently it requires moonlight. And the Allies are bound to worry about dangerous information leaking, so they'll want to move at the earliest date possible."

Macurdy couldn't help remembering the snafus in Algeria and on Sicily. Both had turned out all right—the Sicilian drops had been remarkably effective despite everything that had gone wrong—but this was so much bigger! So much was riding on it! So many lives would be invested!

"We'll act as soon as possible," he said.

"Good." Anna yawned. "Goodnight, Kurt. I'm going to bed."

He watched as she stepped to the bed, lay down and pulled the cover over her, then he lay down on his pallet across the room. Hansi considered Anna sexually desirable, he thought, and he was right. She was not actually pretty, but her features were pleasant. Attractive. And despite Berta's appraisal, she was not scrawny, just small. Wiry perhaps. Wiry might be exciting in bed.

From across the room, Anna spoke in an undertone. "Kurt?"

"*Ja?*"

"Come and sit by me. I have things to tell you."

With a sense of unease, he went to her bed and sat on the edge. She sat up, holding the covers to her shoulders. Her aura told him she was sexually aroused.

"We are a strange pair," she murmured. "I read minds, or in your case moods, and you read auras. We do not easily keep secrets from one another."

He nodded, saying nothing, recalling how neither of them had discerned the other's intention to turn themselves in.

"I have not had much affection in my life," she went on, "particularly in recent years. I have had to be very watchful, very guarded, avoid friendships. At times I have been horribly lonely." Her voice dropped to a whisper. In English. "Curtis, I want you to hold me. Make love to me."

He stared at her in the darkness, feeling both dismay and desire.

"Your conscience is troubling you."

"Yes."

"If your Mary knew the situation we're in, would she feel deeply aggrieved if . . . ?"

He knew the answer to that: She'd feel hurt, if she knew, but she'd also understand and forgive; before too long it would be almost forgotten. But would that excuse him?

He tried to make out Anna's features in the dark. "Have you ever had a man?" he murmured.

Anna chuckled softly. "A man? When I was fourteen, there was my cousin Steffan, who probably weighed forty-five kilos. He was also fourteen, and had been seduced by a woman. His parents had a summer place in Pommern, on the Baltic coast, and that July we went there with them, Papa and Mama and I. On the second day, Steffan asked me to hike in the forest with him. I knew what he wanted of course, but it sounded exciting, so I went."

She chuckled again. "In fact, we took walks in the woods each day for three days. Then our parents became suspicious. They didn't accuse us of anything, but Papa and Mama and I went home early." She sighed theatrically. "But have I had a man? No. Only a boy." She giggled then. "Though I'm lucky I didn't get pregnant."

She slipped a hand inside Macurdy's shorts then, and for a moment froze. "My God, Curtis," she whispered. He turned and threw back the covers. She was naked, had pulled off her gown beneath it before she'd called him over.

And suddenly Anna was unsure. "I don't want you to feel guilty," she murmured.

He didn't answer. He'd feel guilty all right; he knew it. But he would also make love to her. As he took off his shorts, she lay back, and crouching on the bed, he began kissing her.

After each had used the bathroom, Macurdy lay down on his pallet. Anna already lay curled in bed awaiting sleep. Where, he asked himself, was the strength of will he'd shown when he'd been married to Varia, and Melody had tried repeatedly to seduce him over the months? With Berta he'd been able to rationalize, and with Rillissa he'd had little choice, but he could easily have said no to Anna, and she wouldn't have been upset with him. She'd even offered him grounds for refusing. Guilt. He felt enough of that, for sure.

So what now, Macurdy? he asked himself. What about tomorrow night? And the next? Another reason to complete this mission quickly. What were the benefits of delay? At best a few more underlings reeled in.

Abruptly he sat up. *Call headquarters now,* he told himself. *Use the phone here. If anyone tries to stop you, kill them.*

Then answered, *easier said than done.* To support his Montag role, he'd deliberately brought nothing more than a pocket knife, in case they were searched. He could, of course, take Anna's Beretta, if it came down to it. Pulling on shorts and trousers, he cloaked himself, then slipped barefoot into the hallway and down it to the living room. The phone table was by the day bed, where Bahn lay sleeping in flowered pajamas, the phone twenty inches from his head. Macurdy turned back down the hall to Hansi's office, where he'd seen another.

By light from the hallway, he found the office light switch, turned it on, closed the door softly, and stepped to the desk. There by the phone was a thick file folder titled *Operation Overlord (3)*. Was Operation Overlord the code name for the invasion? Reaching, he picked up the folder instead of the phone.

He'd hardly looked inside it when the door opened and Hansi peered in, Luger in hand, frowning uncertainly, not seeing through the cloak. Macurdy froze—and the folder tilted, papers spilling onto floor and desk. Hansi's eyes widened.

"Montag!" he hissed. "What is this? You're a damned spy!"

"*Ja, für Reichsführer Himmler!* There are reports you've been turned, that you gave away Captain Streicher."

"You lie. Who would . . ." Hansi stopped in mid-sentence. "I know you!"

"That's right." Macurdy straightened, speaking American. "I'm the man who saved your life at Severtson's camp. The friend who took you and your suitcase to the depot when you left Nehtaka."

Hansi stared without speaking, confused by the mixture of coincidences, and by Macurdy seeming to materialize before his eyes. Suddenly his pistol was too hot to hold, and reflexively he flung it from him with a loud cry. Macurdy pounced, striking him powerfully in the forehead with the heel of his hand, and letting him fall, went for the gun. Aware of heavy running in the hallway, he snatched it from the floor—to him it wasn't hot—then jumped behind the metal desk. A gun fired multiple slugs into the file cabinet, desk, wall, and Macurdy popped up to fire the heavy Luger once. Bahn, crouched in the doorway, rose almost upright, then toppled, and behind him a woman screamed. Macurdy scrambled, dove, slid on the waxed oak floor to the open door, on his side, gun ready. Alice Gwynne stood wild-eyed in the hallway, a pistol in her hand. He fired at her leg, and she fell heavily, grabbing it with both hands, screaming again.

Anna, Beretta in hand, was peering out the bedroom door, then scampered naked into the hall and picked up Alice's gun.

"That's all of them," Macurdy said to her, and getting up, stepped to the phone. *Probably everyone else in the building is headed for the phone too,* he thought. With one eye on the unconscious station chief, he dialed the confidential OSS number. "Hansi," he murmured while he listened to the phone ring on the other end, "I'm really sorry it came to this. But goddamn it, your dad was right."

PART FOUR
The Spoiler

32

A Captive for the General

The OSS duty officer got Von Lutzow on the line within a minute or so. Von Lutzow said he'd have a team on the way within ten minutes. He didn't notify MI5—British counter-espionage—till after his own people were well on their way.

The bobbies arrived well before any of them, of course—soon after Macurdy was off the phone. Anna answered the door. By then she'd dressed; even had her shoes on. Macurdy had tied Hansi's wrists and ankles with electric cord, and begun to work on Alice Gwynne's thigh wound. He told the bobbies a team from MI5 was on its way; actually they weren't, but they soon would be. As additional police arrived, they cordoned off the place, and after a few perfunctory questions, left him and Anna alone. Their functions did not include interfering with intelligence agencies.

Nonetheless, when the OSS team pulled up in front, led by Von Lutzow, the police lieutenant in charge wouldn't let them enter the building till MI5 arrived. That was fine with Von Lutzow; he'd just wanted to arrive first, to cover Anna, and of course Macurdy. When MI5 got there, they were welcome to Hansi and Alice, the corpse of Bahn, and everything they might find in the flat. Then, in the care of Von Lutzow, and with another lieutenant from MI5, Macurdy and Anna rode off in an army staff car for middle of the night debriefs. The custody of Anna was never brought up; probably the lieutenant didn't know his office wanted her. And with copies of the debriefs in hand, they had little grounds for demanding she be turned over to them. She was, after all, on the OSS payroll.

With the debrief finally over, Macurdy went to bed and slept till after midday. The duty officer had him wakened in time for lunch, and to shower and shave for an interview with "the general."

Macurdy had never seen Wild Bill Donovan, who was gone a lot, but during training he'd heard stories about him, some no doubt apocryphal. They'd included World War One exploits and the Medal of Honor; he'd been a regimental commander noted for his boldness. Overall, Macurdy had gotten an image of a short, stocky, charismatic dynamo who could absorb a book in an hour and discuss it in detail, who believed in exercising his creative imagination and enthusiasm, and letting his people exercise theirs. Within limits, of course, but the limits were broad. He also had a large tolerance of eccentricity.

He recruited men on the basis of their self-confidence, a degree of daring, and established skill in some demanding and relevant area, even if only athletic. Usually they brought with them a competence in one or more useful foreign languages. Then they were thoroughly trained, and within their mission orders, given a large degree of operating independence. Some lacked judgment, some accountability, and more than a few humility, but as a covert operations organization, the OSS was a good outfit.

And Donovan was its father, its founding genius.

So Macurdy looked forward to the interview. He had no real notion of what it would be like, or what Donovan would want him to do, but he knew exactly what he intended to ask for and get.

The commander stood up when Macurdy entered, and shook his hand. His white hair was parted just off center and crookedly, as if he hadn't used a mirror, and he was older than Macurdy had expected. But at age 61, his blue eyes were sharp, his grin genuine, and his aura reflected a rare combination of aggressiveness and patience.

"I just read your debriefs," he said. "Last night's, and the earlier one on the Voitik Project. Major Von Lutzow is very strong on you, thinks you're better than Wheaties. I also read his report on your airborne history. Remarkable! Remarkable! I wanted to know you myself before we assign you anything further."

Even given the general's reputation as a reader, Macurdy wondered when the man had found time for all that. The debriefs were thick, and the latest, he suspected, were still only handwritten.

"And you knew Oberleutnant Schweiger as a boy! Makes one believe in destiny! You recommended leniency for him. Why? He'd been made welcome in America, then turned on her. And against family pressure, you said."

"He was a good kid," Macurdy answered, "but didn't know much. And I saved his life earlier that year, so I feel kind of responsible for him."

Donovan didn't look convinced, but he dropped the matter. "What do you recommend we do with Anna Hofstetter?" he asked.

"She's a functioning telepath," Macurdy answered, "and they're supposed to be really rare; at least those who can do it at will. She's also smart, experienced, knows German and the Germans, including the SS, and hates the Nazis. She'd be valuable as hell in an outfit like this, especially in internal security. Especially if people don't know what she can do."

Lips pursed, Donovan let his gaze slide away in thought, then returned it to Macurdy. "The debrief of your *Weutische* mission includes things some people find hard to believe. How would you answer them?"

"I'd offer to light their cigarette," Macurdy answered wryly. "Or—would you turn around a minute and look at the bookcase behind you? There's something I didn't include in either debrief. Something that can make the rest of it more believable."

Donovan's black eyebrows raised, but without speaking, he turned away. Macurdy cloaked himself, moved quietly several steps toward one side of the room, and waited.

"Are you ready?" Donovan asked. Macurdy didn't answer. The general turned back, saw nothing, and frowned, then stood up again as if Macurdy might be crouching out of sight against the desk. Still seeing nothing, Donovan stepped around it.

"Right here," Macurdy said, and dropped the cloak. He was

only four feet from the general, who took a quick step back. "I can make myself hard to see," Macurdy said. "It's one of quite a few things my first wife taught me."

Donovan peered intently at him, then sat down. "You're right. That does make things more believable. Not all of them, but some." He paused. "You said in your *Weutische* debrief that you regard the mission as incomplete. What would you recommend to complete it?"

"Drop me on some cow pasture near the schloss. At night. I need to destroy it, the aliens at least, and the gate if I can."

Donovan frowned. "You just put your finger on some of the things I find difficult to accept: the gate, the world on the other side, and what you say their threat is to the invasion. I can't go to SHAEF and tell them they need to watch out for monsters set loose by sorcerers from another world. I can't even recommend something to do about it!"

"The solution is to destroy the ones on this side, and close the gate to more."

The general looked troubled. He'd suddenly remembered a report he'd seen that morning, that fitted nicely with Macurdy's debrief: An English lawyer and suspected German agent, Wesley Perham, had died of a heart attack the day before, in his office across from Tenley Park.

"What would you think of having the schloss bombed?" he asked. "Wouldn't that take care of it? With no harder evidence than I have, I can't get a squadron of 17s for a target like that, but I can get a flight of Mitchells with 500 pounders. I can't talk about sorcerers from another world, but I can come up with something acceptable to Bomber Command."

Macurdy shook his head. "It's too uncertain. The walls are thick, big stone blocks. They might make a wreck of it, but they'd need to put at least a couple of bombs right through the roof into more or less the right places. There are two rooms of TNT stored in the basement—that's in my debrief—but they wouldn't likely blow, much short of taking a direct hit.

"But I could blow them." Tension had tightened Macurdy's chest, his guts; this was really important to him. "I can blow them, and I can probably shut the gate. For good. To keep any more of them from getting through."

He changed tack. "If you think there's one chance in 50 that I'm right and they're real, it ought to be worth it to invest one man in the mission."

The general blew through pursed lips. "I'll tell you what, lieutenant. Bring me one of those aliens. I'll land you on the lake at night with half a dozen good men and a rubber raft. You grab one of the aliens, get him to the plane, and fly him to Naples, where we can examine him. You can even do the interrogating. The whole thing can be over with ten days from today." He paused, his eyes challenging. "What do you say?"

Despite himself, Macurdy grinned. "If I can do it my way."

"What way is that?"

"Alone. Plus a pilot. Because stealth is the key. But if I get you one, I want authority to go back and blow the schloss. And the gate."

Donovan stared at him. This was a compelling man, but his story was strange! Strange! Also, it seemed to Donovan that Macurdy wasn't being entirely candid. He still looked troubled when he stood up and shook Macurdy's hand. "Young man," he said, "you've got a deal. If you keep your half, I'll keep mine. But don't talk about it to anyone except Major Von Lutzow. He'll be your mission officer again. He believes in you, and you've worked well together."

Macurdy's only moderately fictitious plan required making the flight on consecutive nights—the first to land him on the lake, the second to pick him up. The general signed it approved.

His pilot was a character out of *Blue Book* magazine: a burly, mustachioed, heavily tattooed man named MacNab, who looked part oriental and liked to wear kilts. The word was, he was a quarter Samoan, a quarter Chinese, and half Scot, and had learned French as a boy in Samoa. It was Von Lutzow who'd tabbed him for the mission. He claimed the man could fly a garbage truck, had the right mixture of caution and fearlessness, and was the best night navigator in the OSS, giving examples from missions over southern France.

With information from the Air Force's meteorological office at Norfolk House, Macurdy scheduled their departure a couple of days later than he might have, to take advantage of the moon.

On the night selected, it would cross the meridian of the schloss at 1:02, and on the next at 1:56, which was important to the part of the mission plan he was keeping to himself: gating into Hithmearc to get his captive. To take one from the schloss would be much harder, and alarming both the SS and the crown prince, would make his followup mission almost impossible.

Also important, it was near the end of April, and the nights were getting short. It would only be fully night for about six hours at the schloss, and a route was necessary that avoided Axis airspace by day, while limiting exposure to German air defenses.

On the night of their flight, MacNab wore not kilt but a coverall, while Macurdy wore a paratrooper's jumpsuit. They took off from Naples at dusk, in a light flying boat: a twin-engined, three-seat Grumman Widgeon. They would cross the boot of Italy, and avoid German-held territory as long as possible by flying northwestward up the Adriatic for more than two hours. This left a hop of less than an hour and a half across Veneto and the Italo-Austrian Alps to land on *der Kiefersee,* the pilot gliding in the last few miles with reduced power.

Macurdy's experiences with long flights over water had left him apprehensive about coming down on target. MacNab, on the other hand, took it all casually, and Macurdy kept his concern to himself.

MacNab found *der Kiefersee* without difficulty. After deliberately bypassing it three miles to the west, he made their approach from the north, gliding lengthwise over the long narrow lake. After landing, they taxied a short distance almost to the heavily shadowed west shore. There Macurdy dropped the anchor in water surprisingly deep, and helped MacNab refuel the overhead gas tanks from 4-gallon jerry cans. Then, after inflating his small rubber boat from the attached CO_2 bottle, he paddled to shore, where he deflated it, then carried it and the paddle back into the woods. There, by a jutting rock outcrop that marked the place, he hid them in a patch of fir saplings.

From there he hiked around the end, traveling light, his only weapons a Fairbairn knife and his .45 caliber Colt automatic. An incendiary device, a pair of handcuffs, and some nylon suspension cord rode in appropriate pockets.

Shortly he came to the four-wheel-drive road and started up the Witches' Ridge. He might have hurried, but the forest was too dark for jogging, even with the nearly full moon. He was having second thoughts now: It would be far easier to ignore his agreement with the general—sneak into the schloss, hole up in the cellar, and blow up the building. He knew what he was up against there, or thought he did, and had already worked out how to pull it off. This capture mission, on the other hand, was full of unknowns. But a deal was a deal.

The gate hadn't opened yet. He couldn't be sure, of course, that it would, but if it remained on the schedule it had followed after that night of Voitik sorcery, it would open within—he looked at his phosphorescent watch face—within twenty minutes.

He'd nearly reached the crest when he felt the gate activate. If it stayed open as long as it had before, he had more than enough time. On the top he could feel it tug at him, and there, where the trees were more sparse, the moonlight let him trot, feeling the pull more and more strongly. Abruptly he experienced the now familiar indigo darkness, the bass resonance as much felt as heard—and tumbled sprawling into straw. He was in Hithmearc, in the gatehouse.

Scrambling to his feet, he crouched, drew his Fairbairn knife, and looked around. Here it was early afternoon. No one had been expected; no one was there waiting. Hopefully someone was around, but for now . . .

The only exit faced the hostel, so he sat down next to the doorway, back to the wall, and resheathed his knife. If necessary he'd wait till evening, he decided, before snooping around. His cloak had collapsed in transit—he could feel the difference—and he left it deactivated.

Three minutes later he heard footfalls, as someone stepped in no more than five feet from him—a uniformed, spear-carrying Voitu who failed to see him. Macurdy let him get well inside, then spoke in German: *"Guten Tag, mein Herr."*

The man left the floor with both feet, spinning, and came down with spear at the ready.

"Who are you?" The German words came robotically and ill pronounced—drawn undrilled from the hive mind.

Macurdy answered slowly, distinctly. "I am Lieutenant Montag. I do not know how I came here."

The Voitu stared, slowly relaxing, and after a moment raised the spear to a casual port arms. "You not expected."

"I did not expect to be here. Where am I?"

"You in Hithmearc. I take to corporal. He know what to do."

A corporal in charge? That meant only a handful of Voitar, half a dozen at most, plus human servants. Macurdy got to his feet and deliberately staggered, almost fell. "I feel sick," he said. "I have already puked."

The Voitu said nothing, and Macurdy straightened a bit. He looked at the possibility of jumping him then and there—this one would serve the general's needs as well as any—but the Voitu was armed and suspicious, and having him on the other side through an entire day? Kurqôsz and his people would surely pick up his presence.

Scowling, the Voitu jabbed the air with the spear, a gesture with more than a hint of threat. "You come with me now," he said.

"Of course." Macurdy turned and stepped out the door. He twitched all the way to the hostel, remembering the wounds he'd received the last time he'd been herded from a gate by a man with a spear, fourteen years earlier. That, he told himself, had worked out well enough in the long run, but this had to work out in the short.

He'd been right about the number; there were a corporal and four privates. The domestic staff of five humans was enough to serve if a group came through from the other side. Macurdy hoped devoutly that it wouldn't happen.

The corporal's name was Trosza, and he spoke German much better than the spearman. Macurdy talked him into letting him spend the night and return the next day, meanwhile asking questions. At first about the Voitusotar, and what it was like to be a Voitik soldier. By supper they were on relaxed and congenial terms.

He slept till late morning, but that was no problem. He

had till afternoon, sleeping had killed time, and he'd been hit by what in later years would be known as jet lag. After lunch he talked with the corporal again, until they felt the gate activate.

"It is time," the corporal said.

"Yes, I suppose we should leave soon. Perhaps I could have one more cup of your tea. We have nothing like it where I come from. It is very good."

He lingered over the refill, talking, deliberately using up time. The gate always remained open for close to an hour, and he didn't want to be followed. While they finished their tea, Macurdy slipped an object from a thigh pocket and pressed it against the underside of the table, where it stuck. About midnight, if the device worked on this side, it would flash into dripping flame, and hopefully burn the place to the ground. Perhaps even killing any eye witnesses to his being there. At least it would fix their minds on something else.

Finally he and the corporal went to the gatehouse. By the time they reached its doorway, they felt the repulsion quite distinctly, the reverse of the attraction on the other side.

"I will stop here," said Trosza. "I wish you well."

I wish you well! Macurdy had a job to do, but the Voitu's words would trouble him afterward. He reached as if to shake Trosza's hand, a civility the Voitusotar shared with humans. When they clasped, Macurdy pivoted abruptly away, pulling sharply on the hand, bending, kicking backward and upward, all in a fraction of a second. The pull half turned the startled Voitu, the kick striking him below the right ribs, compressing the abdomen, and though Macurdy didn't know it, tearing the liver. In someone shorter, it would have broken ribs, collapsed a lung, perhaps resulted in heart spasm.

Trosza blacked out instantly, and Macurdy, hoping no one had seen, dragged him by the ankles into the gatehouse. If he was pursued, his .45 would be operable on the other side, but Macurdy wanted to avoid attention on either side.

As before, he had to lean and push against the gate's repulsion, but within half a minute experienced the utter blackness, the utter silence, the sense of absolute nothingness of the return transit. Then, knees buckling, he dropped on the crest of the Witches' Ridge, the unconscious Trosza behind him.

✧ ✧ ✧

After handcuffing his captive and tying his ankles, Macurdy struggled the ungainly burden across his shoulders and started down the road. The Voitu was slender, but at nearly seven feet, he weighed at least two hundred pounds. Still it was downhill, and Trosza remained unconscious, which so far as Macurdy knew, meant that any wakeful Voitu in the schloss wouldn't pick up via the hive mind that he'd been captured. If necessary he could kill him; judging by his aura, he was badly hurt already. A Voitik corpse would establish their reality for Donovan, but the general wanted him questioned. A live Trosza could verify from the hive mind what the threat was.

A live Trosza. But if Voitar could die of seasickness, might they also die of airsickness?

He could make out the plane in the deep shadow of lakeside forest, and lay the unconscious Trosza on the shore nearby. From the Voitu's aura, it was clear now that he had serious internal damage. Silently, Macurdy cursed the force of his kick. After getting the raft and inflating it, he loaded his captive, then paddled the dozen or so yards to the plane, where a curious MacNab helped him fold the Voitu inside. The pilot had worn his kilt this time.

"Long skinny son of a bitch," he commented.

"Got a flashlight?"

"Sure." MacNab took one from a compartment and turned it on the Voitu's face. "Jesus Christ! Look at those goddamn ears! They all look like that?"

"Yep. Really tall, really slim, red-headed, and ears like a goat."

"How'd you get him?"

"Trickery and a close-combat move."

"Huh! Did he carry a gun?"

"A spear and a sword. I left them there."

MacNab put the flashlight away, shaking his head. Macurdy's replies had posed more questions than they'd answered. "We've got a complication," he said, as if in passing.

"What's that?"

"Fuel. Some flak batteries fired at me when I crossed the coast near Venice. Took a hole in one of the wing tanks. Lost the gas it still had in it, and it won't hold any now. And the other one won't hold enough to get us to Naples."

Hell, Macurdy thought, *I didn't need that.* "How is this crate for crash landing on dry ground?"

"Good, if we could stay in the air long enough to reach allied territory. But I can guarantee we won't."

"Can't we land on the water when we run low, and refuel the other tank with what's left in the cans?"

"Maybe; I've got my fingers crossed. But it's windy down there, and the forecast's for more of it. The chop will make it tricky at best."

MacNab climbed atop the wing, Macurdy handing the cans up to him, and refilled the other tank, then taxied to mid-lake and took off. *Well,* Macurdy thought, *at least I've got a pilot who knows how to navigate.* Meanwhile he hoped earnestly that the weather down south would ease off.

After take-off, Macurdy spent about half an hour working on the energy threads in Trosza's aura. They responded, but the results held only briefly. Within seconds they "unraveled," so to speak, lapsing into chaos. He hoped that bit by bit he'd get them to hold—that gradually the effects of even such brief normalization would bring improvement. But after 30 minutes they seemed more chaotic than when he'd started, and reluctantly he gave up. It was, he told himself, up to God now, and he wasn't at all sure that God intervened in things like this, especially to lighten the killer's conscience.

Crossing the coast brought no flak this time. "How's the wind?" Macurdy asked.

"Worse. You might as well put on a life jacket. Get me one too."

Macurdy followed his advice. Trosza's aura told him his captive's grip on life was tenuous, and he decided not to struggle him into a life jacket unless it became necessary. Instead he worked again on the chaotic energy threads in the vicinity of the damage. The disorganization was more severe and widespread than before, and the threads, when he adjusted them, didn't remain adjusted even for a moment.

Glumly he quit, thinking that at least the Voitu wasn't airsick, and sat down beside MacNab again. He remembered something Arbel had told him: A body can be too damaged to save; a shaman had to be prepared for that.

Closing his eyes, Macurdy dozed, to dream about the fuel gauge.

After an uncertain time, he awoke to dawnlight, gray and grim, and with an odd sense of detachment watched the slate-colored Adriatic for several minutes. The fuel gauge needle was very near the peg.

"How are we doing?" he asked.

"Better than I'd expected. We're almost far enough south to angle toward the coast. Better put a life jacket on your passenger though."

Macurdy got in back with Trosza. What Arbel had termed "the spirit aura" was gone, and properly speaking the body aura too. All that was left was residue: the energy of tissues that survived, temporarily, the death of the integrated organism.

Meanwhile MacNab radioed a mayday call, giving their location, bearing, and intended course, then reported "urgent living cargo." Macurdy removed the handcuffs and put a life jacket on the corpse; a lot better to bring in a dead Voitu than none at all. When he had the laces tied, he got back in front again.

"How's your goat-eared buddy?" MacNab asked.

"Dead. His name was Trosza. He wished me well, and shook my hand. That's when I did it to him."

MacNab recognized contrition when he heard it; he nodded and said nothing more until, a few minutes later, he repeated his mayday with a new location and bearing. And got an answer. Three destroyer escorts operating out of Termoli were on an intercept course. Macurdy resisted asking what the prospects were. In the distance he could see the Abruzzi coast now, farther ahead than he liked.

Again MacNab repeated his mayday, with location and bearing. "I'm at 3,600 feet," he finished, "and starting my letdown."

"The engine hasn't quit," Macurdy pointed out.

"I have to land crosswind, and have fuel left to maintain steerageway. Otherwise forget it. The weather's worse than predicted. Those are storm seas down there.

Several miles farther on, Macurdy made out the three

warships moving toward them in the distance, and wondered if they'd seen or heard the plane. The altimeter read 640 feet, and MacNab had cut power, radioing that the ships were in sight and on course. Short minutes later they were close above the water. No way in hell, Macurdy realized, could they refuel in waves like those. MacNab touched her down, running parallel with the seas along a crest, skipping once. Contact slowed them abruptly, and shortly they were an enclosed boat, not an aircraft. Rolling heavily, they rose like a cork on a large wave, then slid sideways into the trough. Macurdy didn't know if they were in trouble or not.

"How's it look?" he asked.

"If the fuel holds out, we should be okay."

"Should I inflate a life raft?"

"Not in the plane. I'll tell you when."

The fuel nearly did hold out. The destroyer escorts were perhaps a half-mile away when the engine quit. Almost at once the Widgeon weather-vaned, the wind on the rudder surface turning her into the seas. She nosed into the next wave, water washing over the windshield. With a pang of fear, Macurdy wondered if they'd recover, but the plane rose, shedding gray-green sea water, then slid into the trough and buried her nose in the next wave, staggering again as it washed over her.

"Get in back," MacNab ordered, "and be ready to evacuate through the cabin door, with the life raft. I'll tell you when. It'll be a helluva lot easier for them to take us aboard from a raft than from the plane. As you go out, *then* pull the inflation cord—and for chrissake hang onto the lifeline! Pull yourself on if you can, but the important thing is to hang on to that lifeline."

"What about you?"

"I'll be right behind you."

"What about Trosza?"

"I'll bring him out. You get the raft out."

Macurdy waited at the door, the pilot close behind, gripping Trosza's collar. "Now!" MacNab barked, and Macurdy opened the cabin door just as the Widgeon nosed downward into the trough. The abrupt change in tilt drove him back, and briefly water poured in. As the plane rose again, he made it out the door, face down on the rubber raft, gripping the lifeline with one hand, pulling the inflation cord with the other. Then he was in the water and under it, shocked by its cold. The raft popped to the surface, Macurdy somehow spread-eagled on top. MacNab was not with him, and he looked around as best he could.

Long seconds later Macurdy saw him; he'd gotten out. The plane was riding another wave, tail higher, the open cabin door briefly clear of the water again, then it disappeared behind the crest. Macurdy rolled off the raft on the side toward the pilot, who was swimming laboriously toward him. Keeping a death grip on the lifeline, Macurdy tried with some success to stroke toward him. After a minute their hands met and gripped, then MacNab reached the lifeline and held on, coughing and gagging on salt water.

He didn't try to climb on, just held on. The Widgeon crested another wave, tail skyward now. They didn't see her again. What they could see were two circling DEs, with the other moving in on them at "slow ahead," men in life jackets and swimming trunks at the rail.

"Sorry," MacNab said.

"About what?"

"That I didn't get your goat-eared buddy out. She was tilting to the bow too much, and I had to let him go. It was that or we'd both go down."

"He was dead anyway," Macurdy answered. He wished to hell he had the body though. It would make his story a lot more convincing.

Then the DE was beside them, and seamen jumped in with lines. A couple of minutes later, they were hoisted aboard.

They got some strange looks from the crew and officers—Macurdy in jumpsuit and jump boots, MacNab in a kilt. Macurdy found himself grinning despite his loss. *At least I've got another witness to what they look like*, he told himself. That wouldn't answer the questions the general wanted asked, but Donovan would still okay the other half of the bargain.

The thought didn't actually convince Macurdy, but it made him feel better.

33

Bypassing Authority

It was Thursday the 27th of April, when Macurdy and MacNab arrived back at OSS headquarters in Grosvenor Square. Both were debriefed by Von Lutzow, MacNab first. Then the pilot was sent to the medical officer, because he'd come down with a bad cold and sore throat. When it was Macurdy's turn, he asked if Donovan was going to sit in. No, Von Lutzow said, the general couldn't be there. He'd read the debrief later.

It wasn't till afterward that Vonnie told him the general had been called to Washington, and wasn't expected back for a week or ten days.

Which left Macurdy apprehensive. "We had an oral agreement," he said. "If I pulled this mission off, I could do a second one. And I kind of did, but not entirely. I hoped I could do the follow up."

He described his discussion with the general. "Don't worry about it," Von Lutzow told him. "I've got to write up my comments on your debriefs now—your's and MacNab's—but you and I will talk in the morning."

Macurdy took that as hopeful, and looked up Anna. She'd already had supper, but went to a restaurant with him, to keep him company while he ate. She'd been signed on as a civilian internal security specialist, she told him. There was nothing like that on the TO; but after she'd demonstrated her talent for him, the general had improvised.

"What are you doing next?" she asked. "Or—that's the kind of question you're not supposed to answer, isn't it."

"Right. But I don't expect to be in town long." He paused, not meeting her eyes. "There's something I need to talk about with you."

"I think I know." She reached across the table and put her small hand on his. "I'm not sorry we did what we did. It was lovely.

"But I do sincerely regret any unhappiness it caused you. I admire you, I envy and respect your Mary, and I will not ask for a repeat performance. Believe me I'd enjoy one, but I will neither ask for nor agree to it."

She withdrew her hand. "And on that cheery note, there's an American film I'd love to see tonight, at the Leicester: *Casablanca.* People are talking about it, and I'm starved for a good film. I do hope you'll keep me company—my treat. I haven't yet had a payday here, but I held back a few pounds when your—*our*—organization impounded the lovely counterfeit British money I was given before we left Germany."

He went with her, and enjoyed the film. But not the drink afterward, because he found himself feeling something which, if it wasn't love, was something very like it—fondness and appreciation, spiced with desire. He'd had somewhat the same feeling for Melody, only more strongly, when he'd thought himself still married to Varia, so he knew it was possible to be "in love" with two women at once. But knowing didn't make it any easier. When he left Anna at her quarters, both knew without saying that they wouldn't see one another again except in passing or on duty.

In the morning Macurdy had a message from Von Lutzow to be at his office at 0815. He arrived just after eight, and the WAC clerk-typist sent him in at once. When he entered, Von Lutzow stood and shook his hand.

"The bad news first," he said. "Paul Berntvoll is Acting C.O. while the general's away. You've probably heard his reputation. If he ever saw your debriefs, he'd want you put away somewhere, or at least off-loaded on a Section 8. So I'm not going to propose the mission you want, because anything like that would require his signature, and we wouldn't get it."

Unexpectedly, Von Lutzow grinned. "The good news is, I'm writing it as an extension to your existing mission orders, instead. That sort of thing's not uncommon, but so far as I know, it's always been initialed by the general or his acting. I'm justifying it on the basis of the general's oral agreement with you. You did kidnap an alien for him—MacNab's debrief verifies that—and you lost it due to enemy fire, the flak that holed your gas tank. Then there's the timing you mentioned in your earlier debrief—Anna's verifies it, incidentally, and specifies a date—that the aliens would be shipped to Von Rundstedt's command on or about May 10th. Which makes action urgent."

Macurdy's gaze had sharpened. "Berntvoll will shit a brick if he finds out."

"Right. And as the general's acting, he will find out. It'll reach his desk this afternoon; that's standard routing." Von Lutzow smirked. "But it'll be late this afternoon, I'll make sure of that, and I happen to know he's leaving at 1500 hours. He's been seeing a daughter of General Postlethwaite, and she's taking him home to meet her mum this weekend."

"What will you do when he gets back?"

Von Lutzow's smile went lopsided. "I won't be here. You need a pilot, and MacNab's too sick. So I'm it. By the time we get back, the general should be here." He grinned. "I'll admit I'm not as good a navigator as MacNab, but who is? I can get you there, get you down, and get you back. That's all you need.

"Meanwhile, you need to round up whatever you need *muy pronto*. Today. I've already arranged a ride in a gooney bird to Casablanca tonight, and with any luck, we'll get another one to Naples or Salerno tomorrow. When Berntvoll finds out about this on Monday, he'll be pissed—may even radio a stop on it to our offices in Algiers and Naples. I don't actually expect him to, because of your oral agreement with the general, but I can't be sure, so I want us on our way to Bavaria by then."

Macurdy was impressed: Von Lutzow was as wild as Doc Alden or Captain Szczpura. And with Von Lutzow out on a limb for him like this, damned if he was going to worry about the navigating.

He did though, a little.

Meanwhile he'd picked up his mail: two letters from Mary and one from his parents. He saved Mary's for last, savoring them, realizing how much he loved her.

Macurdy had known almost nothing about Von Lutzow's past, but on their flight south, the young major talked about himself. He'd graduated in civil engineering from Northwestern in 1932, and flying the Stearman biplane his father had bought him three years earlier, had spent three summers on a barnstorming tour. He'd worked literally hundreds of small towns from New England to New Mexico, taking people for ten-minute "rides in the sky," mostly at fifty cents each, had flown stunts for cash at county fairs, and occasionally hauled some well-to-do passenger to a meeting somewhere, on business or amours.

In the off-seasons he'd tried prize-fighting; he'd been a light-heavy on the Northwestern boxing team. "I only had nine pro fights," he said. "I discovered my limitations early. But I hung around boxing gyms and worked as a sparring partner a lot—learned and improved—and it was interesting. I thought of it as collecting characters and experiences for the stories I'd write someday." He laughed. "You're one of them.

"My mother, of course, was having a breakdown about the way I lived, especially the fighting." Laughing again, Von Lutzow touched his nose; it had been broken, that was apparent though not conspicuous. "And Dad was doing pretty well, considering the times, so when I quit, he paid to get it fixed; it looked worse than yours. He also lined me up with an engineering job. But respectability got old, and in the fall of '40, when the draft started, I enlisted. And because I'd done two years of ROTC in college, they sent me to OCS."

Eventually the talk petered out, and briefly Macurdy watched the ocean below. *That Von Lutzow's led a really interesting life,* he thought. Entirely overlooking his own.

Then he turned his thoughts to the mission, rehearsing its

steps from arrival to completion. In his rehearsal, nothing went wrong, not a thing.

They arrived in Casablanca as intended, and almost at once caught another 47 to Algiers, where they were told nothing was flying to Italy because of bad weather there. They did, however, catch a flight to Tunis, and from there, Von Lutzow talked their way onto a B25, an urgent flight taking several high-ranking CID officers to Trapani in western Sicily.

The next noon, Monday, found them in Naples, but Von Lutzow was reluctant to tap the standard OSS sources of equipment: He was afraid there'd be an order waiting for him from Berntvoll, to return at once to London. Evading orders was one thing; disobeying them was something else. And anyway he assumed he could manage with charm and bullshit.

But things had changed. The 5th army was there, waiting for better weather to dry the roads—waiting to launch a major offensive northward and liberate the army at Anzio, trapped on its beachhead and pounded on by the Germans since January. Resources were tight, and the base in Naples ran pretty much "by the book." People weren't dealing fast and loose the way they had when a fluid situation required it.

The next day, Von Lutzow said they might have to settle for a land plane. Aside from twin-engined PBYs, large and noisy, there were very few amphibians at the base, and he hadn't come close to getting one of them.

The following morning, he took the risk he'd hoped to avoid: He contacted the OSS project that flew support to Yugoslav guerrillas across the Adriatic. Yes, there'd been a message from the acting CO, but the project commander disliked Berntvoll—"the stick," he called him—and was willing to ignore the order, on the grounds that the general would be back soon, and hopefully overrule the man. Besides, he said, it'd be a shame to let the OSS become just another chicken-shit, by-the-book outfit.

He didn't have an amphibian Von Lutzow could borrow, but he could loan him a single-engined utility aircraft. A pair of freefall chutes came with it, and he could throw in supply chutes if needed. It also had an improvised interior gas tank for refueling in the air from 4 or 5-gallon cans. Using it stank up the cabin pretty badly and carried a risk of explosion, but it was useful for long flights.

That afternoon, the two mavericks reviewed their plan. The plane, of course, could not be landed on the lake, and the waning moon, slender now, wouldn't rise till almost 0230 AM; landing on the country road would be hellaciously risky. So Macurdy would jump; he insisted on it. He had what he needed: From England he'd brought a musette bag stuffed with K rations, a towel, and a few other things, plus a curved plywood pack frame, a canvas supply-drop bag fitted with lashing rings, and a coil of nylon line for lashing it onto the pack frame. And the working tools: blasting caps and 30 feet of fuse.

"I hate like hell to leave you there," Von Lutzow said.

"I'll be okay. I was well trained for getting out crosscountry before I went the first time. And I'm in uniform; if they catch me, there's a decent chance they won't shoot me."

Von Lutzow took a deep breath: He was skeptical of that "decent chance." This didn't seem as good an idea as it had in London, but then, he reminded himself, things seldom did. "No second thoughts?" he asked.

Macurdy shook his head firmly. "I know what the stakes are," he said. "I'm probably the only one who does. Even Anna doesn't, really. The Voitar didn't give her the depth of training they gave me, nor anything like the close contact." He grinned, taking Von Lutzow by surprise. "Besides, no one's going to see me unless I screw up."

"Well," Von Lutzow said, "let's pray for decent weather."

The forecast had not been favorable, but it seemed to him, just then, that the weather would be fine.

34

Troll in the Cellar

Late that afternoon, Von Lutzow and Macurdy filled the auxiliary tank. Then, stinking of aviation gas, they ate supper in the visiting officers' mess at the airfield, and took off after dark, headed east. The sky was clear—a break in the weather—but the moon wouldn't rise till well after two, and only a sickle moon then.

They scarcely spoke, all the way up the Adriatic. Macurdy dozed much of the time; he didn't know when he'd have a chance to sleep again. And dozing, dreamed of Corporal Trosza. They were walking along a beach below chalk cliffs, and he was trying to tell Trosza something. Meanwhile Trosza had severe stomach cramps. Macurdy could see inside him—the Voitu's abdomen was half full of blood—and he tried to distract him so he wouldn't notice.

Trosza put an arm around Macurdy's shoulder and squeezed him lightly. "I'll be all right," he said, "I'll be all right."

It was Von Lutzow's voice that wakened Macurdy. "We're crossing the north shore," he said. "Venice is off west a bit. If you've had any further thoughts, now's the time to talk them over."

Macurdy straightened in his seat, contemplating the dream still vivid in his mind. It was not, he thought, one that would slip away and be forgotten. He'd have no qualms about killing Kurqôsz or Greszak, or even Landgraf, for whom he felt affinity. This was war, and they were the enemy. But Trosza? The Voitik corporal had had no part in this war. He'd even been friendly.

He shook free of the dregs, but not of the dark mood the dream left him with.

Von Lutzow's comment seemed an invitation to cancel, but he wasn't about to do that. Mentally, Macurdy reviewed his plans and gear: He'd never jumped with a freefall chute before, but felt comfortable about it. What he didn't feel comfortable about was the predicted wind; his preflight optimism had died in his sleep. The Air Corps' meteorological office in Naples had told him to expect winds of fifteen to twenty-five mph in southern Bavaria, and he worried about trusting his gear to a supply chute which might get lost in the night.

So far the drop bag contained little except his musette bag, fuse, and blasting caps. It was lashed to the pack frame and didn't weigh much. Now, given the wind, he decided not to drop it with a supply chute. Instead, he'd tie it to his web belt with a length of nylon cord, and toss it ahead of him when he stepped out the door. It would hang about a dozen feet below him, hitting the ground a fraction of a second before he did.

The blasting caps were in a small drawstring bag, and originally he'd planned to carry it in one of his numerous pockets. But he'd thought better of it. He had a thing about caps—they were touchy—so instead he'd packed them in the drop bag, with the fuse. Now he had third thoughts. Suppose he came down *on* the bag?

He knew from his OSS training there'd be small orange drift chutes aboard, used before making supply drops. Leaving his seat, he took one from an equipment chest, and digging caps and fuse from the drop bag, stuffed them into the drift chute's small ballast bag. He'd jump with it, then toss it three or four seconds before he hit the ground.

By the time he had everything repacked and ready, the Dolomitic Alps loomed in front of them, peaks snow-covered in the starlight, and he sat back down with the drift chute in his thigh pocket. His next concern was Von Lutzow finding the jump site.

He was prepared to jump in any open field though, if need be, and find his way to the schloss as best he could.

✧ ✧ ✧

Von Lutzow found *der Kiefersee* without difficulty. Like MacNab, he bypassed it at a distance, then approached it from the north. It was dark enough that Macurdy could distinguish nothing except lake, forest, and open ground. There remained the problem of the wind, which Von Lutzow estimated at 20 miles per hour.

Macurdy knew the drop site he wanted—a pasture near the lake's south end, less than a mile from the schloss. Between pasture and lake lay a stretch of woods where he could hide his chute. Crouching by the door, he peered out, pack frame in one hand. Von Lutzow had cut power and lost altitude; despite the wind, they were to be at 1,000 feet when Macurdy jumped. He'd have preferred 400 to reduce wind drift, but they'd agreed that Von Lutzow should glide in on reduced power till after he was well past the schloss, and that required more elevation.

Macurdy's eyes strained at the blackness. He forgot to breathe, made out the shoreside woods and jumped, tossing the pack ahead of him, and counting aloud—"one thousand, two thousand"—pulled the ripcord, felt the silk and lines pull from the chute pack, felt the shock as the canopy popped open, felt the tug as his plummeting pack jerked on his web belt.

He'd estimated time to the ground at about 40 seconds, and picked up the count again at six thousand. He'd begun at once to oscillate in the wind, and looking downward, discovered he had little sense of how far he was from the ground. Meanwhile the wind was carrying him backward, and he couldn't spill air from his chute to turn himself, because he had to get the drift chute from his thigh pocket, which occupied his hands. At about 25 seconds he smelled grass and cow manure, and taking that to mean he was very near touchdown, tossed the drift chute with its small cargo of fuse and blasting caps, then reached back and gripped his risers, anticipating impact.

It took much longer than he'd expected. Another dozen seconds elapsed before he hit, heavily, swinging backward. And his risers were twisted; the wind in his chute dragged him along the ground until he pulled it to him. Scrambling to his feet, he wadded the canopy and briefly knelt on it. While dragging, he'd run into and over the pack frame and drop bag; now, taking the tether in his hands, he pulled it to him. When he couldn't see it even at his feet, he felt a foreboding about the drift chute with its small but important cargo.

The wind in his face told him the direction from which he'd been dragged, and he had some sense of the distance, so after stuffing his chute into the drop bag, he slung the packframe over one shoulder and backtracked. The drift chute had had 10 or 15 seconds to drift on its own. Its course shouldn't have differed from his, but it might have descended more slowly, thus drifting longer. And worse, if it had blown along the ground after landing, where might it be now?

He wished it were white instead of orange.

At his guessed point of impact, he stopped and peered around. *It could be right in front of you, a foot away,* he told himself. *Best stay where you are till the moon rises, and then hunt for it. Even a sickle moon will help.*

Meanwhile he realized, to his disgust, that the smell of manure was too strong to come from his surroundings. The wind must have dragged him through a fairly fresh cow plop, presumably smeared down the back of his jumpsuit. He was also aware that the wind was chilly, so he tapped into the Web of the World for warmth, then laid back on the ground to wait the necessary hour and a half for moonrise.

"Macurdy," he muttered, "this better not be an omen, that's all to hell I've got to say," then sat berating himself for not putting the fuse and caps in the bag with his other gear. *You should have known better,* he thought glumly. *If you don't find the sonofabitch, you've got a serious problem.*

After a few minutes of futile cycling through failure, imagined consequences, and blame, he took himself by the figurative scruff, and sitting up, began the meditation Varia had taught him: breathing with his diaphragm, inhaling through his nose and exhaling through pursed lips. Given the circumstances, it took awhile, but after a bit his mind smoothed out, and he let the occasional vagrant thought drift past and disappear.

One of those thoughts was the realization that as he'd blown along the ground, there'd been a thudding of hooves nearby.

Cows, he knew, saw better in the dark than humans; apparently he'd spooked some.

Even before it rose, the moon paled the night a bit, and when it cleared the ridge east of the lake, it made more difference than he'd expected. But still he could see no drift chute. Vaguely he discerned cows grazing in a loose band some distance away.

It was light enough now to orient himself. He was about halfway between the road on the east, with its bordering trees, the lakeside woods on the west, and a bit farther from the forest at the pasture's south end. He'd come down perfectly on target, despite the wind and visibility. *If you're going to believe in omens,* he told himself, *that's the one to believe in.*

Meanwhile he needed to be out of sight before daylight; he and his chute. Someone would arrive about sunup, perhaps earlier, to drive the cows to the barn for milking. And while his invisibility cloak might hide him from a farmer, whoever came for the cows might have a dog to help them, and he wasn't at all sure the cloak would hide him from a dog.

In less than an hour, dawn paled the sky, its thin gray light exposing details. Cloaking himself, Macurdy started toward the lakeside woods, going out of his way to approach the cows. They looked up as he came, poised to run, so he veered off. They saw through his spell; dogs would too.

The lakeside woods, he discovered, consisted entirely of old trees, mostly beeches fire-scarred and hollow, standing above thin grass speckled with violets. Browsing had eliminated brush and young trees, except for ground juniper, which grew in scattered patches, prostrate and dense. He selected a patch, and lying on his belly, shoved the white chute as far as he could beneath the sprawling evergreen shrubs, shoving his helmet after it. Then, shouldering his packframe, he sat waiting on a rock, still cloaked, thinking he'd have to do something about the stink on his jumpsuit. Close up or in a closed space, he might be unseen, but hardly unnoticed.

He didn't wait long. His watch read local 0512, and the sun was up, when he saw the herd girl walking up the road. Reaching the pasture gate, she swung it open and yodelled.

The cows started briskly toward her, ready for the relief of being milked, and the grain that went with it.

When they were gone, he spent half an hour quartering the pasture in the sunlit morning, protected by his cloak, looking for anything orange. In the downwind direction, he went all the way to the pasture fence; to hunt upwind made no sense. While searching, three ways occurred to him of bypassing his need for the missing fuse and caps; two were iffy, the other suicidal. Iffy meant possible failure, but he wasn't at all sure he was ready for deliberate suicide, even if it saved far more lives than the one he'd lose.

Then another thought occurred to him: Suppose the drift chute had come down on a cow, and caught on a horn? Although the odds of it happening were minute, it was possible. On the other hand, any cow he'd ever known, and he'd known many, would have bolted, run to the woods if a chute had settled on its head. And he'd surely have noticed when it came out to answer the herd girl's call.

Nonetheless, for a while he wandered about the woods, looking, because if it had happened that way, the cow would have tried to rid herself of the chute, and perhaps rubbed it off against a tree. After a bit, though, he gave it up and went down to the shore, where he ate a K ration, topped off his canteen, then removed his jumpsuit and used moss and icy lake water to scrub off the cow manure. Most of it had been on his chute pack, but there was some on a shoulder and one pants leg. When he'd finished, they remained stained, but the manure was gone, and after it dried, it wouldn't smell nearly as strong.

As far as he could see, there was nothing useful left to do there, so he started for the schloss, hiking along the lakeshore to avoid sharp eyes that might otherwise penetrate his cloak in the bright sunlight.

Avoiding the road, Macurdy approached the schloss through the forest. On this lovely, if chill and breezy spring morning, the SS platoon was doing morning exercises on the large front lawn, shouting cadence, young voices strong and vigorous. So he crossed the lawn behind the building, to the end of the near wing and the cellar's rear entryway. Presumably the whole platoon was in front. No one would be in a position to see him unless they were on duty in the stable, perhaps feeding the colonel's horses.

Moving quietly down the entryway steps, he tried the door to the cellar. It was Thursday, and he didn't really expect to find it unbarred, except perhaps on Friday and Saturday evenings when guardsmen would bring party girls from town. But to his surprise, it gave. Opening it a few inches, he listened hard, and hearing nothing, peered in. The long corridor was empty, so he entered, closing the door behind him, beginning to feel optimistic again. Someone, he noticed, had put fresh bulbs in two fixtures that had been lightless before. It was still poorly lit, but lighter than it had been.

Though his initial business was not in this wing, he paused to pick the lock of the first explosives magazine, to make sure the TNT was still there. It was. He checked the second with the same result, then moved on into unknown territory, the cellar beneath the south wing, the Voitar's wing. It seemed indistinguishable from the wing he knew, except that it had no back entrance. Nor did it open into the sacrificial chamber at the base of the tower.

From its end, he worked his way back toward the main section, trying doors. None that he checked were locked. Three were half full of furnishings protected by large sheets. The others had nothing more than sowbugs and a damp earthy smell until, halfway to the ell, he found the one he'd use.

It appeared to have been a machine shop, and later, storage for old plumbing and other junk, most of it since hauled away, probably melted down for the war effort. What remained was non-metallic, except for small odds and ends: pipe caps, tee joints, short cut-off pieces of pipe, rusty bolts, a corroded brass hinge, cuttings from threading pipes. . . . Beside the door was a light fixture with its bulb burned out.

The room's most important feature was a long dining table, lying on its side near the back wall, shoulder high. When it had graced some dining room, it would have seated 20, he thought. Now its veneer was warped and curled, but for him it looked ideal—a bonus he'd never imagined.

This is the room, he thought. Taking the dead bulb from its fixture, he went into the corridor and exchanged it with one of the good bulbs there. Back in the room, he installed and lit it, then digging the towel from the drop bag, blocked the space beneath the door so the light couldn't be seen from the corridor. Next he moved the heavy table some 10 feet from the wall, and emptied the drop bag on the floor behind it.

Finally, taking the towel, packframe and drop bag with him, he went back to the SS wing, to one of the magazines, closed the door behind him, turned on the light, and put the folded towel against the crack.

So far, so good, he told himself, *now the work begins.*

Taking the packframe from his back, he went behind the large pile of TNT and began loading half-kilo blocks into the drop bag till it was full. After hoisting the now-heavy packframe onto his shoulders, he peered up and down the corridor, then lugged the explosive to the south wing and unloaded it behind the concealing table top. Cat-footed and quick, he repeated the procedure, trip after trip without a break, till he'd transferred 800 blocks, almost 900 pounds of the powerful explosive, none of it visible from the door.

In the magazines, he'd taken only from the back of the stacks. From the door, they looked undisturbed. Far more remained than he'd taken.

There'd been no interruption, no guard patrol, no one at all but himself. Clearly the SS considered their building security satisfactory, for who but they and the Voitar knew the magazines existed? Besides, there was always a guard outside the main entrance, and another in the foyer.

Phase two of his plan had to be carried out that night, Thursday, because the guardsmen would probably have party girls in on Friday and Saturday nights. One squad would be given passes on one night, another on the other, while the other two would have theirs the following week. So it was important he rest now, by day. He looked for a mattress in one of the rooms where furniture was stored, and settled for three large sofa cushions, which he lay as a bed behind his stack of transplanted TNT. Taking a K ration from his musette bag, he ate, then drank from his canteen, turned out the light, and removed the towel from the bottom of the door. Finally, using his GI penlight, he went to the cushions and lay down.

For a minute or two he lay awake thinking: He still didn't know how to blow the building, short of suicide, but he'd come up with something. Meanwhile first things first: He *did* know how he'd blow the gate. The problem there was the timing; if it wasn't just right, it wouldn't work.

He awoke having to relieve himself. Taking the toilet paper from the K ration he'd eaten, he cloaked himself, checked the corridor, returned to the unbarred entryway and left the building. It was still daylight but the sun was low, the side yard mostly shadowed by bordering trees.

Even so, crossing it made him twitchy. This was the SS wing, and if someone saw him through a window . . . His jumpsuit didn't look remotely like an SS uniform, or anyone's uniform except the American airborne.

Macurdy, he told himself, *quit your damned worrying. It's worked every time. Even Hansi didn't see you till you fumbled that file folder.*

After relieving himself in the forest, he walked to the lake, and in the early dusk, refilled his canteen. Then he returned to the building, to one of the magazines. Once more he filled the drop bag with TNT, this time taking it not to the stack behind the old table, but out the back entryway. He packed it about 500 yards, including a couple hundred feet up the four-wheel-drive road that climbed the Witches' Ridge. There he stashed it behind a patch of fir saplings, cloaking the stash. He marked the place—it would soon be too dark to find it otherwise—by breaking off a dead fir sapling and laying it across the truck trail. Using the pen light would be risky, so near the county road.

That trip too he repeated, till he'd transferred some 300 half-kilo blocks, and had started back for more. By that time it was fully night, and moonless. When he'd almost reached the graveled road, he heard footsteps walking in the direction of the schloss. Motionless, he listened while the person passed, invisible to him in the moonless, tree-shadowed dark. Even after he could no longer hear the sounds, he waited a couple of minutes before following. Sound could betray him.

But he did take something for granted. In the entryway he opened the door—to find two SS men coming toward him down the corridor, talking! One glanced toward him, stopped and stared, then swore. "That damned Josef! The fool left the door wide open! If Mueller or Lipanov find it like that, it will ruin everything!"

"It could have been the woman."

"That's beside the point! It's Josef's responsibility!" He strode toward Macurdy, who backed away, holding his breath. Grabbing the door, the soldier closed it in his face. Chagrined, Macurdy climbed the dozen steps to the yard and retreated to the forest's edge. The person who'd passed on the road had been "the woman," it seemed to him: some farmer's wife or daughter whose husband or boy friend was fighting in the Ukraine, or sitting in a bunker on the Channel coast. A woman feeling desperate with life, and perhaps short of money.

How long would she be in there? He'd planned to take twice as much TNT to the hill, then perhaps start packing it up the ridge, if it wasn't too damned dark.

But hell, even with his tiny pen light, it *was* too dark. The best thing to do was resign himself to patience. He still had a few days.

Or did he? What if they decided to transfer the Voitar early?

With a muttered curse, Macurdy moved back to the entryway and down the stairs, to try the door. It was not barred, and he opened it a few slow inches. No one was in the corridor, so he slipped inside, moved quickly to the nearest magazine, picked the lock and entered. Again he blocked the space beneath the door and turned on the light. Working faster than before, he filled the bag with blocks, shouldered it, turned the light out again, removed the towel, and listened hard with an ear against the door. The party room was just a few yards away across the corridor.

Listened with worry and self-anger. What he'd just done was foolhardy, had endangered his whole mission for no adequate reason. The best thing to do now, he told himself, was catch a few hours sleep behind the stack of TNT.

But hearing nothing, and driven by a sense of urgency, he held his breath, opened the door, and peered out. No one. Quickly he stepped into the corridor, closed the door silently behind him, and without locking it, went to the entryway and left. Then, crossing the lawn, he hiked to his stash by the ridge road, where he unloaded the bag and considered. He decided to go back for one more load, but not go inside till after the woman came out. When she left, the guardsmen would surely go up to bed.

But waiting for her by the entryway, the question again became how many she'd serve, and how long it would take. He'd assumed there was only Josef and the two he'd seen, but there might be more. And would some demand seconds?

After a bit he grew sleepy. Rather than fight it, he drank as much water as he comfortably could, then went a few yards into the forest and lay down, ordering his mental alarm clock to waken him in two hours. If it failed, his bladder would remind him.

He awoke as intended, rolled quickly to his feet, slung the pack frame on one shoulder, relieved his bladder, then padded to the schloss. The corridor was clear, and listening at the party room door, he heard nothing. Working steadily, he packed two more loads of TNT to his stash in the woods, before stopping to rest.

Was it enough? Was it possible to destroy the gate with any amount? "Wrong damn question, Macurdy," he muttered. The operating assumption had to be that it *was* possible. And as for how much it would take, the only rational response was to use all he could while still doing it that day, that morning at 0857, when the weather office had said the moon would cross the local meridian. The explosive had to be there at the gate, waiting—*he* had to be there waiting—before it opened.

And it was doubtful he could even lug what he had up the mile of truck trail to the gate between dawn and 0857. Yet to start lugging it now, in utter darkness, would be stupid; even coming a slow, groping 200 feet up the ridge road had involved stumbling, straying off the rocky road, even bumping into trees. And he would not risk it all by using the pen light. He'd wait for dawn.

Still driven by the urgency of his mission, he went back to the schloss and hauled more TNT to his new stack beneath the Voitar's wing, till he had 1,800 blocks stacked there—nearly a metric ton. For good measure, he loaded another sackful to take with him, then returned to his stash in the forest. There, with the deadly burden still on his shoulders, he sat back against his pack to doze, with the strict admonition to be on his feet at the first dawnlight that reached him through the trees.

He half-wakened various times over the next hours, till he became aware that the darkness was thick gray, not black, and he could make out, vaguely, the tree trunks around him. With a lurch he got to his knees, then his feet, found the rough road, and started uphill for the gate. Twice he stumbled, not quite falling, but charged hard nonetheless, jogging on the easy stretches, sweating profusely in the chill morning. By the time he reached the crest, it was light enough to see that the SS had no guards there. He recognized the gate itself by memory, and by a psychic buzz so faint, he'd have missed it had he not been concentrating.

He unloaded his burden, not taking time to stack or cloak it, then shouldered the pack frame again and started back down at a lope, not concerned with falling or the noise of his descent. Subsequent trips were even faster, Macurdy drawing energy from the Web of the World to keep up his furious pace. The last load was less than full, and he made it in a shambling run, driven by the fear that the gate would activate before he arrived, yet unwilling to leave any of the explosive behind. When he arrived at the loose heap of TNT at the gate, he dumped his load, then ran back to the place he'd chosen earlier in passing. Facing the heap, he looked at his watch: 0854.

Within a minute he felt activation begin, and concentrated on the TNT 120 feet away—close enough that he could see it clearly, sharply, but far enough that the gate wouldn't suck him in. If he didn't time it right—if it blew too soon—it seemed unlikely he'd survive. That was an awfully big stack of explosive.

He raised both arms in front of him, palms forward, level with his shoulders, saw the margins of the heap begin to waver, blur, made himself hold back for brief seconds. Then the heap shimmered, and he pumped plasma spheres at it, almost too swift to see in the morning light.

Abruptly the field collapsed and was gone, as if it hadn't been, leaving not even a psychic echo. There was no shock wave, and to his eyes, nothing had changed—except that the heap had disappeared. There wasn't even a hole where it had been.

He collapsed on the ground, and for several minutes lay exhausted, unseeing, numb with relief. He'd timed it right.

But there was nothing resembling jubilation. For one thing, he couldn't be sure—not really sure—that he'd actually destroyed the gate. He might simply have interrupted it, or altered the timing again.

At any rate, the more dangerous task remained.

35

Points of View

Greszak had long since lost any real interest in the training project. Life had grown monotonous, boring, to the point that all he looked forward to—all any of them looked forward to—was returning to Hithmearc. Next to the boredom, the worst thing about this place was being cut off from the hive mind—except for the fragment consisting of their own small group. One got used to it, but only to a degree.

For him, the high point had come to be the spring birds caroling in the new day—he'd been getting up at daybreak to hear them—and the low point, this week, had been the antics of the human guardsmen bouncing and shouting on the lawn in some grotesque rite of spring. Watching through a window, he wished them ill as they filed back into the building.

At first, training Germans in magic had seemed a challenge, but had become essentially a defeat. In Hithmearc, training humans in magic had never even been contemplated, of course; first it was undesirable, and secondly, few showed talent. Even in the two races that had—the Saanit and the Ylver—the talent had been quite limited. As a precaution, both peoples had been dispersed—destroyed so far as possible. The remnants of the Saanit had fled into the vast harsh taiga east of the grasslands. While the Ylver who'd survived—the island Ylver—had fled west across the ocean sea, an escape his people would never forgive.

The Germans had no more talent than usual for humans: A few showed one or another ability, but always minor. Still, it had been interesting for a while to see what could be made of them. Some had gained modestly, but soon reached a limit, perhaps because they lacked the hive mind. The most successful had been the one named Montag—amusing to be named for a calendar day—but even Montag had reached his limit well below adept.

Nonetheless it had heartened Landgraf and Kupfer to send him off against their enemies, and in fact, Montag should prove useful to them. But overall, as a magician he was no more powerful than the Ylvin magicians of ancient record.

Meanwhile Greszak's staff went through the motions of teaching, while looking forward to going home. The Crown Prince would arrive through the gate shortly, bringing a circle of seven adepts and a power master, and after two days of acclimation and briefing, would send them with the Germans to some meaningless place on the northwest coast, to repel invaders.

And when they'd been sent, the Germans would complete their part of the bargain. They'd already delivered detailed diagrams for building large sailing vessels—their most vital contribution—and had tried to deliver powerful explosives. Now they would deliver tools, models, and less utilitarian artifacts, along with a medicine they claimed to have against seasickness.

It would be interesting to go north themselves, he and his staff, and in an early stage of planning, it had been considered. But the Crown Prince had decided otherwise. There were risks, and they all were masters, well beyond the level needed by the Germans; adepts would serve nicely.

A sensation touched Greszak: The gate had begun its daily activation. He felt its energy rising, shaping. In perhaps half an hour, the Crown Prince and the team he was bringing would arrive at the schloss on foot, their disorientation and queasiness repaired by the run.

A bird landed on the window sill and looked in at Greszak. The baron didn't know the names of Bavarian birds, but this one looked rather like the speckled thrush at home. He grinned at it, and it cocked its head as if to say, "Who are you?"

"I am Baron Greszak," the Voitu replied, "and who are you?"

Its answer was to flirt its tail and fly. Probably, Greszak thought, it had a nest close by, perhaps under the eaves.

He returned his attention to the gate energy. Activation involved frequency acceleration, and he sensed it culminate. Then, after the brief and customary waver, it stabilized—and at that same moment cut sharply off.

Greszak's face froze. Aborted! What had happened to the gate?

His consternation lasted only a moment. Nothing was wrong with the gate itself. Their spell had simply collapsed. It had been inevitable, but Kurqôsz's calculations had predicted eleven lunar cycles before it happened. After a period of dangerous irregularity, it should settle on its natural timing—midnights nearest the full moon. Meanwhile he would salvage the situation on this side; in the absence of the new team, he'd fulfill the agreement using his staff, himself acting as power master. To panic a human army would be no challenge at all. More like entertainment.

Colonel Landgraf had been disturbed at Greszak's news. The Crown Prince's magnetism and power had more than made up for his arrogance, and the colonel had felt assured by his presence. But Greszak had promised that the project would be carried out despite the mishap, and Landgraf did not doubt him.

The buzzer on his desk rasped.

"What is it, Kupfer?"

"There is a local farmer to see you, sir, about a matter that seems quite important. I believe he should tell you himself."

Landgraf frowned. What would a local farmer have to say that Kupfer couldn't take care of? "Send him in, Kupfer."

A moment later the farmer entered, a middle-aged man of middle-height and sturdy build, in work clothes, his battered felt hat clutched in a thick-fingered hand. In the other was a large paper bag. His bald skull was ivory above sun-reddened cheeks, his eyebrows yellow-brown, the eyes beneath them blue. In all, he resembled many of the farmers in Landgraf's home district, though Landgraf knew that when the man spoke, his dialect would spoil the resemblance.

"Guten Tag, Herr Oberst," *the farmer said apologetically, and bobbed an almost bow. "I have found something the colonel may wish to know about."*

"Let us see it, sir."

The farmer opened the paper bag and took out a small orange parachute perhaps seventy centimeters across, with a long, orange sack attached, both of some silk-like material.

"It was caught on the wire fence at the north end of my pasture woods," he said. "I do not know how it came there, but it seems to have been deposited forcibly. See how it was torn!" He spread the material to show a ragged tear.

"And in its sack I found this." He drew from it what the colonel recognized as either fuse or detonation cord, depending on its origin. The farmer laid it on the colonel's desk, and reached in the bag again. "And these," he added. Taking out a drawstring pouch, he emptied it carefully into his hand, and gently laid a handful of brass capsules beside the fuse. "I was a sapper in the Kaiser's army," he said. "These are detonators, as for dynamite."

Landgraf's face went wooden. What did this mean? "In your pasture woods?" he said. "Let me see the parachute."

The farmer handed it to him. Numbers were stenciled along its edge, and in small block letters, "U.S. ARMY."

Lieber Gott! *Landgraf breathed, and looked up at the farmer. "You are to be commended for bringing this to me. What is your name?"*

"Gruber, Herr Oberst. Wilhelm Gruber."

Landgraf turned his gaze to the door and stood up. "Hauptsturmführer Kupfer!" *he called, "see that Herr Gruber receives a proper commendation for this!"*

Kupfer had been waiting by the door, and looked in. "Yes sir, Colonel."

Landgraf extended a hand. After brief hesitation, the farmer took it, and they shook. "You are dismissed, Herr Gruber."

"Yessir, colonel sir," Gruber replied, did a rusty about face, and left. Kupfer closed the door behind him, then Landgraf keyed the intercom to the watch room and snapped an order. In scarcely a minute, Lieutenant Lipanov arrived with three men. The colonel showed him what the farmer had brought.

"I do not know what this means," Landgraf said, "but you and I are going to visit the magazines."

They marched from his office then, not through Kupfer's, but directly into the hallway, downstairs into the cellar corridor, and down the corridor to the magazines. A corporal unlocked the first magazine door and opened it. To Landgraf's eyes, everything seemed all right.

"Search it!" he ordered, and the three enlisted men entered, all of them for the first time. A minute later the corporal looked apologetically at the commanding officer.

"Sir, I find nothing out of order!"

"Good. Let us look at the other."

They moved to the next room. It too passed.

Landgraf stood frowning. "Are there ways into the cellar from outside?"

"Yes sir, colonel," Lipanov said. "At the end is a back entryway, with a door that is kept barred. And the coal bunker off the furnace room has a small door for a coal chute, that a man could crawl through."

"Have them both checked immediately. And Lieutenant, I want two men on guard here at the magazines. At all times. Also one in the furnace room, and double the guards at the front entrance. This finding may have nothing at all to do with us, but we must take no chances."

Then he turned and left the cellar, muttering about phoning Munich. He'd tell them once again that they really needed to remove this high explosive. Since the aliens could not use it, it served no purpose here.

Lipanov watched him leave. Was that all? he wondered. Three guards in the cellar and two more at the entrance? Who had dropped that parachute? Americans, obviously. And to whom? A demolitions team, of course. As for why: This was the only military installation for many kilometers, so obviously the schloss was the target, the schloss or perhaps the aliens. Yet the colonel was treating the affair as if they were dealing with ordinary criminals. What he should *do was request a battalion be sent to hunt them down.*

Well. Perhaps he intended to; he'd mumbled something about

Munich. And after all, he did wear the Iron Cross, the old one that really meant something. At some time in his life he'd been a warrior and a hero.

Meanwhile, *Lipanov told himself,* I'll set lookouts on balconies during the day. And guards outside at night, in pairs, with orders to shoot anything that moves. American paratroops are all criminals—rapists and murderers released from prisons to fight us—everyone knows that. They scruple at nothing.

36

Crescendo

Macurdy's collapse was cut short by a realization: Kurqôsz would have noticed when the gate opening cut short, and be concerned. Guardsmen might be sent. Grunting, he got to his feet and started down the truck trail, still cloaked, though he'd hear any vehicle grinding its way up the steep grade.

He reached the foot of the ridge without seeing or hearing anyone. Meanwhile his legs and buttocks were stiffening from his furious exertions of the morning, and the ends of his toes were sore from his downhill runs. Out of shape again, he thought, and headed back to the schloss, not by the county road, but through the woods, pausing at the edge of the lawn till a cloud obscured the sun.

The cellar's rear entryway was locked, which disappointed but didn't surprise him. Slipping around the corner into the shadow of the north wing, he leaned against the wall and thought for a bit, reviewing his plans. He was stiffening seriously now—thighs, buttocks, calves, even tibialis. By noon he'd have trouble walking, let alone running if necessary, unless he did something about it. And before long, the shortage of sleep would dull him.

Macurdy, old horse, he told himself, *it's time to take care of yourself for a change.* With that he crossed the lawn again and hiked back into the woods. Feeling thirsty, he reached for his canteen. Empty. He must, he thought, have drunk it all that morning, and in the intensity of his focus, never noticed; only now did he realize his clothes were wet with sweat. So he continued to the lake, where he refilled his canteen, drank deeply from it, and topped it off again.

By that time he was hobbling badly, so he went well back among the trees, sat down against one, and focused on the dark and murky aura around his legs. *You did good work,* he told them, *damn good, and I appreciate it. Now let's see what I can do for you.*

He began to touch the sore places, willing increased blood flow into them, touched the energy vortices in his hip joints, knees, ankles, feeling their energy. Then he began manipulating the energy threads. The tissues were heavily loaded with fatigue acids, and responded more slowly than he'd expected. After 30 minutes though, the soreness was much reduced, and he got to his knees, to work on his buttocks by feel and visualization. That done, he took off his boots and gave attention to his blood-blistered toes. Finally he found a patch of feather moss, and lying down on it, went to sleep almost at once.

He awoke famished, and realized he had nothing with him to eat. In his intensity of the day and evening before, he'd failed to put any rations in his pockets; they lay in his musette bag, behind the TNT he'd piled in the south wing room.

His watch read 1833 hours. He'd slept the whole afternoon. And to his surprise, his legs had stiffened again, somewhat, so he sat down and began to work on them. *Guys,* he told them, *I'm sorry, but I really didn't have any choice.* He'd never "talked" to his body before while healing it—not as if its parts had a sentience of their own. When he'd thought to them, it had been to direct them, guide them, not apologize or acknowledge. But somehow it seemed the thing to do now.

This time he continued till the soreness was gone. His watch read 1911. He drank again, to put *something* in his stomach, and gave his attention to the evening.

Tonight some of the SS men would be on pass, would ride a truck to Kaufbeuren, probably; it was somewhat nearer than Kempten, and not a lot smaller. He really didn't know much about their lives, he realized. Presumably they'd bring back girls, and the cellar beneath the north wing would be dangerous for him. If he could blow the stack he'd made beneath the south wing, though, that should collapse the south wing interior, and the Voitar would end up part of the rubble. A train of gunpowder could serve as a fuse, with a candle for a timer if he could find one. But he'd need a detonator of some kind in lieu of the blasting caps.

He could always blow the stack with a plasma ball, as he'd done on the ridge, but it would be his dying act.

So. Detonators. Somewhere in the north wing, probably on the first floor, the SS would have its ordnance room. Find it, steal a few grenades, get the detonators out of them . . . The potato masher grenade was one German weapon he hadn't been taught to dismantle, but it was easy enough with American grenades; the German were probably no harder. The tricky part would be getting the grenades.

Once again he topped off his canteen at the lake, then headed briskly for the schloss. Dusk was settling. The guardsmen on pass would have left for town already; maybe the cellar door would be unbarred.

When he reached the manor's grounds, he stopped, chagrined. Two men stood guard by the cellar entryway, one on each side. Clearly something had happened, and the only thing he could think of was, they'd discovered that a large amount of TNT was missing from the magazines. If so, they might have searched, maybe found the stash he'd made beneath the south wing.

For a moment he stood uncertain, then crossed the yard opposite the north ell and moved along the front of the building just far enough from the wall not to leave tracks in the flowerbeds. There were two guards at the front door, too; there'd been only one before. On the porch, he used the additional concealment of a pillar, and waited. Within a few minutes, Captain Kupfer arrived, a driver letting him off in front of the entrance. Daring, Macurdy followed him closely through the door.

And stopped. A guard now stood at the door to the cellar stairway, and another on the second floor landing, overlooking the foyer. Then it struck him: this evening they had submachine guns. Before, they'd had bolt-action Mausers, varnished and polished—fire one shot, then work the bolt—much more accurate at a distance, but close up, far less dangerous.

Deciding, Macurdy walked toward the guard at the cellar stairway. The man's aura reflected boredom, resentment, inattentiveness. Heart in throat, Macurdy slipped past him and down the stairs, then turned toward the north wing. At the ell he saw the guards at the magazine doors. Now he had no doubt: His thefts had been discovered.

That left the question of his south wing stash, so he started for it. Peering around the south ell, he saw no one, so he continued to the room he'd made a bomb of. Was it booby-trapped? Wired to an alarm? He turned its knob and pushed; it made hardly a sound. Stepping inside, he closed it behind him and turned on the light. Things weren't as bad as he'd feared. The stack of TNT, and the musette bag on top of it, still were cloaked. Again he folded the towel against the bottom of the door, then ate a K ration and drank some water.

Now, he thought, to find the SS ordnance room and steal some grenades. Intent and somehow confident again, he retraced his way up the cellar stairs and past the guard, who, like the others, held his weapon at port arms, ready for quick use.

Macurdy, he told himself, *the guards aren't your main problem. Just find their damned ordnance room.*

There might, he thought, be a building diagram in Landgraf's office. Slipping past the staircase, he entered the corridor, stopped in front of the colonel's door, and put an ear to the panel. And heard the colonel's voice, apparently on the phone.

Macurdy straightened. He'd planned to warn Edouard Schurz before he blew the place; he might as well do it now. Warning Schurz was one of the details he'd deliberately omitted from his mission plan. He was confident the professor wouldn't expose him, but even Von Lutzow might object to warning the man: The reaction would be, why take the chance? So rather than disobey an order, Macurdy had said nothing about it.

Going to the staircase, he slipped past the guard and up to the second floor. Normally Edouard would be in the recreation room in mid-evening, so he peered in. Something new had been added—a radio, a large floor model, from which music issued—from Lohengrin, though he didn't know it. The only woman there was Berta, playing cards with a girl about 10 years old. Macurdy had never seen the child before. Otto was absent; Philipp sat turning cards as always, aimlessly it seemed; Manfred Eich sat in the broken-down easy chair by the window, reading. Edouard dozed with a magazine in his lap.

On an impulse, Macurdy tried to project a thought into Edouard's mind, but got no response, so he walked softly into the room and leaned near his ear from behind.

"Edouard," he whispered, "I am in the men's quarters. Come to me. Pretend that nothing unusual is happening. There is something urgent you must know."

Edouard opened his eyes, and for a long moment stared straight ahead, then got to his feet, lay the magazine on a shelf, and left. By that time Macurdy had backed out the door and moved quickly to the room, where he stood by the open latrine door. Edouard entered, looked around, and still failed to see him.

"In the latrine," Macurdy murmured, "in case anyone looks in," and watched a frowning Edouard walk past him not five feet away. Following him inside, Macurdy dropped his cloak and closed the door. "Here," he said quietly.

Turning, Edouard stared first at the strange uniform, then at Macurdy's face. *"Lieber Gott!"* he breathed.

"Where is Otto?"

"Sent away. Back to the farm; he is too old even for the *Volkssturm.* And Marie is gone; the old woman. And Sofia, the red-haired gypsy, God knows where. What has become of Anna?"

"As soon as we reached England, she turned us in. She is working for the Americans now. As I have been, all along, investigating the aliens, though she didn't know it."

Edouard's mouth was as round as his eyes.

"You need to get out of here, you and Berta. Tonight. I will take you to Switzerland with me. That's all I can tell you, except that if you stay, you will die."

"But—why? How will we die? I need to know more about this!"

Macurdy put his hands on Edouard's shoulders. "Look at my aura, Edouard, and trust me. I beg you!"

Edouard looked a long moment, licked dry lips. "How do we get out?"

"At midnight, I want you to open the window and throw out the fire rope, then climb down. If Berta cannot climb down, tie it beneath her arms and lower her over the window sill."

"But how do I get her? That will be after lights out."

"You are the Herr Doctor Professor. The guard will allow it. Just do it."

Edouard look unconvinced.

"What if she doesn't want to go?"

"She will. She told me before how much she longs to escape this country."

"She will never go without Lotta. You do not know Lotta; she is new here, a child 10 years old. She is like Marie; she does not speak. Colonel Landgraf has told me something of her history; her experience of life has been—ugly. Berta is very good for her."

"Then lower her, too. And when you get outside, move as quietly as you can. There may be guards, but there is no moon. Go to the forest and wait for me at the edge, near the stable." Macurdy glanced toward the door. "I haven't much time," he said, and from an inside pocket, took the folding stiletto he'd been issued in the 505th. "If Eich wakes up, and he probably will, he will try to stop you, cause an alarm. So use this first, through an eye socket into the brain. To the handle. If you simply cut his throat, you'll be a bloody mess."

He paused, then added, "Edouard, I know this is hard for you. But if you cannot do it for yourself, do it for the child. Give her a new life, with Berta."

He pressed the weapon into Edouard's hand, fearing as he did so that this man could never murder someone in their sleep. *That's all you can do for them,* he told himself. *From here it's up to Edouard.* He clapped the German on the shoulder, then opened the latrine door and peered into the room. No one was there, so he left, closed the door behind him and reactivated his cloak.

Edouard Schurz stared at the door that had closed in his face. Then, for a long moment, he regarded the small but deadly instrument in his hand, as if it might bite him. Before returning to the recreation room, he put it under his pillow.

Feeling more confidence than ever in his cloak, Macurdy returned to the first floor, meeting no one enroute except the unknowing guard on the second-floor landing. In the first floor corridor, he was alone except for the rather distant guards at the ells. His ear against Landgraf's door heard nothing. Still listening, he scratched softly, then tapped with a finger nail. Again nothing, so he took the set of lock picks from a tunic pocket. The bolt opened with an audible "cluck," and Macurdy glanced left and right down the corridor. No one had heard. Opening the door, he went in and closed it behind him, grateful that it swung inward.

The blackout curtains were drawn, and the corridor well enough lit that light wouldn't show beneath the door, so he switched on the ceiling light. *Now,* he thought, scanning around, *where . . .*

Shock gripped him, followed by a surge of excitement: On a table in front of the window lay the bright orange chute and ballast bag, and on top of them, the coil of fuse and the drawstring pouch. Quickly he stepped to them, and with hands that shook, opened the pouch, checked the contents, then tucked it into a tunic pocket. The coiled fuse he stuffed into a thigh pocket. Then, after a long deep breath, he tightened and relaxed his muscles to steady himself, and stepped quickly to the door. Again he heard nothing, but as the first floor was carpeted, that simply meant that no one was talking nearby in the corridor.

He switched off the light and pulled the door open—to see the corporal of the guard about to pass as he made his periodic round of the guard posts. The sight of the colonel's door opening jerked his gaze toward it—and reflexively, Macurdy's empty hand pumped a plasma charge into the corporal's head. The skull popped as if the contents had boiled, and the corporal fell bonelessly to the floor. From the south ell, the guard called, "What is wrong? What happened?"

Macurdy stepped into the hall at once; the corridors would soon be crowded, and it wouldn't do to be cornered in

Landgraf's office. He slipped silently but quickly to the foyer, going under instead of around the staircase, avoiding the view of the guard on the second-floor landing. But the man on guard at the cellar stairway stepped away from his post to look toward the disturbance, and seeing a body in front of Landgraf's door, hurried toward it. Macurdy barely got out of his way, then grasping the opportunity, stepped quickly to the cellar stairs and down them.

Moments later he was in the room with his TNT stash. There he cut off a long length of fuse, inserted it into a blasting cap, pressed the cap into a block of TNT, willed a bright bead of hot plasma at a fingertip—then stopped. If he blew the stack now, Edouard and Berta would die, and the child. If he didn't, the building would surely be searched, but . . .

So far his concealment spell had worked better than he'd ever expected. He would, he decided, sit on the TNT and wait. If they came in and looked, hopefully, probably, they'd see neither him nor the evidence. If they did see him, he'd pump a plasma charge into the stack.

The decision left him calm, even serene. Sitting on a ton of TNT, he assumed the meditation posture Varia had taught him, and began to meditate. Seldom had it gone so well. Remarkably, not even his ankles complained. After 20 minutes the door opened, the light turned on, soldiers peered behind the table, then the light went off again, the door closed, and they were gone.

Macurdy sat calmly through the hours, aware when midnight came and passed, and after a bit stood up without stiffness in knees or ankles. Using his penlight, he went to the switch and turned on the light, then put the towel in place. Next he cut a TNT block into four cubes, cut four short lengths of fuse and capped them with detonators, pressed a detonator into each cube, and put all four quarter-pound bombs inside his tunic. His remaining K rations he distributed in pockets.

Finally he lit the long fuse, turned out the light and left the room. He had only one thing more to accomplish—blow the magazines as quickly as possible, before something went irretrievably wrong.

At the north ell he paused a moment, peering around the corner at the guards outside the magazines. No longer bored or heedless, they were looking in his direction, submachine guns ready. He drew his .45. If he stepped out and snapped off two quick shots on target . . . But only one of the two needed to fire a burst in his direction, and even unaimed . . . Any significant wound would be deadly. So he compromised: His .45 ready but silent, he stepped out and started toward them.

It was obvious at once they didn't see him, but every step of the way he half-expected at least one of them to start firing. Both stood in mid-corridor, so he moved along one wall, and when he reached them, slipped by slowly, to avoid making an eddy of air. His senses were preternaturally sharp; he smelled his own stale sweat, with a lingering trace of cow manure, and wondered that the two Germans didn't. Ten feet past them he speeded up, and at the end of the corridor, opened the door to the room nearest the entryway. Then, quietly, he lifted the bar from the exit door, took it into the room, laid it by the wall, and stepped back into the corridor.

A hundred feet away, the magazine guards still stood with their backs to him. His .45 boomed twice, the shots so close together, the second man had hardly started to turn before a heavy slug smashed through a rib into the heart. Both men fell without firing.

Turning, Macurdy pushed open the entryway door, and with as little Baltic accent as he could manage, called: "For the love of God, come quickly!", then stepped back out of the way. He heard a brief exchange above the entryway, then one man ran down. As he passed, Macurdy shot him too, then stepped back into the room, took out one of his small, short-fuse blocks of TNT and lit it, intending to throw it out of the entryway and take out the other guard. With an eye on the sparking fuse, he stepped into the corridor—colliding with the other guard, who'd heard the unfamiliar boom of the .45, and after brief indecision, had run down to back up his buddy.

Both men recoiled with shock, then Macurdy pounced, at the same time tossing the block of TNT into the entryway. Wrapping powerful arms around the guardsman, he pinned the submachine gun between them, and wrestled him against the wall, out of line with the door. Felt, heard, smelled the man's weapon fire, bullets pocking the concrete near their feet. Squeezing with more strength than he knew he had—strength multiplied by desperation—he compressed the man's rib cage. For a long moment they struggled, the man's eyes bulging, then Macurdy found an added surge of strength, felt the man go limp, and staggered with him into the corner next to the entryway door. A quarter pound of TNT exploded just outside it. Macurdy let the German fall, and picking up the man's submachine gun, pointed it at him and squeezed the trigger, three rounds slamming into the fallen guard before the gun was empty.

Meanwhile there'd been a shout from somewhere up the corridor. Picking up the other guard's submachine gun, Macurdy started toward the magazines at a lope, then became aware of boots pounding on concrete, running toward the ell, so he slipped through an unlocked door, leaving a crack to peer through.

Landgraf himself rounded the ell first, followed by four guardsmen. An image imprinted on Macurdy's mind, of the colonel, tall riding boots freshly shined and a Luger in his hand. The others carried submachine guns. Seeing the bodies, they faltered, then one shouted, "Colonel! The door at the end of the corridor! It is open!"

The colonel led them on, half crouched now, no longer running. They'd almost reached the first two bodies when 1,800 half-kilo blocks of TNT exploded under the south wing. Even in the stone-walled cellar the sound was stupefying, and followed by the roar of floors, ceilings, roof, even sections of exterior walls collapsing into the cellar beneath. A thick cloud of dust rolled swiftly down the corridor and around the ell, and Macurdy closed his door, keeping it shut for half a minute, listening in darkness to the explosion's rumbling aftermath. Then he peered out again. The men in the corridor stood coughing in the settling dust, the colonel slightly bent, brushing it from his breeches, his tunic.

Turning to a sergeant, he chuckled. "Giesl, we are still alive! Is that not remarkable? One wonders why."

The five Germans were looking away, toward the ell.

Macurdy stepped into the corridor and fired two long bursts into them at a range of thirty feet. Then, willing his hands not to shake, he quickly picked the locks on both magazines, swung their doors open, lit the fuses on two of his remaining pieces of TNT, tossed them gently onto the two stacks of explosive—and sprinted down the corridor, up the steps of the entryway, and across dewy grass toward the trees.

He'd almost reached the forest when the north wing blew. Glass flew. The roof heaved upward. Sections of wall burst out, others, an instant later, fell inward. Macurdy sprawled headlong, hands pressed tardily to his ears.

He lay there for perhaps a minute, perhaps several, while additional stone blocks fell individually and in masses onto the rubble. Temporarily deaf, he did not hear them. Stunned but still functional, he got up, groped in a pocket, and replaced the magazine in his .45. He would not, it seemed to him, be finished until he was sure no Voitu had escaped.

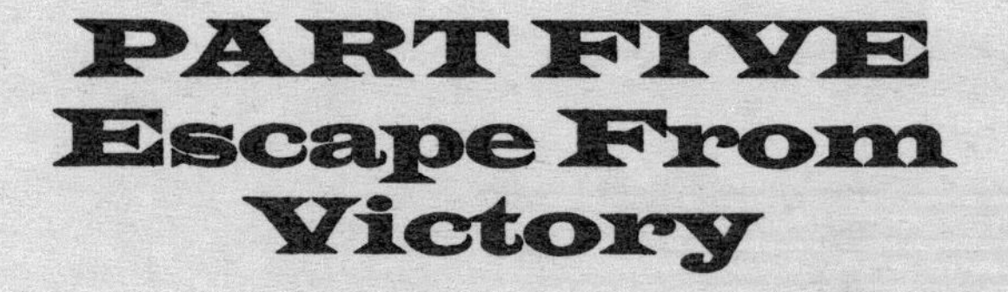
PART FIVE
Escape From
Victory

37

Flight

If Edouard and Berta had escaped the schloss, they should be at the forest's edge near the stable, but for now, Macurdy decided, he'd leave them there. It was more important, and more urgent, to find and kill any SS and Voitar who might have escaped. He doubted that any Voitar had; their wing had blown without warning. The SS, on the other hand, had been warned in time for at least some, perhaps most, to evacuate the building.

And it seemed to Macurdy that any who had would be in front, on the lawn or by the road, probably stunned. His cloak had persisted through the shock, and with his .45 in hand, he trotted across the turf toward the front of the building.

As he cleared the building's northwest corner, he saw auras glowing softly in the night, eight of them, almost at the road, their owners no doubt staring at the ruin some seventy yards in front of them. As he drew nearer, he saw that none were Voitar. He wished now he'd brought one of the loaded submachine guns from the cellar. From close up, he could have taken these nine from a flank with a couple of long bursts.

As it was . . . There were problems with using the .45. The muzzle blasts would mark his location, and one or more of the SS would have submachine guns, depending on how many had been on duty, and how many rousted out of bed by the south wing blast, to flee without stopping for weapons. And the .45's clip held only seven rounds.

Closing in, he became aware that not all were SS: He

recognized Edouard's aura, and Berta's. Another, which he'd missed before, was pressed close to Berta and much smaller; Lotta's. From their auras, all nine, psychics and SS, were more or less in shock, though none seemed wounded. Both blasts had taken them by surprise, whereas he'd been prepared, as much as he could be, for the enormity of sound and destruction. And probably, hopefully, their hearing hadn't fully recovered, as his hadn't. From ten yards he could see that both Edouard and Berta had their hands together in front of them, as if manacled.

Macurdy chose his target—the SS man beside Edouard—and Fairbairn in hand, moved up behind him. Quickly, smoothly, he reached around him with his left arm, clamping his forearm hard on the man's mouth, his hand gripping the submachine gun by the end of the short barrel, while the right slammed the fighting knife upward beneath the ribs, double edges slashing about, driven by a powerful wrist. Warm blood flowed down hand, wrist, forearm. He let the man down carefully, aware without seeing that Edouard stared, perhaps comprehending. He'd heard no sound—no gas or groan, no thrashing or kicking, no clatter of weapon falling. But even so, it seemed incredible that no one had reacted, that only Edouard had noticed.

He wiped his blood-slick right hand on the dead man's woolen tunic, then hissed in Edouard's ear: *"Bitte! Finde seine Schlüssel!"* Softly he stepped back and moved past Berta and Lotta. Berta still seemed unaware that anything had happened, even when Edouard, heeding Macurdy's order, knelt to find the dead guard's key ring. Macurdy transferred the guard's submachine gun from his left hand to his right, and fired a burst from it, sweeping it across the five remaining SS men at a distance of four to eight feet, right to left, then back before they'd had time to fall. Only one turned part way around, legs twisting and collapsing as he squeezed off a short burst of his own, into the ground, or perhaps a comrade.

Berta had screamed, but for an instant the sound didn't register on Macurdy. Nothing registered, except that it was finished—the Voitar and the blackbacks dead. He sank to his knees, emotionally spent.

"Montag?" The voice was Edouard's.

"Yes?"

"What do we do now?"

Thank you, professor, for the good question, Macurdy thought, and hands on thighs, got slowly to his feet. *Don't get weak on me now,* he told himself. *You're* not *finished. You won't be till we're all four out of Germany.* "Is there anyone else alive around here?" he asked.

"Only Manfred, I think. It was he who got us caught."

"You should have killed him, as I told you."

"I could not do it. And he seemed to be asleep. I thought we could get out without waking him."

"What about Philipp?"

"He is dead. When the south wing blew up, he ran crying toward the building, and a guard shot him." He paused. "Kurt, I cannot see you. It's hard to talk with you when I cannot see you."

Macurdy dropped his cloak, telling himself it worked a *lot* better than he'd thought, if Edouard couldn't see him, even hearing his voice and knowing where to look. Apparently it concealed his aura, too.

"What about it, Berta? Any possibilities besides Manfred?"

"I don't think so, not even any of the blackbacks. Three of these were the guards Captain Kupfer told to take us outside. The other three ran out after the south wing blew up. No one else came out. When we left, they were running around in there like terriers chasing rats.

"How much does Manfred know?"

It was Edouard who answered. "Too much. Berta asked questions, and I told her about you. That you were American, in a uniform with many pockets. Then she told me you could make yourself invisible, and us when we were together. I was about to tie the rope under her arms. Then Manfred jumped out of bed shouting, and began to grapple with me. A hall guard came at once."

Macurdy scowled in consternation. "And Manfred overheard all of it."

"Yes, and made up more to go with it. He told Kupfer you were a commando, and more were in the forest, come to kidnap the Voitar." He paused. "You are right, of course. I should have killed him."

Macurdy looked into the forest, seeing nothing but darkness. With a little luck he could find Manfred, whose aura would give him away at night, but there wasn't time. The explosions would have been heard for miles. People would have called the authorities, and they'd arrive soon, even if they had to come from Kempten. "It's time to leave," he said. "We will take one of the trucks."

He picked up another submachine gun, then they hurried to the machine shed, Berta holding the silently compliant Lotta by a hand. Macurdy started a truck, backed it to the stable, then found a flashlight in the glove compartment and went inside. There he found a loading ramp and stock rack, and with Edouard's help, wrestled them into place on the truck. The colonel's horses he loaded and secured without help; Edouard's only experience with large animals had been riding rented horses on holidays.

By the time the horses were secured, Edouard had grown visibly agitated; it seemed to him the police or SS would arrive before they could possibly get away. Macurdy, on the other hand, was intent and intense. Working swiftly, he found and loaded saddles, bridles, and extra horse blankets, rough and coarse; the horses already wore large quilted blankets belted on. After everything else was loaded, he helped Berta and Lotta in back, wrapped the extra blankets around them, and had them sit against a side rack.

That done, he paused, squatting, and peered at Lotta, whose eyes avoided his not by shifting away, but by focusing inward. In the "mental" layer of her aura were several small vortices. A moment's concentration turned one into an image that clarified for him what Edouard had meant by "ugly experiences."

"Herr Schurz told me your name is Lotta," he said quietly. "Berta and he call me Kurt Montag, but my name is really Curtis Macurdy, and I am American. You are the first person in Germany I have ever told my real name. I hope that when you know me better, you will be my friend, but that is up to you."

Then he cloaked Berta and the girl with a spell, got off the truck, and set the gate rack in place. "All right," he said to Edouard, "get in and let's go. You will drive."

"Um, Kurt—" Edouard spoke hesitantly. "I have never driven anything larger than a Volkswagen. Also I do not know how to get to Switzerland from here."

Macurdy frowned. With his bloody jumpsuit, he'd planned on sitting invisible beside Edouard, as navigator. But if anyone stopped them, they were out of luck anyway. With Berta and Lotta in back, and horses, they'd be in trouble if stopped. He'd probably gotten blood on things, too. So nodding but displeased, he got behind the wheel and drove away.

Alone, Macurdy could have walked to Switzerland unnoticed, even with the Alps in his way. But with two sedentary urban adults and a child . . . The truck greatly increased the risk of detection, but it could also take them a long way to start with. The urgent first thing to do was get onto some other road, one that wouldn't be used by military or police vehicles headed for the schloss.

They met no one, and Macurdy turned off at the first crossroad, in the village of Wiesenbach, nine kilometers from the schloss. The relief he felt showed him how tense he'd been. The road sign said LINDENDORF 11 KM, but neither he nor Edouard knew anything about Lindendorf. This was not a route he'd studied in training.

Well outside Wiesenbach, he stopped. "Look in my pack," he said. "There is a flat canvas holder with folded silk maps. Let's see where we go next."

Edouard dug them out and handed them to him without a word. Macurdy unfolded one, and using the flashlight, plotted a course with his eyes. Lindendorf was not on a direct route to anywhere helpful, but at least this road wasn't so immediately dangerous. He thought of bringing Berta and Lotta in front with them—they would be miserably cold in back, but crowded in the front seat, whoever sat by him would get blood on their clothing, and that needed to be avoided.

The back roads they took kept them clear of anything larger than a village, and again they met no other vehicle. He wasn't surprised. Not only was it night and the country lightly populated; shortages of fuel, parts, and civilian vehicles, and distance from the war zones, dictated little traffic even by day. When dawnlight began to spill from the east, they were in higher, more rugged country than before, its farms mostly along the road, and even along the road, forest predominated. Pausing, he rechecked the map, not for the first time, then drove slowly on. After a few minutes he spotted a narrow truck trail that disappeared into the forest, and turned in on it.

"Where are we going?" Edouard asked.

"To hide the truck and take a nap."

"But—it is too cold out there to sleep."

Macurdy thinned his lips. He drove some 300 yards to the end of the road, then stopped, got out, and opened the door on the other side. "Out," he said to Edouard, and gestured with a thumb. Edouard got out. Then he had Berta and Lotta get in; any blood on the seat should have dried by now. "Get some sleep," he told them. "We have a long day ahead of us. Then he climbed in back, and without asking for help, manhandled the heavy ramp quickly into place, led the horses down it, tied their halter ropes to stout saplings, and removed their blankets.

"Here," he said, holding the blankets out to Edouard. "Take them. They won't be enough, but they'll help."

Edouard stared, not taking them. "What will you use?"

"Take the goddamn things!" Macurdy said sharply in English. "I know how to keep warm without them."

Flinching, Edouard took them, and Macurdy switched back to German. "You need to understand something: I am trying to save your life, yours and theirs." He gestured toward the cab. "I could have avoided a lot of trouble by forgetting you. You would be dead back there in the schloss, buried in the rubble, and I would be gone. Nobody could see me, and I would have no trouble hiking out of here. But you were my friends. I could not abandon you.

"Last evening I gave you a tool, a weapon, and told you to use it. You didn't. I was afraid you wouldn't, but I trusted you anyway. My error. By giving in to your own squeamishness, you have put us all in needless danger. Because if Manfred was dead, the police and SS would assume that everyone there had died in the explosions, except the handful of SS that I butchered outside. They would be watching for a force of airborne raiders, not a man, a woman, and a child; and me they would not see."

He took a deep breath. "So listen well: I am the commander on this mission. In emergencies, do what I tell you without questioning. Without hesitation! More lives than your own may depend on it. If it is *not* an emergency, and you have an objection, tell it to me once. If I do not agree, that is the end of it."

Macurdy paused. "If you cannot abide by those rules, tell me now. I will leave you a blanket and one of the four field rations I have left, and take Berta and Lotta with me."

Edouard's face had reddened, turned wooden. After a long moment he replied. "I understand, and I will accept your orders. I appreciate what you have done for us, and you have every right to be angry. I regret that I had not learned to think like a soldier."

Macurdy gripped his shoulder, and his words were mild. "Thank you. It is not surprising you thought like a civilian, but it was unfortunate. For the next few days, you will think like a soldier." He smiled, and his voice softened further. "When we get to Switzerland, you can think like a civilian again, and in a year or so, when this war is over, I can too. Now scrape some fir needles together and lie down. I will set my mental alarm clock for three hours, then we will be on our way again."

Few motor vehicles passed them on the road. Now and then, in the vicinity of farms, a woman, older man, or youngster passed on foot, or riding a wagon or draft horse. What the passersby saw was a family on a day off, an outing. Usually a rather tall slender man on a horse, riding slowly southward, followed by a woman on another, their daughter holding on to her mother's waist from behind. The man and woman would wave cheerily, and sometimes received a wave in return. The daughter neither waved nor loosed her grip. Others, however, saw only one horse, led by the slender man on foot. On those occasions, Macurdy was riding, and had cloaked his horse as well as himself.

The passersby, of course, did not exchange notes. They saw,

then dismissed the sight as unimportant. Few even noted that the horses were remarkably well-bred for such undistinguished riders, or for the district.

Occasionally the family paused to let the horses graze the burgeoning spring grass beside the road, or drink from the ditch. Then the woman and girl got down to walk around stiffly.

Once, as they passed an elderly man trudging toward them headed north, horse apples appeared noisily out of nowhere and dropped onto the graveled road. Stopping, the old man gawped. For the first time the girl made a sound, giggling behind a hand. The old man seemed not to hear, as if his ears were faulty, merely stared at the pile of new dung steaming in the morning sun, while the family rode on. After a pause, he continued down the road, seeming dazed. He'd tell no one; he valued his reputation.

When they were well past him, the mother joined in the giggling. For the next several minutes both mother and daughter giggled from time to time, while the father smiled. Both "parents" were thrilled at the sound from their "daughter"; neither had heard her laugh before.

The family had learned to see their companion when they tried. Presumably others, unaware and less talented, would not. His very foreign-looking khaki jumpsuit showed extensive stains, especially the right sleeve and trouser leg—blood browned from drying, but recognizable. A web-belt rode at his waist, with a holstered pistol and a sheathed knife. A Schmeisser submachine gun was slung on a shoulder. On his back was a plywood pack frame with a large green canvas bag, fat with horse blankets. Had a passerby seen him, they'd certainly have reported it.

From time to time the riders got down and led the horses back into the forest, where they all rested out of sight, the humans sometimes nibbling morsels from an unheated ration, passing a container around, sharing, then burying the small green can or wrapper, hiding the evidence. Occasionally one of them refilled the canteen from some mountain stream passing beneath the road. Their waters might not have passed a purity test, but generations of farmers and herd girls had drunk from them with few ill effects.

The sun was in the west when they approached the village of Schöndorf, in a broad bowl occupied mostly by farms, the road keeping to one side, along the forest edge—the sort of scene described in travelguides as "picturesque." Limping a bit, the father led the horse out of sight among the trees. His feet had blistered. When he stopped, his wife and daughter climbed down from the horse, clearly saddle sore.

Their invisible companion left his horse with them, and trotted back to the edge of the woods on foot, where he stood appraising a small house some two hundred yards away. His stomach growled; he'd eaten nothing all day, explaining to the others that he drew energy from the Web of the World. Considering all the other unlikely things he'd done, they took his word for it. His stomach on the other hand, wasn't convinced, and there were only two rations left. By the time they slept that night, there'd be none.

The SS had no doubt checked maps for possible routes to Switzerland. This seemed one of the least likely, but they'd no doubt look into it, and one of the things they'd check would be places where food could be bought.

Macurdy heard a screendoor slam. A woman came into the yard, carrying a large basket, set it down beside the laundry hanging in the sun, and disappeared into the privy. Macurdy headed for the house at a strong lope; he'd hardly get a better chance in this village.

Hopefully there wouldn't be a dog.

There wasn't. When he returned to the family in the woods, his tunic bulged with a loaf of rye bread and an eight-inch wheel of cheese. He'd been tempted to leave two reichsmark notes in payment, reichsmarks printed by the British SIS, and issued to him by the OSS, good enough that even a banker with a magnifying glass wouldn't recognize them as counterfeit. But payment would surely cause talk, while as it was, the woman might simply be puzzled, and say nothing beyond her own living room.

He hoped, though, that the absence would go unnoticed until he and his wards were well away. With that in mind, he ordered them back onto their horses, and trotting ahead of them, backtracked a half mile to the edge of the open basin, where a lane ran along the forest's edge, toward the higher mountains at the head of the valley.

They camped two miles above the basin, beside a mountain stream. There was a cattle trail along it, leading to an alpine pasture with what, on his map, seemed to be a cow camp. The map showed not only contours—the terrain—but forest, colored pale green, with openings in white, and buildings shown as tiny squares. The trail they'd followed was marked by a curling line of tiny dashes. In Oregon the cattle would be untended, but here, he suspected, someone would be with them.

Sooner or later, someone would come across the truck and report it, hopefully only after several days. But it might already have happened. Then the SS would know in what area to look. That meant pushing on as fast as they could, faster than Edouard and Berta might think possible.

Dusk had begun to settle, and Macurdy ate with the others, though lightly, appeasing his surly stomach. He'd chosen the hard tough heel from each end of the loaf, along with a slice of cheese, taking small bites, chewing slowly and thoroughly.

Tomorrow was important. They had a long way to go. He could only hope no one would find the truck for a while.

38

Bruno Krieger

The Munich airport felt like summer. Lt. Karl Hintz perspired in his black winter uniform. The only protection from the midafternoon sun was the black command car he'd arrived in, and it was like an oven. If the damned plane had been on time . . . Or had it been sent to the wrong airfield? Perhaps the officer he waited for had landed at the fighter base.

At any rate here he was, melting into his boots.

A plane approached from the north—most did, here—and grew larger to his hopeful eyes. The hope faded: It was a nondescript, single-engined craft resembling some used for civilian purposes before the war. Idly he watched it assume a landing course and make its approach, flaps down. It lifted its nose, and the wheels hit the runway smoothly, the plane slowing as she rolled, finally to taxi toward the SS parking strip and black sedan. The plane too was black, and now he could see the SS death's head emblem on its fuselage, and a swivel-mounted machine gun by the door.

Apparently, Hintz decided, this was it after all.

It stopped, propeller feathered, engine idling, and a man wearing fatigue coveralls swung easily out the door; a crew member, Hintz decided. Clearly not the important man from Berlin he'd been sent to meet.

Still, the man walked directly toward him, remarkably tall despite round shoulders, and with indecently long arms that hung like an ape's. Hintz stared. The nearer the man came, the more alarming he looked, swarthy as a Greek and lantern-jawed, with cheekbones like russet doorknobs. Despite his complexion, the deep-socketed eyes were pale blue. Hintz stared. The creature stopped in front of him, its slight smile sardonic. It had been stared at before.

"I am Captain Bruno Krieger," he said, adding "Heil Hitler!" and saluting. The salute, it seemed to Hintz, held something between disdain and contempt; he wasn't sure if it reflected disrespect for the salute or for himself.

The man stood as if waiting, and abruptly Hintz realized he hadn't returned the salute! And neither had his driver!

"Heil Hitler!" His heels clacked, his arm shot out, and he almost shouted the words, the driver echoing them.

The pale eyes washed over him, leaving heat and queasiness behind. "Well? Are you going to take me to Major Hauser? Or must I stand in the sun the rest of the day?"

"Of course," Hintz said, then realized his answer could be taken either way, and hurriedly opened the car door for the visiting captain. Contempt, he decided. The captain's tone had definitely been contempt, and directed at him. As they drove away, he thought, *Wait till you report to Major Hauser in that fatigue coverall. He will rake you over the coals till you cry for mercy.*

Major Hauser did no such thing. He'd never before seen Bruno Krieger, but he knew his reputation. The disgraceful-looking troll had been one of General Heydrich's favorites, a hunter and triggerman who, after Heydrich's death, had remained popular with headquarters in Berlin, despite his well-known lack of courtesy. For he was more than a faithful and deadly hound; they were numerous in the SS. Krieger had a reputation as uncannily skilled in tracking, getting close to, and destroying the victims assigned him. There were even some—notably Reichsführer Himmler—who credited Krieger with occult powers. He was said to have terminated, decisively, several conspiracies against important figures, including, it was claimed, one against *der Führer*.

It was also said that Heydrich had intended to promote him to major, but Krieger had demurred. Promotion, he'd said, would weaken his position. As a captain—a common enough rank—most saw him as the sword of the general who'd sent him, representing the authority of his commander. As a major, that perception would be reduced; some would look at him as having only his own authority.

It was also told that when *der Führer* heard the story—and Heydrich had made sure he heard it—he dictated a letter to the captain, with a copy to his personnel file, expressing his admiration.

Thus Hauser was cordial, though maintaining his nominal seniority, and Krieger did not bait him as he had the young lieutenant.

"What can you tell me about this Kurt Montag?" Krieger asked.

"Essentially nothing that was not in my report to Berlin, or in their reports to me. He presented himself as mentally and physically defective, and became the most promising psychic in *das Weutische Projekt*. Then he was sent to England to make difficulties for Anglo-American headquarters there, using some confidential means, reputedly psychic. But in fact he was an American officer, who then captured the Abwehr's London station chief and his staff. Which of course resulted in a chain of arrests, and collapsed the entire London-area operation.

"A London informant reports that 'Kurt Montag's' real name is Chris McCarthy. He is a decorated American *Fallschirmjäger* from the fighting in North Africa and Sicily, a man with neither conscience nor mercy.

"Our Captain Reiter investigated the destruction at Schloss Tannenberg. With information from a neighboring farmer and a surviving psychic, he established that Montag-McCarthy returned via parachute, apparently alone, and destroyed the Schloss not only with its entire complement of our people, but with the Voitar quartered there. Our records show there were five tons of TNT stored in the cellar. It was undoubtedly this he used, after transferring part of it to the other wing to ensure that no one escaped alive. All this while a guard platoon was stationed in the building.

"The TNT had been taken there for use in bargaining with

the Voitar, but for some reason they lost interest in it. Colonel Landgraf three times requested its removal, but Berlin had not gotten around to it." He shrugged. "The manpower shortage, I suppose. It was certainly not something they'd send interned Balts or Frenchmen to do."

Hauser spread a map on his desk. "Your quarry escaped the Schloss in one of our trucks there, taking with him three of the four surviving psychics: a man, a woman, and a ten-year-old girl. They left with him willingly. Yesterday, forest workers discovered the truck abandoned here, hidden in the forest." He pointed at an X penciled on the map. "Obviously they intend to escape via Liechtenstein. He was undoubtedly provided with military maps, and well-briefed on routes out of the country. So he knows he will have to take one of these." The finger moved decisively, there and there and there. "He will know that with a woman and child, anything more difficult is impossible, whether on horseback or on foot.

"If pressed, he will no doubt abandon the horses first, then his companions, but he will set out on one of those routes. Even so . . ."

Hauser paused, clearing his throat like a lecturer. "The nature of the terrain and the shortage of men make it impossible to scour the country looking for them. Too much is forest, and there are small, boulder-littered ravines beyond count. *But*, there are a limited number of places through which he can cross. That is the key."

Again he paused, looking uncomfortable with what he was about to add. "I must mention that the other psychic insists this Montag-McCarthy can make himself literally invisible. I would reject the notion out of hand, except for two things: the havoc he has wreaked, and that he is a certified psychic. Even with confederates inside, to accomplish what he did . . ." Hauser shook his head. "And it is questionable that the people he took with him could have contributed much. A nurse, an academic, and a child. They are not the type."

Krieger grunted. Listening to Hauser's lecture, he'd gotten a deep, intuitive sense of his quarry. This Montag would not abandon the people with him, of that he was certain. And as for routes—he was likely to select one which men like Hauser would not expect, perhaps carrying the child and bullying the others. As for invisibility— If it was real, Krieger had no doubt he could see through it.

"Anything else?" he asked.

"There was one thing, but Captain Reiter rejects it, and I agree with him. The psychic who informed on them believed that Montag-McCarthy had outside confederates, other *Fallschirmjäger*. A small parachute was found caught on a nearby pasture fence. It was marked U.S. Army, and carried fuse and detonators, so we had the surroundings searched. Only a single large parachute was found, concealed beneath shrubs in the woods. There was no evidence, none at all, of any other intruders. And in such an operation, to such a man, stealth is more practical than firepower."

His Captain Reiter is a sound detective, Krieger decided, *and seemingly the major himself is not bereft of intelligence. Or integrity; he gave credit where credit was due.*

"I am told," Hauser went on, "that you will hunt them from the air. That should simplify matters. If you find them, you need simply fly past and machine-gun them."

"I will take him alive."

"Alive?!"

"I have two squads of our own *Fallschirmjäger* at my disposal."

Parachutists? Landing in the high Alps? Lunacy! The air is too thin! "But if this McCarthy is invisible, how will they find him? How will *you* find him?"

Krieger half grunted, half snorted, and his eyes seemed to glow. "I will find him," he said. "In daylight or dark, I will find him. I always do."

Hauser's short hair bristled, and any doubt he'd had, died.

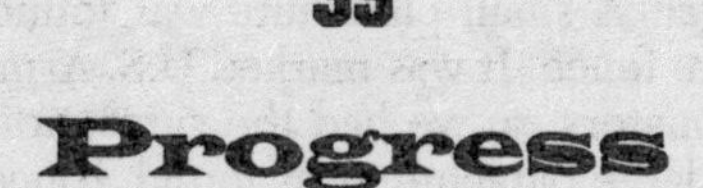

39

Progress

The four fugitives started their second day before sunup, and by midmorning came to a high pasture, with what in Oregon would be called a cow camp, though here the cows were milk cows, not beef. They bypassed it, keeping out of sight in the forest. Afterward they worked their way up a rocky draw above it, riding at first, then leading their horses. The draw topped out at a notch, which on the other side overlooked a deep and narrow valley that Macurdy thought of as a canyon. He hadn't been sure, from the map, if they could take the horses down into it or not, but one way or another, they had to reach the bottom.

The horses had enough trouble just getting to the notch. The other side was worse—a steep declivity. Partly the trail crossed treacherous scree that by itself prohibited horses, and partly it crossed open sideslopes, mostly of bare rock, almost too steep for burros. The way was marked by summer cairns, scattered and minimal, mostly just two or three rocks tall.

They had no choice but to leave the horses behind, and travel afoot. Macurdy would have set the animals free, but if he did, they'd soon find the chalet, and the herd girls there would stable or hobble them. Then, if soldiers came searching, they'd know, and capture would be probable.

So he had the others wait, resting, and led the horses back to the last patch of forest, shading a remnant of old snow, dirty with fallen needles. There he took them behind a thickly limbed spruce blowdown, some hundred feet from the trail, tied their reins to branches, and pumped a plasma charge into each beautiful head. It was not the easiest thing he'd ever done. Then he cast his spell of concealment over them, uncertain how long it would last.

Hopefully the herd girls would tell any soldiers that no one could ride horses over the mountain, and after a search of the woods around the pasture, they'd go back. Unless, of course, they found the prints of shod horses, and he'd skirted the trail itself to minimize the risk.

So presumably, if soldiers followed it to the notch, they'd miss the carcasses. Then, seeing what the trail was like on the south side, and assuming their quarry was mounted, they'd conclude that this route had been a false lead.

Unless carrion birds found the horses, and drew the soldiers' attention. He'd seen ravens earlier that day, and an eagle soaring.

He rejoined the others and they started down, all of them walking except on the scree slopes, where Macurdy carried Lotta on his shoulders. Instead of ankle-high SS boots, she wore sandals buckled on with straps; the sharp, frost-broken scree would have crippled her. Carrying her on his shoulders gave him a higher center of gravity than was safe, and made a crick in his neck, but there was no place for her on his back. He was carrying the packframe, with the two large, quilted and belted horse blankets stuffed into the drop bag. And neither Edouard nor Berta was physically up to carrying Lotta or the pack, at least not more than briefly. Each carried one of the smaller woolen blankets, rolled, and tied over a shoulder.

At least, Macurdy told himself, it was downhill today. Tough on the feet, of course, but easier on the thighs and buttocks than the uphill grind they'd face later.

Finally they crossed the forested lower slope, and turned west up the canyon bottom, guiding on Macurdy's map, keeping to the trees when possible. He didn't want some herd girl to see them, even though the route was unlikely.

Later they crossed the canyon, wading a swift icy stream, to reach the descending side canyon Macurdy had decided on. It too had a trail, that led steeply up and up to two large high meadows occupying basins, the lower of them with a cow camp.

More and more, Lotta rode on Macurdy's shoulders, her trust

in him seeming absolute now, though still she didn't speak. Each of the fugitives, even Lotta, had blistered feet from hiking on steep slopes, but they pushed steadily on, no one complaining. Macurdy had promised to heal them when they stopped at day's end. Edouard, although he tried, couldn't entirely believe him, but knew that Berta believed, so he hoped. Otherwise—there'd be time to heal in Switzerland.

As they got higher, the forested and north-facing stretches had old snow, newly trampled by cattle being driven to the high pastures. Eventually, well up on the mountain, they reached the first grassy bowl, with deep old drifts around the edges. At the lower edge was a set of small, steep-roofed log buildings. The elevation was considerably higher than they'd reached that morning, even at the notch.

It was time to replenish their food supply. The stolen bread and cheese were mostly gone, and there were hard miles to hike before they came to the villages and farms along the road to Liechtenstein.

The road to Liechtenstein. There lay the greatest danger, with little he could do about it except avoid attention. Meanwhile they needed rest as well as food. He'd carried Lotta much of the time—most of the time that afternoon—grateful she was small, and Edouard and Berta were a lot more tired than he. He wished he was in the shape he'd been in at Oujda or Chilton Foliat, or Benning or Camp Robinson, but even so he was doing pretty well, tapping the Web of the World. If it weren't for the damn blisters . . .

Close below the lower basin, he cloaked the others and left them to rest near the trail, then scouted till he found a secluded opening facing the late sun. He led the others there, and they unshipped the blankets. Then Macurdy worked on their feet until, to Edouard's awe, they could actually see new pink skin covering the rawness. Finally Macurdy worked at flushing the fatigue acids from their legs and buttocks; after a day like this, they'd stiffen seriously if nothing effective was done. With Berta and Lotta, he worked without touching legs or buttocks. Berta he didn't want to excite. As for Lotta—he remembered the images in her trauma vortices.

Berta watched everything he did, asking questions, intent on learning. She couldn't see the energy threads, but perhaps with practice . . . Certainly Kurt's methods were much more precise than those she'd used.

Lotta too had watched and listened, and still without speaking, duplicated his actions. When Macurdy asked her if she saw clouds of light around people, she looked away shyly. *At least,* he thought, *it wasn't fearfully.*

When he'd finished his healings, they napped. He intended later to send Edouard and Berta to the cow camp to buy food. In these times, a couple hiking in the mountains might well seem suspicious, certainly if they weren't wearing hiking clothes. But that suspicion would be less for the two of them alone than if they had a child with them wearing sandals.

It was near evening when Edouard and Berta approached the cow camp, Edouard carrying the pack now. The camp consisted of a cabin that housed the herd girls, along with the pans and utensils they used to make butter and cheese; and a springhouse, woodshed, storage shed, two long cow sheds, the hay shed, a privy, and a guest cabin for the men when they came to make hay.

A large dog bounded toward the couple, but kept some distance, not threatening, or even barking after sounding his initial alarm. His strong tail waved tentatively.

Meanwhile Macurdy and Lotta waited a couple of hundred feet away, invisible. The dog paid them no heed—either couldn't see them, or simply didn't notice them standing motionless against a background of forest.

The barking brought two aproned "herd girls" from the cabin, one a graying woman in her fifties, square, with strong square hands, the other a shy-seeming girl, slight and blond, perhaps twelve years old. The older woman, Edouard supposed, provided the know-how and confidence. The younger no doubt helped her milk and cut firewood, herded the cows and learned the trade. Their auras reflected basic mild contentment, but just now, the older did not entirely trust the visitors.

Both Edouard and Berta tried to look as fit and vigorous

as they could, which was easier now that they weren't limping. Edouard told the women they were on a hiking holiday. Macurdy's pack tended to support the story, though it would have been better had it resembled the usual German rucksack.

Using some of Macurdy's counterfeit reichsmarks, Edouard bought new butter, uncured cheese, freshly baked bread, and a jug of buttermilk, promising to return the jug before they left.

"Where will you sleep tonight?" the woman asked. "It gets very cold at night, with so much snow left. The sun goes down, and 'poof' it is freezing! We always keep the cows in at night until after it has melted."

Edouard and Berta looked at one another, then back at the woman. "What do you suggest?" he asked.

"You can stay in the hay shed tonight. I will charge you—" The woman thought a moment. "One reichsmark."

Edouard didn't hesitate. Reaching into his pocket, he gave her another reichsmark, and thanked her.

Macurdy watched the woman take Edouard and Berta to the hay shed, leave them there and return to the cabin. Moments later Edouard reappeared, and looking toward where they'd parted, motioned to him. Macurdy and Lotta joined them, and Edouard told what he'd arranged. Macurdy agreed: Sleeping in the hay shed seemed a good idea, and a very good bargain. And both Edouard and Berta could see and read auras; they should know—suspect at least—if the woman was a threat.

After they'd eaten, they went outside in the failing daylight, to a nearby outcrop of dark rock still warm from the sun. There the invisible Macurdy worked on their feet and legs again. Meanwhile the two herd girls went to the hay shed with pitchforks, and for a while carried hay to the cow shed a few yards distant.

Despite himself, Macurdy worried again. "Are you sure the woman can be trusted?"

"I would know if she couldn't," Edouard answered, and Berta agreed. Then Berta asked Macurdy to show them again how he healed, and this time Edouard also tried to see, or at least feel the energy threads.

The dusk thickened, dew began to form on the grass, and they returned to the hay shed to sleep, Berta holding Lotta in her arms like a mother might hold her child. Edouard had told Macurdy, the evening before, why the Occult Bureau had been interested in Lotta. Macurdy wondered what kind of dreams she had.

40

Lotta

Bruno Krieger's mood was deteriorating. To start the day, the plane's engine had failed the pre-flight checklist, and he'd waited on the ground in Munich for more than two hours while the pilot and a mechanic had worked and cursed, getting it ready to fly. Then, after several hours of flying, they'd had to land at Kempten and refuel, and their luck had not improved since. If they didn't find his quarry fairly soon, they'd have to leave and refuel again, which would take them till evening.

Where in hell was the American bastard?

He turned and spoke to his pilot. "Fly over the Vorarlberg Highway," he said. "West from Bludenz."

It was unreasonable to expect he'd gotten that far, but this Montag was an unreasonable man, an extraordinary man, aside from any occult powers he might have. The paratrooper of whatever nationality was trained to exceptional performance, reflecting determined will even more than physical toughness.

And among them, some stood out. And among those . . .

The pilot had said nothing, responding to the order by banking and gaining altitude, to clear the mountain ridge to the south. Short, compact, hard-looking, he was a taciturn man who smoked incessantly. Different though they were, he and Krieger were highly compatible, and through Krieger's influence, he received enough assignments to keep more or less busy, and in food and cigarettes. Like Krieger, he was non-political and non-military, a highly skilled professional who mouthed party slogans only when he had to, and with reservations. Politically he was a complete cynic, militarily part cynic, part pragmatist. For him, the important thing was to fly, preferably on interesting missions, though they were the exception. In the first war he'd been a decorated fighter pilot with twenty-three kills, but at age fifty-six and with a heart murmur, the Luftwaffe was not interested in him. Nor was the SS, except as a civilian sometime-employee, which was how he preferred it.

They cleared a high crest, Krieger's calm eyes taking in the landscape to the south. Ahead lay the Ill Valley, with broad pastures, areas of dark forest, and along the river a railroad and narrow paved highway, with cultivated fields on the better ground. Here and there, tongues of forest led down to it from steep slopes higher up, mostly accompanying small streams that flowed into the Ill.

Krieger's attention became more focused as they approached the highway. If the people he hunted were on the road, it seemed to him they'd be easily seen. If they were keeping to the forested land, steeper and rougher, that was something else, but the going there would be much more difficult for them.

The pilot turned west above the road, and Krieger aimed his binoculars along it. Soon he saw a man and woman walking beside the pavement, each carrying something over a shoulder. A rolled blanket perhaps. But what might there be that he wasn't seeing? His focus sharpened. Something, something—

Abruptly a retinal image popped into his consciousness, of a man in uniform, wearing a pack and with a child on his shoulders! It was as if the man had suddenly materialized a few meters ahead of the couple. A chill surged over Krieger, accompanied by exultation, then the plane was past, and not wanting to alarm them, he let the pilot continue west.

"Did you see the couple we passed on the road?" he asked.

"Yes."

"How many were with them?"

"With them?" It seemed a strange question. "None."

If verification were needed, *Krieger thought,* that was it. I saw the third and fourth, he did not. Therefore, the man carrying the child is Montag, hidden in some sort of concealment spell. *He'd heard of concealment spells: Because of his own talents, he'd read rather widely on the occult—the traditional as well as popular and quasi-technical literature—but had never seen evidence that concealment spells were real. "Continue down the valley," he said, "then circle back, wide, so they do not see you. They must not suspect our interest."*

He took the microphone from its mount and called a young officer waiting at the airfield outside Kempten, giving him instructions. The officer listened intently, jotting notes on a map, then got his squads quickly aboard their plane. While the twin engines warmed, he briefed the pilot. Ten minutes after the call, the planeload of SS Fallschirmjäger *rolled down the runway, lifting sluggishly with little tarmac to spare, then climbed and turned south. It would, the pilot told himself, fly better after his human cargo had jumped.*

Macurdy had been only mildly concerned about planes. A couple walking along a road didn't seem terribly suspicious. A couple on a mountain trail had been another matter, but they were over with now. And with a road that led directly to a border crossing, it made sense to use it, even though it ran mostly through open ground, with occasional villages.

He traveled with Lotta sharing his cloak, holding her hand or carrying her. Presumably, hopefully, Edouard and Berta wouldn't attract attention, but even so, approaching and passing through villages they'd played it safe, all four clustered under Macurdy's cloak. It was awkward, requiring coordination, but near the border, where candidate routes narrowed to a few crossings, they'd play it safe. The truck had probably been found by now, a compelling clue to their route.

Three times in the past hour or two he'd heard a plane, and twice had seen one, perhaps the same one. It worried him, perhaps needlessly. He could have been written off as unlikely to cause further harm, and not worth committing German manpower to hunt down. Or perhaps the truck hadn't been found after all. Something might even have happened to Manfred.

But it seemed more likely that Manfred *had* talked to the SS, that the truck *had* been found, and that the SS wanted very much to nail him, along with any presumed accomplices.

Then surely they'd have warned the authorities to watch for them, not only as a foursome, but as separate individuals. They'd have descriptions, and if he were one of those authorities, he'd have notified village storekeepers and constables to watch for them. Perhaps even warned the local population by radio, those who had electricity.

Meanwhile all four were limping again, Berta worst of all. He'd healed blisters and muscles each night, and treated them at breaks during the day. Without the healing they'd have been much worse, but even so, they limped.

There'd been more forest the last couple of miles, providing cover for breaks, but Macurdy was waiting for a brook or creek. There they'd have a real rest. He'd work on their feet, then they'd nap until dusk, and continue to Feldkirch after dark.

And reach the border crossing that night. There'd be guards, of course, but with a little luck, they'd get across in a tight group, cloaked.

The road was passing through wide hay meadows, their grass knee high, when a movement caught his attention from a tongue of forest some eighty yards ahead. "Stop," he said quietly, and gestured the others back. They stopped, and for a moment nothing happened, then uniformed men stepped from behind trees, weapons aimed toward them, or at least toward Edouard and Berta.

"All four of you!" one shouted. "Do not move. You are under arrest!"

All four! They saw him *then!* Slowly he set Lotta on the ground as the men started toward him. "When I say *down,*" Macurdy murmured, "I want you all to fall flat on the ground." He gave them a second to digest the order, then snapped "Down!"

And dropped himself, not quite flat, his left elbow holding his upper torso off the ground, his right hand raised as gunfire erupted ahead of him. Two-centimeter plasma charges pumped from his slightly cupped right palm, quick as bullets but without gunshots. And more accurate, as if they sought their targets.

The gunfire stopped, and he rolled from the roadside into the shallow ditch beside it, then looked at Lotta lying on the shoulder a few feet away, her eyes wide with fear. "Lotta!" he hissed. "Roll into the ditch! Now!"

He hadn't been sure she would, had thought she might be frozen with fear. He was partly right; she didn't roll. She stood half up, then threw herself almost on top of him.

And no one fired!

He looked back. Edouard and Berta still lay on the road, seemingly unhit, eyes as wide with fear as Lotta's, though theirs were on the forest, not on him. "Edouard, Berta," he husked, "roll to the ditch!"

As soon as they moved, the silence was torn by three or four seconds of gunfire that made Macurdy press his cheek against the ground. When it was over, he looked up again. The men ahead had moved back into the concealment of tree trunks.

From behind him, Berta called, "Kurt! They have shot Edouard," and looking back, Macurdy saw the professor lying on the shoulder, doubled at waist and knees, making tiny grunting sounds: "Uh, uh, uh!"

Macurdy dismissed it for the moment—there was nothing he could do about it—and gave his attention to something else: The enemy hadn't fired when he'd rolled, or when Lotta had gotten up. "Berta, listen to me," he said tautly. "I am going to cloak you, you and Edouard, but you must stay where you are. Do not move! The cloaks cannot follow you. And stay as flat as you can; cloaks don't fool bullets."

After casting his spell he stood up, slowly, carefully, arms above his head as if surrendering. Nothing happened. He lowered his arms; still nothing. *They don't see me*, he thought. *They only* assume *there are four of us*. But how did they know he was there? Manfred! Manfred had told them he could make himself invisible, and they'd believed him!

Then someone emerged from behind a pine, holding a submachine gun. Macurdy froze, then lowered himself to the ground again. After a moment, three others stepped from the woods, guns ready, and all four began advancing. As they drew near, Macurdy made out the leader's collar patch—a lieutenant—and after a few more yards, saw the color of the intent eyes. Blue. They flicked around as if seeking.

Macurdy raised both palms, pumped plasma charges toward the approaching men, then flattened himself against the ground, peering through the roadside grass. All four were down, dead.

It took a moment, as if the troopers left behind hadn't fully grasped what they'd seen. There'd been no gunshots, and in the afternoon sunlight, they shouldn't have spotted the darting plasma charges. Certainly not at that distance. Then a voice called from the forest: "Lieutenant! Are you all right?"

When there was no answer, a tentative rifle shot was fired, then another. When that brought no response, they let loose an intense flurry of gunfire, lasting three or four seconds.

After that it was quiet again. It had to be damned spooky for them; presumably they couldn't see Edouard or Berta any longer either. For a long half minute he didn't move, then turned onto his side and now cast a separate cloak over Lotta, lying beside him in the grass. "Lotta," he said, "do not get up. They cannot see you if you stay where you are, and the bullets won't hit you if you lie flat." He hoped.

Again he got up, and again no one fired. Slowly, watchfully, he started toward the woods, but had gone only about a dozen yards when four more troopers dashed from the sheltering trees, staying low, well dispersed, to hit the ground a few yards into the field.

At that same instant, Macurdy hit the ground too. A moment later the four were on their feet again, this time covered by a flurry of gunfire from the woods. When it stopped, he raised his head. A moment later the four were up and dashing another few yards, again with covering fire. This time Macurdy kept his head up enough to watch. The fire came from four men, in the forest somewhat off to his right, and having drawn no return fire, they didn't retire so completely behind their sheltering tree trunks when they finished.

Again the four on the ground dashed forward, bolder now, covering ten or twelve yards before hitting the ground. Again they had covering fire from the woods. The instant the covering fire stopped, Macurdy rose to his knees, pumping silent plasma charges toward the men who'd shot, then dropped prone again. At almost the same moment, the men on the ground got up and dashed forward once more, as if they hadn't noticed his return fire.

It was then he became aware of a sound he'd been ignoring. A plane was circling at a little distance. Still his attention focused on the men in front of him. Their dash not accompanied by covering fire, they lay for perhaps half a minute before one raised himself cautiously to an elbow, then a knee. When nothing happened, he looked back toward the trees—and shouted. Then Macurdy stood, and pumped out half a dozen more plasma charges. The man fell; the others moved not at all, or only twitched.

The plane's engine was louder. Macurdy started back to the others, somehow certain that the plane was dangerous. "Berta!" he shouted, "take Lotta and run to the forest! Now! I will bring Edouard!"

Confused, she rose only to her knees. The forest was where the danger had been. He gripped her arm and pulled her to her feet. "The forest is safe now! They are all dead there! The plane is the threat now!"

Berta did run then, only pausing to pull Lotta to her feet, and they ran hard toward the woods. Macurdy bent, lifted the marionette-jointed Edouard, and struggled him over a shoulder, then started after them. Now exertion showed him what he'd overlooked: the cost in energy of firing so many plasma charges. He stumbled, nearly collapsing beneath Edouard's weight, then staggered on. Through the aircraft's engine noise, he heard its machine gun hosing bullets, and ten yards in front of him, dirt and asphalt spurted. He stopped, nearly fell, heard the engine yowl as the plane banked sharply. Again he started running, heavily, his lungs heaving as if he'd raced a hundred yards with his burden.

And heard Lotta running back to him, crying, "Herr Montag! Herr Montag!"

Dismayed, he shouted, telling her to go back.

Hands on its sides, Krieger leaned out the door, watching the troopers dash forward, hit the ground. From his vantage he couldn't see the others deliver covering fire, but had no doubt they did. They knew—at least he'd told them—that they might be unable to see the man they had to deal with, an American in a khaki jumpsuit. But he hadn't realized the man might be able to confer invisibility on the others. He wondered if his troopers realized their unseen targets were lying prone.

After a few seconds the soldiers were on their feet again, sprinting, cast themselves on the ground, and now, as the plane banked, he could see the others deliver covering fire—and fall!

His consternation almost choked him. "Closer!" He shouted into his throat mike. "Quickly! I need to lay down accurate fire." Then jerking the door gunner out of his way, he took the gun over and set himself. From behind it he had a smaller field of view than before, but as the plane banked, he saw Montag running, now with a body over his shoulder. Staggering; he must be wounded! Krieger laid down fire in front of him, his goal to stop instead of kill. Alive, Montag was valuable for what he knew, what he could do.

As he fired, he saw Montag stop, actually barely pause, then lumber on again. The plane banked steeply, but Krieger kept his prey in view. In seconds the American would reach the forest, unless he killed him. Krieger pivoted the gun on its mount; he dared not spare the man again.

He never noticed the child running toward Montag.

It was then the pain struck, like an explosion in his skull. With a bellow, a roar, Krieger let go the gun, clasping both hands to his temples, and unconscious, plunged headfirst out the door.

In the cockpit, hornets attacked the pilot, hornets large as his thumb, swarming about his head, stabbing face, eyes, hands with liquid fire. He roared, raging, holding the stick with one hand, swatting and snatching with the other. The pain was excruciating . . . .

Macurdy *felt* Lotta's fear, her desperation, and fell to his knees, suddenly too weak to stand. Heard but didn't see the plane crash and explode on the far side of the river. Lotta ran to him and flung her thin arms around his neck, sobbing wildly. "I couldn't help it!" she cried. "I couldn't help it! They were going to kill you! They were going to kill you!" He hugged her, patted her, telling her it was all right, all right, that it was over with. Then Berta was there too, sobbing, her arms around both of them.

It seemed to Macurdy he couldn't get up. How many charges had he fired in those few minutes? In that one minute alone? More than there'd been targets. Then it occurred to him that when he'd picked Edouard up, the man was still alive. His aura had shown it. But he might not be for long, unless something was done for him. It took a major effort to lift him again, this time in his arms. Slowly, Macurdy staggered with him to the forest, then carried him a hundred yards farther, to get well away from the road.

He sent Berta to hide by the roadside and watch; if anyone came, she was to return and tell him. Nearby farmers might well have heard the gunfire—almost surely someone had—but how long it might be before the authorities arrived, he could only guess. He didn't think local police would investigate that much gunfire. Surely no farmer would. There'd be soldiers at Feldkirch, manning the border checkpoint, but surely not many, and probably in their forties and older. *Landsturm*, perhaps *Volkssturm*. The tiny nation of Liechtenstein, more or less a Swiss protectorate, was hardly a threat to Hitler's Third Reich.

Edouard's aura reflected the severity of his wounds. He'd been hit twice. One bullet had punctured the lower lobe of his right lung and collapsed the pleurum. The other had entered the lower abdomen on the right side, and exited his back on the left without hitting the liver or either kidney. Macurdy didn't know the details, of course, only that no major blood vessels had been ruptured, or Edouard would already have bled to death. But he assumed the intestine had been perforated, and infection would follow.

He also knew that Edouard could hardly have gotten those wounds rolling toward the ditch. Perhaps in the scramble he'd crawled, trying to shield Berta.

With a shivering Lotta beside him, Macurdy worked on Edouard beneath a cloak, manipulating energy threads with mind, eyes, and fingers, and bit by bit the threads stayed where he wanted them. After 20 minutes, Berta trotted up, whispering that a truck, a kind of van, was coming up the road from the west. Without speaking, Macurdy motioned her to kneel beside himself and Lotta, within the perimeter of his cloak. Then he continued manipulating and visualizing while they watched.

Visualized not only Edouard whole and well. Visualized white cells and antibodies, like microscopic cartoon soldiers rampant in Edouard's bloodstream, vaporizing germs in tiny black uniforms. For it was not enough simply to save his life. He had to create enough healing that Edouard could survive being carried to the border and across. It was a challenge he didn't doubt he'd win.

Distant voices reached them, barely, but he ignored them. A second truck arrived. Dead soldiers were loaded on it and covered by a tarp; then it left. Minutes later the Gestapo van followed it. Macurdy continued, till he'd done what he could for the moment.

It was only then he realized that during his efforts—perhaps because of his efforts—his energy had returned, and his confidence. Pulling the large quilted horse blankets from his pack, he helped Berta wrap Edouard in them. Then he knelt by his three co-fugitives. "I'll be back soon," he said. "I'm going to get something to eat. Talk to him. Tell him to get well. Tell him—tell him you need him."

Macurdy trotted easily through the dusk of early evening, passing two farms before he came to one without a dog. Never hesitating, he entered the chicken house, and in the midst of squawking flapping chickens, wrung three necks and left carrying supper, unseen by the farmer who stormed from his back door with a shotgun. Let a polecat or fox take the blame, he thought. Tomorrow night I'll come and get that wheelbarrow by your woodpile, and leave a few reichsmarks by your door.

After a supper of creek water and scorched chicken, Macurdy gave Berta a lesson in concealment spells. She was short on confidence, but before they stopped, she'd succeeded in making herself—obscure. Easy to overlook. He told her to work on it, that she'd be responsible for Lotta and for foraging. He'd be busy wheeling Edouard to Liechtenstien.

Then he scraped together a bed of conifer needles and lay down. Waiting for sleep, he examined the day's wild climax. He did not doubt that someone in the plane had seen through his cloaks, had guided the soldiers and fired the machine gun.

He also knew what had saved him, knew with certainty. The night before, Edouard had told him that Lotta was "a terror poltergeist." Macurdy had assumed that meant a poltergeist who caused terror, and perhaps it did. But it was *her* terror that triggered it.

Perhaps in Switzerland, with Berta, she'd lose her need of it. He had no doubt they'd make it there.

PART SIX
May 1945

41

The Schurz Family

Flying over in still another C47, it seemed to Macurdy that Bern, Switzerland must be one of the world's more beautiful cities.

A year earlier he'd been interned there, briefly. Then Colonel Dulles had gotten him released and flown to Algiers, from where he'd returned to London. There he'd learned that a naval vessel on patrol in the Adriatic had picked up a body floating in a life jacket. A very peculiar body—Trosza's. That had been about the time he and MacNab arrived back in London, but word wouldn't find its way to Grosvenor Square for three weeks. When Macurdy had returned from Switzerland, General Donovan had pinned 1st lieutenant's bars on him: He'd not only provided proof positive of the aliens; he'd blown up the schloss, alone.

The promotion hadn't been Macurdy's only surprise. Anna Hofstetter was dating Vonnie Von Lutzow.

With his fluency in German, and experience in the Bavarian and Austrian Alps, Macurdy had next been assigned to a project to undermine Hitler's bitter-end "National Redoubt" plan, a plan that never remotely came to pass.

Now the war in Europe was over, and as of 19 June, 1945, Macurdy would officially be stationed in Washington D.C. Until then, he was on leave. With new captain's bars on his collar, and the DSC, silver star, purple heart, jump wings, and combat infantry insignia on his Ike jacket, he could have caught an Air Corps transport to the States via Reykjavik and Gander, and been in Nehtaka five days after leaving London.

Instead he was landing at Bern. There were things he had to check on, had to know. If he flew home without following through, he never would. He was still in Europe; things were still fluid and opportunities available. The chicken-shit specialists hadn't taken over yet, though they were working on it, and this was the time to do what he had to.

He'd already learned how the old 509th had fared. In Belgium it had been in extended heavy combat, and so badly chewed up, instead of replacing the casualties (again), the Pentagon had sent the survivors to other airborne outfits.

A letter from Berta had arrived for him in London at the end of August, 1944. Edouard was out of the hospital, and working in Bern as a janitor, but had been accepted as a lecturer in the University beginning in September. They had married, and begun proceedings to adopt Lotta, who was living with them. They'd been living in a single room, but with Edouard's new position, they'd be able to afford an apartment.

Macurdy had been in France then, and the letter had followed him from London, then followed him again, reaching him at last in mid-September. He hadn't written back for more than a month. When he had, his letter hadn't reached Bern for more than two weeks, and was returned as not deliverable.

He'd heard nothing since.

But the OSS office in Bern had resources. When the Peace was signed, he'd radioed, and they'd easily gotten Edouard's address and phone number for him.

So he phoned from the airport. Berta answered, and sounding delighted, invited him to supper. He suggested instead that they all eat at a restaurant, at his expense, but she insisted. "I am actually quite a good cook," she said. "And while many things are hard to get here, I have learned to do nicely."

Lotta would be home at about 4:30, she said, and Edouard by 6:00. If he could be there at 6:30 . . .

A taxi delivered him at the curb at 6:34, and putting down the two suitcases he carried, he rang their bell. It was Berta's voice that answered, and Edouard who came down to meet him. Edouard's eyebrows rose at the suitcases.

Macurdy gestured. "A few presents," he said, "mostly for Lotta."

They went upstairs together, neither of them making even small talk. They'd have to get used to each other again, Macurdy decided.

The apartment was on the third floor, at the end of a hallway smelling faintly of varnish and cleaning compound. At first it was Berta who carried the conversation. Lotta had grown and changed in 12 months, but was still shy. By the time they'd finished the custard Berta had made for dessert, Macurdy and Edouard had loosened up and warmed up. Then Lotta, though still less than talkative, brought out almost every possession she had, for Macurdy to see and admire.

Which led him to open one of the suitcases he'd brought, the larger, with things for her. Anna Von Lutzow had helped him shop. Mostly they were dolls and stuffed animals, but there was also a bright orange rain cape and a gold-plated fountain pen. It earned him a hard hug and a kiss on the cheek from Lotta, and moist eyes from Edouard and Berta.

For Berta he'd bought a white nylon blouse—Anna had helped him—and a purse with several compartments; for Edouard a heavy sweater of Scottish wool, and a camera. For the two of them together he'd brought a liter of good cognac, and the suitcases, which they were to keep.

Afterward they sat in the living room and sampled the cognac while they talked. They told him about their new life—neither wanted to return to Germany, despite the end of the war, though "someday we shall visit"—and he told them a bit about his life before the war, leaving out the years in Yuulith, of course, and his first two marriages.

"You seem too young for all that," Edouard said. "I would have guessed your age at, oh, twenty-five perhaps. Although already in Germany I had decided you were older." He cocked an eyebrow. "How old are you?"

"Thirty-one." He'd been tempted to say forty-one, his actual age, but that would require difficult explanations. It occurred to Macurdy that with the secrets he had, close friendships of long duration would be few.

"Remarkable," Edouard said. "Don't you think so, Berta?"

"Yes, remarkable, but somehow I am not surprised." She laughed. "After the things we have seen you do, Herr Macurdy—Curtis—we are not so easily surprised as we might have been."

He didn't stay late. At nine they sent Lotta off to bed. She hugged and kissed Macurdy again before she left. Shortly afterward he phoned for a cab. Before he and Edouard went downstairs to wait, Berta too hugged him, and kissed his cheek.

"We will write to you," she said, "and you must write to us. Because you are Lotta's uncle Curtis, which makes you our brother." She paused. "You were a soldier, but also you were a human being. We have talked of you often. You have our highest respect and admiration."

"Thank you," Macurdy said, feeling awkward. "I am honored. You both have my respect and admiration, and not only because of what you are doing for Lotta."

While he and Edouard waited in the foyer for the cab, they found little to say again. Then the cab arrived, and before Macurdy left, the two men shook hands, a long process, as if there was more to say but they didn't know what.

Macurdy rode back to his hotel feeling pensive. Getting ready for bed, he spotted two of the reasons: Edouard and Berta not only had a child, they had a future in which, with any luck, they'd grow old together.

He doubted their love could be as strong as his and Mary's, but there'd been all those pregnancies without results. And as for growing old together . . .

Life, he told himself, *is a string of choices, a web of them, choosing and living with the results, good and bad, and making future choices on top of the old. Hopefully learning as you go, getting smarter.* He paused. *No, not smarter. The word is* wiser. *And hoping that at the end of your life, the overall results will be good.*

Which, he realized, was why he was flying to Bavaria in the morning: He had more results to check on.

42

The Bavarian Gate: Goodbye

Lieutenant Colonel William Von Lutzow, stationed now in Munich, met Macurdy at the Bern airport shortly before noon, in a borrowed OSS plane. They had supper that evening at the officers' mess in Kempten, where the army ran the airfield, exercised authority over civil administration, and undertook to supplement the district's inadequate food supplies. Afterward, walking uniformed around town in the long spring evening, Macurdy saw little sign of resentment. Stoicism was more the mode, and poverty. Two young women accosted them, but they declined.

The next morning at ten-thirty, Vonnie checked out a jeep from the motor pool and they headed for Schloss Tannenberg, Macurdy driving. May was verging on June, and though the morning was cool, the day was glorious. The villages along the way showed the drabness of war and defeat, the long shortage of means and manpower. But here and there, flowerbeds and planters were bright with color, and the roadsides were spangled with wildflowers. The beech trees and larches were a fresh and lovely green.

A truck was parked beside what had been the schloss, and using a ramp, block and tackle, and crowbars, several civilians were loading stone blocks. Two of them wore German army uniforms, perhaps the only clothes they had. Clearly gasoline was not entirely unavailable to civilians; presumably, entrepreneurial GIs in the Red Ball Express had set up a black market.

Macurdy barely paused at the schloss—he had no doubt of his results there—but turned up the truck trail to the top of the Witches' Ridge, where he parked on a patch of rock outcrop not far from the gate site. The moon would be full that night; if the gate still functioned, he should be able to feel it at local noon, as a distinct buzz in the Web.

Meanwhile they ate an early lunch in the sun: fried-egg sandwiches, Hershey bars and oranges, bagged for them at the officers' mess, along with two cans each of army three-two beer.

"So this is the place," Von Lutzow said.

"Yep."

Vonnie did not doubt the Voitar were real. He'd always had faith in Macurdy, had talked with Anna and MacNab about them, and had read the report on the body, with photographs. And they had to come from somewhere. But it was still hard to believe in the gate; his face and aura reflected—not skepticism so much as discomfort.

Macurdy looked at him and smiled. "I know where there's one in the Missouri Ozarks," he said, "that I'm pretty sure still operates. If you'd like, we can go visit it sometime." He laughed then. " 'When the spirit comes ahootin'.' "

Von Lutzow gave him a sideways look, and Macurdy laughed again. "An old Ozarks conjure woman described it that way. She's the one who took me there the first time."

"So what happened?"

Macurdy's smile turned wry. "Don't ask. I might tell you, and ruin a good friendship."

Von Lutzow shifted uncomfortably on his seat, and let matters lie. Macurdy didn't, however, not entirely. "The birthdate on my personnel record is false," he added. "By ten years."

Vonnie knew the comment was not a non sequitur, regardless of how it sounded, but he let that be too.

After several minutes of digesting in the sun, Von Lutzow drove the jeep into the shade and lay down in the back seat, eyes closed. Within a minute he slept. Macurdy, on the other hand, needed to be awake and alert at noon, so he got out and walked along the crest a bit, checking his watch every few minutes. A squirrel scolded; birds chirped and occasionally sang; a hawk whistled shrilly in the sky. He was back at the jeep a few minutes before local noon, and felt nothing, nothing at all. At 12:30 he wakened Von Lutzow, and with minimal conversation drove back to Kempten, ninety-nine percent sure the gate had either been destroyed or rendered inoperable.

That afternoon, the two Americans visited the *Rathaus*, where the police had charge of the records left by the local Gestapo office. There Macurdy learned that "Gerda Montag" and her grandparents had been arrested by the Gestapo on Wednesday, 10 May 1944, charged with spying and harboring a spy, and been executed on Sunday, 14 May, of the same year. Just as he'd feared.

That night Macurdy drove back to the ridge again, this time alone; ninety-nine percent was not sure enough. The pasture he'd jumped on, more than a year earlier, was flooded by a full moon. Cows, no doubt the same cows who'd been there a year earlier, grazed in the moonlight, a sight he somehow found ineffably beautiful.

Again he drove to the ridgetop, where he parked and waited for midnight. Waited and felt—what? For one thing, an old love, buried but not dead. But this was the wrong gate, and that marriage long past.

Local midnight came and went, and still nothing happened. He gave it an extra forty minutes, then feeling dry as old leaves, started the jeep, drove back down the ridge, and headed up the road to Kempten.

That night too, sleep did not come quickly. Too many memories, too many thoughts. *Except for Mary,* he told himself, *you've had no luck with wives.* Varia stolen and married to someone else, which had worked out well for her and Cyncaidh. And Melody, drowned with their unborn child. And Gerda Schwabe, who hadn't really been married to him, though the marriage had been real enough to the Gestapo. A marriage never consummated, though she'd wanted to. All she got out of it was dead.

He tried to shake his mood. *Macurdy* he told himself, *get your head out of your butt and look at the facts.* Gerda had been living on borrowed time, and the loan had been foreclosed. She'd been a spy for the British in Lübeck, and was executed as a spy, a German who despised the Nazis. Like millions in the war, damned near including himself, she'd died as a soldier, in her case without a uniform.

And what of Landgraf? He'd been no Nazi, despite being an SS *Obersturmbannführer.* Decency and patriotism had been his central traits. And loyalty. A decent man supporting a monster! There was no understanding such things.

Rising up on an elbow, Macurdy looked at the watch on his bedside stand. The luminous hands told him it was past three, and the officers' mess stopped serving breakfast at 0800. Tiredly he got up and sat on a metal folding chair, to still his mind through meditation.

In a few minutes he was nodding off, and lying back down, fell quickly asleep. To dream of Yuulith—of Vulkan and Varia and dwarves—and Kurqôsz. Though he wouldn't remember it when he awoke.

The next morning he flew to Munich with Von Lutzow, and by noon was on a plane to London. Within hours he was on another, to New York, via Reykjavik and Gander.

Beginning to feel eager. He was done with war, he told himself. There was still Japan, but he'd get around that. Something would intervene. Maybe he'd start limping again; he was good at that.

And he was done with gates. He and Mary would make a new life for themselves, in Nehtaka to start with, then elsewhere. The problems weren't that great. If he looked at them right, they weren't problems at all.